Changeling Thirteen Changeling Thirteen Changeling Thirteen

R

Hanuman's Travels

by Andrei Ivanov

translated by Matthew Hyde

Vagabond Voices
Glasgow

The original Estonian edition was published in 2009 as Путешествие Ханумана на Лолланд (Таллин: Авенариус, 2009)

Translation copyright © Vagabond Voices 2018

This translation first published in July 2018 by
Vagabond Voices Publishing Ltd.,
Glasgow,
Scotland.

ISBN 978-1-908251-97-8

Printed and bound in Poland

Cover design by Mark Mechan

Typeset by Park Productions

The publisher acknowledges subsidy towards the translation from the Estonian Cultural Endowment

EESTI KULTUURKAPITAL

The publisher acknowledges subsidy towards this publication from Creative Scotland

ALBA | CHRUTHACHAIL

For further information on Vagabond Voices, see the website,
www.vagabondvoices.co.uk

Contents

Introduction

Hanuman's Travels is based on the experiences of its Russian-Estonian author, Andrei Ivanov, a native of Tallinn who lived in Denmark during the nineties as an illegal immigrant, and more specifically the period he concealed his presence there by submerging himself in the entangled world of a camp for asylum seekers. In this he was similar to his narrator who also keeps close company with an Indian illegal immigrant who is the novel's real protagonist and the Hanuman whose erratic charisma guides most of their travels, that is the travels they dream of and the travels they manage to turn into a chaotic reality, though circumstance and happenchance also play their part.

This work is therefore copied from life – at least in part – and belongs to an illustrious tradition that examines the marginalised lives of those who cannot find a home in their own societies – except here we're talking about the global rather than the national society laid bare by its antecedents. The French authors Jean Genet and the lesser known Jean-Paul Clébert spring to mind, and suggest that perhaps in France such authors find a wider audience, as confirmed by the success of the recent publication of *Hanuman's Travels* in French. Clébert loved the poor so much and found them so fascinating and creative that the reader almost feels that he would like them to remain poor, and he himself embraced poverty as a kind of liberation. The marginalised of Ivanov's work are different and more a caricature of the society they would like to become part of, though more honest because they have to struggle harder. Certainly my own instinct is to connect it with Émile Zola's *The Earth*, a coruscating and brutal examination of peasant life during the Second Empire, though in his case autobiography is supplanted by comprehensive research in accordance with his naturalistic vocation. When published in English, the book was considered so shocking that both translator and publisher were sent to prison, though the law was quite happy for the book to circulate in England in its original French version as, it was felt, in French there was no danger of it getting into the wrong hands. In this tradition, if you're shocked, then you're shocked by humanity, because the purpose is to describe humanity as it is and not as it should be.

Ivanov, like the authors mentioned above, often suggests that whatever the marginalised get up to, it is never as bad as the apparently orderly society that looks down on them with an air of moral superiority. He deals with these aspects principally in the early part of the book, and the mordant satire absolutely sparkles, as it does later in the narrator's reflections and Hanuman's extraordinary set pieces (brilliantly translated by Matthew Hyde). He differs from the other writers in that he does not identify with the left or indeed any political movement, but this is not an apolitical work. Its viewpoint, as expressed through the narrator and the protagonist, is cynical, hopeless and largely misanthropic. Paradoxically this engenders much of the vibrancy and humour in the work. I will make one last comparison, hazardous and more tenuous, to a writer very probably unknown to Ivanov: Evelyn Waugh who wrote about a very different milieu, the English middle classes, with a similar misanthropic zeal – and both authors succeed because of their vicious self-deprecation, most noticeably here in *Hanuman's Travels* and in Waugh's highly autobiographical novel, *The Ordeal of Gilbert Pinfold*. I should also make clear that the author himself claims as his influences two writers much closer to home, James Kelman and Irvine Welsh (that is to our home not his).

In our politically correct times, words and sentiments are banned but often held by people who would never express them in public – for now. When you enter the world of *Hanuman's Travels*, you enter a world of the grotesque inhabited by a large and expansive cosmopolitan cast of characters who seem remarkably free of any moral constraints and without scruples when it comes to terms of abuse, though on closer examination that is not entirely true. It is not hell, though the narrator often refers to it as that, but rather purgatory where existence is on hold for an indeterminate period and governed by dreams and chimeras. Though the camp, which is apparently quite simple to leave and return to, appears to be more liberal than the British ones, it is almost its own state with its own very limited regulations. The police rarely get involved unless they wish to pick up a failed asylum seeker for deportation. In the camp, the strongest rule over and control the weak, who live in a state of fear and desperation. Life is a constant struggle and inevitably scams are devised and a black economy created along with an extreme free-market culture, almost a parody of Western society. Hanuman explains this to the narrator's girlfriend with his typical bluntness:

Well you know my dear, everyone sells themselves, everyone! Especially the artistically inclined! Artists, actors, they all sell themselves! Just take a look around, all these squeaky-clean millionaires are rotten to the core, there's corruption everywhere, corruption! The world is a market – a huge market…! We're all selling something! The clever guys sell for the highest price possible! Everyone in this camp is trying to sell their homeland in return for a yes! And you're a real beauty! You're a work of art in your own right! So sell yourself for such a good price that it leaves no nasty mercantile aftertaste! Sell yourself like a piece of jewellery! Sell yourself like a diamond or a pearl! But sweeten the deal with some emotions, with some illusions! Convince yourself that you love the person you're sleeping with, that you don't need his passport, or his wealth, or his country with its redistributive social security system, but that you really love him... (p. 345)

In the early seventies before Britain entered the EU (or rather its forebear, the Common Market or more correctly the European Economic Community), I was an illegal living in Italy and in those days there were no camps and few problems with the police. I shared a room with Algerian immigrants, and none of us had the required permit, which meant lower wages and no secure employment. However, our lives were distant from the illegals and asylum seekers in *Hanuman's Travels*. Work was easy to find, and it was clearly easier to survive within society then than it is now, though we were slightly hidden from view in poky and remote rooms of cheap hotels and *pensioni*. The migrant workers were part of a fairly cohesive community and sometimes the wider community came together, meeting in public places such as the cathedral steps. Money was short, but money did not govern our actions or thoughts as it does the immigrants in *Hanuman's Travels*. The interesting and for me depressing truth that emerges from the novel is that since the advent of neo-liberalism and the decline of social-democracy (not without its own problems), all collective consciousness has disappeared from society, including those whose often traumatic journeys bring them to our shores (though very few of them to British shores, in spite of the Brexiteers' protestations). The bottom of society sometimes follows the top, and sometimes the top follows the bottom. Our society is now of the former kind. And Ivanov's description of it has authenticity although, in keeping with the picaresque tradition that goes back to sixteenth-century Spain, there may be the odd exaggeration and certainly a degree of selection.

The picaresque is the other side of this work: a delight in storytelling about the life of the underdog, which has elements of the heroic as well. The premise for Henry Fielding's *Jonathan Wild the Great* was that the "virtues" required of a thief and confidence trickster are the same as those required of a politician and a general. The genius and persistence of our band of illegal immigrants knows no bounds. If they fail, they persevere, and if they succeed, they spend their ill-gotten gains on drugs and prostitutes a little too quickly, so it's a moot point as to whether success is better than failure, because success always appears to end in despair or even depression. The courage and cunning is worthy of Odysseus, as can be inferred from this account of Hanuman's serious and apparently irreversible depression:

Mister Lee said the same thing when he came floating into our room chasing a rare butterfly which he had been stalking with his net for three days, clad in his dressing gown. He stood by the bed, listened to my account of what was happening, which involved a short overview of Hanuman's life up to now, his erotic dreams, his passion for photography, his first experience with a lady who was much older than him in the shadows of his small photo studio, illuminated by the occasional flashes of a red lamp, as well as his expedition through the mountain villages of Himalaya, where he was brought flat-breads sprinkled with cannabis seeds by fairies dancing in gay dresses with lilies woven into their hair from which hummingbirds and butterflies fluttered, not to mention his journey to New Zealand, where he danced with aborigines, and transformed himself into a multicoloured fountain. From there he went to the island of Crete via the island of Bali, where he had wandered through the gloom onto a showground full of fireworks and other pyrotechnics while a carnival was in full swing – and when it all went up in smoke, he came out in one piece and was taken for a New Avatar. I spoke about his life on Cyprus and Capri, about his wives in Bucharest, Prague, Riga, Gå on the outskirts of Stockholm, about everything which had befallen us in Denmark, our travels from Frederikshavn to Copenhagen, from Copenhagen to Farstrup, up to Aalborg, down to Langeland, to Svendborg, Silkeborg, and eventually to Huskegaard. Mister Lee listened, attentive and unruffled throughout, frozen in a fixed pose: his right hand was raised, holding the net, and the long sleeve of his dressing gown, which looked like a ceremonial robe, had slipped down, exposing an elbow with a wart on it. He had shifted the weight of his body onto his half-bent right leg, while he was holding his left leg in the air – he was the spitting image of Mercury! He let me finish, and then he said, "His mesolimbic system has collapsed, that's all. The patient used narcotic substances in excessive quantities. He also suffered overexposure to gambling, both in the casino and with his own fate. Recklessness, thrill-seeking, risk-taking, an unhealthy obsession with making money from nothing accompanied by an ever greater gift for spending it – all these things led to mental exhaustion. He needs peace and quiet, tea, and weed. It's not psychosis or a coma. It's just his nucleus accumbens. Nothing more." (pp. 386–87)

There's little to add to his monumental biography or Mister Lee's analysis.

Hanuman's Travels has also been published in French, German and Estonian, and even adapted for the German stage, and was to be published in Danish, appropriately as Denmark is the home to this global epic, and the author speaks the language fluently. The Danish publisher withdrew because they felt that the asylum seekers' various escapades could provide ammunition for the xenophobic right, but the fear, though understandable, misses the point. Leaving aside the obvious arguments that xenophobes are continuously fed a diet of hate by the tabloids and they're unlikely to read this book anyway, the fragmented lives of the camp-dwellers are the products of a global economy that is entirely out of kilter and the global aspirations that go with it. This is humanity as it is now. It has changed, and will change again, and it's the job of literature to engage with realities as they are and not as the author or polite society would like them to be. Nothing in this book detracts from the need to treat asylum seekers who come to our shores with compassion and support, particularly as many of them are driven by wars that we fomented.

Primarily this is a story of resilience and comradeship – often, it's true, driven by necessity. The narrator hates his neighbour and fellow Russian-speaker, Potapov, who is a fool, hypocrite, abusive stepfather, talentless artist and incompetent. And yet the neighbours are constantly collaborating on absurd schemes to make money. This book is the story of a world that is almost totally ignored and rarely viewed from inside. For that reason alone, it is worth reading, but it is much more: it is a fine work of literature, and widely accepted as such.

Allan Cameron, Glasgow, June 2018

Hanuman's Travels

Part One

1

Hanuman was sick of the Danish provinces and the *gammel kro*, with the pretty baskets of flowers on every windowsill, and behind every window, like fish in an aquarium, the stooped old men, slicing sausage with fear in their faces.[1]

Everything about this world was foreign to him. The smallest of details made him recoil: the odd shape of the paving stones, the decorative reliefs on the walls, the wickerwork fences, the bronze doorknobs. The tangle of streets, the ornamental hedges, the snort of lawnmowers, and hidden behind high walls, the factories, workshops and scrapyards...

"It's like some laboratory maze!" Hanuman said, nudging me in the ribs. "Just right for a pair of rats like me and you, Euge! One black, one white! Heh! Which will survive? Every town is the same! Exactly the same!"

And so they were. The bright red postbox, with its gold crest bearing a bugle and crown. The neat flower bed beside the petrol pump. The freckle-faced girl in the little store at the crossroads. The gradually approaching murmur of town, like the wheezing of bellows. Cables disappearing into the industrial horizon. Roads racing rapidly in the same direction. Every road marking perfectly painted. Every road rolled dead flat. The cars didn't even need engines! They glided along so smoothly, as if they were on conveyor belts, heading straight for the sky. We watched them pass as we meandered between bus stops, sheltering from the wind and rain in dark-green metal containers, smoking cigarettes, twisting our map this way and that. The buses floated past with reptilian indifference. The important-looking drivers in their uniforms made us feel uneasy. Gold

1   *Gammel kro*: a traditional Danish guest house/bed and breakfast.

buttons, rosettes, cuffs; all standard issue. Bushy whiskers under heavy bulldog cheeks. Eyes filled to the brim with tedium. Hanuman squinted at them apprehensively, tugging agitatedly at his braces.

"Can't say I envy them," he said, forcing a grin. "Imagine trundling up and down these roads day in day out... you'd go out of your mind with boredom! We've only been trudging along a few days and we're dog-tired, but they have to do it every single day!"

Now and again one of the buses would stop and the driver would get out to help some elderly woman off, or just to empty the coffee dregs from his thermos flask, and he would fix a stern gaze in our direction. Hanuman watched them constantly out of the corner of his eye, reminding me not to let my guard down; he was sure that the drivers were on the police payroll.

"They have to report everything they see," he said out of the corner of his mouth. "Believe me! They have to sign an agreement... they get called to the office, that's where they get given their instructions... they get half an hour to read them, then they have to sign. The slightest problem, and they'll call... they have a special phone number... there's a rapid deployment squad at the police station for those kinds of alerts. What did you expect? They'll arrive in a flash. It's the best way to enforce control! You don't think it looks suspicious? Two guys like us sitting here... and one of them black. Who could they be? Better check their papers..."

"Then maybe it's best we clear off?" I said, and we got up and started to walk away. Hanuman was singing something to himself.

He always had some tune on his mind, but he would keep it from everyone, behind firmly closed lips; protecting it from the wind and the prevailing circumstances; furtively tapping out the rhythm, one foot after the other. Striving for every note. But the wind plucked the words from his lips. The noise penetrated his skull. It filled him with a foreign substance. It knocked the rhythm from his chest, like an articulated lorry thundering into his soul, a motor scooter tearing into his heart. That sputtering flame of melody could be extinguished by yapping Danish voices, mighty pneumatic drills, rumbling engines, or the hubbub of supermarkets. Traps, dead ends, red brick walls turned yellow by time, all weighed on Hanuman's soul. There was red brick all around us, glowing with patriotic pride. Dense walls of it, one on top of the other, it made your flesh creep. Windswept squares. Sterilised, stylised see-through stations, issuing echolalia instead of timetables and tickets. Impenetrable schedules for buses, trains and ferries. Wherever you went. To stop you getting lost, going off course, so that you only had yourself to blame...

Every eventuality had been taken care of in that carefully compartmentalised world; it was all but impossible for a couple of rats like Hanny and me to find ourselves a bolthole. There were cameras and eyes everywhere. Everyone was phoning someone. There were even trees specially planted to keep track of us and send signals to someone who kept track of the trees. All these tiny details were woven into the fabric of a life which was incomprehensible to the two of us. All of it had been smelted in the same crucible. Platforms with people dignifiedly looking askance, impatiently awaiting their trains, all of it had crawled from the same giant crater, coagulated, and manoeuvred itself in front of us, terrifying in its unity. But the most frightening of all were the people. Unapproachable, like bastions. Sleek coats, well-practised gestures. Cold, like the remorseless steel rails. The glare of spectacles; bright white teeth. All of them effectively deployed, standing like columns propping up the drab sky. Every one of them had made their contribution. Their usefulness to society was enhanced by a series of regular training courses. The eternal star of specialisation shone brightly above every one of them. Mighty corporations protected them under an invisible shroud. Beings intended for many years' service. The insurance companies covered the entire guarantee period. Every eventuality had been taken care of. Even chance itself...

The intercity trains sped into the distance. Carrying those precious lives in their bowels. Some of the passengers were conversing, others reading, noticing nothing, some sleeping or looking dreamily out of the window at us, past us, through us. There was no room for the likes of us on those trains. The ticket inspectors would chuck us off: a boot up the árse for Hanuman, an elbow in the back for me. The inspectors' peaked caps nodded, ticket machines punching holes in the air, kilometre upon kilometre of steel: click! *Vaersgo!*[2] Click! *Vaersgo*...

We trudged onwards. Level-crossing barriers sprung up from underground; cars appeared, indicators flashing; locked doors everywhere, gates, signs reading "*ingen adgang*",[3] "*forbudt!*", "*privat*". Hanuman was preoccupied. His eyes shone glassily. It was cold, and windy. The taxi drivers looked at us suspiciously. A flag in every yard. A flag flapping like a rag.

"They wipe the wind down with patriotism here, to make sure no one ever comes down with a dose of disloyalty," Hanuman said, teeth chattering. "It's just impossible, Euge! It's sickening to behold! Man, what sort of country is this! What kind of a kingdom!"

"A kingdom with a clean conscience and cleaner toilets, man," I mumbled, half asleep.

The tiredness was getting the better of us now. We were rolling down a slope, careering downhill, being sucked into a funnel. Something bad was afoot. Apparitions spun round us. Little gnomes in red caps paraded past. People in red uniforms, just like the gnomes, marching past with heavy brass instruments, shooing on fat crows. They were amateurs, but they were marching and blowing their trumpets just

2   *Vaersgo*: Tickets please! (Danish)
3   No entry (Danish)

8

like professional performers. They spun round the square like clockwork toys: Hup! Hup! They were getting ready for some sort of event. People were hanging up garlands. Old women put dolls in their windows. Frightened birds hung in the sky like pieces of rubbish. The sun frowned and started beaming down at the polished brass trumpets again. Shop windows announced discounts. Girls and boys walked around the street, handing out invitations and postcards. The rattle of tractors from the fields roused foreboding. A bearded man circled round, holding a pen and piece of paper, hassling passers-by, asking them to sign up to something, to donate... Someone had put a ladder up against the wall. A dodgy-looking character reached for his phone...

We entered the station. Blended in with the crowd. More timetables. Signs and arrows. The same booklets, tourist brochures, museum guides, historical pamphlets, leaflets strongly advising you that "If you went to Jutland but didn't see ... and ..., then it's safe to say you haven't experienced the real Denmark."

"How tedious!" Hanuman moaned. "Heh, I'd prefer not to see Denmark at all! I wish I'd been struck blind as soon as I stepped off the ferry into this cursed country!"

I caught the booklet which he chucked at me, and started reading: "...take the opportunity of visiting a restaurant at one of the provincial *gammel kro*, which is the only way of experiencing real Danish cooking..." And naturally, while you are there you can also visit "Aquapark, Legoland, the aquarium, the Old Town at Aarhus, a national park containing the burial mounds of the first Viking kings, the gardens with magnolias, orchids too ... the museum of ancient ships used to conquer London and Paris, to discover Iceland, Greenland, America, and the rest of the world..." Well of course, "the rest of the world". That's right! How could one expect anything less... And yet more train timetables, "with the assistance of which you too can visit all these wonderful Danish destinations."

"There you go then, Euge," Hanuman continued. "Half an hour on the ferry, no more than half an hour! A piffling half an hour... From Helsingborg to Helsingør is no more than half an hour... You start off in a proper country, and after half an hour's ferry ride you're God knows where! Man it's just so tedious!"

It was true, it really was tedious enough to make you want to howl into the wind.

Those timetables drove us to distraction. At first Hanuman didn't dare look at them. Later he developed a full-blown aversion. One time we got stuck at some bus station (somewhere near Odense). We had time on our hands and didn't know what to do with ourselves. So we sat there spitting on to the ground, smoking our last three cigarettes. Even the thought that we had tongues in our mouths which could be used for talking to each other made us feel sick.

Hanuman had nothing better to do so he went up to one of the timetables to check whether what was written on it tallied with what was actually happening at the bus station. Some of it evidently did. And from that moment he started to believe that he knew how to navigate Danish time and space just like any Danish person! He travelled a few stops full of a newfound belief that he had somehow connected with the true spirit of this country, a belief that he was no longer just an ape, but a proper human being. He stuffed his briefcase full of timetables, insisting that everything now made perfect sense, that they would be sure to be come in handy; he got so carried away that he couldn't shut his case properly. But it ended badly: he eventually became convinced not just that the timetables were useless but that he was entirely incapable of comprehending the true order of things in this country. He realised that he would never be able to truly make sense of all those schedules, and so he threw them away and swore never to look at them again.

That happened on the platform of the main train station of some little town, maybe Randers, maybe Horsens. We hadn't eaten for three days, and the worst thing was that we were doing nothing to improve this state of affairs. We got stuck in that town because of a drug dealer who nabbed our last krone through the window of his flat. We ended up sleeping at a breaker's yard, in an old car which even started and kept us warm for a while, until we used up the last drops of petrol which the previous owner had saved for the car's final journey. And when we started to freeze we lit a fire in a large metal canister, using the porno mags which Hanuman carried in his briefcase and newspapers which we found in the car boots, but we still couldn't get warm. We fumigated ourselves with filthy smoke, but we just couldn't get warm. We smoked all our hash without getting the slightest bit high. We smoked hundreds of cigarette butts which we unearthed from the ashtrays of the more-or-less respectable-looking cars. We ate all the apples off the single apple tree which was willing to grow out here on the outskirts of town. We used up all the matches, all our cigarette lighters died; we drank all the water in Hanuman's litre bottle; eventually the fire in our canister went out, then the last of the embers stopped smouldering, and we crawled to the station to try to get warm. On the way I vomited on a street with the revolting name of Krapgade. I threw my guts up. Hanny said that I might have overdone the apples and cigarette butts. He added, "Maybe it's a stomach ulcer."

He said that without looking at me, he just uttered it into the emptiness, looking somewhere directly ahead. The thought that I might have an ulcer made me feel even worse. But I pulled myself together, stood up and dragged myself to the station. We drank some water in the WC. Hanuman sat on the toilet for three hours with the timetable, trying to get his frostbitten brain to work out when the train to Aarhus would arrive, and at what platform...

For some reason, Aarhus was associated in our minds with

11

the wild, ill-defined hopes which had been tormenting us over the three days we were in Randers. I can't remember why and in what circumstances these thoughts had first started to haunt us. These hopes had crept into our heads like apparitions creep up on a madman; they bit us to pieces like flees; we had scratched our souls red raw by the end of those three days in that damned Horsens! I can remember how Hanuman suddenly flared up, he got carried away by his usual rush of fiery emotions. He started really coming up on one! A proper high! The words seemed to spew from his mouth. He was ready to run for it right there and then, foaming at the mouth, forcing his way, pounding on locked doors… just to get out of that wretched Randers!

"We need to go to Aarhus! Take my word for it, man," Hanuman said, slapping me on the back. "We need to get the hell out of Horsens. Aarhus, man! That's where we need to go! To Aarhus! Why didn't I realise that right away?! Fuck me in the mouth! Fuck me up the ass! What a cretin! We should have gone to Aarhus straight away!"

I also started getting worked up, but I soon cooled off. Just like the embers smouldering in our canister. By now I didn't care: Horsens, Aarhus, it was all the same to me… But I said nothing to Hanuman so as not to complicate an already impossible situation. I pretended I was also set on going. The previous night in the car had taken a heavy toll… I didn't even have the strength to grumble.

Hanny smoked cigarette butt after cigarette butt, continuing his agitated commentary:

"Mmm, that's right, we need to go to Aarhus! Yeah, man, yeah… it's a big city, lots of foreigners, it's easy to blend into the crowd, to go unnoticed, get stuff done, feel like a proper human being. You get it, Euge? It's easier to make contacts there. Maybe we'll pull some girls. Maybe we'll get lucky with work. I heard that there's a proper Asian market there. They say it's a big one. Yeah! There must be some Indian restaurants as well. There just must be. What sort of place doesn't have an Indian restaurant? Even Frederikshavn has got one. Aarhus must have one. Heh! Who knows, if we're lucky…"

But first we had to get to Aarhus. Hanuman thought that with any luck we wouldn't get caught. He liked saying "with any luck". If we weren't lucky he would simply say it was "bad luck". And that was that. But for some reason, this time he wouldn't let it lie:

"We're bound to be lucky. No chance we won't. We haven't been lucky in ages. We can't be unlucky all the time. Eventually we have to be lucky. Aarhus is spitting distance from here! This is a district train line. They almost never check. After Aarhus they'll check, but before Aarhus, no way. You know that yourself. We change at Aarhus. In any case, it's even closer than from Roskilde to Copenhagen. They check once in a blue moon, if that. They'll let us go anyway… just think how many times they've let us go already… eh?"

"Yeah, yeah, of course," I agreed sleepily.

Hanuman got more and more worked up, almost as if someone had injected him with something when he went for a piss. Maybe that was where he got the idea from. From behind the fence at the scrapheap… I can't remember. It's not important anyway. The thought of Aarhus, or the place he imagined it to be, got him really agitated! Even the word "Aarhus" produced a rush of adrenaline, and that was why he was repeating it constantly like an incantation.

"Aarhus – it's not some petrol station with a supermarket attached… it's not some inbred little village where everyone fucked each other three hundred years ago! Aarhus – it's the historical capital! It's virtually a megalopolis! That's where the king had his residence! And it's a student city, which means music, parties… the cultural capital of Denmark! I read about it in one of the tourist brochures."

"Yeah, yeah, sure," I said.

Hanuman was pestering me. On my case every ten

minutes. Wrenching my consciousness from a starving torpor. On the final night he just couldn't sit still any longer. He suddenly wanted to go for a ride somewhere. He imagined being on the intercity train again! Hanuman really liked those Scandinavian trains. He was totally in love with the DSB[4]. He felt like a proper human being when he was on the train. And he actually became one. He metamorphosed into a citizen of the world. He took on the form of a German Indian. An Indian who was born in some place called Scheißwurstbach to a stout German woman and a skinny refugee, but had never set foot in India. He was even happy to be mistaken for a Pakistani, as long as it was assumed that he was born in Europe. There were plenty of loons like that around. Wandering aimlessly from place to place, trying to compensate for their dark skin with their European ways. And he would do exactly the same: smirking as if he found everything a bit tedious, just like them, propping his legs up on the opposite seat just like them, unbuttoning his shirt to show off his amulets just like them, leafing through "Tag med[5]" just like them. It was phenomenal. I would worry about my presence detracting from his finessed performance, that I would spoil it all for him. He would turn to the window, observing the intolerable views with a weary expression, repeating "det er så kedeligt, man, så kedeligt"[6] with such a natural look of boredom on his face, that it seemed as if he had felt an aversion to these fields and towns since childhood. He pulled it off so convincingly that the inspectors decided not to ask him for his ticket. They walked right past us, pecking at the air above the seats with their peaked caps, like thrushes on a freshly ploughed field. And Hanuman followed them with a look of contempt on his face. He was

4   Dansker Statsbaner, Danish national railway
5   "Take with" (Danish), a magazine usually found on the intercity trains.
6   "It's so boring, mate, just so boring" (Danish).

a fare dodger by vocation. Ticketless train travel gave him a rush. That's how he got his kicks. It was more potent than a line of coke. For him the very best start to the day involved travelling a couple of stops without a ticket. He couldn't get by without it. With a kick-start like that the day might well conclude with some successful shoplifting, or even a chick on his arm!

Then I started to suspect that there must be a reason why Aarhus had crept into Hanuman's thoughts. He just wanted to go for a ride on the train without worrying about ticket inspectors. Going to Aarhus was just as pointless as going anywhere else. There was nowhere worth going to! Wherever you stuck the pin on the map, there was nothing for us there. Nothing and no one at all. Apart from the cops, and trouble.

I couldn't bear thinking about what was waiting for me back in Estonia, and he just didn't want to return to his past. He would often say, "Going back to India would be like travelling from the future back to the dark ages. Man, if you were lucky enough to find yourself a time machine, then it would be stupid to go back to the past! Full steam ahead! The further the better!" He didn't like going back anywhere. "It's like betraying what you've achieved," he would say. "Onwards!" He might have a wife waiting for him in India; or a woman with a child in Bucharest; or a girlfriend in Prague; or some new love interest in Stockholm. But he didn't want to go to any of those places. He wanted to go to America. America was to be the place where his journey into the future would culminate. It was in America that his future would become his present. But obviously there wasn't a single Danish train which could take him there. So he had reached a state of despair. And it was from despair that he thought up Aarhus. Aarhus was just a pretext, anything to get moving, anything to get out of this wretched little town. Whatever it was called: Randers, Horsens… what was the difference! It didn't matter where to. Wherever! Anything to get out. By now we were properly pissed off. I felt the hopelessness of the situation like an aching in my guts. I felt sick to the core. I was ready to croak right there, at the station, in the toilets. There were such powerful eruptions coming from inside me that I felt like a cannon about to discharge. Eventually I heard Hanny say from the other cubicle, "Spor two. Quick! We've got five minutes!" We dashed to platform two and waited. But our train arrived at platform three. Cursing, we rushed back. But we didn't make it. The underpass was blocked with an effluence of fellow passengers, all carrying sacks of some sort. The whole place suddenly felt clammy and constricted, impassable like a waterlogged trench. We just managed to get to the steps. To see the train departing, right under our noses. Hanny flew into a rage. He lost it completely. He twisted himself out of his jacket and started trampling it, baring a big mouthful of teeth. He was swearing so loudly that I even stepped to one side and stood by the ticket machine as if I was buying a ticket. I stood there grimacing, ready to flake out. I wanted to disappear into thin air. Evaporate the hell out of there! I knew there were other people about. I knew that they were watching. I felt a shiver of paranoia run through me. I huddled into my own shadow, eyelids pressing tight on to my eyeballs, anything not to start weeping there and then. Right behind me Hanuman was bleating like a goat, fulminating away. Foaming at the mouth for all to see. Gesticulating. Hissing. Bellowing. Writhing this way and that like a loose hosepipe. He couldn't give a damn that people were looking at him. Fuck the police! He was giving it all he had. Giving it to each and every one of them. He struck terror into people's hearts, like Cú Chulainn before battle. He'd had it with everything and everyone. The other passengers looked on in stunned silence as he chucked the timetables on to the tracks, yelling after them: "Oh it must be a practical joke! This schedule does not make any sense at all! What do we need it for, if we can't fucking use it! I see no fucking point!"

All the ruses we had learned in Copenhagen were of no use to us at all in Jutland. The ticket machines wouldn't take our fake tickets. Hanuman couldn't crack them, all his reproductions proved worthless. The machine just made a horrible whining sound, and we had to extract ourselves, turn around and walk off. It was exactly the same with the buses! We were virtually booted off when our home-made tickets got stuck in the driver's ticket machine; he started swearing, we backed away; the driver grabbed his phone, we started leaving hurriedly; the other passengers watched us, slack-jawed; we picked up our pace.

Hanuman was not used to days which dragged by so slowly, or weeks which passed so pointlessly. We were in the doldrums, he would say, making no progress. He couldn't get used to public holidays with endless winds tearing through them. He was wary of the empty little towns with narrow little streets edged with hollyhocks. He detested lupins at first sight! And there were plenty of them around... a row in front of every fence. The narrow, cardboard cut-out streets weaved this way and that, and there were lupins growing everywhere: pink ones, lilac; violet, red, blue, yellow...

"They sure do love their flowers! The damned fools are trying to compete with the Dutch! They must think that if they plant a load of flowers, then they'll make the country just that little bit better! A rose revolution! Flower power... fuck that!" Hanuman ranted.

He was always leading us the wrong way. We were constantly getting lost, ending up down dead ends, having to trudge back the way we came. People watched us from their windows, gardens and cars. We had to pretend that we were looking for someone, checking the map or a scrap of paper, looking about us like tourists. It was madness! Hanuman choked on obscenities as he moaned that all those little streets were no better than the timetables.

"Their streets lead nowhere. They're all dead ends," he said. "They made them like this on purpose, so they could catch thieves easier!"

But they didn't have to try very hard to catch us. We virtually handed ourselves in. Just open up that pig wagon! Every time we ended up in a dead end we would find ourselves next to a little gate with a silver plaque on it, and we would be met by the same old woman in a fashionable, prim raincoat. She would ask us a question which we were incapable of answering, because we couldn't even understand the words coming from her lisping lips. We would turn round and walk off, feeling her gaze stuck to our backs, hearing the breathing coming from her fishlike mouth.

Hanuman couldn't get used to the silence which filled the weekends, he couldn't get the knack of decoding the sounds which came screeching out of the gloom, or the rattle of petrol station chains and bells, the specific Jutland accent, or the way the old people walked, shuffling their feet. He couldn't work out which way the doors were supposed to open. That was probably the worst thing.

Hanuman's inability to comprehend this foreign world drove him to commit petty crimes. He unwound lengths of toilet paper in the toilets and stole stacks of serviettes. He would never leave a café without an ashtray or salt cellar. He could have passed for a kleptomaniac, or maybe just an ordinary madman. But he was neither. He was simply wreaking his revenge on the world for all the offence it caused him, and he hated anyone who seemed comfortable in that world. He had his reasons, plenty of them... He hated people for nothing more than their neat outward appearance; for their nice, tidy, brightly coloured clothes. He hated the fact that even the pensioners dressed like teenagers, with their rucksacks, pink hoods, green mittens, and red trainers...

"These people look like marzipan dolls," Hanuman said one time.

I agreed with him. The worst thing was that these marzipan men had eyes, and these eyes were goggling the whole time. I was constantly catching their gaze... it was a particular kind of look. You could see that gaze slide across the crowd, across the street, across the shopfronts, and come to a halt when it reached you. Their eyes narrowed, they studied you, trying to decipher you like a sign, trying to place you in their inventory, to classify you... but to no avail. There was no place on the list for the likes of us. We were different to the local tramps and vagabonds. They were used to their own lot. They were inoculated against them. They didn't have to worry, they knew what to expect; they had corrective procedures and registers for their down-and-outs; they could train them to behave. But we clearly didn't fit the mould. We didn't look like the kind of people who had been told which way was left and which way was right since childhood, what was permitted and what wasn't. That's what made these marzipan men twitchy. That's right, they were worried. We stressed them out just by the way we looked.

"Heh, Euge! Stress, that's the last thing they want," Hanuman explained. "Although we're the ones who could end up being sent down!"

People kept their distance from us; they looked at us askance. Every one of them had a mobile phone on them. If we saw a hand rise to a temple, we got up and left, in unison.

"Better safe than sorry, Euge, better safe than sorry," Hanuman forced the words through gritted teeth, spitting on to the doll's-house pavements, cursing the neat road markings, the musical level crossing lights, and the displays of schoolkids' drawings.

He cursed every last McDonalds and Spar kiosk, and the trees festooned with balloons by the kids' cafés.

One evening Hanuman pissed all over a shiny new Mac-Burger restaurant which had sidled up to a decrepit, but still-functioning little church. "Heh! They respect religion here, just like they respect pensioners," he said as he unzipped his flies. "But they still can't wait to throw their old folk into the *plejehjem*.[7] In this country religion exists in only the most rudimentary form. Somewhere in a *plejehjem*. A dusty skeleton in the closet... God is recuperating in the loony bin... Jesus is wearing a straightjacket... the pastor is like Judas administering vitamin injections, sedating his congregation with sermons..." And so on, and so forth...

He chuckled as he let loose a lazy arc of urine all over what must previously have been a church porch, which had now made way for a drive-through. He strode round the car park on long bandy legs, pissing as he went. There were oval lanterns shining, bringing streaks of spilt ketchup into view. Hanuman pissed noisily on a yellow plastic chair. The skin of a dead balloon was drooping lifelessly from the fence, the trees sighed silently. Hanuman pissed all over an oval table. The stars quivered, flags fluttered. Hanuman pissed on the little silver fir in its tub. Hanuman pissed on the counter. Hanuman pissed on the rubbish bins. Hanuman pissed on the glass door. He shook off the last drops with the words "take that, take that, all over your brand new Mac-Burger religion... take that, I did it, take that, fuck you..."

With the words "and you sold out too" he entered the Aalborg pub, where a wooden Red Indian was standing by the door with a mug full of foaming wooden beer, and a sign on his chest reading "Make mine a Tuborg too."

Hanuman would grimace every time he walked past an insurance agency. "That's where the worst bloodsucking ghouls live," he would say. "They make money out of people's fear!"

He laughed at me when I said that I felt sad as I watched the ferries depart for Sweden or Norway.

"Don't get down, Euge. You won't get far on one of those

7   *Plejehjem*: retirement home (Danish).

ferries anyway," he said, slapping me on the shoulder. "A boat with a Danish flag is going to Denmark, and nowhere else…"

It would drive him crazy to see anything more than twice. The rainbow in every single garden. The dark-skinned bloke selling candyfloss. The deafening Looney Tunes song playing from the gaudy ice cream van as it trundled round town. Wherever we went we heard the piercing wail from the loudspeaker and the chuckle of Daffy Duck, and then the stupid van covered in cartoon characters would materialise. I said that maybe we were being followed, but Hanuman just poured scorn on me: "There are dozens of vans like that! Don't be paranoid, Euge!"

When the weather was fine there were girls assembled outside every school, getting ready for their performances. Pretty majorettes dressed in red and gold, tossing their whatnots into the air with a flash of silver, spinning on the spot before deftly catching them. A little way off, fat, freckled girls in leotards were doing gymnastic moves to "Gimme baby one more chance". We sat on the bench smoking, smoking and watching them do their exercises, drinking our water and licking our lips.

Signs, inscriptions at every turn, third-generation graffiti on every other wall; roadside illuminations, a reflector on every trouser leg and sleeve, pictures, stripes, columns, arrows for cyclists, neatly tended graves. The postman dressed in red, on his brown bicycle. Road sweepers wearing orange. The postman signals, and waves at them. They wave back, and then return to chasing the fluttering red, yellow, brown leaves with their plume of air… the leaves shoot upwards, spin round, fall downwards, rebound upwards, rolling, tumbling onwards, combining in a heap, to be devoured by the miniature vehicle driven by a thin middle-aged woman.

"He-ha-ho!" bellowed Hanuman. "What sort of country is this! It's like it's been assembled from a Meccano kit, and now it can't be taken apart... it's been put together in such a way that you can understand it only if you were born here... just like their damned language, fuck it..."

"Just look at these people, Euge!" he yelled at me. "They're not alive, they're just playing at being alive. They're playing at life, just like a game of Monopoly or Bingo. They weigh up every word like the Egyptian gods weighed human hearts! They check you out like the detector alarms in the shop doorways. They know if you've smoked grass, even if it was a year ago. They can tell from the smell of your piss that your visa has long since expired. They can read a genetic history of alcoholism and subjugation in your eyes. They'll steal your heart from your chest before you can even remember that you had one. And then they'll get into their humble Volkswagen and drive off to their grill party, and you'll be left standing in the middle of the field like a disembowelled scarecrow. The crows will be crapping on you, and they'll be standing in their friend's garden scoffing sausages and swilling beer, and they won't give a damn about you! They'll forget you ever existed! They'll just stand there with bored expressions on their faces! Got it?! Expect nothing less from those fuckers..."

He would tend to come over all eloquent whenever we were deep in fog. We would often stumble into fog, because we were normally trudging around on foot, like real Danish *laengevej ridder*.[8] We couldn't scrape enough money together for the bus. We couldn't get the hang of forging tickets. And anyway, we didn't have anywhere to go.

"What's the point of spending money on a ticket,

8 *Laengevej ridder*: literally "knights of the open road" (Danish), the ironic term used to describe homeless vagrants who tend to have a recognisable appearance – they are covered in badges and dressed unconventionally, they drag rucksacks, teapots, and rolled-up mattresses about with them, and they usually have a trolley and a dog; this lifestyle is generally seen as an act of protest.

if we don't know where we're going?" said Hanuman despondently. "Do you know where we're going?" he asked me. I said that I didn't.

"And nor do I!" Hanuman bellowed. "I don't know either!"

He was being completely honest with me. He no longer knew where we were going, and he didn't hide it. He wasn't trying to get to Aarhus any more – he didn't give a damn about Aarhus – that idea had gone, together with the rage, the spittle, the sweat, and the shouting. As soon as that fit had passed he forgot all about Aarhus and he never thought about it again, it was as if the place had never existed! So I never got to go there, and never got to see if there really was an Asian market there. Aarhus was forgotten, and we no longer had a goal – we were like lost souls, wandering from town to town with an eye out for anything which wasn't nailed down. Jutland's hinterland sucked us in, deeper and deeper, like a quagmire.

We gutted the tins of loose change which we found on the untended stalls, where strawberries, radishes, leeks and flowers were put out for sale: they turned up quite frequently, left out in good faith, but the tins never had much money in them, and it took a lot of plodding to find them. We stuffed our pockets with whatever came our way, and trudged onwards, chomping on carrots and radishes. Hanuman jangled the loose change in his pocket, mumbling that some money had appeared in his pockets; that was something, at least that was something...

We drank the cold milk from the farmers' refrigerators, which they also left out by the roadside, we stuffed our pockets with cheese and coins, then we bunked off. I tried to persuade Hanuman to turn off the road, on to the fields, in case the farmers discovered that the money had disappeared from their fridges or stalls and decided to come after us in their cars. He grumbled for a while and agreed. We ended up in fog, became bogged down in mud, we got lost, and when we found the road we discovered that we had accidentally wandered back to the stall which we had turned over just before the last fridge we had looted. Hanuman lost his temper, and swore he would never turn off the road again. He came out with all sorts of nonsense. He told me he had a childhood fear of water vapour, geysers, thermal springs and mists. He claimed it was a kind of phobia. He even told me a childhood story, about how he and his mates had been messing about in some factory in Chandigarh, and his stupid brother had tugged on a lever, or twisted a valve, and steam had billowed out in all directions with a terrible hissing sound. Hanuman's glasses misted over, he was temporarily blinded, he careered around the factory, knocking into pipes. That was where he had his first epileptic fit, in a pool of fuel oil mixed with his own piss. He lost consciousness. Eventually the factory workers found him and pulled him from the steam.

I laughed and said that a one-off event couldn't cause a phobia, that no such phobia existed, and that even if it did, it couldn't develop just like that, from some sort of silly thing like that! To say nothing of epilepsy. I told him he needed to see a therapist. Hanuman was fuming, but I tried to persuade him to turn off the road on to the fields again. I told him that at least on the fields no cars could run us over, but if we were on the road when the fog set in, and we had no reflectors (he flatly refused to wear them), a car could easily knock us down. Or I'd think up some other argument...

I wasn't really worried about a car knocking us over. That was the last thing I was worried about, because I was already totally hacked off with the life we were living. It would have been easier to snuff it than to carry on wandering around in the constant drizzle, swapping a south-easterly breeze for a westerly one, followed by a northerly one, and so on. The wind buffeted us, poking its freezing fingers under our scarves, down our sleeves, up our trouser legs, it crept through our flies, wafted up our arses, tore our hats from our heads, ripped the plastic bags out of our hands, stripped us bare, prancing around us like a frenzied pack of phantoms. No, I would have been grateful to have been knocked down by a car, killed even. Worrying about that would have been silly, and anyway, it would have been nothing to be ashamed of.

The thing I was most worried about was that the police would stop and check us. Two guys like us wandering about, one of them black… now then, what do we have here? Better check their papers… And that would have resulted in so much hassle that it didn't bear thinking about. Because the police wouldn't put you up before the firing squad straight away, they'd do everything by the book, string the whole process out, let you slowly marinate. But I didn't want to admit that I was worried about that to Hanuman. He was ready to hand himself in, to start legal proceedings, apply for asylum, and he had the grounds to do so. It was just that he wanted to do it on his own initiative, not after being caught. He had a fake "blue card" in the name of some Indian guy. Or at least a copy of one. Knowing him, he would somehow find a way of wriggling out of trouble if it came our way. But he was constantly contradicting himself. Sometimes he was on edge like me, but sometimes he said there was no reason to worry about meeting the cops on the empty roads; there was no one around anyway! He didn't believe that the cops could just appear out of nowhere, he didn't believe in bad luck. But I did! I'd known since I was a kid that cops were like devils! But in Denmark they wouldn't come out on to the fields. Not for anything. If you wanted to avoid the Danish police all you had to do was sit there up to your neck in horseshit. I found hundreds of pretexts for turning off the road without revealing my true fears to Hanuman. I thought up different routes – "a shortcut closer to the coast", "a shortcut further from the coast", "closer to the farm, to check if they've put anything

out, maybe there's a fridge, or some vegetables there" –
and eventually he would give in. He followed me, and we
would always end up in fog. Hanuman started to lose all
self-control when he was in the fog. He yelled at me that
he'd been terrified of fog since he was a child. He once got
lost in the mountains, he said. And there was fog in those
mountains. So he was scared he might take a wrong step
and fall off a cliff. He had been just a kid back then. That
was when he started having panic attacks! I tried to calm
him down, told him that we weren't in the mountains, that
there weren't any cliffs here, that there was no chance of
any appearing, but nothing worked, he didn't listen, he just
carried on muttering under his breath.

It turned out that there were several reasons he was
scared of fog. It wasn't just that he was afraid of getting
lost. He had actually developed a kind of ontological fear
of fog. He was scared that he might forget something, not
just anything, but something fundamental. He was scared
that the fog might steal away his memory, or his soul, and
insert someone else's there in its place, and then Hanuman
would come out of the fog a changed man. He might, for
example, come out of the fog as Amarjit, who was another
person altogether. Or as Arjuna, and that would mean big
trouble. As far as his family was concerned, fog was the
bearer of bad news, uncertainty, change, disorder, discord,
destitution. I wasn't in the least bit worried about all that
stuff, because as far as I was concerned it had all happened
to me already, and the only thing which could be worse was
the cops.

Sometimes when we were lost in the fog Hanuman would
start trying to explain something, and his language would
overflow with expletives. But his self-expression would have
been incomplete without swearing, it would have been like
Indian food without chilli pepper, swearing was an elixir for
his eloquence. There in the fog he told me about his first
family, and his first wife, and about the unfortunate souls

whom he had robbed to get from Greece to Italy. He wove his stories with such skill that it was hard to be sure what was truth and what was fabrication, or even to discern a shadow of truth behind the mountains of invention. He filled his phantasmagorical monologues with historical personalities who had never existed, and with events which he thought up on the spot. If he started crying, it would always end with coughing and hiccupping. He would choke on his hysteria. He would have fits of remorse. He would confess to all manner of terrible things. I would have to take him by the arm and lead him onwards, like a child or a blind man. When he reached the peak of despair, when he was foaming at the mouth and barely able to carry on, he would take a sip of water from his bottle and make an unexpected announcement, as if he had just experienced some kind of enlightenment. But then he would switch the monologue back on, and carry on defaming Denmark. He could curse Denmark left, right and centre, starting from any subject and from any letter in the alphabet. Starting with the Queen and ending up wherever you please. Sometimes he got carried away, and he would stumble onwards, blathering like a madman as he went.

"These fools have still got a royal family. Hah! Just look at them! They didn't kill them off like in Russia. Of course not, this is a developed country, a civilised society! Fuck no! Of course they didn't! They evolved directly from Vikings into cosmopolitans, they only needed to take one small step to get there. We should fall at their feet! But for some reason they still need their aristocracy. It's part of their history, which is just so important to them! Because they just love their traditions! Their bloodless revolution was finished in half an hour. The masses assemble, in the form of fifteen postmen, three lackeys and a snotty, spec-faced student carrying a big banner; the king chucks a manifesto out of the window, written by his lover with the king's sperm still wet on her lips; they shut the window so they can carry on

27

the fun; it starts to rain, the postmen get wet, they have a smoke, then they all head off to the tavern to celebrate their new democracy; the lackeys grab their brooms, and the student hangs the banner on the wall – now it's in the national museum. And that was their revolution. No blood, no machine guns. Not a single man hanged! Not like Russia. Hey, they didn't kill the king; they still need him. Just like in England. But why not like France? Because it's their ancestors still ruling in England. Well, maybe not ancestors exactly, but the same genes, the blood cells from the Normans, Danes, Goths... They still remember that, and that's why they respect the English. They hold them in esteem, as if they were cousins, they reckon they're civilised. Of course they do, the English managed to dispatch all their maniacs and insurrectionaries to America and Australia. What a clever move. Bravo! He-ha-ho! They gave themselves a bit more room to breathe. But not too soon: have this lot from India and Africa instead! The Europeans dealt with those countries pretty sensibly too. They calmly divvied up both continents, drawing such straight borders it makes you giddy just to look at them. Peace and love all round! But how were we supposed to live there after that? It was some kind of cartographic perfectionism. They cut the countries into even sections, exquisite geometrical forms, like slicing a cake. Into reservations! There's a bit for you, here's a bit for me, that bit's for the Dutchman, that bit's for the Frenchman, and let them have that bit for themselves, there's nothing there but sand. He-he, the English have the most precise measuring equipment of them all. They tested it out on us. All of those measures were drawn up in the House of Lords, the measurer of all measures, its membership determined by hereditary right. By the forefather of Marlborough and Darlington, a spirit level in one hand, scales in the other. And a microscope in place of his left eye, so as not to miss a thing. A telescope in place of the right one, so as to stride into the future, clad in Wellington boots. *Andiamo!* The world which Jack built is measured in feet and weighed in pounds. And of course they need their Queen. Although they didn't need the princess, she was far too pretty, fairy-tale pretty. But England is not a mythical land of bluebirds and roses... it's a land where policemen kill black boys on mopeds...[9] And there are more mopeds in Denmark than anywhere, more mopeds than there are bikes in Holland. I never saw so many mopeds in all my life. They even thought up their own word for them, *knallert*.[10] Amazing! Did you know that? Or was it you that told me? I believe that a relative told you, if I'm not wrong? Anyway, it's not important. There are no relatives in the fog. There's nothing at all in the fog. There are just words, words which lose all their meaning. Those two words, they're the only new words to enter Danish in forty years: one of them is "moped", the other is "hydrogen". Hahaha! They don't need the hydrogen bomb, they thought up their own word for it. But they'd be better off dispersing the fog and getting rid of those sponging royals. But no, they need to have a queen, sitting there in her palace. Of course, how could they leave the palace empty! It's a museum, complete with living relics. Even better than Madame Tussaud's. Hah, it's like some sort of historical fun-park, but with a living queen. Just take a look at her, that woman has the blood of Holger the Dane flowing through her veins! Hoho! That's better than any dinosaur. Or a woolly mammoth. Or even a visitor from outer space. Their very own queen. These people are like ants. Or like bees, damn them. They're insects. And they need their royal family so that they can photograph them, read about them in the tabloids, dress up the queen, feed her, and discuss her family amongst themselves. It's like a big village. They've got nothing better to talk about. Whose cow gave the most milk? How many piglets did so-and-so's

9   Lyrics by Sinead O'Connor
10   *Knallert*: moped (Danish)

29

pig have? And in between the cow and the tractor let's say a few words about the queen. But then back to Jens' chicken which lays bigger eggs than Nils' chicken. And Heidi's got bigger tits than Birte. And Nils's cock is longer than Jens's. But how do you know that? He-ha-ho!"

He would stop without warning and stand dead still, his scarf hanging lifelessly from him, like some kind of ancient agricultural implement, a pole with a weighted rope dangling off it. There he stood, like a man struck by lightning, a man who had just had some profound truth revealed to him, or something terrible told to him. He could stand like that for seven minutes flat, without budging. Without showing any outward signs of life. Without blinking an eye. Like he'd been switched off. In the midst of the fog, the thick wall of fog through which the outlines or lights of some nearby farm were just visible, or maybe they weren't. He stood there without reacting to anything, and that made me feel so lonely, catastrophically lonely. Then he put his arms on my shoulders, leaned in towards me, and looked into my eyes, as if he were trying to discern if they had turned yellow from hepatitis. And then, after a long pause dominated by the sound of heavy breathing, Hanuman spoke, making ample use of the "f" word: "Euge! You stupid son of a bitch! Do you not understand me? Eh? When are you going to understand? When will you see the full picture? Eh? When, I ask you? When are you going to stop being such an idiot? Don't you understand what deep shit we're in? It's not the real world here, it's just a huge pile of dung. It's a silage pit, for fuck's sake!"

Hanuman held my head between both hands and looked at me, as if he were staring into a crystal ball in which he hoped to see other worlds, and then he whispered, "Surely you remember? Or have you forgotten? You fucking bastard, you've forgotten it all! In this godforsaken world we can't hope to do anything more than survive! Those hyenas left us no choice! Those jackals have plundered the lot!

30

We've been thrown the bones of a decaying dog! There's nothing left for us! We have to prostrate ourselves just to get a corner of the blanket, a minute of sleep is all we're given. But why? Because those overfed swine have taken all the heat from the radiators. All the heat in the room! All the heat has gone down the tubes. Down the damned tubes! Euge! You know I'm right! They're bloodsuckers! They've locked love up in jars, in safes! The shares have already been issued! Now there's inflation! It's the dole queue for the likes of us! A bowl of soup for the flea-ridden tramps! And these scumbags, these flabby characters of unspecified gender, they're magisterial and magnanimous enough to give us our heating on credit! They'll take the dying breath from our chests! A ticket to the cinema, that's the limit of their love! For five minutes only! In return for a whole life! Shit polished to a sheen! Celluloid humanoids! Deiform androids in limousines! A champagne cork in your arsehole! You understand? You hear me? The Europeans ruined everything! The Goth, the Hun, the Houyhnhnm! The Western European mind corrupted everything! You're a Slav, for fuck's sake! You are, aren't you? I hope I'm not mistaken... You're not a Finn or something are you? Not a German deportee from Kazakhstan? You're a Slav! And I'm an Indian! Both of us are victims of European civilisation! How can you not understand! Haven't you read Castaneda?" And so it went, on and on...

Of course I could have pretended that I remembered everything, that I understood it all perfectly. Yes, right you are Hanny, of course! The role of Western European thought in the rapid descent to doomsday, apocalypse in a three-minute ride in a Beamer down the Autobahn, yeah! Of course, Hanny! You and me against the world! I remember about the oil. I remember about the gas! I remember everything, every single word you said is engraved on my heart! I remember about our mission! And so on, and so forth. You couldn't let your guard down with Hanuman.

You had to play up to him, humour him. And there was no way you could contradict him. That would be suicide. He was being tossed this way and that, like a boat in a storm. So much as a squeak, and you'd be swallowed up in the abyss of his insanity.

Hanuman let go of my head. He took a step forwards, then another, stuck out his lower lip and spat out his words in disdain, as if he were clearing his way forwards with spit. Starting with queens, chickens, eggs, he could jump to the economy, social security, and then deeper still, ending up with the Vikings and how they spread vulgarity, vandalism, and carnage throughout the world, how they were worse than any plague. He would say DK for Denmark, and pronounce the two letters like "decay". Then he would start to juxtapose Denmark (and Europe with its Germanic tribes) with India, which he would praise unconditionally, and grandiloquently, with words which were nothing short of poetry.

"Oh, India, cradle of civilisation and source of all tongues! My native Punjab! Land of five rivers, oh ancient land! Mohenjo-daro – have you not heard of it? You should be ashamed of yourself, Euge! Not knowing that is worse than ignorance, it's a sin! The land where the Gods of all mythologies were born. Where Kush and Luv sing the Ramayan. Where Shiva dances, where rocks grow in the gardens. Where golden wasps swarm, where diamond deposits nestle in the folds of mammary tissue. Oh, my native Chandigarh! The city of flowers, the city which Le Corbusier himself built. And the university, where I, now a vagrant, had the honour and good fortune to study and create my unrecognised masterpieces! That five-star university was designed in its entirety by Le Corbusier, and in a way which allowed the students to draw, construct, write, dance, sketch and drink whatever they wanted – twenty-four hours a day, always by natural light, just by moving from auditorium to auditorium, following the sun, to infinity. He-ha-ho! That beats even UCLA. Oh, India! A country with such long monsoons, and such perfect but perhaps not entirely essential irrigation systems, a country of long rivers and long roads, stuffed full of trains and empty purses, a country of poets, culture, love and creation. A country of colours and smiles. A country of song and dance. And Denmark… what kind of country is it? There's not even room to spit. It's not a country, it's a chemist's!" Hanuman yelled.

But what Hanuman could stand least of all was that particular male representative of the species whom you would commonly come across in the Danish provinces. Men in blue overalls, paint splattered like bird droppings across their shoulders, pencils tucked behind brace straps, a mobile phone poking out of the breast pocket, a packet of cigarettes in their belt bag, exuding a complex odour: toothpaste, coffee, tobacco and eau de cologne. They were everywhere. And they were always in demand. The world in which Hanuman simply couldn't find his place depended on men like that. Because they had built this world, and they had done so without ever considering the possibility that two characters like Hanuman and I might appear in it. Hanuman felt uncomfortable in the presence of these people, he started to shiver, he flinched at their gaze, he fidgeted, tugging at his left earlobe or checking his mobile phone. He couldn't handle the way these people always spoke loudly, always walked with a long stride, with a deliberate, heavy footfall, swinging their hefty arms in rolled-up sleeves. Hanuman always started to tremble when he came across their distinct footprints, pressed into the ground. And as if to spite him, these footprints were everywhere. That's what he hated most of all. These footprints were like a reproach to him. They reminded him of the phantasmal nature of his own existence, of how he skated across the world's surface leaving virtually no trace, of how he failed to gain any foothold on the world as it disappeared from under his feet or slipped out of his

33

hands like an incredibly thin piece of silk. This would drive Hanny to despair, and he would start to hate everything and everyone around him with renewed intensity.

He hated the farmers with their crooked cud-chewing mouths. He hated the farms on the edges of the fields which were always divided neatly down the middle, farms frozen still like a contemplative chess move, with the sleepy forms of cows moving sedately across the board. He couldn't bear the sound of the Danish language. He hated the kiosks and the shops and the boys and girls in red Brugsen supermarket uniforms or blue Rema 1000 retailer's outfit; their little peaked caps hurt his eyes, their yapping voices made his ears bleed. The smell of fish mixed with cheap Aalborg schnapps made him weak at the knees. The fumes of *Gammel Densk*[11] wafting through clouds of Samson cigarette smoke gave him heartburn. He would start to hiccup when he saw those grizzly, sour-faced losers who found comfort in horticulture. The coffee from the vending machines took its toll on his liver, the cheap Carlsberg did for his kidneys, he suffered from indigestion, and he complained of pains in his stomach. He suspected every passer-by of being a snitch. He saw a copper at every window. He was a chronic paranoiac. It wasn't easy to get on with him. He could snap like a brittle twig; his moods could change abruptly, just like equipment designed for the tropics went haywire in Europe. He would contradict himself and everyone else too. He could start an argument from nothing. He was capricious, impossible to please. If I wasn't prepared to be as morose as him he would take offence, and start to lump me together with all the things against which we had vowed to wage merciless war. He could become deeply and lastingly depressed in a moment, and any reason would do, there was no point in trying to find out what it could be. There were plenty of reasons all around us. Cast your gaze in any direction

11   "Old Dane", a Danish alcoholic drink with an unusual aftertaste.

and you could immediately find a hundred reasons to be depressed. For example, the Eskimos of Greenland would make him despondent due to their inability to come out of their perpetual hangover. He felt so deeply for them. India continued carrying out its nuclear tests, which drove him to distraction. He announced that he would never go back. "A country which could come up with Buddhism and then test a nuclear weapon has to be the most hypocritical place in the world – I refuse to live there!"

His moods were always changing. Sometimes he seemed bitter. He might barge contemptuously, shoulder-first, into some old man. He could readily insult some little old lady. Those girls with their limpid eyes, multicoloured seaweed for hair, pierced navels, and tattoos in the smalls of their backs aroused animal feelings in him verging on a lust for violence. When Hanuman saw the Unicorn bank attached to the post office building which you could find in nearly every paltry little town, he would clench his teeth, and the muscles of his face would twitch ominously. These powerful emotions were worthy only of respect, but even they could quickly subside, and Hanuman would grow sad and retreat so deeply into himself that you couldn't get through to him at all.

The stupidity and slowness of the farmers drove him wild; he would grow despondent from the endless sea breeze, which spat rain into his face, or wet snow, like phlegm from an expectorating camel. He was oppressed by the twilight into which everything around us would dissolve, he was scared that he would dissolve too, so he stayed close to the lamp posts as we moved around town. But he also hated the bilious yellow hue of those lights. Rustling, whispers, footsteps and echoes would proliferate in the twilight hours. Hanny thought that soon nothing would be left of him but an echo of his former self, and then it would be too late, he would never be able to return. All he could do was shatter into shards like a glass bottle.

The situation in the refugee camp, where we got stuck for several months, got him down. The camp was like a station with far too few tracks for all the trains, and far too few tickets on sale for all the trains which shot through. And even if there were tickets on sale somewhere, it wasn't clear who was selling them and how, and where the ticket office was located, or even the ticket clerk. And as ever, the timetables were totally muddled...

For some time he was preoccupied with the mystery of the Directorate, which everyone was always talking about, and which my uncle wrote to me about over the course of many years. Back then I thought that my uncle was messing about with me because I was a silly student, that he had dreamt up the Directorate and decided to write to me about it, but it turned out I was wrong. The Directorate did in fact exist, this was confirmed by the replies which Nepalino got to his appeal letters. Just like my uncle before him, Hanuman bustled about with documents, traipsed from corridor to corridor, listened to conversations, took notes, assembled papers, read them, tried to analyse them, tracked down evidence of the Directorate's virtual existence via the Internet, he even mastered a significant assortment of Danish bureaucratic terms and phrases. But again, this might have been enough to create the impression of being knowledgeable on the subject, but it was far from sufficient to understand how the whole machine operated. He quickly came to a grinding halt, started to despair and then gave up altogether, arguing that if he was never going to get right of abode then at least he could put down roots on some rubbish dump, spin his web somewhere, go into hiding.

The constant flow of nomads through the camp put Hanuman on edge; the rotation of different characters left a bitter residue, a sense of things left unsaid. With every day the feeling he had missed his train loomed ever larger, a feeling that he had to wait, but that it was now too late – that train had been withdrawn from service, it wouldn't ever be back, and now he had to run, only he didn't know where he was running to. That feeling swelled in him, crushing his chest. He started to get migraines. The pain gnawed at him, tormented him, like a toothache. He had no idea what to do. He turned ashen grey, he started to grind his teeth and groan in his sleep. He must have still been trying to solve the mystery of the Directorate as he slept.

He started to suffer from a migraine from the very first days of our acquaintance, when we were both living in a refuge for illegal immigrants under the protection of an entrepreneurial Kurd who knew how to find work for people without papers – and how not to pay them for it. We stayed at his hostel while we were waiting for illegal documents, which the Kurd had assured us would set us up like gods on earth. Or we were waiting for the person who would supply those documents, or maybe they weren't documents but some kind of key, the right form of words, which would open all doors for us… in any case, we were waiting for something improbable there, and slogging away like dogs for the Kurd! We never got to leave our little room. The window was boarded up so fast that not even the faintest glimmer of light could get through. Our days were so thoroughly planned out that we didn't have so much as a second to think about anything other than work. It was a twenty-four-hour shift. We had to do the lot: chop vegetables for the salads, stuff shawarma kebabs, brew litres and litres of coffee, mop the floors, and fix toys of some sort. Our boss didn't give us a moment to catch our breath, we called him Hotello behind his back. That hostel was on the coast, in a little harbour town called Frederikshavn. Right up north, well off the beaten track. Hanny found a tourist attraction for us up there. It was a window of a little two-storey building. The building itself was old, probably around a hundred years old, but it was just as well preserved as those Danish centenarians who rode about on scooters:

we often saw them gliding pluckily into supermarkets, or barging their way through the crowds of young people at the harbour, with their shopping bags and suitcases on wheels. That window was the masterpiece of Frederikshavn. Hanuman described it as an outstanding work of art which fully encapsulated the true wretchedness of life in this Danish backwater, in all its deathly dreariness. Whenever we looked into this window we saw one and the same sight: a girl sprawled on the sofa in front of the television, legs propped up on a coffee table, smoking one cigarette after the other; she was sleepily watching television, the look of boredom on her face slowly giving way to revulsion, the kind of revulsion you experience when you've smoked too many cigarettes.

Hanuman was fascinated by this window. He would say, "Look at this window Euge! It's so low! It's at waist height. And there's no curtains or blind. It's completely open for all to see, more open than a wide-open door. There's no privacy at all. What's the point of a room like that?"

Later Hanuman would talk about that fake openness, that "velkommen-ness", the soul with ice at its core. Back then, during one of our first cautious walks around Frederikshavn he watched that girl sitting in front of the television, sucked his teeth and said, "Just look at that Euge. Feel the full tedium of human existence… it's Friday evening and that girl is sitting watching TV. Alone! Watching TV and smoking. She's already sick of smoking and whatever she's watching. Soon the life she's living is going to make her sick enough to vomit. But she's still sitting there, gawping at the screen! How wonderful!"

A few days later we went out for a walk, and walked past her window again; and there she was, sitting in front of the television, smoking. The light from the screen was playing across her face, she was sitting there puffing out clouds of smoke, and watching TV. After that we started making a point of going to check if she was still sitting there, and she was always there without fail, sitting in the same spot, as if she were at work in some office. Later Hanuman said to me, "You can find out so much about Denmark just by looking through people's windows. Pretty much everything. Everything you need to know about the people of this country. You don't need to read any books. Just go and take a look in their windows. Firstly, they never cover up those windows. And secondly, their lives are empty, but stuffed full of trinkets, like those little china boys in straw hats with their trousers at half-mast. Or those mermaids. They're everywhere! And their flags! And gnomes, and trolls. He-ha-ho! They've got the lot! And thirdly, buried under those piles of junk they're dying of boredom, because they're total idiots, half-witted numbskulls, that's why it's like taking candy off a baby, Euge!"

But as it turned out, he wasn't completely right, not completely...

The smell of Danish provincial life was another thing which drove Hanuman crazy. Twice a year – once in spring, once in autumn – all the fields of the Jutland peninsula were treated with fertiliser. The process lasted two or three weeks, and during that short period life in Jutland became totally unbearable. Once Hanny said that it felt like living through a plague epidemic which had killed off the whole population, but there was no one to bury the corpses, so they were left lying about, rotting – just that for some reason you couldn't see them.

The smell coming off the field outside the only window of that little room of ours was particularly bitter and acrid, most probably because it mingled with the stench of the refugee camp refuse. That smell could make your eyes water. It would drive Hanuman into a frenzy. Overcome with disgust, he would leap up and rush off, jumping into the first bus which came along, and riding until the fields came to an end, until the blue strip of sea appeared, swelling and sighing under the heavy, leaden wall of sky. He would get out of the bus and head for the water, footsteps sinking into the sand. And as he walked, he blindly extracted a cigarette from the pack with trembling fingers. He approached the water's edge, and bowed before the giant frothing medusa as if he was bowing before his mother. Then he would say his *namaste*, lightly touching the water with his fingers as if touching the hem of a sari, before lighting his cigarette. He could stand there like that for ages, completely alone, back turned to us, completely oblivious to us all.

Later, when he voiced certain thoughts, he would describe the thoughts as being of "littoral" origins; he would say the thought had come to him by the sea.

I counted three such thoughts; maybe there were more, but I remember three. The first concerned global domination through enforcing an absolutist form of leftist taste and aesthetic terrorism. I had only the vaguest understanding of what "leftist taste" could mean, in fact I had no idea whatsoever. I didn't even want to think about what aesthetic terrorism could mean. He shared the second thought, which had also apparently come to him by the sea, at one of our regular dope-smoking sessions, probably at Mr Skov's castle: "I wonder," he said from a cloud of smoke, "did Jesus get his feet wet when he walked on water? What does the Bible say on that point, Euge? Do you remember? That thought came to me by the sea, that time when you were choking on the stench of refuse and asylum-seeker shit, and I was at the beach, relaxing on the sand… Hahaha!" And the third thought… the third thought was connected with Lolland: he said that when he was by the sea he had realised that he wanted to go to Lolland. To be more precise, he had been talking about that for a long time, but before then Lolland had only cropped up in his monologues as some sort of mirage or daydream, an idle thought and nothing more. But after one of his regular escapes to the sea, fleeing the unbearable reek of fertiliser, he became obsessed with the idea. He spoke of nothing else but Lolland, insisting we should go there right away. "To Lolland! To the Scandinavian paradise!" he yelled as he traversed the football pitch with the long strides of an agronomist. "Forwards! To Lolland!" he cried, like a military commander. "Right away! To the place where half-naked girls writhe in the swimming pools like seals, to the place where ecstasy tablets drop into wide-open mouths like meteorites into the ocean's maw. To the place of music and revelry. To Denmark's Ibiza, to Lolland!"

But unfortunately I can't remember why he had decided on Lolland in particular. I remember him saying that the fantastic idea first came to him when he was by the sea; he had even walked knee-deep into the icy water, lured by a vision which emerged from the frothy waves. I remember what he was like when he came back – agitated, electrified, insane. He walked into our cold, dark room with the words "Euge, we're heading to Lolland", and two days later he upped and left again. And I could no longer remember why exactly he had wanted to go to Lolland.

The reason I couldn't remember was probably because I didn't pay much attention to anything back then. I didn't give a damn about anything much. And I didn't believe in all those asylum-seeker fairy tales about paradise. I was sceptical about Lolland right from the very start, even before I heard that Mais, the young Armenian guy, apparently knew all about it. He could tell me a thing or two about a place called Lolland, or so that windbag claimed. With an authoritative air, pulling his rosary beads across his knuckles, he proceeded to inform me, out of the corner of his mouth, that the only reason anyone went to Lolland was to let loose, to get laid, and once you had got there you wouldn't have any trouble finding yourself a girl. But I didn't believe him. That idiot wasn't even a competent thief, but he was so greedy that he couldn't resist trying. He would steal whatever came his way, one time it was even bras, and he would always get nabbed for something stupid (a lump of meat which dropped out of his coat right by the till, for example). We once asked why he stole the bras, joking that he must be some sort of pervert, and he answered in total seriousness that he stole them to sell to Arab women. But no one believed him of course. Arab women never bought anything, they had no money, their husbands kept hold of all the money. Mais didn't even know that! He ate almost nothing. He didn't want to spend his pocket money on food. He used to hang about in the kitchen while the others were cooking. They would feed him out of pity. He would say that he didn't buy food because he didn't know how to cook. He was a fan of Ajax football team, he once stole a pair of football shorts in the team colours and wore them like some kind of trophy. He somehow never managed to get the shirt. He dreamed about going to Germany, and he would stand for hours on end in front of the map, running his finger up and down it, showing everyone the place where he planned to cross the border... A line even appeared on the map, a streak left by his dirty finger, like a slug trail on a leaf. He never did go, I think it was because they were rumoured to pay asylum seekers less in Germany, and he wouldn't be able to handle that. He wasn't capable of taking decisions. All he could do was hang about and gossip; he was particularly good at gossiping. He told us that the Tamils were all homos. He had apparently seen them drawing lots one time. Then when our Chinese neighbour got himself a girlfriend, Mais told us in disgust that he had peeked through a crack in the window and seen the Chinaman buried between her legs, munching away like a pig! "For a whole hour! And he does your cleaning too!" he said, spitting out the words with disdain. There was no knowing what stories he might have concocted about us. But he definitely wouldn't have said anything good! He sucked up to us because everyone else sent him packing, particularly his own people, whom he shamed by being so stupid, so unwashed, and so unshaven. For Armenians all that stuff was very important; suited and booted, creases ironed. Culture! That runt was a blockhead, he dressed in dirty tracksuits, crawled into any open window, and stole anything he could lay his hands on. He often ripped his trousers too. Of course he never found anything of any worth because everyone had stopped keeping stuff in their rooms. Hanuman once told Mais that if he tried to crawl into our window and steal anything, or if Hanuman noticed that something had gone missing or was out of place, then he would go straight round to see him and whip his ass. At which Mais just grinned like a cretin and said, "But how would you know it was me?"

But he never did try and crawl through our window, even though Hanny kept it open at all times. He stole irons and calculators from the discount shops where there were no alarm gates, where no one gave a damn, where an iron might cost fifty kroner, at a generous guess. He was king of those kinds of places. Sometimes he stole three irons at once. Of course, no one bought them off him! But he had to come back with some booty, he couldn't return empty-handed. With his plastic bag, or rucksack, full of something heavy, no matter what it might be, even rocks; the main thing was that the girls in the kitchen saw Mais drag something to his room. What it was exactly, and how soon it would be chucked into the rubbish container – that was less important! And so, I asked myself, what on earth could he know about Lolland! Absolutely nothing! He might be able to muse on the prices for various trains and ferries, granted. Somehow he knew, or pretended to know, how much it would cost to get to Lolland...

"Just three hundred kroner," he said with an authoritative air. "Yep! Three hundred kroner is all I would need to get to Lolland!"

He talked as if he had nothing put aside, as if he didn't have three hundred kroner to his name!

"Much less than going from Bornholm, my friend! From Bornholm you'd have to pay a clean five hundred."

I couldn't bear listening to him. It was total nonsense. Hanuman was smirking too: "Five hundred from Bornholm... where to? Mais, why would you go to Bornholm? So you can go from Bornholm to Lolland?"

"Why does he talk to me like that?" Mais asked me indignantly. "Tell him that I know very well that you can get to Lolland by train... at two hundred kilometres an hour!"

I translated this for Hanuman, trying not to laugh. He looked dumbfounded: could there really be a train to Lolland?

"Of course there is! How could there not be! Without a shadow of doubt! You can go anywhere by train... Their trains go two hundred kilometres an hour! Even to Sweden! And to Germany! Two hundred kilometres per hour! Blink and you're there! One day you set off, and the next day you've already arrived! You have to make sure you've got your passport with you, sometimes they check..."

"Mais, there are no trains to Sweden or Germany, none at all!"

"What do you mean? I saw the proposal myself!"

"That was just a proposal!" Hanuman bellowed. "A projected route, understand! A proposal! For the future... Euge, translate that for him..."

"You don't need to translate! You think I don't understand or something? I understand very well! A proposal! What's to understand, proposal-shmosal. Tell him that there's ferries and trains there... there's even a bus! Choose whichever route you want... three hundred kroner! Costs the same whichever way you go! Five hundred from Bornholm!"

"It costs five hundred to get to Copenhagen and back! From Bornholm! But what has Bornholm got to do with it Mais? We're talking about Lolland here! Lolland, Mais!"

"I know we're talking about Lolland... I'm not an idiot! I'm just comparing the prices."

"Ah, so he's comparing the prices is he… How would you travel from here to Lolland then?" Hanuman asked.

Mais clicked his tongue, rose slowly (first a wrinkle on his forehead, then his backside) and beckoned us to the map of Denmark which Tiko had hung up in their building.

"There's Farstrup, OK brother-dzan. Translate for him, Zhenya-dzan, my English isn't very good…" and he carried on: "there's the station… that's where you get the train, right? To Ringsted, understand? Remember that! Then you have to change trains. It should say Nykøbing F… Remember the F… from there you can get to Lolland… and there's ferries too… From Copenhagen it's three hundred kroner by ferry to Lolland… I know that very well… from Lolland there's ferries to Germany as well, brother-dzan! Were you thinking I was going to Lolland just like that? No sir, I'm thinking about how Mais is going to get to Germany… the ferry – that's an option, my friend, it's an option…"

It was all total nonsense. He didn't have a clue what he was talking about. Why were we all standing there, gawping at the map? The map just served as a visual representation of his deranged thought processes: Germany, Germany, three hundred kroner! From Farstrup to Copenhagen was no less than five hundred. We all knew that.

"I reckon it could be even less," Hanuman said when we had shaken off Mais. "One hundred kroner or so, no more… It's right nearby after all! Just a stone's throw. The main thing is to get to Zealand… we'll need some cash for that… but once we get there, if we manage to forge a ticket… I wonder, can you use the travel card there, or do you need to buy a ticket at the ticket office? What do you reckon, Euge?"

"No idea," I blurted. "But one thing is clear, and that's that Mais is a total idiot, and everything he just said made no sense at all!"

It was true that Mais was a total clown. A clown! All he could do was dream about going somewhere. I could imagine him lying to the younger guys in the other camps, telling them that he'd already been to Lolland, and to Germany, and he'd gone to Sweden on the ferry from Helsingør, and wherever he went he had pulled off some amazing feats, which basically meant he'd knocked off some shops... It wasn't hard to imagine!

He hadn't been anywhere, and he knew absolutely nothing! All he could do was wank over pictures of places. That's all he could do. What was the point of him going to Lolland anyway? What chance did he have of getting laid? What had he actually seen in his life? What was that drivel about Belgium? About the jewellery shops which he'd supposedly robbed? About the jeep which he'd supposedly flipped over when the police were chasing him? His fantasies were on roughly the same level as a low-budget war film. One time we were walking down a street in Aalborg with him when two pretty Danish girls walked past; for some reason he started talking to me loudly in French, which basically meant a random selection of the French words he knew: "*Alyor mon ami, tu t'apple Ezhen eh mwa apple Mais eh nu vivon isi a Danmark eh se byen, nes pa, mon ami? Kes ke tu pans, twa, eh?* Let's make them think that we're frogs, alright? Say something, go on... maybe we'll get lucky..."

Oh the idiot! The complete fool! Why did he latch on to us at Aalborg? He totally embarrassed himself back there! He hadn't been anywhere apart from the transit camps. Maybe Taastrup and Roskilde as well. He spent his time there stealing torches and kids' air pistols. As soon as he got to Aalborg he came a cropper at the mobile phone shop. "Wait right here, my friend; I'm getting to work. Zhenya-dzan, watch, brother-djan, watch Mais at work, soon Mais will be chatting on his very own phone." He went into the shop, and I lit up a cigarette. I didn't even manage to finish it before the alarms started wailing; an awful din, like at a fairground. We calmly got up from the bench and moved on.

"Phew... thank God for that, he got caught," Hanuman sighed.

"Yeah, thank God, we won't see that idiot until the evening..."

But he didn't show himself in the camp for a whole week; he was too embarrassed, he hid himself away, the proud eagle couldn't handle the shame. The cretin. What could he know about Lolland? Nothing, that's what. Mais was an idiot. A cretin. A dumb bastard. No, if you listened to fools like Mais you needed diagnosing yourself. Because everything they said about Lolland was gibberish. Those stories were like a skin rash, or dandruff, which you could catch through a handshake. They were an infection which spread from the empty, idle minds of the asylum seekers. I didn't understand, nor did I want to understand, what was Hanuman's interest in that little island? What was it for? Why did he suddenly want to go to places in Lolland, like Maribo or Nakskov, if he'd been planning to go to America for as long as I had known him? He was crazy about SoHo! He could reel off a list of every cosy spot, all his favourite bars, restaurants, shops; he talked about SoHo and its denizens as if he had already lived there, as if he were personally acquainted with every pooch, as if he felt genuine nostalgia for New York. He had already planned his life's trajectory. He wasn't going to just sit about, not Hanuman, he was going to America. His whole life revolved around going to America, whichever way he could, by whatever means of transport, via whichever countries necessary. To start with he was planning to go via Greenland and Canada. Then via Iceland, which he would reach via the Faroe Islands. Then via Argentina, changing in Cardiff. But the final destination never changed, because there was no other point on the planet which could ever be final. Nothing was as important as the States. And then, all of a sudden... Maribo, Nakskov... What was Lolland compared to Manhattan and California? Or SoHo? Come off it! It just sounded silly. It had no shock value. It wasn't going to impress anyone. Whoever you told you were going to Lolland would just laugh in your face. We were always going to New York, Hanuman... to our Babylon... what happened, Hanny!

The new direction didn't make any sense to me. What was the point? I had already got used to the idea that he was going to America, and I had got used to the idea that I was somehow going there with him... what was Lolland for? America was the place for us! It was his indefatigable belief that sooner or later he would definitely get there which was what made Hanuman so special. In my imagination he was already living there. Twisting time inside out, I spoke with him as if he had already come back from America. For me Hanuman was no ordinary person, for me he was part of a myth, in my mind he was "Hanuman SoHo-man".

That was why it was so hard for me to get used to the new direction of his dreams. Everything which conflicted with the myth of America made me uneasy. He had no right to diverge from the dream. Everything depended on it! His dedication to the myth had instilled an illusory sense of security. I reckoned that he should hold on tight to his America, like Aladdin to his lamp! Without America he was nothing. A nonentity. I reckon he knew that himself... But the most important thing was the formula which I had devised for myself, the formula which only my mushroom-addled brain could have come up with: until Hanuman went to America, I wouldn't go home. An ideal equilibrium! A fantastic balance! The longer it took Hanuman to get to America, the longer I would take not going home. Judging by the pace at which Hanuman was nearing the country of his dreams, I would never have to go back to Estonia at all. And that suited me just fine. The rest of it didn't bother me much. That was why I helped him any way I could. We had struck the deal in the attic at Hotello's; I swore that I would help him realise his goal, if he guaranteed me eternal non-return. We sealed our deal with a bottle of contraband whisky from the Kurd's stocks. It was that night in the attic, to the accompaniment of the howling draft and creaking floorboards, that I discovered that Hanuman knew thousands of stories about people going to America; he'd been collecting them since childhood. He had wandered around backyards listening to old blokes' stories. He had hassled the sailors in Bombay, as if he were begging them for alms. He had slept outside young girls' windows after soldiers had sneaked in, because "soldiers spin all sorts of yarns to their girls when they're in the sack, and the favourite story is about their trip to America!" That night he told me the latest story, which he had heard from a Somali in Sweden, not long before he hopped across to Denmark. It was a sad story about twenty-three Somalians setting course for America by ship, about how the captain discovered that there were suddenly twenty-four of them, and ordered that one be chucked overboard, because he had only been paid for twenty-three. That was why Hanny always told me that he would never join forces with anyone. "Just you and me, that's it. No one else! No groups of any sort! Travelling in a group is dangerous," he would say, "especially if you can't negotiate with the trafficker yourself."

His favourite literary character was Sinbad the Sailor. His favourite book, *One Thousand and One Nights*. He was headed for America with every single ounce of his being. Even the Soviet Union's missiles weren't as closely trained on America. That was why he was already there, as far as I was concerned. If he really had to then he would hijack a plane. He talked about it all the time… it was just that he hadn't yet found the right plane. It's not every day that you meet someone who would be capable of such a thing.

It was hard to catch Hanuman out with a silly question like, "So what are you up to Hanuman?" He always had one and the same answer. "Me? Well, I'm going to America." Even if he happened to be shaving, or puffing on a joint

49

at the time. Even if he was just standing in a queue with a beer and a piece of cheese stashed inside his coat. Even if he was leafing through a porno mag, with the little Nepali wriggling about under his quilt. Even if the boss caught him in the storeroom with a stolen bottle of whisky in his hand. What do you think he was doing? Hah, he was going to America! Even if his spindly, nimble fingers were sneaking into someone's knickers, he was only going to America! Even if his sparkling snow-white line was three times fatter than the other three, he was just going to America – he just needed a bit of a boost to get there. He wouldn't just steal a bike, he needed it to ride to America. He wouldn't climb into a rubbish container just to rummage about for some grub; no, he was preparing for a journey and was going no other place than America. What if he had slipped his hand into the pocket of an old man sleeping on the train, to steal his ticket to Copenhagen? No, Copenhagen was just a stopping-off point, his real destination was America. And whatever else he got up to, whatever else that happened to him, he was just passing through, it was life in the rear-view mirror on his journey to America.

Hanuman had been on his way to America ever since he had started watching *Star Trek*, ever since he had started reading comics, ever since he had pulled on his very first pair of jeans. From then on he had constantly been going to America. But Lolland – he'd been going there for just a few days. No, it was nonsense... That's why I wasn't particularly upset when he came and announced to us all that he was going to Lolland; I assumed that it didn't mean anything, it was just a whim, a short detour which basically changed nothing, we were still going to America. And then, two days after we used up our supply of rice and mutton, and the Nepali refused to feed us, and the Tamil didn't show up with the supplies, and the Chinaman finally did for the heater with his damp rag, Hanuman upped and left again, and I even felt glad... I assumed that this time it was for good. I decided that this time he must have left for America. For good. At long last. How much longer was he going to mess about! It was time for action. He had left so many times before, and every time it was supposed to be for good. He would shout, "I've had enough of it here," and "finito!", grab his leather jacket and his case, and with his war cry "Hasta la vista!" and a yell of "see ya guys in the USA!" he would leave, clicking the heels of his Camels as he went. Then the bang of the door would reach us from the corridor, the thin wall of the building would shudder slightly, and for a while we would hear the gentle grumble of gravel as his footsteps departed across the yard, and that was it, he was gone without a trace. Apart from a few shirts strewn here and there, the porno mags on the shelf, and his old phone charger. Nothing, apart from the ashtray full of cigarette butts and ash. Nothing, apart from the scent of eau de cologne, which was swiftly devoured by the stench from the field. Nothing apart from the little Batman he'd drawn on the wall. That was it.

And although I was sure he wouldn't come back, I never followed him. Not because I hadn't given a damn about the States for ages now, or to be precise, not only because of that. Mostly because I couldn't walk any more. After enduring the torture of my shoddy Polish boots my feet simply refused to make contact with the Earth's surface; for me, the Earth was medically proscribed. Hanuman once said to me, "If you write poetry, Earth is no place for you. You should live up in the sky! What do you want to go to America for? Forget it!"

He was right. Yep, he was so right... I didn't know how to live on Earth. Whatever Earth used to hold a man to its surface was missing in me; I was lacking that certain something which was necessary for my feet to get a firm purchase on it... It was physically impossible for me to walk! I couldn't even pull my socks on, let alone my boots. It was silly to think about going to America. The roads there were endlessly long, and petrol was so expensive… it was getting more and more expensive by the day – by the time we got to America, the prices would have risen so much that it didn't bear thinking about! And anyway, I never did learn to drive… I would have to hobble along on my poor old feet! They were so swollen and ached so much. No way, you could do as you pleased, but I definitely wasn't going to America, there was nothing for me there, not with feet like mine. You must be joking! God, sometimes I thought I could hear my feet moaning! So I did nothing, I just lay there and didn't even dare think about the possibility that I might have to get up and go somewhere.

Before we settled in the camp I had probably walked around two hundred kilometres, and the boots which I found in some rubbish bin had left my feet crippled, finishing off the job that football had started several years earlier. And so when the Nepali and Tamil let us stay with them I immediately clambered up on to the top bunk and settled there, up high, as far above ground level as possible. And I tried not to think about footwear at all. Every time Hanuman left, I thought I would never see him again. "Farewell, Hanny," I thought to myself as I filled my pipe.

But Hanuman came back; after a few days, he always came back. And then he suffered all the more. He said that he returned because he had seen some foolish glimmer of hope; maybe the smell would have dissipated and everything would go back to normal. But as soon as he had passed through the Løgstør district, where the fields started again, the smell wafting off them was just as before.

The stench rose from the fields and formed a thick wall around our settlement, poisoning us, like a chemical weapon or gas attack. Like the village which, according to the Kurds, Saddam had destroyed (that village figured in every Kurdish asylum case, the Kurds in our camp seemed to be constantly recounting, with wavering voices, how a relative had perished there, although I never could remember the name). Surrounded on all sides by fields, caught in that trap, Hanuman began to perish, like a soldier without a gas mask.

"Wherever you go in this town it stinks," he cursed, "damned farmers! Everywhere you look you see the same little houses, with their little gardens full of pretty little flowers. Mimosas, lupins, rhododendrons, anything you please! Your eyes see one thing, but at the same time there's this stench, and it's no laughing matter! It's like everything else in this country. You see one thing, but what you get is something completely different. They even say their numbers back-to-front. Five and twenty. Three and eighty. One hundred six and thirty. And it's totally impossible to tell the difference between seventy and ninety. It's a coded country. We need to get Gulliver here. Gulliver!"

"Scowl all you like," I said with a yawn, "that's nothing... In Germany they write their numbers like that too, but France is something else altogether... all you want to say is ninety-three, but you have to tie your tongue in knots with 'four times twenty and thirteen', how do you like that?"

"Piffle," he muttered. "At least in France they don't promise you anything. They don't even look at your case. They don't suck your blood from you drop by drop. They just shove you on a plane or a boat, and send you back where you came from. At least they're honest about it. Some of the local black and Middle Eastern guys are even scared to go to the airport in case they get mistaken for illegal immigrants and deported. But here... they talk a lot, promise you this and that, but you end up with something completely different. Starting with their damned language. Don't believe your eyes! And you'd be best off bunging up your ears too. It looks like one thing on paper, but when you try to read it out, no one will understand a word you're saying. And if they tell you something, you won't know how to write it down. You try to buy a ticket to Frederikshavn, and you end up in Fredericia. Further away from Frederikshavn than when you started off. There's this town, it's written Mariager but it's pronounced "Maya", for god's sake! They write *nogen*, but they say *nue*. And they've got dozens of words which sound just like *nue*. Just try and understand which of them means what. And then there's this eternal stink… Frederikshavn suffocated me, wore me down, but I survived. Copenhagen poisoned me, tried to kill me, set the cops on me, but I got away. But this little bug-infested town… can't be more than a thousand people living here. And all the streets have such pretty names: *Klevervej, Anemonevej, Margeritevej, Industrievej, Fabrikvej, Brandstasjonvej*, and last but not least *Bensinstasjonvej*… but it's all so deadly dull, and wherever you go there's this vile stench, it's enough to make you top yourself!"

It got me down as well, but not as much; for Hanuman it was pure torture. He started to hallucinate, he lost touch with reality. Quite literally. He couldn't eat because he immediately started vomiting. The deepest melancholy overcame him, and he would look at the same three pictures of his wife for hours on end, sobbing. He couldn't sleep. And if he did manage to get to sleep, then he'd start raving. Of course I couldn't understand what he said in his sleep. But the Nepali guy laughed. He laughed, but he wouldn't wake Hanuman. He lay there, wrapped up like a mummy, listening to Hanuman raving, and giggling. But he obviously understood what the exhausted Indian was saying. That's why he lay there giggling. But he also giggled because he found the smell pretty easy to handle himself. He had lived in the jungle, in the swamps, for him malarial mosquito bites were nothing, he wasn't going to let some fertiliser smell bother him. Decay was his native habitat. So he took pleasure in watching the Indian suffer.

Whenever Hanuman woke up and saw the smile on the Nepali's face, he'd get up right away and start beating him, swearing like even my dear departed dad didn't know how to. Eventually he stopped even bothering to check if the smile had appeared on the Nepali's face. He just made eye contact with him, bellowed, "What are you looking at?" and started whacking him, using a sandal so as to spare his soft hands. The Nepali resigned himself to that state of affairs surprisingly quickly, and seemed prepared to permanently play the humiliated and downtrodden role he even seemed to welcome. For Hanuman, beating the Nepali turned into a kind of obligation, a ritual without which no day would be complete. Having beaten the little rascal, Hanuman started smoking, exhaling noisily, trying to drive away the stench of the fertiliser. He smoked and paced up and down the room, he smoked and paced and swore. Sometimes, if he wasn't swearing, he would complain of a migraine and curse the farmers and the maize. But he would never shut the window. He always kept the window open. Always. Without fail.

I was lying looking at the ceiling when the smell first arrived. Actually, no… I was lying there with my eyes shut, and in my slumbering brain, which was already seriously addled by grass, picture postcard memories floated by, mingling with bizarre images of the reality of camp life. And then suddenly I realised that something was not quite right, something was awry. Something had changed. Something had joined the customary sensations, which by now were quite familiar in all their disgustingness. One other spice which was not previously present had been mixed in with the bitter taste which normally accompanied my troubled excursions into the past. I normally returned to my past as a ghost, or a demon, or as some bystander (a Herbalife salesman, or a Jehovah's Witness with a stack of leaflets), but now another serpent had slithered in. It was that smell.

At first I thought that some animal had snuffed it, maybe a cat, or the Potapovs' rat. But it was the field, or to be more precise, the fertiliser.

It was vile. Hanuman sensed it too and woke, uttering "yuck!" and adding, "Has our Nepali friend shat himself or something? Oi, you bastard, wake up!"

Hanuman started kicking him awake; then he switched to Hindi for greater persuasion. Naturally the Nepali ended up getting a beating (and Hanuman hurt his finger again).

The smell was of exceptionally lethal strength. It had ripened in the vats of asylum seekers' shit, mixed with the stench of rotten compost and the pure organic fertiliser, growing unprecedentedly powerful. Once the fertiliser had been dumped on to the field it would start creeping outwards in all directions, reaching as far as twenty kilometres. Then, joining forces with similar smells which emanated from the neighbouring fields, it would begin its assault. The ring tightened its grip until the stink held sway everywhere, leaving not a single spot in the whole district to take refuge. On one fateful day the whole of Farstrup (that miserable little Danish town stranded in the middle of Jutland's wilderness) became a zone of malodour in a matter of hours.

Hanny and I put our heads together... we had to decide where to go next, because it was impossible to tolerate this place a moment longer. But there was nowhere to go. We didn't have the money to get to Lolland, not even for the ticket there, to say nothing of board and lodging, or entertainments.

"Unless you've got at least two thousand in hard currency you can't do anything there," Hanny-Manny argued, "that's the minimum you'll need just to get started. That's as clear as day! And how much do we have? A measly three hundred. We're just kids, little kids... maybe we should strangle our Nepali cat. Pull his savings out of his arsehole and do a runner?"

"We'll get caught," I said, trying to put him off the idea.

"Yes, of course we will," he agreed without hesitation. "They catch people fast here. But we still need to get a move-on, it's unbearable here. Look what kinds of thoughts this stench is driving me to. You see? This could all end very badly..."

We were both superstitious, so we couldn't help seeing the onset of the stink as some sort of omen. We decided that it could mean only one thing: it was time to move on.

Every day he found more and more reasons to complain. One time he shouted, "Everywhere in this place stinks like the Gents. Wherever you turn, it smells of shit… You go to the bar for a drink and it's full of shit. You go to a nightclub, and it's full of shit! To the library – and even that's full of shit. Nothing left for it but to plug up your nose… or cut it off altogether!"

He started smoking more and more, and pacing round the room talking to himself.

"Things wouldn't be too bad if it wasn't for that stench," he said trying to look on the bright side of things, cracking his knuckles as he spoke. "In principle we could stay here, in the camp. While they're yet to deport the Nepali, while they're still processing that queer's case, we can stay at his place. They'll take a long time on him. They have to observe all the formalities, everything has to be done by the rulebook. He pretends to be a refugee by the rulebook, and they reject his application by the rule book; they can't just put him on a plane and chuck him out with a parachute somewhere over Nepal. What were you thinking! They're humane, not like that French lot! That's what the French did with those Malians. But those Mali guys are no pushovers. They smashed the plane to bits in mid-air, the pilot almost couldn't land, and then they never took off again, because the Malians took the plane to pieces, and threatened to do the same thing to every single French plane used to deport Malians. The Danish are in the same position. They've got to think up some way of dressing it all up with nice words, the nicest way of sending that Nepali queer back home without infringing his rights or breaking the law. And they need full assurance that he won't be killed when he gets back, right there in the airport, like what happened with those forty-five Iraqi refugees. That was a big scandal. From then on they started granting asylum to every single Iraqi. They'll let them stew for a while, but they always grant it in the end. And if an Iraqi refugee can prove he's a Kurd, then they'll roll out the red carpet! But the Nepali won't be shot when he gets back. In Nepal they let them rot in prison instead. They've got it all worked out there. No one will ever know a thing. One more Nepali cat coughs it, one more Nepali toad smothered in his own excrement. No one cares. The world won't stop turning, so who cares. The illustrious humanitarian agency manages to save face. Nepal takes back its prodigal son, and no one gives a damn about what happens next. But – they still need to deport him quietly, and preferably at minimal expense, that's the main thing. Ha, no one needs a scandal. Who wants a scandal? Everyone wants to keep their hands nice and clean. So he dies later. At least there'll be no articles in the local papers, no fuss over the Nepali shrimp. They don't need people nattering on trains, they don't want homos demonstrating with banners in support of the Nepali queer. No, they'll deport the Nepali any way they can, as long as it's quietly. They don't need another Nepali arse bandit in the Kingdom of Denmark. They've got enough arses of their own. They have to deport him, but they need to maintain the appearance of a caring humanitarian agency, which decides who to grant leave to remain, who not to, in accordance with the regulations as set out in some document. But those regulations are formulated in such a convoluted way that people have to spend years and years and submit tons of paperwork to prove that they satisfy just one of the points. And over the years the situation might change, and the requirements might be reviewed. Who's going to spend years examining your case anyway? In any case it's the cops who decide everything here, not some humanitarian agency. In this police state it's the spooks who are in charge, and they're the ones who will decide whether our Nepalino gets to stay in Denmark or whether he has to go back to the chaos he came from. To be precise, they decided it straight away, they decided ages ago that he would be going home. Then they handed the case over to the humanitarian agency, whose task it is to dress up the refusal in nice words and inform this sorry soul, to provide firm grounds for the refusal, to explain to him on paper why he's going home. But he already knows, he doesn't need it explained, he understands perfectly well, the only use of the explanation letter is to gain time: the longer it takes them to explain to him why he is going home, the better. They write him one rejection letter, and he responds with fifty letters to fifteen different organisations. He's pretty well informed, his uncle gave him all the blank appeal and petition forms, he's got a whole heap of documents, and he just sits there filling them out. Good for him. What else is he supposed to do? That way he kills time, and writing all those letters helps him learn the language, and the money keeps trickling in. He writes his letters – and they have to reply. And he couldn't be happier, because every reply means more time. He's happy that all the red tape drags on and on. The longer it drags on, the more benefits he stashes up his backside. And maybe in a year or so the situation will change, maybe he'll get the chance to move on somewhere else, or maybe he'll slope off back to Germany, back to his bum buddy, and there he'll go back to chopping up vegetables, stirring Chinese soups with his ladle, giving his boss a Thai massage. Anything could happen, maybe an opportunity will come his way for a sham marriage with some other queer just like him. And there's also the option of making an appeal, and the appeal process looks like it could last forever. All you need is some silly little article on Nepal off the Internet, and the situation could radically change... a typhoid epidemic breaks out, and end of story! A massive landslide, diseased cattle, the spread of an intestinal bacteria which is harmful to human life. That's it! His life is in danger. Who is going to send the sorry soul to his certain death in Nepal when it is in the grips of typhoid or the plague? In other words, the whole thing might drag on, and as long as all that bureaucratic hassle continues, while the legal and administrative processes run their course, while the Nepali presents more and more papers, evidence of the flagrant infringement of his rights as a queer, as a human being, moreover as a human being of Nepali origin, as long as he carries on praying that civil war flares up in Nepal, that a revolution takes place, or that China invades, or India, or that good old mass typhus breaks out, while a solicitor gets involved in his case, while all that nonsense carries on, we could just calmly sit it out here, clambering in rubbish bins, knocking about town, cutting ourselves a hunk of someone's mutton from the communal cold store for a modest meal, collecting bottles, swapping ten empty ones for a bottle of cheap plonk, however vile… at the end of the day, as long as they don't throw our arses in jail we could live here, it wouldn't be too bad… If only it weren't for that damned smell!"

Hanuman claimed he was ready to live in that camp for eternity. He was even ready to give up on America. For him that was a major sacrifice. He was ready to fester in that camp until the end of his days. He said that he was used to keeping one ear cocked at night, and waking every morning to expect the most unpleasant thing which could befall an illegal immigrant. He was resigned to the fact that the Serbs were rowdy halfwits, that the Muslims sounded like zombies when they sang their prayers. He was used to this ghostly existence, he was resigned to the fact that he would never reach his second homeland, that America would remain just a dream, and that even if all of his efforts were directed at that single goal, he would never move closer to it physically. He was resigned to it all, was going with the flow and was prepared not to ever acquire life's baggage, or new passport data, or settle down with a lawful wedded wife and a bevy of children. He had stopped dreaming of having his own bank account, with its own code, where his state benefits could slowly accrue. Hanuman was ready for all those sacrifices! He had even given up on God, because God had long since given up on him. He was ready to put up with a life of penury and prison, he had resigned himself to all the likely and unlikely unpleasantness which could befall his sorry soul, which he had long been in mourning over, and he was ready for anything. "Bring it on!" he shouted, "Bring it on, whatever you've got! Anything but that smell. Anything but that vile fertiliser. Anything but that tractor and the stench coming off that field!"

Yes, Hanuman was ready for anything: he was even ready for all his plans to end in a fiasco, to be awarded the lifelong appellation of "loser". Whatever you like! It's no problem at all! Anything you please... It was nothing for him. Hanuman had had all sorts of things happen to him. He'd put up with far worse. And he'd lived to tell the tale. He'd experienced pretty much the lot. He'd suffered worse than you can ever imagine. He'd put up with a bullying older brother who slipped a snake into his bed and put bugs into his food. He'd put up with a father who drilled them like soldiers preparing for the next war with Pakistan or China, or maybe even America. He'd put up with the grotty neighbourhood boys who envied him for his light-toned skin, so much so that they blushed as dark as Tamils, and chucked clods of earth at him every day on the way to school, so he would be dirty-brown like them too. He'd put up with the cheating girlfriend who favoured rich Babuji the businessman, who had pockets deeper than her vagina and a drooping lower lip longer than his dick.

He had even survived the cellar where his old granny locked him to try and cure him of onanism. The cellar containing the corpse which the monks had brought from the graveyard on granny's orders. He even survived that wretched cellar with the stinking corpse, teeming with maggots and flies feasting noisily on the old man's putrefying body. He survived his time in prison, he didn't allow himself to be humiliated. He survived starvation and a heroin overdose. He survived a ship's hold, where he sat for three months without seeing the sun. Without seeing anything, anything at all. He didn't hear a word spoken in his own language. He saw nothing apart from his own vomit and the bucket he crapped in. The bucket which tipped over hundreds of times, leaving him sprawling on all fours in his own sick and shit. He lived through that, and he survived… But he simply couldn't bear that smell. That smell drove him crazy. That smell was worse than anything… worse than the decaying corpse in the cellar… worse than the vomit in the ship's hold. Worse than the snake in his bed and the insects in his rice… even the horny-skinned toad, the warty toad which they shoved into his pants… even that toad was nothing compared to the smell coming off those fields.

"Something is rotten in the state of Denmark," he concluded. "The whole country is decomposing, like a corpse. Now I'm convinced of that. He-ha-ho! The Danish kingdom is decomposing before our very eyes. What's the point of them fertilising anything?"

"That's a maize field, Hanny," I said calmly, without opening my eyes. I reminded him that we had recently eaten sweetcorn from that very field.

"Even the rotten potatoes which the Albanians fry up on Thursdays don't smell as vile as that," Hanny said in revulsion.

I had to agree with him, they didn't; that much was certain.

Every morning at the camp was like a mental blackout. Real life came to an abrupt end as soon as I woke. Reason deserted me. Insanity ensued. The loss of all sensations. Chaos. Anarchy. Spiritual collapse. Morning poisoned my blood, seeking to displace all that was human in me, to destroy the last defences of my immune system, to eradicate the last traces of my being, just like they exterminate lice. So that, gelded and eviscerated, with my soul sucked out of me, I would go and hand myself over to the cops. Every morning was the same, exactly the same. Like a rehearsal for the most excruciating play. Like the return of the same nightmare. Morning manifested itself in every bend of the corridor, in every creak of the door, in every sigh of the soul, in every bird's shriek, in every flush of the toilet. And it was always exactly the same, down to the most tedious of details. It was so uniform that any sensation of progression through time evaporated. It was a repeat of one and the same day. The needle was stuck in the groove. Hey, you, the nearest to the record player, blow on that needle!

Everything about the situation oppressed me, tormented me, gnawed away at me, made me want to run away, tested my resolve, drove me slowly out of my mind. It was as if someone were whispering to me, "Aha! A nice mess you got yourself into! Well, if you call yourself a refugee, then go ahead and enjoy the full emotional spectrum of the outcast's life." Try the timeless terror which has oppressed the human race since the moment of its appearance on earth; the gut-wrenching umbrage, indignation, jealousy; the biblical fear of being hounded until the end of one's days; nostalgia, maybe in fashion now, but no less of a torment; loneliness of mythical proportions; the burden of memories which grows heavier with every day; a looming wall of hatred for the world; self-pity; humiliation, and a readiness to be humiliated; disgust at oneself, even more disgust at everyone else; the dead weight of bureaucracy; your readiness to become nothing under its pressure, to diminish into nothingness; learning to measure the loss of any genuine human virtues by your own example; to become free of all those virtues forever; to become smaller than nothing; to know the full boundlessness of hatred for the rest of the world; despair in its purest form, multiplied by an impureness of thought, and so on and so forth...

Those are the typical symptoms written on the face of every asylum seeker, allowing him to be identified from a crowd of locals just as easily as identifying a hepatitis sufferer by his jaundiced complexion. It's what the refugee has to live with every God-given day. It's what, in essence, makes him a refugee, even if he is yet to be classified as one. It makes no difference if his village hasn't been bombed, he fears being deported even more than someone whose village has. Those kinds of feelings have a levelling effect. And so someone whose village is sleeping peacefully at night can't sleep peacefully himself, because it means he could be sent straight home; he envies the guy whose village has been blitzed, and secretly wishes that his village would be destroyed too.

In the refugee camp people would wake with a complex tangle of emotions pressing on their chests, gripping at their throats. People would start the day with that noose around their necks, with a lump of resentment in their throats, with that tight knot of emotions in their stomachs. With inflamed eyes, bedraggled, they groped their way out of their rooms, stumbling off in search of someone on whom to unload their burdens, someone who could help to loosen that knot, someone they could cough up the lump in their throat on to. People sloped round the camp like gallows birds. They bumped into each other in the corridors and started sharing their worries, recounting their nightmares, infecting each other with their anxieties (as if it made them feel better to make someone else suffer too). They wound up getting into conversations, and these conversations got them more wound up, and they shuffled off like mechanical toys, blighted, agitated, looking for someone to soothe their souls. Other people tagged on, others who were also afflicted, sick, dishevelled. Their numbers grew and grew... that build-up of fear and disquiet started from dawn.

The thoughts and feelings which troubled the typical asylum seeker built up overnight and then burst free with accumulated force. As if you had died in your sleep, and then in the morning you were reanimated, sliced open, brought back to life with an electric shock, and ordered to carry on living. And you lie in bed groaning, asking yourself the eternal question, "Why the hell…"

That's how the mornings went in the Farstrup camp. They would jolt into life like some kind of mechanical device. They progressed, step by step, like some kind of ritual, or medical procedure. They ground us to a polish, like military training. Mornings would arrive like an executioner, with a set of instruments for corrective torture, as prescribed by the disciplinary commission. The instruments were of the most ordinary kind: morning light, a slight chill, sounds of various kinds.

The light entered barefooted and shivering, cautious and unsure, like a timid young thief. But then, having quickly appraised the situation and got its bearings, it became surer of itself, cockier, it started to show an interest in its surroundings, it grew inquisitive, importunate; now it was blue and pale, stealing into your soul like a pathologist's probe, turning your being inside out.

This light somehow had a metallic quality, glassy even, it was surreal and cynical, it intruded unobstructed, and it started pressing, pressing like it was being pumped in by a dynamo which was hidden away in a cellar somewhere, its machinery grinding away. That barely perceptible tremor made you ill at ease – unusually agitated – and then the shuddering started. That was the cold. It stole in like a ghost in a mortuary, like a wayward wraith which had just shuffled off its mortal coil, still not sure what to do with itself, where to perch, wandering about, prodding sleeping forms at random, hoping to find somewhere to slip in.

Morning always let the light in first, it groped its way across objects in the twilight, making things visible which it would be preferable never to see. Then the cold would follow, led by the light on a lead. And after them marched that raucous rabble of sounds which always came with the start of day. They advanced from every corner, japing and jeering, mincing and mocking...

The sounds of the camp, the sounds of these outcasts' lives, of these bedraggled refugees from life. Who were they? Nature's surplus, disdained by the societies of various countries? Offcuts from the otherwise perfect form of this wondrous world? The ones who had managed to escape with their lives, the sole survivors, tossed up by merciful elements on to the shores of Denmark – or, still worse, of Jutland – with its maize, cows, chicken coops and the rest of that respectable dross. Had the world seemed too round for them? Was it spinning too fast under their feet? For many of them it was burning, hissing, spitting shards of exploding mines, pumping geysers of blood. Pyramids crumbled, tectonic plates formed many eons ago shifted, archipelagos of states split asunder, rock tumbled after rock, and life came crashing down around them like an avalanche; life disintegrated and collapsed like a landslide, it raced off like a steam engine at full speed, branches flashed past windows, sighing farewells, while fear, horror, wailing, and death trod on their heels. And so they ended up in the sewage canal of the Danish provinces. Stuck between the lavishly fertilised maize fields and football pitches where walking was forbidden. They ended up locked in the deathly dead end of the eternal weekend, in a cramped train carriage which was headed nowhere, going round and round in circles, circles which made you sick from the monotony. And they would hear the same phrase again and again, spoken in a heavy Danish accent: "You must wait a bit longer." And so they waited, trudging here and there, jostling in queues for handouts, cursing, stealing, drinking, brawling, going stale, rotten like vegetables no one wanted to buy. They waited to be fed to the cattle, to be sent back into the inferno, they waited for an answer... That is what they fell asleep to, every single night. And every single morning it started afresh: the brazen cold, the stench from the field, the viscous quivering light, restoring things to their material forms. With the situation exactly the same – an endless feeling of inevitability.

Inexorably, the square outlines of our useless, clunking old television took form from the gloom. Underneath it, like a pedestal, the coffee table revealed itself, with its revoltingly rounded, bright-yellow handles. Hanging on the wall was a calendar open at April 1995 (that had been a lie for more than three years now). And a poster of three German girls called Tic, Tac and Toc (I had no idea which was which, but of course Hanuman knew the family tree of every one of those dusky vixens; they were his darlings). Distended metal cupboards, greyish blue. As the light gained dominion the ceiling seemed to get lower and lower, and the smeared corpses of the flies which perished in a summer psychosis became more clearly visible. Vile! One and the same motif, every single morning.

It felt like it all been predetermined. This nightmare seemed to be the work of a cunning designer. He had planned everything so that morning would deliver all the filth of the world straight into my soul, as if it were exacting vengeance for everything I had smoked, drunk, or injected the night before. The stench from the field made me nauseous, my drowsy, groggy brain started raving and conjuring up visions. And in my delirious state, still half-asleep, I asked myself what kind of a world this could be; a world where I had tripped and fallen face down, just like falling into shit, all because I was born under the wrong star. During the comedown it occurred to me that all of this must have been preordained. Having fallen from my customary environment, having been separated from my grim, but familiar former life, from the normal order of things, I was like a wheel detached from the spindle of my native cart. And so I had to roll onwards, eventually coming to rest in this ditch where no other start to the day was possible.

Because all the grimness of the world was collected within these four walls, amidst this rubbish, this filth, these thieves, drug addicts, fugitive terrorists, scammers, speculators, and con men who had come to this country in search of an easy life, and ended up in this pigsty, this stinking cesspit.

When I was high, I thought: "Oh-ho, this is just for starters. The best is yet to come. Hang in there! If the start of the day is so dismal, wouldn't it be best not to wake up at all?"

Or at least it seemed that I was thinking… In fact there were no thoughts as such, just jellyfish, swimming through the aquarium of my see-through head, randomly coalescing, creating some semblance of thought. And in the mornings I was clammy, as if I had been hung up to dry overnight, but hadn't been properly wrung out, like the dripping floorcloth which Chinaman Ni draped on the radiator every evening.

He always hung his things there, repeatedly breaking the rules, but the rest of us were tired of trying to tackle the problem. We'd tried explaining it to him. Every way possible. But every time we started talking to him the Chinaman just produced a grubby piece of paper from his pocket, on which was written, "I speak only china tung."

The note was so old that it looked like it might crumble in his hands, like a piece of parchment. God only knows what kind of illiterate idiot wrote it for him, and how many years ago. And God knows how many times Ni had taken it out and showed it, like some kind of official form, the only document he had of any worth. He had confounded so many people with it. It was phenomenal! The piece of paper was so old that the Chinaman asked the Nepali, who was the only one in the camp who understood a little Mandarin, for his help to write a new one just like it. But for some reason Nepalino refused every time. Evidently the Nepali got some kind of Nepali pleasure every time he saw the Chinaman reach for the note which threatened to disintegrate in full view of everyone. He clearly delighted in seeing the Chinaman's wrinkles stand out in relief from the concentration, even the hair on his head stood on end as if he had been electrified, so that he looked impossibly like a hedgehog which had rolled itself into a ball and stuck out all its needles. Evidently Nepalino was longing for the day he would see the Chinaman embark on his regular search through his pockets for the scrap of paper, only to pull it out in pieces. And then he would have to pick up all those little pieces and try to put them back together again...

But every time any important papers arrived for the Chinaman from the Directorate, Nepalino would go to the office with him to receive them. And he would sit there with an important air, drinking the coffee which the staffers brought them, having suddenly become the centre of attention, because for a few minutes he was invaluable. Nepalino read the documents, which were written in Danish, and with an unbearably self-important expression he would translate them into Chinese.

And even if no one could check how good or bad Nepalino's Mandarin was, everyone knew very well that he couldn't speak a single word of Danish.

I lay there in a comedown delirium, hallucinating all sorts of stuff. I saw the world rolled up into a ball of rubbish, rolling down a hill, and me going with it. Smoke ribbons and seaweed strands of thought floated through me. Fragments of words and phrases rushed past, spinning faster and faster, an echo of something sloshed around, jangling in my head, sobbing and moaning. The wind wailed, flattened faces flashed by, lamp posts rushed at me, demanding answers, lengths of cables receded into the grey murk, a metal roof clattered past. In a squall of cinders, belching clouds of white steam, the train from Farstrup to Eterniton sped past. It was like being in the depths of hell, surrounded by vampires, leaches, and demons. That's how it felt when I heard the Muslims praying, their voices stealing up on me from all sides.

It was a total nightmare. From every corner, from every crevice, the monotonous drone of their prayers crept into your brain. They clambered across your body like Lilliputians, they bound you tight, they seemed to be reading the last rites, or performing some kind of ritual before devouring you alive. Their voices worked like a sedative, even if you wanted to get up and walk away, you couldn't. And then their procession started, down the corridor to the toilet, each of them carrying a bottle to perform their ablutions. The sound of their footsteps inflamed the imagination: the endless lisping shuffle, the slap of flip-flops against the floor, the scuffling... And he just had to be humming some doleful tune to himself, the bastard, or belching noisily, or spitting on the floor, banging the door. Then came the sound of running water, momentarily drowning out the prayer. After him came the next one, then a third, and a fourth... And it would happen all over again: the shuffling, the spitting, the banging, the running water. And if two of them happened to meet in the corridor, they wouldn't fail to greet each other joyously and effusively... then the footsteps would shuffle off, and the water would engulf everything once again. And then it would all start afresh: the knocking, spitting, doleful singing, up and down the corridor. Like the same scene being filmed again and again: a Muslim morning at Farstrup camp, take two, take three, take four...

Hanuman and I were lucky with our room: to the left, on the other side of the wall, was the toilet, and to the right – the room where Mikhail Potapov and his brood lived: his wife Masha and their daughter Liza. And since the people who surrounded us on all sides were too primitive to live any other way, and did exactly the same things day in day out, all our mornings started identically. On the left, the sluicing water, on the right – "Why aren't you eating?" ... "Why don't you say something?" ... "Why are you just sitting there staring at me with those big cow eyes?" ... "Do as you're told and eat something!"

The walls in the camp were thin, and you could hear pretty much everything; it was like living in a cardboard box. Hanuman and I went to bed late, basically towards morning. It was best not to sleep at night; the cops could turn up at night, they could come and raid the place, looking for illegal immigrants evading deportation, for thieves, junkies, other scum just like Hanny and me. And so every morning, just after we had turned in, we were woken by Mikhail Potapov's voice: "What are you gawping at, damn it, eat!"

That voice demolished the walls of my sleep; and the walls of our hen coop shook. Every morning, like a clock chiming – "Well, are you going to eat it or not!" – with Potapov just like the Rabelaisian cockerel inside the clock.

Waking was awful. I awoke in a delirium; no sooner had I gone to bed than the relentless activity restarted, steeped with Allahs on one side and Russian domesticity on the other. And so my spirit was ground between those two millstones every morning. Almost like a cripple, chewed up and spat out by some hammer mechanism, I lay with my eyes shut, disintegrating into innumerable granules of emotion, listening to the Russian bloke cursing his daughter to the right, and the Muslims washing to the left, while from underneath...

Normally I would lie on the top of the fold-up metal bunk bed, while underneath me, cosily wrapped in two quilts, living in blissful oblivion like a mythical creature in his cave, lay my companion in misfortune, Hanuman the Indian. And so we would normally go to bed as morning broke, so that we wouldn't have to hurriedly shove each other through the window, so as not to have to stage that silly scuffle with pounding hearts and heavy breathing in the dark, with that "come on, man, come on" by the window, which we always kept open just in case. One time we almost got caught. The cops turned up, descending on us like ghouls from the gloom, like a tempest with a multitude of arms and legs, with a lamp in every other hand, and baying voices. We heard doors slamming like shutters in the wind, and the slamming started getting closer and closer to our room. We were drunk, so we couldn't comprehend what kind of nocturnal high jinks might be afoot. It could be anyone turning up and frisking the camp dwellers, or maybe the gypsies had nicked something and were looking for buyers... But once we heard them speaking Danish we realised what was going on, and we managed to jump out of the window and scarper into the maize just in time. So from then on we didn't sleep at night, and we kept the window open at all times. The Nepali guy, who the Serb Radenko had nicknamed Nepalino, got his revenge on us the best way he knew how.

Unlike us, the Nepali didn't yet have any reason to fear the cops. He lived in the camp, waiting for official notification that his case had been processed, that it was time to go *Nach Hause*, back home. So for now he had no reason to jump through the window whenever there was a night-time raid; he could sleep soundly, and he would have preferred the window to be closed. But Hanuman kept it open, ignoring Nepalino's wishes, irrespective of his implicit proprietary rights.

Nepalino and his acquaintance the Tamil literally gave us refuge, they took us two vagrant, footloose illegal immigrants in, and warmed our sorry hides, as if we were a couple of stray dogs. I remember how I rejoiced when I was able to take a shower, and with real shampoo too. But I felt the fastidiousness no doubt familiar to every white man when the Tamil gave me his sheet to dry myself in place of a towel; this was the same sheet he wrapped round himself like a toga-wearing demigod after he had taken his own shower. He would walk round the building in it, jingling his sandal clasps. He strode about with a worthy air, leisurely supping his beer, cheap Danish beer, crunching his slightly singed chapatti, intermittently dunking it into a bowl filled with pepper-flavoured dressing.

The Tamil didn't actually live in the camp, he was lodging with an acquaintance somewhere; he did illegal work at a factory, some kind of pulp mill. He turned up quite frequently to check the post, pick up his pocket money – his state benefit – and to create the appearance of being at the camp, which the asylum seeker was forbidden from leaving for any length of time, and to wash. He tried to be sparing with his friend's water, maybe that was because his friend had dropped a hint that he should be more sparing. He came to wash his sheets. He'd throw on his robe, chuck his stuff in the washing machine, crack open a beer and sit there drinking and chomping away on something. He'd have a chat with someone, lose to me at chess, argue with Hanuman in their incomprehensible language, pull his washing out of the machine, bid *farvel* to everyone, and disappear. He would turn up agitated, like a coiled spring; who knew what letters might have come for him while he was away, maybe a deportation notice sending him back to Sri Lanka? (Having savoured the taste of freebie Danish beer what Tamil would want to go back to Sri Lanka, where he might end up puking and shitting blood?) He would normally be covered with a thin layer of dust, not shavings, but a layer of timber dust (although one time he did turn up with a pretty spiral-shaped shaving resting on his sock).

One time Hanuman told me about the work which the Tamil guy and his friend did. It was illegal to employ refugees, that's to say asylum seekers who had made their applications and were waiting to officially become refugees – so the Tamil couldn't work. So his friend, also a Tamil, but one who had already been smiled upon and anointed by the Kingdom of Denmark, came up with the following ploy. He somehow managed to agree with his boss that he would work if not a full twenty-four hours a day, then around sixteen, or two shifts, and he got permission to do so. He put his unflagging capacity for work down to the fact that he had been doing yoga since he was a child, and that he preserved the purity of mind and body; he didn't smoke or drink, he followed a miracle-working diet, and so on.

In fact our asylum seeker and his friend, who were practically identical to the European eye, simply split the work between themselves. It's true that in order to resemble one another as closely as possible, the legally-resident Tamil had to go on an all-out diet and lose three kilograms, while the other, the second-rate one, had to shave off or trim all the facial hair which he had put off shaving and trimming for a full half year. Of course, they both dressed identically, and they even copied the way each other walked, and in a short space of time our Tamil managed to learn to speak Danish as well as his elder friend. Although this was no great achievement – the latter spoke Danish so badly that our Tamil didn't have to strain himself particularly, and the nature of their work meant they didn't really need much Danish anyway; all they had to do all day was cut up sheets of plywood on a giant guillotine. And anyway, Tamils tend to have identical gestures and facial expressions, so no one noticed that there were two of them. They would never show themselves in public together. They never went out to any bars and cafés. They ate exactly the same food, and exactly the same amount, heaven forbid that either of them should put on weight. They turned their lives into a kind of theatre, or a spy game. They took great care of their appearances, almost as if they were male models. They made sure to maintain their resemblance in all things, like a tightrope walker maintaining his balance, although in their case one would have to imagine that this was no ordinary tightrope walker, but Siamese twins walking down the rope.

One question preyed on my mind: how much did our Tamil get from his benefactor? I was sure the enterprising son of a bitch wasn't likely to give him much. Not even half of a half of it.

But our Tamil didn't really care. As long as he got something. Any paltry sum was enough for him to prance about with a sheet of plywood by the guillotine blade. Every day, for eight hours a day, he lugged sheets of plywood about and sawed them up on the guillotine, putting himself at risk of being crippled. What a nutter.

Of course they wouldn't give a Tamil any other kind of work. I wouldn't go anywhere near that kind of machinery, not even for a full wage. I once visited a similar workshop at a furniture factory, and I heard enough stories about saw blades working themselves loose and coming screeching through the air at the workers. I would never go to work in a place like that, not even for double wages.

But that Tamil guy went to work every day, and he was happy to. An opportunity like that wasn't to be sniffed at! And anyway, he never spent his pocket money, he saved every single krone. Like almost all the refugees. That was understandable, you never knew how things were going to turn out. Old lady serendipity had wily ways... These were damaged people, they had plumbed the depths of life. They had seen some sights. They had sniffed the gunpowder, and the smell of freshly exploded human flesh too. They had munched shit sandwich. Who knew what might happen next?

They lived in constant expectation of a "no", and yet their hearts were consumed by hopes of a "yes". They steeled themselves to take the rejection on the chin, and they were ready for it at any moment, ready to drag their miserable itinerant arses off to seek their fortunes elsewhere. And they all dreamed about the States, the land which they believed had united the refugees of the world. They fantasised about how the Statue of Liberty would rise from the waters to greet them, how they would approach her in a white ship, how they would be greeted by music coming from the shore, how their new American passports would be presented to them, already opened, on a plate. They dreamed about moving into their new homes, about how they would sit puffing on a pipe and sipping wine by the open hearth, a blanket on their knees, and a cat sitting on the blanket. Their kids frolic in the meadow, swings squeak, a pony runs in rings, rays of sunshine peek through the hawthorn, the heather is in full bloom, and the pony is still running rings, running rings... "But to start with," said the elder Tamil to the younger, "learn how to value what you have in life, it might not be much, but at least it is yours. You must learn to treasure the little things!" And the younger one learned to do just that; our Tamil was no exception, nor was our Nepali.

Nepalino had an uncle in Copenhagen. Apparently he worked in an Indian restaurant. It was hard for me to understand why he looked so proud as he said that, because I had an uncle too, and he also lived in Copenhagen. But I didn't feel proud. And it wasn't because my uncle cleaned toilets for a living... even if he'd been an artist whose paintings took pride of place in the fanciest galleries of contemporary art, I still wouldn't have been proud... but that's not the point. Maybe Nepalino's chest swelled with pride because it was an Indian restaurant, I don't know. Maybe in Nepal an Indian restaurant is like the Promised Land, the pinnacle of human achievement, I don't know... I also had an auntie in Stockholm, but that too had never been something I took pride in. She looked after old biddies, but that wasn't important... I just never talked about her! I was ashamed that I had an uncle in Copenhagen, and an aunty in Stockholm, while I was the son of a bitch living up to my ears in shit in this stinking Jutland camp! What was I doing here? Why wasn't I relaxing on a down quilt in Stockholm, or reclining in front of a TV in Copenhagen? Actually, there were reasons for that, good reasons... I never could get on with my relatives... as far as I was concerned I would have been better off if I'd had none! They only brought various forms of unpleasantness, headaches, weird telephone calls, and even weirder letters... All of life's troubles started with the damned relatives! Those dear relatives were very the last people who would wish you well. They longed for you to go under, so that they could pull you up by the scruff of the neck like some runt, and with one sole aim: to make you indebted to them for the rest of your life, so they could moralise at you until the end of your days! Our respective well-being is in inverse proportion, my relatives and me: the better things are going for me, the worse they seem to be for them; and the worse they are for me, the better for them! And one other thing about relatives is that they tend to die, leaving you with nothing but the bitter residue of unvoiced resentments... to hell with them all!

So then, about that Nepali guy, and what went on down below. Our Nepalino was a fairy, a real queer, the gayest of gays, and that was the crux of his case. His application for asylum, that is. His story was odd, silly even, and to my unsophisticated mind it was totally incomprehensible. I just couldn't get my head round the fact that being a sodomite could be sufficient grounds for getting asylum in... well, in any country. Even in Gomorrah! But he had applied for asylum. It wasn't clear to me how such a feeble reason could warrant such a serious investigation. But he maintained that in Nepal he had been persecuted for both his political and religious convictions.

"He-ha-ho!" Hanuman laughed. "Poxy, Nepalese arse bandit. He insists that he could only live safely somewhere in Europe, in a democratic country, and all the rest of it... of course Denmark is the best of all, they've even legalised gay marriage here. What total nonsense!"

Although his grounds were only partly genuine, they were still quite plausible compared to the majority of cases. And why not? Who knew what wild ways those mountain tribes had? Maybe there are lost tribes living in some jungle somewhere who still eat each other? Why not entertain the possibility that in tribes where the orientation is strictly heterosexual any signs of sexual disorientation must be eradicated. Why not? The Himalayas are full of all sorts of scum! They eat dogs there!

Why couldn't you argue, for example, that it counts as discrimination against gays for their political convictions when the purpose of tribal lore is to ensure the survival of their race, which means only allowing reproductive relationships, solely between men and women, strictly in the vagina and nowhere nearby, and if you ejaculate, then only inside, no withdrawing allowed! Any alternative, meaning any form of relationship between representatives of the same sex, would be in direct contravention of tribal lore, because it would promote an idea which violated the very principle of intercourse for reproduction, would it not? And so homosexual love was a threat to the very existence of the tribe. Is that a political issue? It sure is. And it's a religious one too. Because religions are always designed to legitimate politics. If you started to argue it that way, you could really go to town! What about all those stone gods ordering you to mate, those ancient cave-wall frescos depicting reproduction rituals, those prayers to Krishna the polygamist, and so on and so forth. It follows that anyone who has ever done it up the arse must be a heretic! Even if it was a woman's arse! And so his case was not so blatantly absurd. No aliens from outer space popping up under his quilt, no undercover agents on his tail, no computer chips up his rectum. It was all quite plausible. No need to invent anything. After all, he didn't make up being gay. Maybe his case was concocted, but at least part of it was true. He wasn't lying about being a queer. He really was one. There could be no doubt about that, especially after what I saw going on under my bunk bed, to the backing track of Muslims vigorously washing on one side and Mikhail Potapov shoving food into his daughter's mouth on the other. Maybe I found Nepalino a pain, but at least he was never boring like the rest of them, with their endless life stories. He never spoke much about himself. Apart from a little bit about his uncle or Germany, where he lived with some old queer; he'd cooked for him, washed his feet, given him massages, and so on. But he never went into the details of his case, he never complained about his lot, he never moaned.

Well no, he did complain sometimes, he did grumble, and he did get on my nerves, but somehow he did it differently to the rest of them. He got his inquisitive arse pretty much everywhere, observing the world through those half-closed, narrow little eyes of his. Having been schooled in European life during his time in Germany, he clearly despised all the rest of the camp dwellers, all those uncouth, uncivilised, unrefined barbarians, who were always telling those same old sob stories. Sometimes those idiots went so far that they started fainting, their bodies convulsing like in the movies. But he just laughed at them. They only did it to get attention, to convince everyone that they were more deserving of a yes than the others, and that they deserved to get it right away. They were always trying to end up in hospital, so they would get more money. But he just snorted contemptuously. He couldn't give a damn about all that stuff. He just squinted, and laughed disdainfully. Our Nepalino was self-sufficient. Of course he never turned down extra cash. But he would prefer to sell his arse or suck someone off for it than to fake fainting or pretend he had epilepsy.

He had a hard time in the camp. Every fucker was on his case. They all hassled him. No one liked him. The young morons would ask him, "So you're gay, Nepal. A gay?" and burst out laughing. He never denied he was queer, but he didn't advertise it either. He wasn't ashamed of it, nor was he proud; for him it was just normal. But his most positive quality was that he never tried to persuade anyone that he had a genuine case, that he deserved a yes more than anyone else, and as soon as possible. You never heard anything like that from him.

He didn't try to pretend to be someone he wasn't. He was gay, nothing more, nothing less. That was the crux of his case. He didn't need to invent stuff. He didn't need to lie. He didn't need to strain the grey matter. When the cops asked him why he was applying for asylum, on what grounds, for what reason, he had apparently looked straight into the light they were shining at him, eyed them for a while from behind his luxuriant lashes, and then calmly said: "Just one reason – I'm gay."

That made him something of a hero. A flawed one. But in that cesspit he was a hero, and a genius too. Because he was natural. He didn't lie, he didn't act up, he didn't dissimulate. The essence of who he was as a person also formed the essence of his case. It was the most honest act of his life. Or at least it seemed that way…

In the mornings he would slither out of bed like an adder. Since the window was open twenty-four hours a day (whether winter or summer), he was always cold. He crawled out from under his seven quilts, and crept up to Hanuman, who was sleeping underneath me, and he would pretend that he just wanted to get warm.

Nepalino was like a pampered, warmth-loving exotic plant which could only survive in greenhouse conditions. That damned open window nearly killed him. He couldn't stand it. Every night I heard his teeth dancing in his mouth. I dozed off to that music: Nepalino's dancing dentures.

He always wore several T-shirts, as if he hoped that would keep him warm. He had a huge, baggy hand-me-down jumper which trailed loose threads everywhere, with some kind of Scandinavian folk motif on it which I totally detested (I generally detested all folk art). He looked comical, and pretty wild, like a scarecrow come to life. He didn't want to buy any clothes from the local second-hand shop, because he saved every øre, every single banknote he got. When he got his allowance every other week, he rolled the notes into a cylinder, tied them up with a rubber band, wrapped them in a little plastic bag and – Lord help me! – shoved them up his back passage. Or that's what Hanuman told me. And if anyone knew it would be him.

Nepalino would only make himself something to eat once every three days, and only if he hadn't managed to catch some crumbs from someone else's table. He was always wandering round the camp buildings, hoping to scrounge a bite to eat, looking for someone who had just got a yes. Someone who had just got right of abode and was putting on a party to celebrate. A party for the whole camp! And what kind of party would it be without Nepalino? He was indispensable. After all, he was such a fine cook! He would take his huge knife and work deftly, as fast as a food processor, chopping the onions into tiny pieces, followed by the chicken. Then he would take a seat and eat with everyone else – completely free of charge! Gratis! Another little victory for him: he'd managed to stuff his face for nothing once again. For him a perfect day was a day lived completely cost-free! That way he saved a whole day of his life, delaying the onset of hard times by another twenty-four hours. It was a small, but by his standards, significant victory. If he didn't manage to get his hands on any free grub then you would see Nepalino trudging slowly and grudgingly across the rainswept football field to the shop; he made a sorry sight. He would buy himself rice, flour or bread, and to try and cheer himself up a bit he would steal something paltry (a pot of pâté, or a tube of mustard). Then he'd go back to the camp, put the rice on the hob, take out his rock-hard lump of mutton from the freezer, cut a thin slice from it, fry it up, and eat. And he would eat with a look of such dismay on his face, as if the hard times had already arrived and there was no point hoping that anything good could ever happen to him again.

He scrimped and saved, preparing for the worst of eventualities – getting a no, and being forced to live illegally at his uncle's, in which case he would have to spend and spend, every last krone which he had saved until now. He would have to live there spending his money for a whole half year, until the allotted time had passed. Then he could take his freshly printed Nepali newspaper, put on his nice new clothes, allegedly purchased in some little Nepali town – as evidenced by a genuine Nepali receipt sent to him by his relatives – and with nothing else on his person he would turn up at the police station to have his case reopened. And over the course of that half year he'd fish those banknotes out of his arse, and month by month that wad would get smaller and smaller, and being quite literally a tight-arse, he would really feel the loss. I could imagine how it pained him just thinking about it. I saw his face turn grey when those thoughts preyed on him. I really felt for him when I saw that…

Nepalino was skinny. He smelled of spices and shit, because whenever he reached up his back passage to top up his savings or count them he would wipe his hands on his trousers. His trousers were always creased, incredibly creased, completely chewed up, like a wad of tobacco in an old Uzbek's mouth; they weren't really trousers, more like scraps of material, rags; he slept in them as well. His hair was long, but he was short, he looked just like a little kid, like a fourteen-year-old boy.

He always seemed to be dirty. Probably because he always was dirty. Even when he had just taken a shower his skin was the same dirty shade it had been before, although with an added greenish hue. And there didn't seem to be any explanation for it… because he didn't do anything which would make him so grimy. But his skin always had a marshy green hue, and patches of it were peeling and shiny like duckweed.

In the mornings, it was always the same story. The Nepali clambered out from under his mountain of quilts, unwrapped his rags, stepped out of his trousers, and started trying to slip into Hanuman's bed, like a cat. Hanuman had let his resolve slip in the past, or at least he had made it understood that Nepalino might just get lucky, if Hanuman happened to really be in the mood; that in principle he had nothing against being with a boy now and again, why not?

In fact, that was how Hanny had persuaded Nepalino to let us come and live with him, by promising carnal pleasures in return for board and lodging, and Nepalino then had no problem talking the Tamil round. There wasn't anyway much talking-round to be done, because the Tamil was almost never at the camp.

But Hanuman was in no hurry to spoil the Nepali with those promised pleasures, which was why the Nepali had to keep making advances, and always in the mornings.

I was sure that he deliberately chose his moments, guided by his knowledge of male physiology. More than likely. But not his own physiology. He would probably have been happy to fuck at any time of the day or night, but he couldn't always persuade someone else to, he couldn't always tempt them with his dirty little orifice. And so he tried his utmost in the mornings.

Early in the morning a lonely man's cock will often ache for something he dreamed about but which then faded away. When he wakes, it's still aching by inertia, and it no longer makes much difference what it was aching for… Nepalino was evidently fully aware of that, so he tried to take advantage of those opportunities, crawling into Hanuman's bed on all fours like a marmoset. Hanuman would chuck him off, kick him, and spit in his face, speaking in Hindi, and Nepalino would crouch on his knees with his arms folded, and jabber something in Hindi in reply, funny words which sounded plaintive, wounded, whining. And then he would crawl back under his quilts and take care of himself – noisily, purposefully noisily, so as to stop Hanuman from sleeping, as if to spite him; you didn't let me in, so now I won't let you sleep.

But sometimes Hanny did let Nepalino in, he decided to give in to his demands, and then the noshing sounds would start, followed by gurgling noises. It would normally happen when Hanuman didn't have the strength to resist, either because he was too drunk, or too stoned, or both.

But back then that didn't happen too often, because we were too poor, and not yet ingenious enough with our moneymaking schemes. Even our thirst for alcohol couldn't drive us to action. We got so lazy that we didn't even bother collecting empty bottles. Our last great triumph was the television set, a fifty-kilo tombstone. It took us the whole night to drag it back from the scrapheap, busting our backs, wrenching our arms from their sockets. Three steps forward, then rest. That's how it went the whole ten kilometres. When we switched it on, we left it on for a whole week, because whenever we turned it off it would take an hour or so to turn it on again. First we would have to spend forty minutes warming it up with a hairdryer (that was Hanuman's trick); in such eventualities we would put Nepalino in position, and he would stand there like a statue, warming the on-switch with the dryer. Then we would watch films for days on end, literally days on end... and we always had the TV turned up loud enough to make us deaf... that was because there was no way of turning it down.

The depression which enveloped camp life had its own smell, and that was the smell coming off the maize fields. One day during a police raid we had to jump through the window and crawl through the field just after it had been sprayed. And there we lay, trying to hide, whispering to each other as if caught in a bombing raid; we lay there until the cops had gone. It wasn't just chemical fertiliser there, but natural stuff as well ("eco product"), the same shit which piled up in the vats outside the camp, asylum-seeker shit, Muslim shit.

And so I lay there in the field, face down in shit, I lay there and thought about the many times I'd heard the Muslim antichrist flushing away his shit in the mornings. But I never thought I would end up lying with my mug in it, and all to prolong my tenuous existence in this country. Was it worth it? Was my pointless illegal existence in this camp worth me lying face down in Muslim shit? Or in anyone's shit! Anyone at all's! What difference does it make whose shit it is when you've got your face full of it?

From that day on I started to ask myself questions like, "Why is my life so strange? What am I hoping will happen? What am I angling for in this camp?"

Really dark thoughts weighed on me in the mornings, when that cursed Nepalino crawled out of bed and then out of his trousers and T-shirts, unwrapping himself like a mummy. Or when one of the Arabs walked down the corridor, bottle in hand, humming some dreary tune to himself. Or when Mikhail Potapov's swearing reached us through the wall, and little Liza made noises which were somewhere between a sob and a whimper.

2

By the time we got to Jutland we had already come off the needle and even started taking care of our health (Hanuman became an advocate of three square meals a day, and gave up burgers). Circumstances initially worked in our favour. We had been staying with a Yugoslav guy for a while who worked as a receiver at the scrapyard. Svenaage had introduced us to him. We had met Svenaage a short time before that; he worked at the Farstrup refugee camp, and we got to know him through the camp lowlifes which we mixed with. He was responsible for children, sport, and leisure activities at the camp, and God knows what else. Basically, he tried to create the appearance of being constantly busy, and given how much surplus energy he had, it worked pretty well. He always seemed to be at the centre of a storm of activity, so that no one doubted that some pretty serious work must be under way. He drank a lot, and whatever they paid him in the Red Cross would never be enough which is why he and the Serb had decided to start up their dodgy business.

They sold all kinds of electrical goods, mostly televisions. It had only taken a few words for Hanuman to convince them that not only could he handle himself around a computer, but he in fact knew absolutely everything there was to know about them. And so he started fixing the computers which people dumped at the scrapyard. After checking what kind of state they were in we stealthily shifted them from there, and then, just like some seasoned professional, Hanuman polished those turds by boosting their memory and installing "Windows 98", some games, and other stuff which Svenaage and Laszlo gave him.

We lived in a small room in the Yugoslav's house. He was just as much Hungarian as a he was a Serb, and he was a bachelor, already completely grey, saggy-skinned, and greedy. He looked ravaged, with an old soak's face which was a criss-cross of capillaries, a vivid violet nose, and watery eyes. But he did know how to cook. "No wife, so I had to learn," he explained gruffly. He was a man of few words, morose, stern even, and he had a few quirks. He could burst out crying for no reason, call me or Hanuman strange names, and sometimes he even started talking to himself without noticing we were there, which felt spooky, a bit like being at a séance. He sometimes suffered from blackouts, a sort of spiritual torpor. He could sit for hours on end doing nothing at all, not only completely inactive, but completely unaware of his surroundings. Then I would have to do the cooking. I made him borscht, and steak with fried potatoes. Once he had eaten he might come to his senses for a bit, even say a few words in his own language, but he could remain in that prostrated state for ages.

Svenaage said that it was OK, the Serb had suffered a bad concussion during the war, and so it was only to be expected. For Svenaage it had indeed become quite normal. As much as he needed people to listen to him and to talk to, he was happy with his own company, and he too had his own quirks. He could look quite satisfied with himself, chuckling into his fist about something known only to him, but we quickly got used to that. Compared to the Serb, Svenaage was a chatterbox, he jabbered on endlessly and talked all sorts of rubbish. But the main thing was that Svenaage always looked after us and bought us booze and cigarettes if the Serb conked out. Or if the Serb was doing his shift at the scrapyard, Hanny phoned Svenaage and he would come back with everything which Hanny ordered – and Hanny would order to his heart's content! But he was allowed to, it all paid for itself, they made their outlay back a hundred times over, as Hanuman worked round the clock. That was partly because, despite his apathy, the Yugoslav couldn't resist the greediness which overcame him whenever he came to his senses; he forced Hanuman to work. As soon as the Yugoslav came round he started up again with double the energy, fetching more and more computers from the scrapheap. Even ones which would never work again. Then he would say to Hanuman, "They might be good for spare parts, you never know."

Yes, yes, sighed Hanuman, and he would send the Yugoslav off to the shop for a bottle of Johnnie Walker, telling him that he was used to drinking Irish coffee when he worked, that he couldn't work without it…

And so the Serb would trudge off to the shop, mumbling to himself as he went. He would bring Hanuman his coffee and whisky, mixing it himself, virtually pouring it into his mouth for him, like someone filling a car with petrol. He would pour the coffee and whisky spitefully, breathing heavily through his nose, watching the monitor as the computer booted, watching the numbers jiggling across the screen. He would watch with a kind of childish delight, as if the activity on the screen was caused directly by the pouring of whisky down Hanuman's throat. As if the growth of his bank balance depended directly on the progress of the computer reboot.

And so we laid low at the Serb's place. And Hanuman started to find life there wearisome… Every single day he had to rummage about inside computer chassis, fishing things out, checking, testing, sometimes he had several computers booting at the same time, and he would wander round the room like a red-eyed lunatic, looking for something without remembering what it was. There were teetering towers of computer chassis stacked up against the walls, and components scattered all over the place, you couldn't walk there barefoot (I cut my foot on something a couple of times).

It was a small room, like a tomb. And we were like two mummies inside it. Hanuman had started putting the computer chassis and other junk out in the corridor, or rather he got me to do it. He said he didn't have air to breathe, and it was true – there were dust strata floating round the room. Boxes and computer chassis cluttered up the corridor. At night we clambered over them on the way to the toilet, and none of the lights worked. Soon boxes started appearing in the kitchen as well. The house filled up with more and more of those computers, just as people started buying less and less of them. And the less they bought, the more junk the Serb brought home. Although it was worse than junk, it was just scrap metal!

But I didn't give a damn: I did nothing, I just loafed about in bed for days on end, watched TV, and had a drink now and again. I didn't care what happened, I didn't care one bit. Anything could happen, as long as no one asked me to do one thing: to show my papers!

The Serb didn't dare take anything out into the street. At least he wouldn't take anything out in broad daylight. Only at night-time, then they would stealthily carry stuff out to Svenaage's van, so they could chuck it away at the scrapyard on the Serb's next shift. But as far as Hanny and I could tell he brought exactly the same stuff back from there later. What would you expect of a psycho!

Those computer chassis piled up because of the Serb's cowardice, because of his paranoia, heaven forbid that the neighbours should find out what he was up to. He was inordinately cowardly, constantly afraid that they would grab him by the short and curlies for that racket. He would mumble something about some government commission, he worried about being rooted out, about his case being re-examined. He sold the computers in the newspaper, through Svenaage, he didn't even dare give his own number.

"You never know," he would say, "There's me working at the scrapyard, and then suddenly all these computers turn up…"

That was why Svenaage took care of selling the computers, and of buying the booze off the ships when they came to port, because the Serb was too afraid to go there too.

"You never know who you might run into on one of those ships," he would say, "some Serb or Bosnian, one jab of his knife and you've had it! Who knows what that lot, those gypsies, have got going on in their heads!"

All the same, he wasn't pure Serbian, and he didn't even think of himself as a Serb. He was only half-Serbian, or so he told us. He was a Serb on his father's side. And his father was a drunk, a shocking drunk who died on one of his binges. But his mother was Hungarian, and so his name was Laszlo. He was Hungarian by name, he told us. But when it came to carousing, his father's genes would reawaken, and he would turn into a real Serb, a Serb through and through! He was always the last to end up under the table, and he would go slowly and gradually, sinking like a submarine – always after everyone else. But then the next day his memory of what had happened the night before was worse than anyone's, and he suffered the worst hangovers.

Sometimes we stayed at Svenaage's place, in Blomstrup. Not far from Farstrup. His house was on a hill, on a huge outcrop, it had a balcony with a view on to the port, and in the morning the seagulls shrieked, stirring nostalgic memories in my hungover mind. Sometimes, I would lie there with my eyes shut, not yet fully awake, listening to the seagulls, and it seemed like I was back home.

One time Svenaage and I boarded one of the ships to buy contraband vodka and cigarettes. A Russian ship had arrived, and Svenaage took me as interpreter, just in case, so he wouldn't get ripped off. He told me the Russian sailors weren't too good at English, "how much" and "okay" was about it, and they pretty much refused to understand anything else, *nicht verstehen*, you could try until you were blue in the face! And so I went with him. And the guys on board not only sold us some booze, but managed to persuade us to have a drink with them. It was someone's birthday. Or maybe it was just one of their regular piss-ups – and a pretty wild one as well! We stupidly joined in, and ended up staying on the boat.

Or rather, I couldn't remember how I ended up staying. I couldn't remember Svenaage leaving. I couldn't remember anything at all. But I woke up in a cabin, and I saw bunk beds of some sort, a porthole, and a sailor's vest, and I felt that we were swaying, oh-ho... Suddenly I was terrified: maybe we'd already left port? Maybe we'd headed out to sea? And I'd forgotten to disembark? What's going to happen? How would I explain myself? I suddenly felt scared, on edge. I panicked, and started to run, multiplying my fear with the trampling of my feet, and my heart was booming, beating every which way, outpacing my legs. My heart was beating, and it felt fear. Just like me, stuck in this metal tin, like a rat in a maze. I clattered down corridor after corridor. "Where are we going?" – I knocked on door after door – "Where are we?"

It was only when I darted out on to the deck and saw Blomstrup that I realised we hadn't left port and sighed a deep sigh of relief. Still I didn't completely calm down. Once

I had left the harbour and started walking down the streets of Blomstrup, once I saw the girls wheeling the goods out of the shops on to the street, with blouses and trousers hung up for display on a carousel, and the postman on his brown bike, dressed in his red jacket, with a heavy leather satchel hanging from his bike frame – only then did I feel the fear subside. But for a long time afterwards the piercing shrieks of seagulls put me on edge, and I didn't crawl out of the Serb's den for ages. I didn't even go to the port, I just sat there smoking, smoking and thinking…

Soon the business started to make a loss. For some reason people started dumping less and less electrical equipment at the scrapyard, and the stuff they brought was only fit for spare parts. It would have been impossible to knock anything sensible together from it. We had made a surplus, and now that was just waiting to be sold, but for some reason no one called, no one wanted to buy second-hand electrical equipment. Or maybe Svenaage had just forgotten to place the advert. You wouldn't put it past him. Meanwhile, the Serb was already fed up with us, and we'd had enough of his paranoia.

We started to venture out of the Serb's hideaway more and more often. The weather cleared up, the heavy rains subsided, it felt good to breathe the fresh air, it would have been wrong to sit out such fine weather in our bunker with only computers and idiots for company.

One day we went to Aalborg to buy some hash. We met an old guy called Hugh in a coffee shop who sold us some strange grass which got us so wasted that we ended up traipsing back to Blomstrup by foot.

It was a pretty weird thing to do, because it took no more than two hours to get to Blomstrup from Aalborg by bus, but walking, walking could take days. It took us a whole week. The only possible explanation for us setting out on such an expedition was the grass. It was atomic-strength weed, they called it Chernobyl Blow! We couldn't remember Hugh leaving, and I can only remember Hanny and me walking down Aalborg's never-ending high street, passing an enormous cigar back and forth between us, and it didn't want to smoke properly, it seemed to last forever, and we were scoffing some sort of Eastern sweet at the same time. Later Hanuman couldn't remember either the cigar or the sweet, but I remember, I remember the sweet because it gave me a toothache.

We walked for ages, because the buses had suddenly stopped running. Some sort of strike was under way. Hugh had warned us about that before we started smoking. He had said that the strike would begin at four o'clock. Hanuman said he didn't care, and Hugh skinned up a joint...

The bus drivers were demanding either more leave, or higher wages, or maybe it was both, in the hope that if they didn't get one they would get the other. The buses were parked up at the bus stops. There were ribbons of some sort tied to them, and in the windscreens there were pieces of cardboard with various phrases ending with multiple exclamation marks written on them; by all appearances these were the slogans announcing their demands. The drivers themselves were standing to one side. It was easy to identify them by their light-blue body warmers and blue-sleeved shirts. They were wearing caps with badges on them. Some of them were drinking coffee from thermos flasks, some of them furtively getting stuck into a beer. All these details impressed themselves on us once we had walked past and started trying to make sense of the situation. Not with a sober head exactly, but more or less...

We sat in the café at the railway station, wondering how we could scrape together enough money for a ticket to Blomstrup. The train was supposed to arrive from Frederikshavn, it was the evening train, and its final destination was Fredericia – it was the most handsome-looking intercity I had ever seen. Me and Hanny had once taken a ride on it...

... on the upper deck, in business class. Opposite us, bronzed thigh resting on golden knee, was a slinky Danish girl, pure "golden brown" like the song goes! Not just any woman, but a magnet for a red-blooded male. A short skirt, a silver snake on her ankle, a ring on one of her toes, so much stuff on her arms that it was enough to dazzle you. She was wearing a suit jacket, a short skirt, and a T-shirt, underneath which, one sensed, dwelled two breasts which were the stuff of dreams. She had a fit body, and was obviously properly pampered by solariums, swimming pools, masseurs, hairdressers and manicurists. Some kind of superstar! Hanuman and I sat there drooling. Hanny bought a coffee, lit up a cigarette, and offered her one. She smiled and said no. He tried to think of some other way of chatting her up, but the ticket inspectors came and asked us to leave; not only did we have no tickets for business class, we had no tickets whatsoever, not for the intercity, not for the goods train! Hanny couldn't handle the humiliation, nearly lost his cool and indignantly showed them his two-zone ticket, which was only valid in Copenhagen, and had long since expired. They refused to take it, and just snapped back at him. They breathed down our necks, and prodded us firmly in the back, towards the doors. They gently had their way with me, taking me from both sides, by each elbow, directing me towards the doors. They huffed and puffed into both earholes, fairly but firmly asking us to get lost, and to do so of our own accord, before they called the police. Looks of derision lit up like flashbulbs. Glances darted at us. Shameful! Everyone else knew how to behave, but look at these two... scandalous! An affront to the entire Danish train network! Shame, shame, poppy shame! But we were happy to make ourselves scarce. No need to make any phone calls! We're more than happy to jump off a moving train, straight on to the speeding asphalt, legs akimbo. What seems to be the problem? Ah, there's no need for any concern! We don't want any trouble. We're very sorry. Just a little blunder. No need to get angry! We just slightly overshot our station. It could happen to anyone! We got the timetable mixed up. Boarded the wrong train. Born under the wrong star. We're already disappearing. We're gone. We don't mind walking!

The intercity film reel spooled away into the distance. We paused for breath. Hanuman tugged at his braces with his long fingers. His lower lip was jutting out. "Get a move on, Euge! Look lively, you son of a bitch!... so they chucked us off the train... big deal!" And that's how we arrived at Horsens.

... but on this occasion, so as to avoid any similar blunders, we decided not to take any risks; as good as the intercity might be, it was expensive. I could see Hanuman licking his lips as his gaze followed every passing train. I knew the temptation was strong: he was chasing the high we got when we were whisked over the Nuborg bridge... for Hanuman the intercity was like a drug, and he needed his fix! But not this time; it was a long way to the bridge – no, not this time. This time he had to get a grip of himself, listen to the voice of reason! And anyway, we didn't have enough money to get to Blomstrup, and definitely not by business class. We didn't have enough to buy a coffee on the intercity. Or even to stand on the platform alongside it. Hanuman was ready to stand there – but I didn't fancy it: we had to get moving, before we were noticed by the spyhole eyes with mobile phones in their pockets!

We said to hell with it and headed off on foot; as always he was spouting some sort of high-flown nonsense, dreaming up his footloose philosophy, again it was "you and me against the world", all as per usual... by nightfall we had somehow managed to plod all the way to Løgstør. Throwing caution to the wind, we broke into a scrapyard on the outskirts of town, by the sea, or maybe it was a canal. We climbed into an old van, had a smoke, conked out, and by morning I had started to get the paranoia.

For several days I didn't want to get out of that van, because I thought it was being watched. I managed to dream up that someone was pacing about outside with a mirror, firing off deadly rays of reflected sunlight. I kept looking out of the van, and I imagined all sorts of stuff, I was suspicious of everything: the rubbish bins standing upright by the wall, like huddled conspirators; rusty containers looming above us, blue, green, brown; barges bobbing by the shore; cables turned brittle from the strain, boulders, the clatter of a moped engine; a wall flooded with sunlight, shadows shifting across it; the shriek of the gulls, piercing my heart again; and the murmur of the sea, fragmenting into clearly voiced sentences, if you wanted to hear them... I was suspicious of everything, including of Hanuman himself.

His mug. It grimaced. It was a mask. Sometimes it looked like my father as a young man – and then I was thrown back twenty-five years, and I started to dribble. Then he started looking horribly like my aunt, and I hurled myself at him, fists flying. I yelled at my aunt: "What right do you have to tell me he's my father! What sort of a father is he, what sort? If you had a dad like that you'd have poisoned him long ago! I swear you would! If my old man had subjected you to the kind of interrogations which Mum and me had to suffer, you'd have found a way of knocking him off long ago!"

That kind of stuff drove Hanuman crazy. He went wild with rage. He yelled at me. Slapped me round the face. Or at least that's what he told me later. I can't remember the details myself. He tried to talk sense into me, he admonished me, he tried to find some way of getting through to me.

None of it worked, all of it was pointless, I was just going out of my mind. Hanuman brought me food, but when the money was used up he insisted that I pull myself together and step out of the van.

"Or..." he said. "Or I will leave alone, right now, and for good!"

Overcoming my fear, I got up, stepped outside, ran across the yard to the rubbish bins, put on my sunglasses, pulled my head down low below my collar, wrapped my scarf around me, completely bandaging myself up like the Invisible Man, and we set off again…

We walked through fields which were full of maize, and past cows which followed us with witless gazes, like patients in a mental hospital.

We walked along the verges of narrow roads, through the rain, steeling our hearts, grinding our teeth, huddling from the wind, hands deep in our pockets, warming our fingers in our armpits, dragging ourselves onwards on all fours.

My bag knocked against my waist, the strap cut into my shoulder, the boots had given me blisters. My feet were stone cold, my toes had almost had it, my soles were covered in dead skin, and my joints creaked. I broke the nail on the big toe of my left foot.

We stopped by a lake. Hanuman went to defecate in a toilet next to some cottages, which seemed to be empty. I was given the task of finding out whether the cottages might be suitable for sleeping in. I dived into one of them, rummaged around a bit, found a stinking old quilt with traces of dried sperm on it (or at least that's what I imagined it was), and for some reason I decided that would be a good place for us to spend the night.

There was a picture of Winnie the Pooh in the window, and some mugs, one of which contained a toothbrush. I decided to take off my boots, so I lay down on the wooden bed. And although it was very cold I took my boots off, then my jacket, and then I noticed that there was a mobile hanging from the ceiling right above me. I started to examine it, for some reason scratching the heel of my right foot with the broken toenail of my left foot. The mobile was a wondrous thing, fluffy, with bits of thread, feathers, and glass hanging from it.

"That's a dreamcatcher," Hanuman said, yawning.

"Invented by the South American Indians. Tonight we will sleep protected by Toltec superstition."

He started to get into bed, and I examined the nail which I had scratched my heel with so hard that it started bleeding. The nail was an awful sight. I asked Hanuman if he had any tweezers for removing bits of nail or dry skin. He said he did, but only for hands, and only for his hands.

"That's an article of personal hygiene," he said with a slightly threatening note in his voice, "you know very well how particular I am when it comes to matters of personal hygiene…"

I knew that there was no point in discussing it any further: he never gave me anything, never. He wouldn't let me use his razor to shave, so I was all hairy, like some gremlin. He wouldn't let me use his eau de cologne, so I stank like a goblin. He wouldn't even give me a piece of his soap, and so I was as filthy as the devil. I was amazed he agreed to sleep in the same cottage as me! If I was in Hanuman's place, if I was in his shoes, then considering his lofty aspirations, his fastidiousness in matters of personal hygiene, his high expectations of people, I would have told myself to fuck off and sleep in the dog kennel!

And as I thought those thoughts I started pulling off the remaining bit of toenail!

I'd done it so many times before, but I would never learn. I would fall into exactly the same trap at least five times a year. I wouldn't ever buy any scissors, wouldn't ever steal any tweezers, I would just tear the nail off with my fingers. Even if I had scissors and tweezers at home I would still just rip it off. I'm hooked on it; every single time I tell myself that I'll do it properly this time, I won't pull the whole thing out root and all, but every single time I end up tearing the nail out attached to a bloody piece of flesh, and I have to quickly find something to stop the bleeding.

Afterwards I couldn't walk, couldn't put my boot on, I didn't even dare pull my sock on.

We had to sit there in that cottage for several days, because I wasn't capable of walking. Eventually Hanny managed to persuade me to set off again. We walked eight kilometres down a meandering road. The weather brightened up. The sky seemed to have smoothed out, outlines had become more distinct, there was a glow of light in the distance. We came across a parking area. A lay-by. There was a truck parked there. It was empty. There was a car as well. With German number plates. There was a sign by the parking space. And a toilet. And a map of the vicinity. Hanny studied the map. Then he said just two words: "I see…" That gave me hope. Those two words, and the thoughtful way they were uttered, instilled optimism in me. The words seeped into me like a churning stream of water.

There was a rubbish bin there, so I immediately peeked into it in the hope of finding something. No such luck. There was some sort of bush which was rustling suspiciously. Voices from over by the strip of sea. A child's voice. Laughter. A loud male voice, pronouncing German words distinctly. Something along the lines of "One, two, three, come on! And again! And again!"

"They must be doing gymnastics," Hanny said with a smile, and rubbed his hands together. "Idiots, uh, ha, ha!"

There was a table and bench behind the car. We hadn't spotted it at first. There was a thermos flask on the table. And there was a basket on the bench. And a towel covering the basket. Inside the basket there was cutlery: plastic plates, knives, forks. Food! A plastic bag containing bread, unopened packs of butter, cheese, cream, and some kind of crackers. We swiped the food and ran off. As fast as we could. We hid in the forest and gobbled it all up. And then walked on quickly. I started getting shooting pains in my stomach again. I had to drink something. All that dry food on an empty stomach! I couldn't go any further. Walking made me feel sick. I lay down on the ground. I looked up at the sky, the low sky. Some pesky flies were buzzing somewhere nearby. Sparse grey clouds were crawling across the sky, indifferent to everything. They crawled along as if it was their job to do so. At that moment I started to sense I was in a trap. It was a simple kind of trap. A bit like a musical jewellery box. I was the little bug which had accidently ended up in the works, and now all the hammers, spindles and springs were going crazy, trying to eject me. I started to feel sick. Then I threw up. Hanuman smoked for a while. I asked him to blow the smoke the other way. "Which way?" he asked in turn.

"Just away from me," I said.

He smoked in the other direction, expanding on my idea about the musical jewellery box. He turned it into jukebox, he made me into a parasite or virus which had corrupted the software, so that all the melodies got muddled up.

"Just imagine," he said, "how awful 'Unchained Melody' would sound if it was combined with 'Wonderful World', eh?"

"I don't know," I said. "I hate them both."

Then I threw up again.

After that we headed down a very rural road; narrow, twisting, unkempt like a pockmarked village crone, with only the occasional road sign. Looming above our heads was the maize, yet more maize, and then sky… Eventually we got fed up with the road and decided to cut straight through the field. Hanuman mumbled, "We're children of the corn, we're children of the corn, fuck me, children of the corn!"

And so we hobbled to Farstrup. At some point the maize fields parted, and we saw the camp, and the washing line, and Eddy's wife hanging clothes up to dry.

"Ooh," said Hanuman reaching into his pocket. "We have to drink to that!"

Over to one side there were children playing, screeching and chucking stones at each other. Hanuman stood there in an ostrich pose, staring at the Iranian woman with her large saggy breasts, and kneading his cock. The men were roasting something on an open fire, behind a fence made from woven ivy branches. Hanuman hunched down low, bent double at the waist, stretched out his neck, straightened his back – and now he looked like a kangaroo ready to jump. He was groping his balls, watching the Iranian woman bend down low to pick up the washing, watching how her skirt rode up, baring her fat calves. I sat on the ground, vacantly observing him as his eyes clouded over with a drowsy film of passion. I witnessed the magical moment when this woman, who was pretty repulsive to look at, was suddenly transformed into the object of his desire. Hanuman's bloodshot eyes filled with lust. He was really yearning for that disgusting bow-legged fatty! That saggy-arsed unshaven hag! He couldn't care less! By now he was working away vigorously with both hands, like a real kangaroo tearing knots of matted hair from its pouch. The Albanians were fixing a car out in the yard. The bonnet had already swallowed up one of them, now it looked like it was about to devour another. A third one was trying to crawl in from underneath. The Iranian woman adjusted her cardigan on her shoulders, then she reached for the washing line, letting the cardigan slips downwards, exposing her neck; Hanny reached a state of ecstasy. The swings creaked, music came floating out of the kitchen together with voices, Arab voices, piercingly shrill. Someone yelped, a ball slapped against the wall, shattering and multiplying, the smell of cooking drifted in our direction, and the maize rustled. By now the hanging washing had completely obscured the Iranian woman from view. Hanuman did up his flies and we decided to go and see what we could lay our hands on in the camp. Hanuman stepped out of the maize, and I followed him.

As we entered the camp Hanuman immediately bumped into his old acquaintance, Nepalino – what a stroke of luck! Hanny somehow managed to make it appear as if he had come especially to see him. After all, he had promised to visit his old Nepali friend, had he not!

"You see Euge!" he said to me with a wink, "didn't I promise I would come? Remember how I gave my word back in Avnstrup, that I would be sure to come and find my little Nepali friend? And have I not kept my word?"

I couldn't remember Hanuman having ever told me about any Nepali friend. There were tons of Nepalis in Avnstrup – all of them with the same face, all of them cunning, dishevelled, downtrodden. I couldn't tell the difference between them. Hanuman had never declared any of those retards to be his friend, not ever. And I certainly couldn't remember him having promised to look any of them up. But his tone of voice caused me to immediately start nodding enthusiastically, as if to demonstrate that I had heard loads of good things about Hanuman's "Nepali friend"... so many good things that I was also "oh-so-happy" that we had finally managed to track him down!

Hanuman didn't give the Nepali the chance to get his wits together.

"Well here I am, my dear friend! Show us where you're living! Tell us how you've been getting on!"

The abundance of attention and backslapping caused Nepalino to start hopping about like he had ants in his pants. He fell for Hanuman's lines as happily as some silly schoolgirl, and he led us to his room. Hanuman heaped praise on everything he saw, from Nepalino's funny clothes to his magazine collection. When he saw a Hindi newspaper he slapped a paw on to it, yelled out something in his language, and shouted to me, "Splendid! A newspaper from Mumbai! That's just the thing! I feel almost like I'm back home again!"

I glanced round the room, and immediately put down roots, they passed right through my bloody, blistered feet into the floor. A moment or so later we met the Tamil. He was about to take a shower, but he was also extremely happy to see us, he behaved exactly like I did when I was humouring Hanuman. But even if he was only pretending, it played right into our hands! He was dressed in a chunky sweater tucked into tracksuit trousers, and his trousers were pulled all the way up to his chest! The Nepali had a word with him, and it was decided that we could stay at their place, in theory for just a few days…

For a while I was happy with the change of scene. I got myself a couple of bottles of beer (on tick), sat down with my notebook, had a smoke, drank the beer, wrote some poems and a single letter home to my mother – with a postcard depicting a pretty little church in Aalborg. It was bathed in rays of sunlight, and behind it was a little cloud, hanging in the dazzling blue sky.

I found myself a friend, and we even lived together in his room for a while. His name was Stepan, and he was from Samara. He had already spent three years trying to crack the bureaucracies of various countries, but completely in vain. He had hoped to settle in lots of places: first in Belgium, then in Germany; he'd spent some time in Switzerland, having crossed from Germany by swimming down a mountain stream, but he fled from there, fearing they might send him to France or back to Germany, where they would have locked him up, clapped cuffs on him, and sent him home. So he fled to Denmark, where he lodged a new application. He didn't tell me what the basis of his asylum request was. The only thing he said to me was that I should avoid making the same mistakes as him, that I shouldn't waste my time, that I should find myself a wife as soon as possible.

"You've got to get yourself a woman," he would drone on. "Then you can arrange a fake marriage, or a marriage of convenience. Otherwise, you've got no chance… there aren't many options here," he sighed, before adding, "Ah, fuck this Denmark, this fucking Denmark, it's just a wetter version of Germany…"

He kept on moaning about how much time he had wasted on this country, how he had saved hardly anything, how he hadn't sent enough money back home, and how his father boozed up what he did send back. It seemed his father had drunk his way through everything they had, even the family home.

"So now there's nowhere left to send parcels and money to, there's not even anywhere to go back to…"

In any case, he knew that he'd be greeted by men in civvies with enquiring smiles on their faces. That's why he had to think something up; how to answer their questions, how to wriggle off the hook. The problem was that he had completely forgotten how to think.

This sleepy kingdom had mummified him, this place called Jutland in particular. He was marinating here in Jutland, just like one of their sweet pickled cucumbers. Farstrup, and our camp, had turned him into aspic, brawn or some sort of jerk. Any free will he'd had was stifled by the routine, the constant waiting for an answer to his appeal, the ungrounded hopes and the prattlers who stupefied him with stories about a legendary lawyer who could win the most hopeless of cases, for the right fee. For a while Stepan even tried to save up for a lawyer just like that.

He was a melancholic, he had no qualms about watching porn in company, and even worse, he wasn't embarrassed about getting horny and telling disgusting stories, in which he was not only narrator, but either the main protagonist or an eye witness. He once told us a story about how he had hitched a lift, when he was living in Germany. He had been wandering down some road for ages, cars were whizzing past, signalling for some reason; he tried to hitch a ride, but most of the drivers just gestured at him like he was crazy, then one eventually stopped and agreed to take him. And so they drove, and they even chatted a bit; Stepan knew some German. The driver was an old man. He told Stepan about how he had been taken captive by the Russians. He told him about the war. He had been just a lad at the time. Then came the prison camp. While he was there he had been, let's say, humiliated. But he had found himself enjoying it. From then on, he had taken a liking to sucking off men.

"So what do you say, do you mind if I suck you off?" And so Stepan let the old man suck him off.

He concluded that story by saying that he didn't see anything wrong in getting sucked off, even if it was by a man, especially if it was a German man. A rich old German sucking off an asylum seeker, a lowly Russian asylum seeker at that; he somehow saw it as a small personal victory over the mighty German state.

He spent virtually nothing from the money which the Red Cross gave him; he collected empty bottles, and showed us which ones you could find where. Then he showed us all the bins where you could find food that was still in a more-or-less decent state, and he showed us where the farmers put out their potatoes, carrots and onions in the autumn.

"It's not far from here," he said. "Five minutes away. Just hop on your bike, trundle along for five minutes, and you've got yourself onions, radishes, potatoes, carrots…"

That's how he lived his life; he spent hardly any money, not even on transport. At first he had a bike, he'd traversed the whole of Jutland on it. He was quite sporty, trim, skinny even. And then he found someone's lost travel card on a bus – a real stroke of luck, unimaginable good fortune. No one had ever had such good luck. He'd never had luck like that his whole life. It wasn't like finding a hundred roubles. It wasn't even like finding one hundred kroner. Or even ten thousand kroner. It meant free travel, across the whole of Denmark, on all forms of public transport!

It was a fancy kind of travel card which had belonged to an inspector for forests, mountain springs, lakes, and other natural water bodies. A travel pass belonging to some kind of Danish Mounty. Practically a military document. Stepan stuck his photo on it, went for a ride, and no one said a word. The driver nodded at him respectfully, he walked down the aisle, took a seat, and sat there worrying that someone might get on and ask him to show his documents. Then he went for another ride, then one more, and no problem! From then on he had travelled completely free of charge!

Just before he was deported he gave me the card. But I didn't use it once. Firstly, the photo booths in the stations didn't print the right kinds of photos, and I didn't want to show my face in a photo studio. Secondly, I wouldn't be able to secure the photo properly, because you had to get it inside the wallet, under the plastic, under the pin which held the whole thing together, you had to somehow wedge your photograph underneath it. I had no idea how Stepan had managed it. He didn't get round to sharing that detail.

Before they came for him he would often look at his travel card and say how sad he was to leave Denmark, especially because of that travel card, there just weren't any scams like that where he was going, unless you were prepared to fake being an invalid or something.

It all happened pretty suddenly, although he had been expecting to be deported any day, he had even been informed about it in advance, but still, but still, it did feel pretty sudden when they came to get him.

I found the ticket, as we had agreed, in the ventilation duct where he kept it. But he still hadn't managed to reveal the secrets of his handicraft to me. When I showed Stepan's work to Potapov, a strange exhilaration seemed to come over him. He rotated the ticket this way and that, and it was clear that he would have been happy to nab it off me right there and then, but I could see that he too was unable to fathom how Stepan had managed to shove his scrawny Russian mug under the plastic casing and the pin, so that it was positioned above the name of the Danish Mounty, Per Ule Pederson.

Stepan managed to show us all the nearest rubbish dumps on the map, he told us what we could expect to find where, who to sell it to, and he even introduced us to some of the people who lived in the immigrant hostels. They were normally three- to five-storey buildings, dirty, smelly, worse than any camp. There were all sorts living there, but they were basically the same as the people in the camps. Only that they were one step closer to acquiring Danish citizenship. They had been granted refugee status, they were no longer under threat of deportation, their benefits were a little larger, which meant that they bore a closer resemblance to human beings than the camp rats. It also meant that they no longer deigned to clamber around rubbish tips themselves, and were willing to buy all sorts of stuff, even if it came from the tip, as long as it was at a rock-bottom price. They eagerly anticipated the next delivery, and were ready to start haggling: brash, drooling, with lewd gestures. They got so bored in their hostel that were prepared to bargain over the most useless piece of crap.

Stepan showed us all of this as if he were entrusting us with his own personal patch. He explained it all like he was briefing his successors. Meanwhile, he gathered his things, tied up his bags and sighed. He reckoned that his case was already heading fast downhill, down such a steep and slippery slope that it might just as well have been a ski run, grab your toboggan and off we go! His lawyer summoned him several times a month, and he would tell Stepan with a sigh, "Have you ever heard of a Russian getting a yes?"

"No," said Stepan, "I haven't."

"Well then," said the lawyer, spreading his arms in resignation, "what more do you want from me..."

"So that's that then," Stepan said to me. "I can feel it in my bones – *Nach Hause* soon, the engine is already running..."

And since he now had nothing to lose, and needed something to live off when he got back to Russia, he made himself a booster bag and set off round the local shops. He mostly nicked CDs, games, all sorts of tat, which he then sold on. But he was unlucky, he got caught. Later when he was drunk, he told me bitterly, "See, Denmark is already giving me the elbow. Whichever way you look it's a dead end!" I had to stop myself blurting – "Wherever you gob, there's a nob," but using the Estonian word for nob would have betrayed my carefully concealed "Estonian origins", although Stepan would hardly have twigged it himself...

Soon afterwards they deported him. Before he left he bequeathed Farstrup's rich seams of rubbish and bottle deposits to us, telling us not to be idle and to collect as many bottles as we could, so we would have the money to go to Aalborg, to the street with all the discos, and pull ourselves a couple of babes.

"The sort you could marry. There's nothing else worth looking for in this country," he said, adding his motto, "Ah, fuck this Denmark, this fucking Denmark, it's just a wetter version of Germany..."

It was a decent way to Aalborg, the nearest big town, and we had no money. So when we decided to have some fun we chose a little town which was closer and a little bit bigger than Farstrup, scraped together enough money for a bottle of something and the fare, and rolled up at a carnival there. The town was renowned for its scrapyard. And because of its name. It was pronounced "Ors", but it was written like the first syllable in Aalborg, that's to say "A" with a little circle above it, so we just called it "arse".

We went there to let loose, and to try and pick up some girls. When we got to the disco there was such a throng that we had to force our way through. All three floors were packed with blokes dressed like girls and girls dressed in next to nothing. And all of them were high on something, maybe it was pills, or maybe they were just stoned. I noticed that when they went to dance they would leave their drinks behind on the table. So I decided to capitalise on the situation. I was already pretty pissed and didn't have any qualms; three of us had necked a bottle of Aalborg vodka between us round the corner. So I set to work on the glasses. Pretty soon I was plastered, and somehow, I had no idea how, I ended up with a group of girls. Hanuman was trying to convince them he was an al-Qaeda terrorist, and that I was an Irish one. Hanuman could pass for an Arab, a Pakistani, or a Peruvian if he wanted. If he was pretending to be an Arab, then he would be called Mohamed. If he was a Pakistani, he would say that his name was Paramjeet. If he was being a Peruvian, then he would play with several names. These might be Eduardo Amaran Santos, Ricardo Santos Amaran, Amaran Santos Eduardo and so on. I suggested he use the name Jurenito, but he said that no such name existed, that I'd made it up. That's how it went this time; everything according to the familiar routine. He introduced himself as Mohamed, and me as Eugene. A few moments later I was outside and feeling up some Danish girl. She was giggling, and I had her wet knickers in my hands. A few more moments later I found myself back at her place, on top of her. Then my knee slid across the cover of the armchair, and my ribs collided with a sturdy wooden armrest... game over! It hurt pretty badly. But at least it sobered me up a bit, and I managed to take care of business again, twice in a row. Then I drank the Cinzano from her parents' drinks cabinet, and ended up on top of her again. It was fun, although by now I was too drunk to have sex. I had some more swigs of the Martini from the drinks cabinet. And then I grabbed what looked like necklaces and a bit of small change off the shelf, a few notes as well, kissed her goodbye, and rushed off to catch a boat, promising to drop by again on the way back from New York. I wandered off across the fields. Through the fog. Up to my ankles in mud. With the rain lashing down. I started feeling sick. I was shaking. I was shivering. I turned on to the road and stopped the first bus which appeared. I used sign language to explain that some yobs from the disco had robbed me, and my travel card had gone walkies, for *helvede*!12 All I

12   Damn them (Danish).

108

had left was this small change. I fished it out of my pocket and unloaded it into the driver's fat palm. It's all I have left, I mumbled in the hope that he would refuse to take it. But the driver weighed the money remorselessly in his hand, and then proceeded to fastidiously pick through it, like he was picking at fish scales. Then he chucked it down the funnel of his cash box. Without bothering to listen to my broken Danish he nodded me towards the seats, summoned forth a crunch from the innards of the bus, and fixed his attention on the road ahead, which was wreathed in fog. The doors of the bus had already slammed shut, but I carried on muttering something about having no travel card, having nothing at all, just drop me at Farstrup... "Ja, ja, ja," the driver grunted in response, "u-ko, u-ko... OK!"

I woke, and tried to stand upright. I felt a shooting pain in my ribs. God, it was painful. I couldn't lie on that side for a month and a half, I had to breathe with one lung. Some party that must have been. I swore I would never go to another nightclub. I became very attached to my bed for a while. But eventually I got better, and I started going out again, exploring the town.

One of Farstrup's notable features was the home – now a museum – of a certain Danish writer, a Nobel laureate. I once tried reading the dross he had written, but it proved impossible. I was too outraged by the fact that he'd won the prize. Back then the Swedes clearly had no idea for what, and to whom, to award the Nobel, and so they chucked it about here, there and everywhere. But it tended not to get very far, it generally landed somewhere close to their friends and neighbours. This must have been the most boring book I had ever had the misfortune of reading, the closest thing to it is probably Tammsaare's *Truth and Justice*. But even old man Tammsaare was quite good fun to read, and with those dogs which crap on the neighbour's doorstep that book is actually not too dull. But this Danish tome was like one of their creaking carts meandering down the rutted, potholed roads, it just dragged on and on, you felt yourself getting hopelessly bogged down, it was just so, so dreary…

Although that pretty much summed up life in Jutland, and Farstrup was a typical Jutland town! Two bars, where there were rarely any more than three customers. One hotel, where no one ever stayed. A scrapheap with nothing worth having, for some reason ringed with barbed wire. And the lake, with its single angler, an old Armenian crouching in the reeds, contriving to catch something from the puddle.

The lake was tiny, like a saucer, with a single constellation floating on its surface. Whenever I wandered round that lake, together with the old men who liked to stroll there, strange, delirious thoughts came upon me.

"Such huge stars," I thought, as I walked by the lake in the evenings, with the poplar leaves rustling overhead and the first fallen leaves crunching underfoot. "Strange," I thought to myself, "how could these stars, which were in reality so huge, fit into such a tiny little lake… although we only see their past, just a reflection… in this lake, every night I see something which used to be a star. Wasn't that what Mallarmé wrote? It's like a dream… more than a dream… it's almost like death… death, with an old devil trying to catch fish!"

Ennui started to swamp me, a growing sensation that I was sinking, like being in a diving bell. A strange melancholy overcame not only my thoughts, but my body too, as if tonnes and tonnes of water were pressing down on me, my body was drained of life and I had stopped trying to return to the surface. I hardly moved my legs, I felt sick, I had stopped trying to get out altogether. And for some reason my legs had started swelling…

"Maybe it's your liver?" Hanuman blurted one time, looking directly ahead, without addressing me.

"What?" I asked, not fully understanding. What was he wittering about? What was he jabbering on about? What liver?

"I mean the liver… I once heard that when people

have some problem with their liver, an underactive liver or underactive bowels, they become passive, quiet and apathetic. Their faces are fixed in some sort of grimace, just like yours. They have the same kind of attitude to life as you do. Do you feel sick?"

"Of course! All the time!"

"You see then, it's definitely your liver!"

"Get lost!"

The weather started to turn much worse, as if Farstrup, and all its flora and fauna, had suddenly fallen ill. The trees coughed and sneezed, scattering handkerchief-leaves, the sky swooned grey. It rained constantly. Some wet snow fell too. Everything seemed unbearably sad. First, I started snuffling. Then my throat felt a bit sore. Then I was completely confined to my room. I just lay there and had come to rest at the very bottom. Like the lead plummet used to sound the ocean depths in olden days. And I was sounding the depths of my own depression, which was the deepest abyss, a bottomless pit. My thoughts were in fixed orbit around the same planets: life as endless suffering, death as release in the form of an eternal absence of life, The Sickness unto Death, purification of the soul... I was slowly going out of my mind. And was it any wonder, how could one stay sane in that stinking camp, amidst those fields, amongst those Muslims, with that kid crying constantly the other side of the wall.

"Someone... sooner or later...," I heard Hanuman mumbling in his sleep down below. He fell silent, dozed for a while and snored. Then I heard him stirring, and he started up again: "Someone... has to teach that bastard how to treat children... someone has to teach him how to behave like a human being. How can he call himself an artist, if he doesn't even know how to be a human being!"

Yes, Mikhail Potapov would stand in front of his easel for hours on end, barrel-shaped belly thrust forwards, crazed jet-black eyes goggling, wet lower lip protruding, thick Tatar eyebrows frowning. With the bushiness of his beard, the fleshiness of his cheeks, his feral nature, his stumpy legs and his crab-claw hands, with the most imposing demeanour he could muster, he tried to embody something between Klimt and Mussolini. But there was more of the despot than the artist in him. And his paintings weren't up to much either… Although you could hardly call them paintings. Actually, you could call them whatever you liked, because they were completely devoid of any content. No one could work out what he'd painted. Of course they were one-dimensional. Of course they were abstract. It was the worst kind of incompetent daubing!

I said to Hanuman that even elephants could draw better.

"What elephants?" he said, clearly not understanding. "What are you on about?"

"The elephants which belonged to those idiots, the ones who fled to America from the Soviet Union!" I explained to Hanuman.

"Which elephants?"

"I told you about them! I told you a thousand times!"

And so I had to tell him the thousand and first time. He never remembered anything! He immediately forgot every single thing I told him.

The elephants had belonged to two Russian artists. To start with these dissidents had tried to impress Western art aficionados with pictures of the Führer hugging Lenin, Stalin embracing Napoleon, Brezhnev with Mao, surrounded by blue aliens with the obligatory large heads and cunningly squinting, almond-shaped eyes. But it didn't work, they quickly realised that no one was interested in their symbolist nostalgia proofed with the yeast of belated imitation and baked in the oven of surrogate surrealism, so they bought an elephant and started to train it, teaching it how to hold a paintbrush in its trunk and draw it across a five-dollar canvas. The results weren't at all bad. People actually bought those daubings! And so those resourceful rogues started up a production line: a second elephant, and a third one with its trunk to the grindstone! And it has to be said that things went well for them: the elephants worked away contentedly, and all the paintings were sold! What exactly took shape on the canvas was something else altogether... but at least no one had any complaints, what could you expect of an elephant anyway...

"Elephant..." Hanuman repeated pensively, although his thoughts were clearly elsewhere.

As usual, he wasn't listening: he was staring into the rain, tapping out some tune...

Yes, elephants, for Christ's sake! That's what I talked about, what I thought about when I looked at Potapov's pictures. His so-called masterpieces were full of ambition, and they were provocatively titled too. Take for example *Time No. 1*, which was a wheel, spokes flashing as it cut through a foaming wave. Or *Time No. 2*, a tyre rolling down a hill. Or *Aristocracy*, which should have been a real masterpiece. At least it could have been and I had suggested the subject. If only he knew how to paint! It was meant to depict a puddle with petrol in it and large, iridescent bubbles floating on top. But it didn't turn out right at all. And then there were *Technocracy*, *Bureaucracy*, and *Hierarchy*, and other such dross.

But he still managed to sell them. Not very often, but occasionally someone would buy one. Because he knew how to talk about the meaning behind the various symbols. You could even say that the worse the picture, the better he was able to talk about it. And the weightier the terminology and symbology which he pronounced, with a look of most pious gravity on his face. Sometimes he got so carried away that he started shouting, and on occasions he would get out of breath and begin to splutter, rasp, and cough. Very often, almost every time, he would say, "Here, of course, the most pressing ontological question is posed." I couldn't understand what that was supposed to mean at all, and I had a hard job not to burst out laughing. When he cranked up his muttering I often had to resort to my tried and tested routine. Like Tristram Shandy's father I reached for my handkerchief, first into one pocket, and then the other, tying myself into knots. Then I proceeded to scoop out all sorts of junk from my pockets – bits of notepaper, tickets which could be given a new lease of life for one more journey, loose change which I often dropped and spent ages picking up. Then I coughed into my fist to hide my laughter, found my handkerchief, removed my glasses, and started polishing one of the lenses, peering into the light. At one time that had been a signal to my friends that I was taking the piss, and they would frantically try to suppress their laughter. But now Hanuman was the only person who knew about it, and he could stay composed in any situation, because, unlike me reaching into my pocket for my handkerchief, he always had a fitting riposte to hand – and he would laugh right in anyone's face if he felt like it, even if it was Mikhail Potapov, who sometimes bought him beer.

Although Potapov's paintings were awful, and the overblown twaddle which he spun was enough to make you vomit, he did manage to sell two of them, by pulling the wool over his customer's eyes and vaunting his string-vested pot-bellied poverty. Svenaage bought one of them, and a couple of Jehovah's Witnesses bought the other. The first bought *Aristocracy*, the other two took *Bureaucracy*. Having earned himself three hundred kroner he got stuck into painting some sort of religious nonsense. But that all came undone when he met Korney.

Korney was quite short too, and he also sported a belly and beard, in fact he looked more like Klimt than Mikhail did, although he bore absolutely no resemblance to *Il Duce*. He painted too, also anything whatsoever, and he would agree to anything whatsoever as well. But he didn't dare give his creations a name. That wasn't necessary, since their obviousness bordered on the primitive, they were so devoid of anything abstract that one was loath to call them art. They were like those simple *lubok* woodcuts. Look, there's a church on a hill. Look, a mill on the same hill. Look, there's a house, or a cow, or a little boy flying a kite, and they're all on that same hill. Those paintings were so direct that they didn't need a name. They were as simple as photographs and – what was really awful – they were like bad photographs. But Korney didn't draw just for fun. His work might have been simple but he was a cunning character. He would start off by buttering up a prospective client, finding out what he liked, and then he would start drawing, as if to order, but without the client actually knowing about it. As if it was a surprise! Then the client would turn up, and Korney would casually direct him towards a picture which seemed to have been painted by telepathy! But he still didn't sell many, he gave more of them away, counting on various favours and assistance in return. After all, he was an asylum seeker, and he hoped to arouse pity in the Danish, to gain a reputation as an undiscovered genius, who could flourish this side of an iron curtain which no longer existed. He tried to act like some kind of holy fool, although he was really just an ordinary alcoholic.

He would give his pictures away, and then ask if it wouldn't be too much trouble for his client to write a letter somewhere on his behalf, for example to the infamous Directorate, requesting that he be transferred to an apartment, or a camp for sick people. Because he was oh so ill...

He also tried to feign invalidity – with great persistence.

He would down various mixtures, pretending he had a stomach ulcer. He tried to wangle some kind of supplementary pension, a modest three hundred kroner extra for medicines, which he could then spend on tobacco. Tobacco was one of his major outgoings. He couldn't cut back on that, even if he did want to save money, because he couldn't do without it; and so he never managed to save a single krone. And he needed his booze too. So he came up with that ulcer, or sometimes it was epilepsy.

One time when he was waiting in the corridor, in the queue to claim his benefits he started retching abjectly, he was on the verge of vomiting blood. They called the ambulance and he was taken away, writhing in agony. He ended up spending three days in hospital, where they violated him with a poorly lubricated three-metre gastric probe, put him on a strict diet, gave him an enema, hooked him up to various pieces of equipment, but still found nothing wrong. He left the hospital skinny, sickly, harrowed, and with a clean bill of health. Falling into a depression he painted what must truly have been his best picture ever, the only one he dared give a name, and what a name it was: *Removing the Heart from Danko's Breast*. What could one expect of a freethinking man of the sixties? He wasn't capable of anything less.

The opened thorax with the heart being ripped from it looked pretty realistic, even if the heart did resemble an alarm clock, and was for some reason being extracted with tongs. They said that he had consulted anatomical charts for the details. In any case, it was definitely better than the windmills, the Russian churches in the snow, and the fields of tulips, which he had apparently seen in the Netherlands (legend had it that he had been transported across Holland to Denmark in the boot of a car, typical asylum-seeker antics).

Having discerned the talent in Korney's brushstrokes, Mikhail took on the role of his impresario, or God knows what. In practice it meant that he brought him paints and canvasses (he later fashioned the frames himself), suggested the subjects, and flogged the pictures in various places. He didn't pay Korney fifty per cent of the proceeds, only thirty, and Korney had no way of checking how much the picture had really fetched. But Mikhail couldn't pocket all the money himself, because his English wasn't up to much, to say nothing of his Danish, so he needed someone to help negotiate with potential clients. And who better suited to that role than Hanuman.

At one point Hanny and me were making a nice little profit out of that. Well, maybe not a profit exactly... Basically, it started with Hanny flogging a couple of pictures to some balding admirer of all things Russian. He was unable to withstand Hanny's onslaught, and so with a scratch of his chin he took the mills with the cow on the hill. Then we smoked all the proceeds that very evening (and the following morning Nepalino was making the same champing noise from down below, damn him).

But then something happened which changed everything, and changed it to the core. Hanuman met some bloke who had his own restaurant, or maybe it was a café, or a shop, or a video rental store (he only had Indian films), or maybe all of those things in one, anyway, hell knows! It was in a shabby little building on one of the backstreets of Aalborg, with a sign above the door announcing that this was not just any old place, but some sort of shop-cum-restaurant, and it was up to you to come in and decide which of the two.

There were loads of odd places like that in Aalborg. Take for example the conspiratorial coffee shop where we bought the hash and the ill-advised grass off that damned Hugh. That was a weird place too, creepy, grim, wreathed in clouds of ganja smoke. The street outside was littered with rusty scooters and bicycles belonging to customers who must have turned up one day and then been unable to leave. Rustling plastic bags, faeces of all forms, from dried-up dog shit to streaks of human excrement. To one side stood a lonely dog, tied to one of the scooters, looking like a down-and-out begging for money. Inside was a pub, with all sorts of strange psychedelic designs scrawled across the walls. And more decor which was even creepier, even grimmer. Take for starters the wizened old man climbing out of a poppy head, a smile on his face and a syringe full of junk in his hand. And the customers weren't much better.

This character who Hanuman discovered was the owner of the restaurant, which he called "Rushdie", and he was busy running it twenty-four hours a day. The old bloke was Indian, and a queer too, and for some reason Hanuman had dragged me to his restaurant. He had apparently promised the old man that he was going to introduce him to a real Russian writer, one who wrote in English. Back then I liked to tell people that I was writing a book, although in reality I was just killing time, putting down all sorts of incoherent drivel on paper. And so one day we walked through driving rain, sheltering under a single umbrella, and turned up at the old man's place. The meeting between the Russian writer and the owner of the Indian restaurant was accompanied by a cannonade of thunder, the applause of slamming shutters, and flashes of lightning, piercing every chink like prying paparazzi. I reckon he must have been seventy, not a day less, and he looked really decrepit, like an ancient relic. I busied myself for a while with my raincoat, which was dripping wet, trickling water all over the place. Then I asked for some tea. The tea had clearly been made well in advance, it had even had time to get cold. I didn't ask for it to be heated up; I realised that it wasn't worth expecting too much from a place like this. The old man was not only the owner, but the cook, the cleaner, the shop assistant, the waiter, and so on. Hanuman tried to relieve him of at least some of the burden, offering to take on one or two roles which the old fart was clearly not coping with. But he reacted strangely to Hanuman's proposal.

"What are you talking about! How could you!" the old man spluttered, gazing upwards into Hanuman's eyes like a dog. "Such an educated, brilliant young man in a place like this? You're just having a laugh at an old fool's expense!"

Not only was the old man queer, but he was an enlightened queer, and crazy about culture. He was particularly crazy about Russia, even though he knew absolutely nothing about the place, and probably didn't want to either. After all, seventy is not the time of life when you acquire any credible new knowledge about things, it is not the age to form any coherent new opinions. You no longer need them. All that a person needs at the age of seventy is to have their breakfast made, and to be given their pills after breakfast. And then the same again for lunch and dinner. At the age of seventy people just need to be kept at room temperature, they don't need to hear anything which could upset their existing world view. They only need their fully formed, slightly rusty, slightly fusty views and preconceptions. In other words, a seventy-year-old only needs the things he can keep close at hand, or retain in his memory, provided he is still of sound mind of course.

This one was. He even read books. He adored Rushdie, of course. I had guessed as much when I saw the sign outside. He proudly showed me his collection of books, displayed on a shelf above the very best table in the restaurant, which was intended for the very best guests. A dozen books by Salman Rushdie, a portrait of the author, and even a piece of paper with some text written in either Farsi or Arabic which he translated for me and which stated that the price on Salman Rushdie's head was ten million dollars – apparently this was the notorious fatwa. "Ah!" exclaimed Hanuman. We sat down at that table and drank the tea, which was cold and tasted quiet strange.

Weaving flower shapes in the air with his fingers, the old man explained that for Indians, people of the East like him, Rushdie was the link with Europe and America, with the

West that is. The usual nonsense, and I could barely restrain myself from making a barbed comment. For example, substituting the umbilical cord, which apparently represented the writer, with the bowels. But Hanuman trod on my foot, and I realised it was best to just nod. With a learned look on my face, I said, "Well yes, that's right, take the collection of short stories *East, West*, well yes, that's right…"

I can't remember what else was said, obviously the conversation was funny, but at the time I found it utterly boring, and I even allowed myself to yawn when Hanuman suggested that we work on the restaurant's interior design. He proposed, for example, painting a picture on one of the walls which he would call *The Moor's Last Sigh*.

"Yes, that would be really cool," said Hanuman, pursing his lips and reclining in the squeaky wickerwork chair. "Imagine a tree with a manuscript nailed to it, and then the Alhambra palace, shrouded in mist…"

The old man was in raptures. Hanuman told him that he would be able to come to an agreement with someone, but that he was too famous to be expected to do the work cheaply, even if he was deaf and dumb, and wretchedly poor…

"All the better," cried the old man, throwing his hands up into the air, "all the better!"

"But," said Hanuman raising an index finger, "it would not be right to take on a dilettante for such serious work…"

The old man concurred without hesitation. And they agreed on a price which was so high that it made me drool. I mentally converted the sum of money into grams of hashish and bottles of wine, and I felt a lightness come over me, together with a slight trepidation. By now their fantasising had infected me too, and I joined in with the conversation. We talked at length, the old man treated us to something, I think it may have even been wine, and then, I don't know why, but completely spontaneously, apropos of nothing, I recalled my old idea about opening a café or a restaurant called "Chez Guevara". At first the old man didn't understand, probably because he didn't speak French. Then Hanuman quickly explained that the name of the Cuban hero sounded like the French preposition, and my unsophisticated and rather lame homonym caused the old man untold delight. Hanny added that he once went to Prague, where he had a wife and child (where didn't he have them?), and he had come across cafés called Kafka on every corner!

"But 'Chez Guevara' would be much cooler," he said.

"Yes, yes, yes," the old Indian jabbered.

He was a fan of all that stuff, it turned out that he loved not only Mahatma Ghandi, but Lenin too, and all those idiots of the same cloth, so Che Guevara kind of fitted with that bunch of reds, and of course he blended with the ideas of global revolution, in other words he was right up the old man's street. I found myself getting quite carried away, and even suggested that the staff of the café should consist only of men, and exclusively young men, who looked like Che Guevara.

"Yes, yes," I said, "curly-locked, hairy-chinned, dashing young men, wearing berets, and T-shirts with a picture of Che on them, just like mine, for example..."

"Wonderful!" exclaimed the old man, flinging up his arms.

"Yes, yes," I continued in a stern tone. "Not a single woman!"

"Yes, yes, yes," agreed the old man appreciatively.

What I was hinting at with some degree of success was that the restaurant would be transformed into an elite, bohemian gay club. And this got the old man really excited, he leapt up, and, throwing his arms behind his back, proceeded to measure out the floor space of the restaurant with blind strides. Without looking up at us, he mused out loud, "Of course, this will be our reply! Our move! Our battle! Our struggle! Our systematic programme for world domination! There'll be nothing to stop us establishing a whole chain of such restaurants or cafés."

"Yes," said Hanny calmly, shrugging of his shoulder.

"Why not the whole world, we just need to put forward the idea, promote it, take out a bank loan, and make contact with the right people. Maybe with the Cuban magnates. Then we need to install the right equipment, and the idea will fly!"

The old man's eyes had glazed over; he had seen a vision of greater things, and he was no longer in his right mind, he had started raving, oblivious to everything around him. Like a virus, the idea was devouring his consciousness. We left him in the grips of that sickness, stepping out into the rain under our single umbrella.

We waited a while for the idea to germinate, and then we all rolled up at his restaurant again. Korney who as agreed was playing the role of deaf and dumb artist, Mikhail Potapov who just pretended he had some role, that his presence was required, and Hanny and I, who would deal with the old man.

But he no longer had much interest in the picture of Alhambra, which was supposed to be rising from the mists somewhere yonder. Instead, emerging from the mists were the "Chez Guevara" restaurants, which would unite all the gays of the world. A chain of restaurants and owners who would be united by the idea of the global ascendancy of the Reds, and the dominion of homosexual over heterosexual love!

So the old man decided against the picture, but promised that he would definitely make use of the artist's services in his new project.

"The restaurant formerly known as Rushdie is now closing," he declared in a fit of some sort of euphoria, and he even chucked out two young women who were about to order something, slamming the door behind them and shouting, "We're opening a new restaurant called 'Chez Guevara'! Understood?"

Potapov latched on to the idea. He insisted that the old man completely redecorate the premises. He said that it was necessary to paint all the walls red, and the ceiling white. He said that they should weave a golden border strip for the wall, with plaster-cast roses, like in the Soviet cultural centres, and then scatter the snow-white sky with bright red stars. He would be happy to take on the work himself, as painter-plasterer, and of course he could be expected to do it all exactly right. Who better than him, a child of the Soviet Union, to know how such things should be done!

But no one was listening to him. Despite his yearning for novelty, the old man was so stingy that he wasn't prepared to go any further than the portrait. He reckoned that it would be enough to paint the portrait and replace the sign outside. He proposed that Hanuman and I work there as waiting boys in red vests, and he kept looking in the direction of Potapov, who he had for some reason taken an immediate disliking to, asking repeatedly, "What's that man doing here?"

Potapov was mooching round the restaurant, not knowing what to do with himself, how to wheedle his way in. He slithered round the edges of the room like a leech, probing for spots which might be in need of a going-over with his palette knife, or for places where the paint was flaking, which could do with the attention of his brush. He suggested tiling the toilet, and making a curtain with pictures of our hero for the front windows, which his wife could sew. He even offered his services as chef, and as speciality of the house he proposed that proletarian staple, borscht. I didn't bother translating that for the old man, after all he had asked Potapov to his face what he was doing there. Potapov had replied that he was waiting for Korney, that he was supposed to be driving him home.

"Ah!" cried the old man, flinging his arms up. "I thought as much, the driver!"

Korney was supposed to be painting a large portrait of Che. Mikhail looked on with undisguised envy as Korney started to make sketches. He clearly sensed that both his money, and his artist, were being taken away from under his nose, and he kept hassling Korney, suggesting that he use the portrait with the Cuban cigar from the photographs which Hanuman provided. But it was decided that the photos with the cigar would be enlarged and hung up as a separate feature in some other part of the restaurant. That was supposed to be Hanuman's job.

We transported some of our things to the old man's place, and moved house; it looked like we could get settled down again. At first I was relieved: no more flip-flops and running water, no more morning shouting, no more Nepalese champing. We could sleep peacefully at night, without constantly stressing, without any agitation; we could calmly visit a nice clean toilet. But it was cold, bitterly cold: the old man was trying to save money.

Hanny and I only just fitted into the tiny room, and we were like a couple of corpses in a mortuary, it was so cramped and cold! Hoping to brighten up our miserable existence, the old man brought us piles of quilts. They made our room look like a gypsy caravan. And with similar maternal care, or a benefactor's concern, the old man brought a funny fold-up bed for deaf-and-dumb Korney, and made it up. And then, maybe just to make it clear what the bed was for, or maybe due to senile dementia, the old man tapped on Korney's shoulder, lay down on the bed, and shouted at him: "So-ve, so-ve, so-ve," which meant "sleep" in Danish.

I remembered my uncle once told me about being brought something to eat at a Danish immigrant reception centre, after he fled the Soviet Union at the end of the 1980s. It was a bit like this occasion, although they didn't treat him like he was deaf and dumb, more as some kind of wild man. The guard had come into the room, put the tray of food down in front of my uncle, and then acted out the process of picking up some food between thumb and forefinger, throwing back his head and placing the imagined morsel inside his wide-open mouth, then saying to my uncle, "Eat, eat!"

Later, in the middle of the night, when Korney had already gone to bed, the old man had come to his room, placed a prehistoric gas heater down on the floor next to him, switched it on, and left. In the morning Korney told us what a fright he had got: "The heater is making such a loud whirring sound, the flame's so bright, it looked like it was going to explode!" He was afraid to turn it off, but he couldn't say anything to the old man, because he was supposed to be dumb. And so he just moved the heater as far away as he could, pushed his camp bed into the far corner of the room, and slept with his face to the wall and a pillow over his head!

Before he finally left the restaurant Mikhail made one last attempt to inveigle himself. He said that he had a family, and that it wasn't that easy for him to move house; he had to transport a lot of stuff, he needed a bed for his daughter, she had already started at school, and so on. At first the old man didn't get what Potapov was prattling on about, then he told him that he hadn't planned to invite him to move in, and certainly not with his family. Potapov could carry on living with his family where they already lived, wherever that might be, he wasn't suggesting that Potapov stay at the restaurant. Then with a dismissive gesture he said, "We don't need the driver any more. The artist is staying with us! No driver required!"

Potapov did manage to nab something, he nabbed a sack which was lying in the corridor leading from the kitchen to the back door, but it later turned out to be full of rubbish. When Mikhail left he was a greenish hue and stony-faced from anger, and then three kilometres from Aalborg he got pulled over by the police. Not only was he breaking the speed limit, but it turned out that he had no driving licence, his MOT was out of date, and he was pissed out of his head. He also had some strumpet in the car with him, and claimed he was just giving her a lift, but it was obvious he was planning to take her into the forest or somewhere, like he normally did.

We settled in at the old man's place, and he started doing the rounds of various banks and agencies. God knows all the places he went. He must have just been trying to get a loan so he could open another couple of restaurants. He was trying to push the idea of opening a whole chain of them. It had all been planned out, put down in writing, and translated into Danish. They looked at him just like they had looked at my uncle in the patents office.

Hanuman kept on trying to persuade me to tell the old man that the whole thing was my idea, that I should get paid for it! It made no difference if I had painted the picture of Che Guevara above the restaurant door or not, I was the one who first proposed the idea of opening a chain of restaurants, I had come up with the whole design, the branding, the theme, and so on…

I told him to forget it.

He told me that I was unlikely to ever have such a good idea again.

I told him I didn't care.

He didn't mention it for a while – for three or four hours we just got on with our own stuff: I went through my notes, he leafed through his porno mag. Then we started drinking the beer which the old man had bought us. And then Hanuman said OK then, sod it, he would squeeze some cash out of the old fart, something at least!

But the old man quickly ran out of steam, and took to his sickbed No one liked his idea – revolutionaries weren't particularly popular in Denmark. Maybe they were amongst the outcasts and underdogs, the would-be punks and outsiders, but setting up a chain of restaurants aimed at that marginal, amoral section of society amounted to breeding more of the bastards, together with the dodgy dens and cesspits where they would multiply, hole up, and lurk, doing their dirty deeds. No way! And so the idea was turned down.

But of course he did get some money. As an entrepreneur, someone who had started up his own business and now wanted to expand. A pretty modest sum, around twenty-five thousand, for him to rent another cellar in some building which was already on its knees, where we could hang up a gaudy sign from the lopsided door canopy. Korney would paint a picture of Che Guevara on the wall, some well-meaning idiot wearing a T-shirt with a profile of our hero would be happy to get behind an improvised counter, and the old man wouldn't need to do a thing. Hanuman's banter worked like opium. He had completely bewitched the old man. Patting his wizened hand with his soft palm and leering at him he whispered, "You don't need to lift a finger, before you know it the business will take off like a runaway tram! You just need to cough up the interest on the bank loan, and you can rake in the rest of the income, the revenue, the profit, the yield…" Oh, those magical words! Who didn't long to hear them? Those deadly, sweet droplets dripped from Hanuman's lips, and like butterflies they flitted around the old man's head, dusting his rusty old brains with magic pollen. The old git looked like he was going to fall into a coma right in front of our eyes! He was exalted, he was floating, carried away on a wave of enthusiasm…

The old man got back on to his feet, summoned all his remaining strength, took out a loan, and promptly went back to bed: he was seized by attacks of asthma, which slowly started to suffocate him, and that was interspersed with chronic migraine. That was the first time I saw genuine sympathy on Hanuman's face. Like many other Indians who came to Europe he suffered from migraine in place of homesickness.

We tended to him for three weeks, pretending that the work was under way, that we were looking for suitable premises for a new Che-restaurant, and we took his money to buy food for everyone, and paint. But we strictly forbade Korney from working, and anyway he couldn't work, because we didn't actually buy any paint. We kept trying to pack the old man off to the hospital, promising to take him by car or carry him there ourselves. But he dug his heels in. He didn't want to be driven to the hospital, or be carried there. He didn't want to see that driver anywhere near his restaurant, so strong was the negative impression Potapov had made on him.

"That vile character – I don't want to see him!" he wheezed between fits of coughing.

"No hospital for me!" the old man bellowed.

His breast cage rose as if he were possessed by demons which Hanuman had sprinkled into his ears together with those whispered promises.

"I hate doctors! They're all liars! They just swindle decent working folk!" he moaned, as if he were talking about clergymen.

He wouldn't go and see a doctor, not ever. He avoided clinics like Satan shuns a chapel. He didn't even go to the hairdresser's. He didn't consult clairvoyants. He didn't use taxis. He knew very well that any use to be had from these people was far exceeded by the amount they would rip you off!

And so he would die at home.

"He's dying," said Hanuman in a serious tone of voice, having once again claimed to be "experienced in the death business".

"He's dying," Hanuman said, in a matter-of-fact tone. "He's definitely dying."

He spoke with the certainty of a surgeon, who had seen people die a thousand times before. He talked as if he had poisoned the old man himself and had no grounds whatsoever to doubt the effectiveness of the chosen concoction.

We wanted to ease the old man's expiration, to make dying more fun for him, so that he could kick the bucket with music in the air and something like heroic pathos in his voice rather than just coughs and groans, so that he could give up the ghost optimistically, jauntily, without dragging the process out, which wouldn't be in anyone's interests. So we hid the truth that he was dying from him, and calmly lied that a second Che-restaurant was being built, that there was more than enough money, that we had found someone who was interested in the project, and that soon more and more Che-restaurants would start to appear.

We would return from the brothel and then wearily, but with the customary post-brothel twinkle in our eyes, we would tell the old man that work was under way, that there were people queuing up for the role of boy-in-T-shirt, that we had made contact with the Cuban magnates who had agreed to support us, and that our cafés would serve only their coffee, real Cuban coffee. To the sound of real live Cuban music! Then Hanny put on a CD which he'd bought for twenty-three kroner, it was second-hand, scuffed, with a crack running through the portrait of Che Guevara like some sort of scar. A little-known album containing seventeen songs by various Cuban and Argentinian musicians, some sort of patriotic tribute to our hero with his portrait, the dates of his birth and death, some of his quotes, and some other nonsense on it, in other words, it was a complete piece of crap! But it turned out to be just what was needed. The old man had a good send-off to that life-affirming jangling. In a croaking voice he said, "Ah, what music! Ah! What music! What a pity I can't understand what they're singing about..."

At that Hanuman exclaimed, "Come now! Eugene will translate right away, no problem! He speaks good Spanish!"

And so under the terrifying gaze of the Hanumaniac I sat down next to the old man, rolled my eyes and started to translate. And I translated knowing no Spanish other than *muchacha*[13] and *una peladura de platano*, and a couple of other things.[14] But if Hanny said that I could speak Spanish, then at least I had to try and create the impression that I could, not just make excuses like a fool. So I sat there and

13   Girl (Spanish)
14   Banana skin (Spanish)

blabbered whatever came into my head in a recitative style, left eye screwed up from the tedium. But it had a strong effect on the old man, my sing-song "translations" seemed to instil a certain melancholy in him. He cried, listened some more, then cried again, and then started coughing so hard he nearly choked. We let him know that we needed more money, for various jobs which had to be done. Hanny dreamed them up: a new toilet, ordering beer with portraits of our hero. We didn't ask him for money, we just presented him with the facts: more money was needed, otherwise the project would come to a standstill, the steam engine needed to climb the hill, otherwise our political enterprise would sputter out before you knew it. Then with the air of a worthy patron he dispatched his hand on the long journey across his chest to reach inside his jacket, clenching his jaw so as not to be knocked off course by coughing. With his eyes screwed up he blindly counted out the money from his leather purse underneath the quilt. Hanuman had caught sight of the purse a couple of times, at which he had whispered feverishly, "Who knows how much he's got there… the purse looked fat to me… bursting with cash!" We took the money and went to a hash bar where we sat and smoked, killing time while we waited for it to kill the old man.

And eventually it did. It was a Thursday. A rainy one. A day for farewells. A day which limped along. Full of heavy goods lorries, crawling along the main road running past our house, heading in the direction of the bridge, the bridge beyond which life began. While on this side was the old man's death. He departed quietly, we found him in the early hours. It was a shivering-cold, murky, hung-over morning, I was so frozen that I could hardly get out of bed. I followed Hanuman's call into the old man's room. He said, "*Finita la Commedia*! Comedian – exit stage left!" and whistled. Then he calmly took the leather purse from the old man's breast pocket, counted the money, and gave me a wink. There was around fifteen thousand kroner there.

Hanuman immediately proposed that we get stoned and go to a brothel. It sounded awful, almost sacrilegious. I refused, I just frowned, I was cold, I felt sick.

The first thing I wanted to do was turn the heating up full. But Hanuman forbade me. He said that the old man would start decomposing, which we definitely didn't want. I didn't understand what he meant. He said that living with a corpse wasn't difficult from a psychological perspective, more from an aesthetic one, because it – the corpse – would start to smell when it decomposed, so we therefore had to limit the influence of the factors which would bring about its decomposition.

I said that I didn't care, I had no intention of living with a corpse, and in any case I at least wanted to get warm, then I tried turning the heating dial up again. But Hanuman said that he wasn't going to desert the old man, that he planned to stay there for a month or so more, and if I wanted to I could leave, but he wasn't going to let me touch the heating dial. I said to hell with it and decided to stay put. Then Hanuman opened the window, explaining that it needed to be cold inside, as cold as a morgue! It seemed like some kind of belated revenge on the old man, as if Hanuman were trying to deep-freeze him because he had forced us to live in such freezing conditions all that time.

Without offering any explanation we sent Korney packing back to the camp, giving him some scraps of food and beer for the road; we basically got shot of him. And we stayed there in the dead man's flat, who despite all our efforts stank so badly that it was enough to make us puke.

I started having nightmares. I dreamt of marshes, bogs, scrap heaps, graveyards, all kinds of grim stuff. Sometimes when I saw the old man in my dreams, he was shuffling from room to room asking the same idiotic question, "Why are there no clocks in any of the rooms? It's Che time, you guys!" And for some reason he was shouting in my father's voice.

When I woke up in the mornings covered in sweat, freezing cold and as stiff as a corpse, I tried to move about to warm myself up, but it was impossible. I would rush to the bathroom, run the shower boiling hot, and wait for the little room to fill with steam, then I would undress and slowly and carefully submit each part of my body to the boiling water, and it would take time, a long time, for me to revive myself.

We spent most of our days in the coffee shops and bars, mooching about looking for kicks and whores. After the protracted stagnation of camp life we wanted to live again, we wanted everything at once, in one big dose! Sometimes we mixed all our thrills into one big pile: alcohol, brothel, grass, speed. Like the Georgians, who brewed up their *koknar* from poppy heads, and mixed heroin and cocaine, an evil concoction. But it was too expensive to go to the brothel every day.

"We won't be going to the brothel again," Hanuman said after the second visit, realising his pockets were empty. And so he decided that we should look for cheap slags on the street instead.

"We're definitely not going to the brothel any more. We won't set foot in one!" he said.

I gave him a long searching look. For me that was the only thing of any value. I couldn't care less about all the powders and weed. What use were they if there was no one to screw? He took the hint, and immediately restored my confidence in him..

"But we're sure to pick up some slags, sure to! They might be old, ugly, misshapen, mangy, gap-toothed, womb-breathed, permanently drunk, with filthy arses and crotches scratched by blunt razors – but they'll be cheap! The cheapest possible! When you live like we do, it's better to shag some dirty beast and feel only repulsion than to yearn for someone more attractive. You know, in our situation it makes sense to experience the utmost disgust at life and

132

all the physiological processes it entails. Some beautiful babe is more likely to cause a pang of despair; it could even be dangerous. We need to be disgusted by life. And what better to arouse disgust than excessive naturalism. And anyway, we can't afford the hot chicks, even if we took one between the two of us, and gave her all the money we've got. And all the cheaper ones, even the ones in the brothel, are all pretty much as disgusting as each other. They're pretty much the same as the ones off the street corner, just that they've been scrubbed up a bit. They're not worth the money. What's the point of overpaying? We just need to overcome our squeamishness! From now on we're going to look for cheap slags, the very cheapest possible. There's something to be said for that, what do you reckon Euge?"

"For what? What are you on about?" I asked him.

"What? What do you mean 'for what'? For cheap sluts! I was talking about cheap slappers!"

"Ah! Well yes, maybe," I answered wearily. "I don't care, it doesn't make any difference."

"That's what I'm saying, it doesn't make any difference! You've definitely got some sort of liver problem... you don't care about anything!"

"Just get lost..."

To start with we didn't have much luck with slags, not until we dived into one fusty cellar bar, just to down a shot of something, warm ourselves up a bit and have a rest. We were tired of mooching around town, hanging about Internet cafés, tourist information offices, and shops. Hanny didn't even know what he was looking for, and I was completely fed up with him by then. My feet were soaking wet, there was a foul wind blowing and the rain was drizzling, starting and stopping, almost like it was playing with us. We sniffled. We shivered. We sat down. Necked our shots. Lit up. Hanuman unfolded something he had printed from the Internet, and laid out all the timetables and brochures he had picked up at the travel agency. This time he handled them completely differently, without any animosity. He laid them out and examined them like someone who could allow himself a good number of the pleasures on offer. He suggested that we go to Grenaa first, then onwards by ferry to Lolland. I just nodded.

"Oh!" he exclaimed, "Not far from Grenaa there's a wonderful little town called Ebeltoft. It says here that there's some sort of museum there, and the old town is really pretty: it has delightful, charming little streets which are over a thousand years old... now that has to be a lie! Narrow streets, just like Paris... we'll see about that! But it means there must be plenty of shops, which means lots of tourists, so it should be easy to, tra-la-la... nick stuff. And it says that there's an aquarium in Grenaa, with sharks, octopuses, all sorts."

I shook my head in disagreement. And then I heard, quite distinctly, Russian being spoken. I pricked up my ears. There were two slags sitting nearby.

"Russian slags," I said.

Hanuman tensed like a drawn bowstring. We sat down next to the girls. Delighted to make your acquaintance, I'm sure!

A blonde and a brunette, both around twenty, one of them dark, the other pale. Something for everyone, as they say. Small tits... sharp nipples under the T-shirts. Coarse, hollow voices... bags under their eyes... dirty glances Both of them from St. Petersburg... a couple of stray cats... horny bitches... just the ticket. They live nearby... round the corner... at Mario the Polish pimp's place. The fat bastard has gone away... OK to drop by then. But three hundred and fifty, no less... they need to eat, don't they. What if we have a snort of something... well if we have a snort then we can manage without food... we can come to an understanding... you can always come to an understanding with one of your own... got a mobile?

A mobile appears... there's a guy we know... he's got some powder.

The light-haired one, Olya, called and said in her dodgy English "I need something two times…"

We waited. Hanuman started leching up to Olya, but she didn't understand what he was saying: she just giggled stupidly. Natulya smiled her crooked smile, yanked a cigarette from my pack, and gazed deep into my eyes.

"How long you been here?"

"A year…"

"You've probably forgotten what it's like to be with a Russian woman?"

"Not really, we were partying in Copenhagen for a while. There's loads of them there…"

"So what are you after?"

"He's wants to party his ass off, can't you tell!" Olya shrieked. Then she started giggling, and her laughter was as vile as the look in Natulya's eyes.

Fifteen minutes later a black-haired Kurdish boy turned up; he made a sniffing gesture, his eyes blazed, he looked at me askance, and then he took Olya to one side. Soon she came back with news: "We're going to the brothel! That fat bastard has gone away for the week, we're so hungry we're about to flake out."

And once again that hideous laughter: "Shit, you said that right… we're going to make out! … Oi, I'm going to piss myself!"

And so we killed a few days there. We left on the bus from Aalborg to Esbjerg (which called in at Farstrup on the way), because we didn't dare go back to see the old man, who would probably be teeming with maggots by now. It must have been the slowest bus in the world! It meandered at a deathly pace through far-flung villages and would-be towns. Towns like this, for example – a petrol pump and a mechanic's workshop, a building next to it, another one behind it, a third one, and that was all. Just fields and tractors which had come to an eternal standstill, rusty memorials to progress which got mired in their own excrement. And as we travelled the Jutland landscape spun past the windows like a fairground carousel, the most leisurely carousel in the world.

The bus drivers, who were always alone, were so sleepy that it seemed they could doze off at the wheel at any moment, they could turn off in the wrong direction and lose the way, and if they didn't go off course themselves, they might mix themselves up with a bus-driving double and set off on another bus's route.

We crawled along dejectedly for several hours. The road twisted and turned like it was mocking us. Several times we passed one and the same apple tree, with a craftsman sitting underneath it making ornamental windmills. They were on display in his garden, on the terrace, the balcony, the porch, by the gates, there was even a little windmill on the roof of his house, sails turning, with pieces of coloured glass in the blades to catch the sunlight, although there was no sun to be seen. A sign on the gates read HÄNDVAERK in large letters.[15] We gawped out of the window, necking whisky straight from the bottle and munching bread rolls and some kind of cheese. Hanuman spent the whole journey trying to work out how he had spent so much money. Eventually he reached a conclusion: on pills, whisky and whores, and on all of the latter's endless whims. He even tried to work out how many times we had called the pimp, how many grams of coke we'd bought, how many times the pimp ripped us off, how many bottles of whisky we bought, how much we'd given the whores for cigarettes and chocolate, and so on. Having counted it all up to the last krone he didn't so much as calm down as run out of steam.

"Prostitutes, drugs, alcohol," he said in quiet resignation. "Damn, if it was possible to live without all that stuff I would have been a millionaire a long time ago!"

I told him that there was no point being a millionaire if you could live without all that stuff.

15   *Händvaerk*: handicrafts (Danish)

He fully agreed.

Once we got back we treated Potapov to wine and hash, which we smoked through a wine-filled bong gave Nepalino enough cheap beer to get drunk, and Korney the wine cork to sniff – he promptly slumped asleep in his chair...

The next morning I woke once again to the sound of the Muslims praying, little Liza weeping, and the Nepali queer hassling Hanuman for sex. Once again I was hung-over, I was depressed, and I didn't want to be alive.

4

In the mornings, those early mornings, mornings filled with babbling voices and shuffling flip-flops, I was woken by nightmares, and they returned during those Farstrup days. I dreamed that I had been entombed alive in dung like Major Gavrilov, the hero of the Brest fortress, that I was lying in dung just like him, only that the dung had spread boundlessly in every direction, round the whole planet, the whole universe was full of dung, and now Hanuman and I, together with the other inhabitants of the universe, were buried alive in that dung!

I spent days on end just loafing around in bed. I resigned myself to the fact that my odyssey was over, I resigned myself to going nowhere. I decided that was it, that I would never move from this spot! Whatever happened! To hell with it all! I told everyone, all the demons who were haunting me, to get lost! I just lay there waiting for the police to turn up. Let them come! Let them check my documents! Let them take me away! *Vaersgo!*[16]

I decided that when they shone the flashlight in my eyes I wouldn't get up, I wouldn't answer their questions.

16   Help yourself! (Danish)

I wouldn't put up a fight – I didn't care any more. Anyway, I didn't have any documents to show them. My name is Yevgeny Sidorov, I'm from Yalta. That was all I was going to tell them. Let them do whatever they wanted with me. I don't care any more, I don't care!

Meanwhile, Hanuman went shopping and elaborated his life philosophy, seeking a rationale for what he called "our" miserable existence. That was when he first told me that we had "lost sight of our goal". I didn't understand what he was talking about, because I couldn't remember him ever saying that we had a goal of any kind. All he had ever said about any kind of goal consisted of inchoate outbursts of emotion, and America. That was it. As far as I could remember he had never said anything concrete, and certainly nothing about "our" goal. But Hanny said that there had been one time up in the attic, when we'd just met and were living with Hotello, when we had taken an oath, and he had outlined our goals and the means of achieving them so clearly and so precisely that there was no point repeating it all now. I could remember the occasion. The attic scene had imprinted itself on my memory oh-so-clearly, but I couldn't remember anything concrete being said. There had been darting hands, inflamed eyes, moist breath, fun and games, cigars and whisky, whisky and cigars...

Hanuman pulled a face like a goat and told me that I had smoked myself silly. At which I reminded him that he had been the first to deviate from the goal, when he decided we should head to Lolland instead of America. Hanuman gestured at me like he was swatting a fly. He told me that Lolland meant nothing, it was just a place to have some fun for a day or two. Then he told me that we shouldn't be frittering away all our money, we shouldn't be spending so much.

"We won't spend that much on hookers again. Let's agree on that right now," he said reproachfully, as if I was the one to blame, as if I had somehow conjured those hookers into existence. "Let's agree that it's OK to spend a bit of money on booze and hash now and again, but not too much, alright? And especially not on hookers... actually let's be firm on that point, let's not spend another krone on hookers, OK?"

I exhaled through pursed lips, demonstrating my indifference. I told him I didn't care. I didn't give a damn. Anything he wanted. And I thought to myself – of course, what's the point of spending money on hookers if you've got that little poof on hand to suck you off every morning!

Hanny announced that he had decided to economise. He said he had a plan, that he had a clear idea of exactly how he was going to save money. I sat there staring at him, staring at him in undisguised amazement as he paced around our tiny room, cracking his joints. Here was this hobo musing about how he was going to economise, as if we actually had some kind of income, a budget and the rest of it. He was talking complete nonsense. Then he demanded that I work on my Spanish. I laughed in his face.

"How does that fit in with your new economic policy, Hanny?"

But my mockery was like water off a duck's back.

"You still don't understand," he blathered. "Euge, you might be OK at chess, but in real life you don't suss the situation more than two moves ahead." And so he started sending the Nepali to the library to fetch all the Spanish phrase books he could find. And he ended up cursing him, because the Nepali always came back with the wrong stuff...

"What do you call that?!" Hanuman yelled, poking the book under the Nepali's mug. "What crap is this, I ask you? It's Italian, you fool! Cretino understands absolutely nothing about textbooks! How did you learn German? You said you learned it from books? Was it books like this one? With books like this you couldn't even ask for directions in Buenos Aires. With books like this you couldn't ask any more than "where's the toilet?... Idiot!"

139

Then he would pass me the books, put on the cassettes, and we would listen to them, listen to them for hours on end… those recordings were full of an uncanny joie de vivre, they radiated sunshine, optimism, and the hubbub of tourists' voices, in them I could hear the murmur of ocean waves, sand crunching underfoot, swishing palm branches and parrots' wings flapping. I closed my eyes and immersed myself in those lisping phrases: *Cabeza, encima de la mesa, una peladura de platano* Hanuman repeated them out loud, and demanded that I did so with him.[17]

He announced that he was getting ready to go travelling; he even made a notch in the wall next to the picture of Batman. He informed me about that in the morning, as he came to get his towel and his toothbrush, in an unusually earnest mood. He told me that he was now in "total preparation" mode, and that I should also start to get ready. And he used a fancy word – "enterprise". Nepalino snorted from under his quilts. Hanuman ignored the grunting. He said, in Spanish, that he was off to the bathroom to wash, shave, and brush his teeth; all of it in Spanish. And he was expecting me to do the same. I just lay there goggling at him – it was so early in the morning!

"What did you expect!" he said, thrusting his wimpy chest forwards determinedly. "How do you ever hope to achieve anything in life if you just fester in bed? It's what they call *clochard* syndrome. Hah! Euge, get up! Get a move on, you bastard! We're going to be in Argentina soon, that's in a completely different time zone, we need to acclimatise, get ready for the time difference. Take a look!" and at that he stretched out his watch arm to me and said with an important, businesslike air, "I've already reset my watch!"

"Yeah, yeah, sure," I said, grinning. He started dragging the quilt off me.

"It's not a joke," he said sternly. "It's all a lot more complicated than you think… I'll explain… now concentrate!"

17   Head, on the table, banana skin (Spanish).

I sat upright, legs dangling off the bed. As soon as he started, I realised he was about to really flip his lid. It turned out that he was still planning to go to the States – but via Argentina! Of all the routes he could think of, this now seemed the most viable. But why... keep listening! And so I listened. And this is what he said: being an expert in computer programming – I was not the only one to be sceptical about that – he now planned to head up some company in Argentina, and had been in correspondence with them for a while. They were apparently waiting for him with open arms. They were already unfurling banners which read "Bienvenido, Hanumancho!!!" He reckoned that in Argentina he would quickly become God-knows-what, an inventor of computer games, viruses, and antivirus programmes. And according to him that would be even better than becoming dictator of Chile or Peru, which is what he had raved on about before. After a while he could easily hop across from Argentina to the States. And with his priceless experience he would of course be asked to take up a position in some fancy corporation. It was hilarious – no one could have dreamed up a sillier way of getting to the States (he might as well have been outlining his plan for becoming king of the world).

Many people had succumbed to this "stateside" sickness, pretty much everyone in the camp dreamt of America, about how one day America would lift the hem of her long green robe and welcome them in, but I had never heard anything quite like Hanuman's plan! America syndrome was the most common ailment among asylum seekers. It was a permanent condition, like paranoia. It had always existed, and it would always exist, a priori. It was a given. At every time in history, and amongst all peoples. Life in the camp meandered along against the backdrop of this *idée fixe*. I would go as far as to say that the majority of them ended up there with that very purpose. In any case, all of them were now striving towards that goal. America was in everyone's soul. The Statue of Liberty was the central axis which grew from the tailbone of every mangy sheep in this factory farm; it was some sort of fixation in the cranium. In their subconscious every one of them was yearning to reach a state of total, unbridled freedom, to ascend to the heavens, and that could happen only in America. In the minds of every one of them, America and heaven were one and the same. That wretched archetype embodied the flame of Prometheus, male fawning upon the feminine ideal, endless coitus, and the Oedipus complex, all of them in one, the whole lot!

But I couldn't care less about America, just like I didn't care about the tumour which half of them claimed to have, a malign growth which could only be removed in a Danish hospital. I couldn't care less about the groaning which echoed from every corner and every corridor. I didn't care that they had turned this pigsty into a stage on which to act out their sordid vaudeville, parading their bedsores, their stumps, and the rashes on their arses. I couldn't care less about any of them, any of these idolaters. And most importantly of all, I felt exactly the same way about every single one of them, without distinction! Jew, Russian, Armenian, Tamil, Arab, Negro... it made no difference to me! They were all exactly the same! I couldn't care less about any of them! Not any of them... When I heard how the Muslims prayed to Allah to send them a yes, I just laughed. Not at the Muslims, but at the jokers who spread that story (I heard it from Mais, from Potapov, God knows who else I'd heard that kind of nonsense from – mostly from Stepan). It made no sense to try and salvage some shred of dignity from this godforsaken mass of humanity, to try to selectively respect one or another of them. All of them were slaves to the American dream, but they were all prepared to settle for a scaled-down version of it on Scandinavian soil, as far as their limited welfare payments would allow. They had all turned into zombies. It was as if the Statue of Liberty radiated some sort of energy, issuing forth a command – "Come to me all you who are weary and burdened" – and they set off like baby turtles to the ocean, or rats following the Pied Piper of Hamelin. But there was nothing to laugh at: was there anything funny in all of this? Hanuman was the worst of all... his ravings sent me into a stupor. No one else could dream about America as elaborately, as abstractly, as audaciously as he could. You couldn't believe your ears. No one I knew was quite as inventive in their imaginings of America, no one had sought out ways of reaching her bosom that were quite as absurd. Casanova, Don Juan, Lovelace and Faublas had nothing on Hanuman. The stuff he said surpassed anything you could invent. I don't know whether he was teasing me, but he told me he could pass for the descendent of an Indian aristocrat from Trinidad or Tobago, like Naipaul (whom he had read a lot of, so he could pull the wool over peoples' eyes and pretend he was from there). He didn't bother explaining why! As if it was supposed to be obvious. I couldn't bring myself to ask him about that. I just inquired, "But why do you want to go to the States? What are you going to do there?" At that he got all puffed up and indignant, and started yelling at me, "Oh man! What sort of question is that! What am I going to do in the States? He-ha-ho! In the States... ooohhh! Well, to start with I've got an uncle there! I wouldn't find myself at a loose end in a place like that! Ooohhhh! I'll get a job! 100% guaranteed!" he said with a click of his fingers.

"What work? What do you know how to do? You?" I asked him. And he answered with an important air, "Pah! Anything you like! To start with I could work as a taxi driver in New York!"

He clearly thought that it was enough to be Indian. If you were Indian, you instantly got given a licence and a taxi, the moment you set foot in Manhattan!

Oh God, if only I could think straight! Who had I got myself mixed up with! How on earth had I fallen for his drivel? How had I let this Hanumania addle my brain?

How could I have thought that... but what was the point now... if someone had been "going to America" since they were a kid... what were you supposed to say to that! But there was something about him, if I was prepared to tag along with him like this, there must have been something. Yes, there was. But all his brains and his energy, all of the limited resources he possessed, everything that nature had bestowed on him, all of it meant absolutely nothing alongside this idiocy about America and Lolland. For some reason I hadn't paid any attention to that, I had just happily drifted along with him. It suited me not to notice the problems. That must have been how my rational side protected itself, the rational me made sure that I didn't ever see a clear picture, it literally forced me to keep smoking something, or to pop some pills, that was how I instinctively staved off insanity. If I had stopped to think, and started to reason rationally, then I would definitely have gone round the bend. No doubt about it. That was why I looked at life through barely parted fingers, and I always kept a couple of fingers crossed for good luck. Let him go to America! Let him go to the moon if he wants to! I couldn't care less. Personally, I wasn't planning to go to America, I wasn't planning to go anywhere. My goal was to sit out five years away from home, after which I could hopefully cast off the chains of trepidation and countenance going back, in whatever shape or form (although preferably in a wheelchair, with a pipe in my mouth, and a pension regularly dripping into my bank account). The only journey I could think of was to Amsterdam or Hamburg, but I would only brave that when I was sure that getting caught would have no fatal consequences. When falling into the hands of the authorities was no longer such a scary thought. I had long since said "good bye!" to my America. I no longer had any need for it. I had outgrown it. I had got over it and other such illusions. I had been cured. But Hanuman still hadn't. That was why he was going to America, and I was tagging along for the ride.

But you could understand where he was coming from. As far as Potapov and his like were concerned, a person needed to have his dreams, his delusions, his Lolland, and his America too. For a while I had raved about Mexico, peyote, and mushrooms. Then it turned out that you could buy those very same mushrooms in Christiania[18] – which I did on more than one occasion – you could buy them, gobble them down, and see all the same stuff which Don Juan showed Carlos Castaneda. You didn't need to go to Mexico! Three grams of mushrooms, and that's my Mexico, right there in my pocket! Three grams of a dream which is far greater than reality! A bridge to eternity, to eternal delusion! A temporary clouding of reason broken by the momentary illumination of something more profound. Clinical death, followed by resurrection! Wey-hey! Eat up those three grams, and you cease to exist for six hours – or at least you still exist, but not here and now – where you are exactly, even you don't know, you've disappeared! No point in anyone calling your name!

Hanuman was exactly the same with his America. He needed America so that he could drift along freely, while maintaining some sort of counterbalance somewhere else to justify everything he did here! In America, Hanuman would become a cab driver, he'd give up smoking hash, he would mow lawns, trim bushes, and try for parts in TV series. The dream of America was worse than heroin and hash combined, worse than anything imaginable, worse than believing in God. It meant losing yourself, succumbing to a living death, turning into a zombie or a scarecrow, with a Chinese calculator in place of a heart, and in place of

18　Christiania is a partly self-governed district of Copenhagen, an unofficial "state within a state"; during the period in which the novel takes place it was possible to buy marijuana and other psychotropic substances there.

brains – Colgate, Head & Shoulders, Pantene Pro-V, Urge, Wash-n-Go, all dependable cars, every time you're eating, never miss your chance, take advantage of…[19]

Potapov also had a dream. His dream was to own a huge mansion. His dream was to recline on a wickerwork chair on his balcony, stark naked. His dream wafted into his lungs with the marijuana smoke. His dream dribbled from his fat lips like the juice of an Astrakhan watermelon. His dream trickled on to his stubbly double chin, down his chest, on to his belly, between his legs, and collected in droplets on the tip of his dick, just as it was being licked by a busty babe, looking up at him dewy-eyed. His dream wandered around the gardens, his own gardens, which he surveyed from his balcony. His dream wandered around those gardens in the form of virgins who had been brought there for him to defile. Mikhail Potapov's dream was one of imperialism and dominion, a dream of tyranny and despotism.

Another person who had a dream was Ivan Durachkov (Ivan had appeared in the camp while we were away, and he was apparently Mikhail's brother-in-law). His dream lived in Paris and spun round a silver pole in her birthday suit every evening. By day she went to college, with a rucksack on her back, clutching her papers and a book tightly to her flat chest. Ivan's dream was a delicate girl dressed in black, with a short haircut, and boyish ways. She walked around Paris, gazing sentimentally into the distance, which was hazy and lilac-coloured, and sometimes at her boots, which were shiny with silver buckles. She wore suit jackets, a silk muffler, a llama-wool shawl, and a scarf which she had knitted herself. His dream could be found in a bistro on the corner of Rue de Musset and Place de Coquillard. There she is, reclining in her chair, holding a cigarette in her outstretched hand, dressed in a jeans skirt cut to her knees (not a centimetre longer or shorter!). His dream could speak French, and a little English too. She was a true

19   Advertising slogans.

146

Parisienne. She had sad, emerald eyes. She wrote poetry in a fat leather-bound exercise book. Her short stories could be found on the disused website www.lesgenscontrelesjaunes. fr, and they were about Arabs who married French girls and mistreated them. She wasn't mocking the Arabs, she was mocking the French girls who married them. She didn't use the metro, because it had disgusting genital associations for her. She drank absinthe and aperitifs, listened to African music, argued with her mother, loved her father like crazy, spoiled Felix her kitten, grew cactuses on every windowsill, smoked hash on Sundays, was opposed to phone sex, didn't vote out of principle, hated going to relatives' birthdays, danced Riverdance on Tuesdays and Thursdays, and by evening she was back in the club, spinning round her silver pole. She kept a diary in which she cussed those same French girls who married Arabs, and every other word she used was an expletive. Her favourites were *merde*, *salope*, *zut-zut-zut*, *bonbon de merde*, *ssssans-culottes* and *nom d'un chien*. Ivan Durachkov's dream had just fallen out with yet another flatmate, and was waiting for Ivan to come to Paris, so she could melt into his arms.

I would have liked to have known what Nepalino's dream was... but he didn't talk about it. Or at least no one asked him. I reckoned that his dream was roaming around some camp somewhere. His dream had long bandy legs, broad shoulders, a firm butt, a long dick, full lips, black skin, long black hair plaited into a ponytail, flared nostrils full of lumps of green snot, a deep belly button where plenty of fluff had accumulated. His dream seduced forty-year-old Danish women, wore sports clothes and trainers, lifted barbells and dumb-bells three times a week, went to all the nightclubs, drank whatever the Danish girls poured him, ate anything and everything, crapped a ton of shit every month, and dreamed of marrying a rich Danish woman so that he could settle in Denmark. Nepalino didn't figure in that black guy's dreams at all.

It seemed like Chinaman Ni's dream had already come true. He found himself a Chinese woman. She moved in with him. She cooked for him. She tidied up after him. They made love for days on end. Sometimes you wouldn't see them for three or four days in a row, but you could certainly hear them, and you could feel the earth move. All of that meant that we now had to wallow in our own muck, but we didn't do anything about it, we just lazed about daydreaming…

Potapov dreamed about his mansion. Ivan about his Parisienne. Hanuman dreamed about his SoHo, New York. Somehow it put me on edge, I was pissed off with it all. And then one time Potapov asked me, "What about you? Have you got a dream?"

"Me? No way. Dreaming is dangerous. Dreaming can land you in the loony bin before you know what's hit you. I've got one particular wish, a specific wish, which contains a few smaller wishes inside it, a kind of package of wishes."

" A dream package," Hanuman inserted caustically.

"Yeah, yeah, something like that…"

"So what is it?" Potapov persisted.

"A little house somewhere in Grenoble or Avignon, it's not important where exactly, cable TV, Internet, a bath, a decent pension, and some sort of harmless disease, something not too serious, the kind that only affects your potency…"

"But why?" Durachkov asked blankly.

"So as not to waste my time, money and energy on women, so as to spare my nerves. And that's not a dream, it's a wish, the kind of thing I would ask for if a golden fish came my way…"

They had a good laugh at my expense and didn't give me the chance to finish, they didn't let me explain why dreams are dangerous, although I could easily have told them.

As I see it dreams are parasites on the soul, and we have to purge ourselves of them just as rigorously as we try to get rid of fleas, computer viruses, bad habits, foibles and excessive self-indulgence. And America is the real bête noire. The most dangerous dream of them all. Like a Siren, she lures you to your doom. She casts Hollywood's nets wide across the world, with advertisements, myths, songs and dolls... and every net contains the promise of Freedom, together with the seed of the American dream, but the dream leads only to catastrophe. It starts with something small, with a harmless promise. A promise which you fail to keep, an innocent lie. One small act of betrayal in the name of a greater dream. America is massive, after all, but a wife is just a rag to wipe your boots on, a hole in which to fulfil a bodily function, like going to the toilet; why not be rid of her altogether in the name of America, in the name of Freedom! A total betrayal of the spirit begins with the declaration of a Glorious Freedom, ushered in by some trivial act. It can start with anything at all: unfaithfulness, theft, gossip which you let go too far, humiliation, cruelty towards your cat... anything at all. It can start from your neighbour's door, where you write "YIDS LIVE HERE" or "Lena is a dumbass". And so word by word, deed by deed, you disappear, you betray something within which made you who you are, you give up on your very self, on the most basic thing you have – your name. And all for the sake of a fiction, a dream. For that alone. You're prepared to do things which would normally seem like idiocy. You're ready to do the most terrible things in the name of that dream. You've already done so many smaller things. But it turns out that the trivial things are the most terrifying of all. The cockroaches in your brain, which it is hardest of all to be free of. Because if you kill an old lady, it happens just once, and then it's done. But if you start to lie, and you get a taste for it, then it's hard to stop. And the longer it carries on, the worse it gets. Day by day, as you nurture the dream within you, the dream which overshadows everything, you run from your former self, you force yourself to be born again, full of disgust at the world and at your very self. In the unsettling company of strangers you acquire new characteristics, born of your imagination. When you start to lie every single day, when you begin to believe your own lies, it's easy, so easy, to lose yourself forever. You yearn to do all those things which you were previously too scared to do, which you turned away from, which you denied yourself. Why not try shooting up? You tell yourself you'll be fine, that you won't overdose, you won't get infected, you won't die. Because it seems that it's not really happening to you, it's happening in your dreams, to the character you invented, who you imagined into existence. And characters cannot die, because they are not alive. They live inside your dreams, in the imagination, fully protected, completely free, like the heroes of comics and books. And so it transpires that dreaming is dangerous – and that the closest thing to dreaming is art. But when art is purged of dreams and polished to a mirror-like smoothness so as to replicate real life, then a dream in the form of art becomes harmless; that is when you understand that there is no better alternative to drugs than art. It's enough to crank up the Butthole Surfers, and that's all you need, take as much inspiration as you need! I could never bear to listen to those stories about great musicians or artists gobbling LSD or getting drunk for inspiration. It always seemed like a kind of depravity. Either it was a flimsy cover, or a feeble pretext. You have to be pretty unimaginative to use art as a justification for getting high! Why do you need to justify it anyway? If you want to get high – just do it! Munch those mushrooms, down those pills! It's your life, anything goes, do what you want! Why do you need to dream up justifications?

And so we had a pathetic sum of money left, and Hanuman spent it on food, chipping in with Nepalino. He told me that the "catlike creature" (that's what we called

Nepalino, although we called him "she" even more often) had ripped him off again, when he bought cheap mutton from some other Nepalese guy who had just got a yes.

"He told me that he paid one hundred for it! Imagine that!" Hanuman said indignantly.

"There you go then," I retorted.

"That little businessman made himself a nice little profit!"

"What did you expect... that way he saves himself another couple of days of his life," I said with a yawn.

"The son of a bitch! I paid for half of it! A whole fifty kroner! And then I found out from Zenon that his father bought mutton off that same Nepali for fifty kroner a kilo. Imagine that! Turns out that the little toad got to scoff mutton for free!"

"That's right!"

They had a noisy argument. I couldn't understand a word of it. But it was pretty funny to watch, like an amateur pantomime set in rural Asia in the Middle Ages. It backfired for the Nepali because Hanuman shooed him away, kicked him, rapped his knuckles on his head, spat in his face, kneed him in the back and prodded him in the nape, not sparing his long slender fingers. But it seemed that this was exactly what the Nepali wanted, he got off on the attention, at least it was better than being ignored.

Hanuman would cook his own food, the most disgusting food ever, seasoning it more generously with chilli pepper than even the Tamils and Mexicans. He brought me his culinary creations as if he were conducting an experiment on me – how long would I last on that kind of diet. He said he was getting me ready for real Latin American cuisine. I ate in silence, staunchly enduring my living hell.

He often did the washing, and he washed my things too, even my underwear, but pretty soon I stopped removing my clothes altogether. I slept in my jumper, in my trousers and socks, because it was so bitterly cold. I was constantly shaking, shaking so hard that I bit my tongue and the insides of my cheeks. There was one thought which consoled me: I might be cold, bitterly cold, but the Nepali was even colder, he was on his last legs, he was already completely green, before you knew it he would freeze to death, and that wouldn't be a day too soon…

If he croaked, we would have to do a runner; if that Nepali queer croaked, then we would have to leave the camp. And thank God for that! So it would be best if he croaked! I'd leg it out of there! We would bunk it, and I'd go first, without glancing over my shoulder, because I knew that before we left, I was certain, one hundred per cent certain, that Hanny would check the dead Nepali's arse, he'd have a poke about up there to confirm if it was true that Nepalino kept his savings up his back passage!

Yes, the Nepalese cat was on his way out, he was turning into a vegetable, he was growing greener and greener, he even seemed to be covered in rind, some kind of scab. You could hear him scratching under his quilts. Or maybe he was just wanking to get warm.

Winter approached like it was performing a dance skipping across the rooftops with torrential rains. The flimsy tin roof didn't want me to sleep, it mocked me. The rain thrashed down, deafening me. Sleeping was impossible, it was worse than any Chinese torture.

Big wet flakes of snow tumbled clumsily downwards, sticking to the window, melting, and sliding down the glass, leaving a dirty wet track, like spit. I spent hours watching them sliding downwards, waiting to see if one would collide into another… one more snowflake would arrive and start melting, and I would be watching to see if it knocked into another, hoping for more of them to accumulate, it was almost like Tetris.

Outside was constant twilight, and the cold was even more bone-numbing now; it was impossible to get warm. Even the noises penetrated me like a draught, making me shiver. I slid into a swooning state, bordering on a coma,

I immersed myself in an abyss of unconsciousness, like a diver. My depression had returned…

Sometime previously, before the old man died, but when we already knew that all his money would soon be ours, and that nothing could get in the way of that, then it had seemed that my depression was ebbing. I felt a kind of inspiration, I even wrote some poetry and celebrated the happy occasion by sending it to my mother, accompanied by an optimistic letter. I left the post office with a light-hearted feeling, like I had fulfilled an obligation and could now relish further affronts on my honour. But after the old man died and the money quickly evaporated, my depression started inexorably returning like a lizard's tail growing back. I feared it would end badly, that something was happening inside my head, something was awry. That was when Hanuman started buying himself shirts. He would buy more and more every day, returning from the shop, showing the shirts to me and trying them on, purring Sinatra songs to himself. He would inform me that he'd bought them at an unbelievable discount.

"It would have been wrong not to! You have to buy something, after all," he would say, trying to justify himself.

"Why?" I moaned, looking down at him from the bunk.

"What do you mean why? To have a memento, that's why. You can put your shirt on and remind yourself: look, I had money back then. And that money wasn't squandered, but spent with a purpose. And here's the evidence of good husbandry – a silk shirt!"

Shirts were a weakness of his. They always had been, and now these ones especially. These shirts were expensive, the fabric was slightly sparkly, or iridescent. They were dark brown, with a golden hue, but the most important thing was that they had metal buttons. Hanuman, who was something of a magpie by nature, just couldn't resist luxuries like that.

He already had several of them. He bought the first one

with some trepidation, brought it home, ripped open the packaging with trembling fingers, and then he tried it on and said with relief, "A good fit, just fine." The next day he came back with another two. He told me he'd got another discount, that he'd spent around five hundred kroner. But however fantastic the discount, I wondered whether the shirt could really be worth that much. You could live a whole month on five hundred kroner! Now our finances were down by a whole month's worth of life in this hole, and we needed to come up with a cunning plan. But I couldn't bear to think about it, I couldn't even roll over on to my other side, let alone... And this guy was spending our last money on shirts, when we could end up on the street at any moment and perish in the gutter.

"How can he!" I asked in amazement, trying to get my head round it. How can he? Hanuman never bought anything! He was saving for a ticket to Argentina. It was one thing to buy stuff from thieves, that was the kind of discount I could understand. He could have asked the Armenian woman to steal that shirt and got it for a third of the price. Or he could have stolen it himself. Why did he have to buy it? Five hundred kroner! In our situation! On shirts! When winter was approaching!

It seemed strange, very strange, and it made me suspicious. It even started to frighten me.

"How can it be," I thought to myself, "why is he suddenly buying himself shirts? What for? Look, there's another three! He talks about economising, he's planning to go to the States, and all of a sudden there's another five hundred kroner down the gutter! Something's not quite right here," I tormented myself.

I looked at Hanuman, and he seemed different, a completely different person, like someone who had gone out of his mind, lost the plot and taken leave of his senses. Or maybe he had ceased to be human altogether, maybe he had transmogrified, been possessed by the demons of this world, or maybe he had just stopped pretending, and had turned back into a demon, reverted to his true self. I started to suspect he was an alien who had been assigned to follow me, assigned to return me to my home planet, assigned to reawaken the alien in me, because I had gone AWOL, I had lost touch with reality, I was losing my mind…

Meanwhile, he paced around the room with a cigarette and a cup of tea, intermittently humming some tune to himself, tapping out some rhythm with his foot, lost in thought, until suddenly – as if coming to his senses – he would start talking, talking animatedly, and saying the following: that it would be best that he bought himself a shirt, yes, that's right, one more shirt, ha ha! Just one more shirt won't hurt! And it's better for him to buy himself a shirt than to give his money to that idiot. He meant Potapov. Obviously. Who else could he mean? Hanuman made it clear by gesturing towards the wall, from where the cries emanated every morning. He pointed his finger in the direction of the Potapovs' room.

"He was round here again," Hanuman announced, without any attempt to look at me.

"What did he want?" I groaned.

"What do you think? He'd had another one of his ideas."

"What kind of idea?"

"What do you mean what kind? One of his usual, stupid ideas. What other ideas could he have? He's an idiot, a complete idiot."

"But you said that you didn't plan to talk to him any more, Hanny…"

"I didn't want to. But I bumped into him at the shop. He had his bag stuffed full of fizzy drinks."

"My God! It's freezing out!"

"That's what I'm saying. It's freezing cold and that idiot is buying fizzy drinks!"

"Why?"

"Because they're cheaper than usual! Imagine it! He-ha-ho!"

155

"He might just as well have bought ice cream."

"That's what I thought. But I didn't say anything. I wanted to walk straight past him, but he latched on to me. He's got another obsession."

"What is it?"

"Another stupid idea. He wants to buy the most beaten-up car he can find, for peanuts, do it up, drive it round the scrapyards, and then sell it."

"Madness, total madness."

"Of course it is, that's what I told him! Then he said that he wanted to do up the car and put it through its MOT."

"Total fantasy!"

"I suspect he somehow got whiff of the fact that we've got money left."

"You shouldn't be buying shirts for five hundred kroner. Any idiot would realise that we've got money."

"I got three for five hundred."

"What's the difference!" I bellowed at him. "In our situation you shouldn't even be spending one hundred kroner. No one is paying us any allowances, unlike him."

"No, I reckon it's nothing to do with the shirts. He just sniffed us out, he's got a good nose."

That was right, Potapov had a good nose, and he also had the gift of the gab. He knew how to persuade weak-willed and susceptible people. But Hanny wasn't like that; he always took a sober view of things, even when he was blind drunk. Somehow Potapov had sniffed out that we had money left, although he didn't know how much exactly.

He'd already had a car for a while. A pathetic little Fiat of paltry proportions and the colour of diarrhoea. The Georgian junkies sold it to him. They had been spotted in it by the police, and in any case it didn't run too well any more; it barely crawled along and stalled at every junction. The Georgians were even more generously endowed with the gift of the gab than Potapov, and they conned him, insisting that the car had passed its MOT and that the number plates weren't nicked – and he had fallen for it.

Then the cops took the car off him, a fine arrived, ten thousand kroner, which he had no hope of paying. He was worried he would be sent down for it. The Georgians tried to console him, telling him that everything was hunky-dory in prison, you got chicken and milk every day, and when you got bored of chicken they'd bring you beef, or sausages with potatoes.

"It's not like some Russian prison, my friend," said Murman. "You're allowed to work, right, you get a television, and every day they knock five hundred kroner off your fine! Once you've been there twenty days, they'll have knocked off the whole ten thousand, then you can go home, my friend, and at home they'll give you a right fucking earful, you bet!"

"No," Hanuman told Potapov once again, when he turned up in our room, partly with the purpose of cadging a cigarette, partly with the purpose of smoking the cigarette while putting forward his proposal of clubbing together to buy a car.

"No, we'll never see our money again," said Hanuman.

"Why do you think that?" Potapov started whining.

"You'll never sell it! You'll drive it until they impound it! You won't pay the money back in instalments, you've got so many excuses! Your family, for example – you've got a family to feed, that's what you always say!"

That was right, Potapov had a family to feed, and feed it he did. Every morning he stuffed the food into little Liza's mouth by force, bellowing, "Eat it, scum! Swallow it, bitch! Just try not swallowing it down!" Oh, that son of a bitch sure did feed his family.

I had even given up feeding myself; I didn't feel like eating any more. And he was feeding his family, he was bending over backwards to. He had a family to feed. Who would feed little Liza full of that vile porridge if he didn't? Who else could do it?

He got given two and a half thousand kroner every two weeks to make sure they all got fed. You could have fed an elephant with that, but he still went around on the scrounge, he always said he'd spent all his money, he never had enough, and he crawled about the scrapheaps on all fours, he collected bottles, just so he could feed his family! The whole time he moaned that you couldn't get hold of decent whole grains in Denmark. No grains, no buckwheat, no semolina! Shit, no semolina! "How am I supposed to feed the kid without semolina!" he whined. If he'd had semolina, he would have fed her it until she choked to death. I knew why the son of a bitch was moaning, I knew it. If he had semolina, he'd feed his kid with nothing but semolina. He'd feed his wife with semolina too. And he'd take Ivan's money off him in exchange for semolina. "It's just such a healthy foodstuff!" he would insist. "It's obvious. It's got everything you need! Carotene, and iodine, and calcium," the bastard would say, counting off the benefits on his fingers. "That's right, it's got everything that a growing body needs! What else has it got? Well, it's got vitamins A, B and C..." Of course it has. And it's oh so economical too! You could buy a car straight off, and a computer, and a Sony PlayStation, and anything you wanted! Semolina – that was the answer to all our problems!

As for me, I was happy that there was no porridge in Denmark, I was simply in seventh heaven that there was no porridge in any form whatsoever! That's the sign of a proper country! They knew what to eat. They knew what was good for humans – not cattle feed, but proper meat. Forget about porridge, give me meat and cheese! That's the stuff! And so much beer, beer was the most important thing of all! But that idiot wanted more grains, he kept moaning there was no porridge, no pearl barley...

I didn't want to hear a single word about pearl barley, but Potapov needed his pearl barley, believe you me. The next thing the cretin will be asking for is wheat bran. Or millet, the son of a bitch will rediscover a taste for millet, the scum!

He stood there scratching his belly, droning on: "They've got this buckwheat here, we tried some of the fucking stuff once, it's green, could barely force the stuff down. No joke, green buckwheat! Fuck me! The finest muck, only fit for feeding pigs! Green buckwheat, would you fucking believe it. It looks just like spinach!"

He had already spewed gutloads of spinach, he'd foraged so much of it from the containers that he couldn't bear the sight of it any more. I had no idea what he did with that crazy sum of money they gave him. I had a good idea where our money went: wine, hash, pills, and whores – that was easy to understand, it didn't require any explanation, it was simple and straightforward. It would have been easy enough to spend even more on that stuff. But scoffing your way through two and a half thousand kroner between three people every two weeks, when they stuffed one of the mouths full of porridge… that was unreal!

On top of all that, he said he was losing weight. Several times he forced me and Zenon to feel his belly, claiming that there was just a thin layer of fat covering his six-pack: "A real six pack, feel it, see how firm it is." So we felt his belly. I prodded a finger into the blubber, and pretended to agree: "Yeah, yeah, it's firm, a pretty firm stomach…" He would tell us his six-pack was made up of striated muscles, nothing less! "Ah, yes," I would say, "yes, of course…"

In reality he was getting fatter and fatter, he was bloating out in all directions! And all the time he would say that he was economising as hard as he possibly could.

"But," he would add, "you can't economise on food! You can't economise on your health! And you can't economise on your family!"

And so he fed his family. He would fill up his trolley to overflowing, load up his car boot, and then fifteen minutes

159

later he would go back into the shop, fill up his trolley with exactly the same list of stuff, and walk out without paying. If they stopped him he would show his receipt and claim that he had come back in with a full trolley to get a bottle of wine. "There she is! My wife's over there! My wife's paying at the till!"

That was an old scam, the Serbs or Somalians had come up with it a hundred years back, everyone was wise to it now, no one ever tried it any more. He managed to pull off the trick a couple of times, and the third time he was politely asked to unload his trolley. He didn't get a fine, because it was impossible to prove anything, but everyone knew it was a scam. He didn't bother kicking up a fuss, he just feigned indignation and told them he would take his custom elsewhere. Whatever you like, they said, it make's no difference to us, there's hundreds of others just like you, and every single one of them is on the nick!

He told that story dozens of times with varying degrees of umbrage. I had no idea why he needed so much food, after all he didn't sell it. He ate it the lot!.

So he had lost his car, and now he had to buy another one at all costs. He didn't feel like a proper person without a car. He couldn't walk far, and had trouble with his legs. I wondered whether he had ever suffered from haemorrhoids. He said he needed a car for business!

"What business is that then?" Hanuman asked him, and Potapov started to offer some examples.

"Going to the scrap heap, for starters. And then there's collecting bottles," he said, counting the activities off on his fingers.

I couldn't bear to listen.

He got two and a half thousand kroner every two weeks, and he still went bottle collecting. It was me and Hanuman who had taught him how to hunt for bottles at the bottle bank, where people sometimes chucked away the ones that could be exchanged for money, the ones with a picture of a bottle with a ring round it. Stepan had taught me and Hanny about those bottles, and every evening we would drag ourselves to the container and rummage about, trying not to make a sound, fishing out bottles with the sign on them from the darkest recesses. At first it was tough, we spent hours there, worrying like crazy in case someone spotted us and called the cops. Then we gradually got the hang of it, and soon we were able to identify the bottles by touch; eventually we became so skilled that we could sense their presence in the darkness, even before we laid our hands on them! We could make up to fifty kroner a night on average. On better days, like public holidays, we could make up to two hundred. On days like that it was worth setting off on one of our fishing expeditions, even if there was wet snow falling and a wind was blowing, even if one of us had a temperature. When we had money we felt it was beneath us to go crawling about in rubbish dumps. But Potapov went crawling, even though he was given two and a half thousand kroner every two weeks!

Sometime long before Ivan arrived, Mikhail stole a bike, took it to bits, and then decided to paint it in our room, explaining that he had an allergy to paints, solvents, and other chemical substances. He left the bike hanging from our ceiling overnight to dry.

He rode about on that bike collecting bottles. We all got drunk together on the money he made, because we were the ones who had led him to the Klondike. I always had the feeling that he lied to us about the number of bottles he found. We could have checked, we could have asked him to show us the receipt, but it seemed petty. We couldn't be bothered going to the shop with him to check, let him say what he wanted...

One time someone spotted him in the shop and commented, "I see you like a drink, my friend." He smiled his crooked smile and made an awkward gesture, as if trying to disown the bottles. After that Potapov sent

Nepalino in his place a few times, but then he started to suspect that the Nepali was filching money, and started going himself again.

Then he said that he needed a car, a decent reliable car, which he could use to drive round the towns in our district, collect bottles, take them to bottle banks, go to scrap heaps. That was when Hanuman had his idea.

"We can gather food as well as bottles," he said. "The food they leave outside the shops. The food that's past its best-before date, the stuff we often take for ourselves. We could sell it as fresh food in the camps. Why not? If we eat it, then there's no reason why other people can't. We can sell it pretty cheap. Just like the Yugoslavs or that Nepali, the ones who bring us food and other stuff to the camp. Heh, it'll go like hot cakes, especially in the camps where people are a bus-ride from the nearest shop! We can always rub out the best-before dates or doctor them."

That got Potapov excited. "Yes, yes, and I can fix the dates! I'm good at that kind of thing!" he said, as if he was trying to persuade me in particular. I told him I didn't give a toss, and turned away, but he just carried on. Apparently he had faked his marks and the teachers' signatures at school, and he did it so well you couldn't tell the difference, he didn't get caught once!

For some reason I didn't doubt him one bit.

We used our remaining money to buy an old Ford which often had trouble starting. Potapov contributed some of his own money and persuaded his wife's "brother" Ivan Durachkov to hand over all his money. I was convinced that couldn't be his real name. I assumed it must have been a figment of Potapov's imagination. Durachkov himself lacked the intelligence to think up a name which meant "Ivan the Fool" and wear it like some kind of badge, a yoke even. I reckoned that Potapov had passed through the same agencies in St. Petersburg or Moscow where many people ended up, where you were greeted with a portentous look and promised the Kingdom of Heaven, paradise on earth, welfare provision and abundance beyond belief – all for a certain fee, of course. Like many of those fools Potapov had traded everything for castles in the sky, but in the end all he got was a house of cards surrounded by bare, stinking fields somewhere on the outer edges of the universe – otherwise known as the arse-end of Denmark – with Albanians and Arabs, puddles on the toilet floor, a dirty kitchen, and a shower which the Iraqi boy shits in. In other words, he'd ended up with a pig in a poke and his family got lumbered with Ivan the Fool into the bargain. At least Potapov got money, and it wasn't a small sum by any means. But what good was money if there was nothing to buy which could compensate for the wretched living conditions? There was nothing to bring any cheer, you could barely call it life. Just this hen coop, no rights, and no light at the end of the tunnel, and every waking day they put the fear of God into you: "Deportation! *Rauss!* Home! *Nach Hause!*"

To be honest, mine and Hanuman's situation was even stranger, we didn't get any money at all. We had voluntarily agreed to breathe in the stench of piss and fertiliser, to listen to the Muslims' incantations, the sound of water sluicing between people's legs and Potapov's muffled howls. Without any particular expectations, Hanuman and I traipsed across the stinking fields and down the nauseously clean roads, looking for adventures, but in essence engaged with just one task: stuffing our stomachs full, finding some place to hole up, to wait things out, to forget about everything, before setting out to look for exactly the same thing all over again. I don't know about Hanuman, but I at least had my reasons for living like that, plenty of reasons…

And so we bought ourselves a Ford. A diesel one of course. That way we didn't have to buy petrol, we could syphon off the agricultural diesel from the tractors in the fields. Their tanks were almost always full. A quick suck on the tube, and the fuel would start flowing, help yourself! Then we hit the road, and started travelling around from town to town. We visited the supermarkets, backyards, rubbish dumps, we collected bottles and plastic bags full of food, and crawled about the waste containers. It was Durachkov who did most of the crawling, he turned out to be the most athletic. We would just prise open the container hatch, and he would dive in like a flash and start passing stuff out. Hanny would shine the torch in, I grabbed hold of the stuff he passed out, and Potapov would sort out what was still fit to eat, sniffing at the food like a rat. We would head back towards morning, wash, towel ourselves dry, sort out the food, try out this and that, and then start rubbing out the best-before dates.

Potapov did indeed turn out to be a dab hand, and wielded his pen masterfully. He was better at drawing numbers than painting pictures, and there was incomparably more to be had from it. He wasn't bad at faking tickets either. But his bragging spoilt everything. It would have been fine if he didn't started singing his own praises, going into raptures over every number he drew.

The next part was the hardest of all. We had to somehow sell that muck, get shot of all our dodgy wares. Any fool could gather the stuff, but trying to persuade some idiot to buy out-of-date food, as quickly as possible, before it started going rancid, while not getting nabbed, not getting spotted by anyone – that took real cunning. We had to drive out to some camp at the back of beyond, then wait for all the Danish people, all the staff, all the Red Cross and social service workers to leave, and then start trying to sell the food. Or the shit which we were trying to pass off as decent grub. And those asylums seekers were a suspicious lot, it wasn't easy to take them for a ride, they would sense something was wrong straight away, especially if you showed the slightest uncertainty.

If it weren't for me and Hanuman it wouldn't have worked at all. To start with Hanuman knew how to talk complete nonsense without batting an eyelid, and people would believe him, and what's more he was a Sikh, and the camps were full of all sorts of Untouchables, Tamils and Bengalis who looked up to Sikhs, and would buy anything off Hanuman just to ingratiate themselves. And secondly, I decided that we needed to take plastic bags with us, as many as possible, bags of every description, stacks of plastic bags, so that we could hand people their stuff in bags, thereby creating the illusion of honest trade, or at least making it seem more like a shop or a mobile market… you generate more trust if you sell the food in plastic bags. And so it was, the bags did their work, that not-insignificant detail gave us an air of respectability and self-assuredness, it won people over. I suggested that we take the Albanian lad Zenon with us too, he could interpret in exchange for beer and cigarettes, which he normally consumed behind his parents' back. He was always hanging round me and Hanuman, and something to smoke and drink would normally come his way in return for intel about various people in the camps he visited.

"He could be our interpreter," I said. "He speaks Albanian and Serbian, and he knows Danish better than any of us, he is sure to win people's trust, especially those greedy, jealous Albanians. And everyone knows him, he's been here ages, everyone knows who he is!"

Hanuman agreed with me. The plastic bags, together with Zenon, and Hanuman's self-assured air guaranteed the success of our undertaking. We trundled round the whole of north Jutland, collecting food from the rubbish dumps, filling up with diesel in the fields, sleeping in the car during the day after a skinful of vodka or whisky, and by evening we were doing a brisk trade at the next camp.

The yoghurts were particularly popular. One time we were lucky enough to find a whole container full of yoghurts which had passed their best-before date. Potapov immediately wrote them off as "fermented milk products", and the others didn't want to take them either, they didn't even want to look in the direction of the tubs of yoghurt, which were standing in a neatly stacked row, illuminated by moonlight.

"It's a dairy product," Potapov barked in the darkness, "it's too risky!"

But I was certain the yoghurts were still OK. I had a feeling that we should take them, so I said, "The Danes always chuck them out too early, they're good for another month!" I said, trying to persuade Hanuman, and so he let me conduct an experiment.

"If you think so, take one, try it yourself!"

Potapov started wittering something about not having enough room in the car, but Hanuman looked at him like he might look at a flea, and Potapov fell silent. I drank down a whole litre of yoghurt on the spot. The others took one look at me, shrugged, and proceeded to load up the boot with dozens of litres of the stuff.

I was always crazy about yoghurts, and there were flavours there which I had never tried, really exotic ones like mango, kiwi, mixed berries, pineapple chunks. I wanted to try them all! But when Potapov saw me starting a second one before I had even finished the first he took the carton off me and told me that we were weren't crawling round rubbish dumps just to stuff our faces – this was business! I was disappointed, and I resented him for it. I'd just got my hands on a litre of yoghurt with tropical fruits depicted on it which I couldn't identify, I had never tried those fruits before, let alone yoghurt made from them! It looked like I would never get the chance, because we sold the lot. The whole time I was hoping that no one would buy that particular one, that I could keep it for myself, or at least try a bit of it. But an Afghan bloke turned up and asked the price in Russian, and when he heard it was seven kroner he grabbed hold of the carton and paid for it without even bothering to look at the date, then he arched his head back, and started drinking it there on the spot. He seemed to like it; his eyes were as big as saucers, and he smacked his lips as he drank! "The swine," I thought.

Those adventures cheered me up a bit, but they didn't last long. The cold was killing me, I couldn't sleep in the car, it was so cramped, we were like sardines in a tin. I never got a proper night's sleep, I was constantly shivering, queasy, dizzy, feeling lousy. I got terrible heartburn from the vodka and whisky. And a nasty stomach ache from eating the crap we were selling. But Potapov forbade me from going to the toilet. He said that it would be a bad advert for our products. He banned everyone from going to the toilet. We were supposed to shit at the railway station or in a field before we set out for the camps. That was Mikhail's idea, and he had a priceless justification for it: "So that no one can say: hey, look at them, some food they've brought us! Look, they've all gone to the bog! They've all got the runs! Some grub they've brought us! You get it? No one's going to buy anything if they hear you farting away in front of them!"

All his directives made me want to go to the toilet even more. All that rummaging round rubbish dumps wore me out, I wasn't cut out for those night-time missions. I always caught a cold, and then the first symptoms of my angina came on. I constantly had to change my socks, my feet got so sweaty. I needed to take a break, recuperate. But the others were completely in the grips of that petty profiteering, and they drove further and further north, where it would have been impossible for me to make a dash for it. I would just perish out there alone. Hanuman said we had to keep going until we had been to all the camps.

"Let's shift our arses!" Potapov yelled.

"Shit our arses?" Zenon asked. He was still getting the hang of Potapov's accent.

I turned my face towards the window. The situation was becoming more and more unbearable. The fog seemed to be getting thicker and thicker, the air colder and colder. I kept hoping that the fields would come to an end, but they never did. I hoped we would stop finding tractors, but they were always there, waiting for us in every other field. I prayed that their fuel tanks would be empty, but they always turned out to be full almost to overflowing. And Potapov kept on driving, further and further north. I hoped more than anything that the car would break down, that a tyre would burst, that the engine would conk out, whatever. But the car seemed to have gained a new lease of life, it was racing faster and faster onwards. One time I took a look at the map which Hanuman printed out, I saw the towns and camps he had marked in the north, and I started to feel unwell. There were at least five of them, we could get bogged down for ages up there. By now I was completely hacked off.

Towards the end of the second week I had developed a morbid aversion to trading in that rinsed-down crap. I wasn't particularly straining myself, I was just bundling up loads of plastic bags from the shops, nothing more. Potapov watched everyone, their every move, and he was keeping a particularly close eye on me. He started to lumber me with all sorts of little tasks. Either he would get me to hold the lid of the rubbish container, or the torch, or to lug the plastic bags about, or he'd tell me to sell the stuff more enthusiastically, to explain to everyone in perfect English how much things cost and where they were from. I couldn't bear the sight of him any more, or of those Albanian mugs, or of those robed women picking at that crap with discerning frowns on their faces. Especially the flour; Potapov had bought two sacks of it on the cheap, and the profits went straight into his pocket, the son of a bitch. The same thing happened with the sweets, Chupa Chups, cola. He bought crates of cheap cola which sat on my and Zenon's knees the whole journey. Then he gleefully sold them for twice the original price. Sometimes they would buy up everything we had in one go, every last nut and stick of chewing gum. And then we were back in the fields. I couldn't bear drinking whisky in that smoke-filled car any more, or listening to the Albanian guy's jokes. The sound of Potapov's guffawing, and the sight of his self-satisfied mug made me sick. I just wanted to jump out of the car and hop away across those endless fields, cawing like a crow.

I always got horribly stressed whenever we had to roll through some town or another. I was worried that the cops would stop us and ask Mikhail for his driving licence, and us for our papers. I was even more worried that the police or someone would raid the camp while trade was in full swing, and grab us red-handed. You could never be sure, someone might grass on us, and then we'd all be fucked.

I decided to walk away from the business, to give up my share in it. We had just come back to Farstrup again, so that they (Potapov, Ivan, Zenon) could collect their pocket money, rest up a bit, rinse down some more of that crap, give the pig-feed a presentable appearance, and try and flog it in our own camp. I announced to everyone that I wouldn't take part in that farce any more.

My first argument with Potapov was what drove me to that decision. It came about over a wager. We had just foraged a massive heap of Brussels sprouts. I was really happy. I loved Brussels sprouts.

"Well now," I thought to myself. "What a stroke of luck! Now I won't let anyone deny me my right to stuff my face!"

We drove on, and I kept on telling them how much I loved Brussels sprouts, that I was really looking forward to eating them, that I was starving hungry, that I could eat three kilos of sprouts!

"Come off it!" Potapov said dismissively. "There's no way you can eat three kilos!"

"Easy!"

"Let's bet on it!"

"Alright then!"

We bet twenty kroner. I quickly calculated that twenty kroner equalled two bottles of the local Master Brew, which was stronger than Baltika #9. For another couple of kroner I could buy two bottles of that caramel-flavoured Hans Christian Andersen beer. And that was stronger than Moldovan port! One bottle of that and beddy-byes... then when I woke up I could neck the second bottle, and doze off again. That way I could sleep two days in a row, without having to see anyone. That was the main thing, killing two whole days. While I was asleep that lot would have gathered up another load of crap and headed up north for another two weeks. What bliss – just lying there without having to talk to anyone or see anyone at all. I could get by without eating, I could survive, just as long as I didn't have to see anyone.

And so I felt happy as we arrived at the camp, and I felt happy as I started cooking the Brussels sprouts. I even put a second saucepan on right away. Everyone came to the kitchen, the whole motley crew, they all wanted to watch me scoffing those sprouts. I got stuck in, and quickly polished off the first bag, then I started on the second. Potapov brought me a glass of water, but I thought to myself: "Hey-ho, not so fast, you're not going to trick me into drinking water." I still remember how a friend of mine from Tallinn, Lehka, won a competition with some guy to eat a metre of sausages. That's a metre side by side, not end to end! A bit different to three kilos of Brussels sprouts, or even five. The other guy, a glutton of gargantuan girth, was ten centimetres from victory while Lehka had still only managed half a metre, but the bloke foolishly drank a glass of water, and his entire sausage-stuffed being promptly forced its way free again, so Lehka won. No way, I thought, I'm not going to drink any water! I started shovelling the sprouts down, while Potapov boiled another saucepan-full and brought it over to me. But as soon as I started eating them I realised they were over-salted!

"They're too salty!" I declared. "I refuse to eat them! You put too much salt in! Boil up another saucepan! Or I'll do it myself!"

But Potapov just yelled at me, "What are you talking about! That's a break! We agreed that there would be no breaks!"

"There was no such condition," I shouted. "You can eat salty Brussels sprouts if you want! I'm not going to!"

"Twenty kroner!" Potapov yelled. "You lost, cough up!"

"Get lost…"

But I couldn't be bothered to finish the sentence. I left, slamming the kitchen door behind me, then I threw myself on to the top bunk, wrapped myself up in my quilt like a mummy, and sank into a deep sleep, hoping I would hibernate the whole of winter, or better still, for the rest of my life!

Part Two

1

Our room was getting colder and colder. My feet were so frozen that I had stopped taking my boots off altogether. They were terrible boots anyway, lousy Polish boots. They were like stocks or little coffins for my tormented feet. Those boots weren't made with any thought to human comfort. They were instruments of torture. They drained me of any remaining will to live. You couldn't call them footwear. They just looked like they might have been. They just gave the impression they were. They had somehow been devised to be passed off as footwear. They could be put on sale, someone could try them on, and even buy them. But you couldn't wear them. Those boots resembled footwear in the same way that those little Polish cars resembled motor vehicles – you couldn't actually go anywhere in them. I had asked Hanuman a thousand times to buy me some kind of replacement, I was already tired of asking. I reminded him every single day. I had never met anyone who was so cloth-eared! He just didn't give a damn! At first I dreamed of buckskin moccasins, but then I just told him that any shoes would do, however sloppily stitched together. I told him I couldn't walk any more, not even as far as the toilet, but he just said that it would be pointless buying shoes, especially in a country like this, which was covered in untraversable mud.

"He-ha-ho," he guffawed, tossing his head back. "It's so muddy, shoes aren't going to be any use to you. Especially not moccasins, what are you on about! Anyway, it would be stupid to pay for them. Best to steal them, and only you can do that. No one can try on the shoes for you. But what do you need shoes for anyway? You don't go anywhere.

Apart from to the toilet. You can go to the toilet barefoot. We can see through the whole winter without having to set foot out of the camp. Actually, we could live our whole lives in the camp without going anywhere. Well, maybe not our whole lives, but a few years at least. And no one at all, not even the Interpols of this world, will have any idea where you are!"

His last sentence left me numb. I started tormenting myself again, feverishly asking myself all kinds of questions. What could he know about Interpol? Why did he mention Interpol? Why not the FSB? Why not the KGB? Why Interpol in particular? Could he know something? Or did I talk in my sleep? If I did, then hopefully I did it in Russian, so he wouldn't understand. Or maybe he knows Russian? A clever guy like him must know lots of languages. Maybe he's been assigned to follow me, to find out who I am, why I'm on the run... maybe he works for Interpol himself?

We had hit the rocks, and we were drifting. But I knew that Hanuman still had some money left. I knew that because of what he said one time, as he was looking out of the window. He was looking at the cops taking the number plates off the car, while Potapov stood there, completely powerless to do anything; he just spread his arms wide as if to demonstrate his innocence, but they still took the plates off, because the car had no MOT, no insurance, and there was some other stuff which wasn't paid for. As he looked out of the window Hanuman said, "We've lost nothing. Not like Potapov! He's lost his car. But we only needed the car to go for a little spin! We don't need it any more, we won't miss it. Let them take it. We earned back all the money we invested in that wreck. We lived three weeks almost completely cost-free, just like we hadn't eaten or drunk anything the whole time, as if we were in suspended animation. We even managed to have a good drink and a smoke without spending a krone from our savings, as if we weren't even alive!"

I pointed out to him, through gritted teeth, "We were scrabbling about in rubbish dumps for three weeks like dogs, that's not the kind of life I want! It would have been better to lie in bed and starve like Gandhi than rummage about in rubbish dumps, telling ourselves that we were living just as if we weren't really alive. That's just self-deception. Wishful thinking. A simulation. We were alive, Hanuman, I tell you that we were alive, and we were living a dismal life those two weeks, we were scrabbling about in rubbish dumps, selling that crap, eating that crap, that's not the kind of thing you can forget easily!"

So now Potapov was going around trying to sell a car without number plates, which could be taken off him at any moment in payment for his debts. Then he found a black guy from the Congo who'd just got a yes. One of a devil's dozen other applicants. They were still investigating the rest of them – they were yet to prove they were from the Congo. This one had already proven it, and he now had a superior air about him – he was waiting to be assigned a municipality and an apartment. He went around saying, "Now they have to find me a flat, they have to." He would look at passers-by on the street as if they personally owed him a flat and all the trappings. He was ready to start living a normal life, but something was getting in the way, they just didn't seem able to find him that flat. He'd already been waiting two months to start living his new, normal life. He used the same phrase which you could hear from all the asylum seekers – "just like a normal human being". That was their favourite phrase, their beloved refrain, their blues, their reggae and rap. That's all you ever heard from them, dozens of times a day – when would they finally be able to live "just like a normal human being", when would they finally be able to relax "just like a normal human being"… that was the sound of the asylum seekers' endless moaning. And so this Congolese guy sighed and made his plans, imagining his future life. And it seemed that in this future life he imagined himself sitting in a car. One could only guess what went on inside the head of a black man who had just been bestowed the blessings of social security and refugee status. It was immediately apparent that he had started getting more money, because the crooks started hassling him, trying to flog him the kind of things that they wouldn't have even bothered to show him before. He told us that the authorities had opened a bank account for him, and were paying money directly into it, which is why we didn't see him in the benefits queue any more. Now he was even getting paid money "just like a normal human being". It wasn't clear what he was thinking of, but he started taking driving lessons with Potapov. He was probably planning ahead. He knew that no Danish person would ever bother helping him. And he knew that the other black guys were even less likely to let him destroy their gearboxes, even if he paid them ten times what he was paying Mikhail.

They would go to the forest and practise driving for a mere twenty-five kroner an hour. Although no one else, not even the richest black man in the world, would have been prepared to pay more for those lessons. Potapov was hoping the Congolese guy would fall in love with the car and agree to buy it, but instead he came to hate it, and he drove it into the ground: the car grew sullen, it started to hiss and sputter and stall at every junction.

We were on the rocks, and we were still drifting, now we'd even started scrounging cigarettes. And Hanuman was doing some improvised translations of letters from the Directorate and the Service for Foreign Nationals, for various Arabs and Kurds. Once he had translated the letters they would ask him to write the answers himself. That made his task easier: he could write whatever came into his head. Occasionally he would come and see me with the latest letter he had opened from the Directorate and read it out to me, rolling about in fits of laughter:

"...in response to your unusual inquiry about herpes we

advise that you visit a nurse. The Red Cross can provide all the necessary…"

Hanuman got beer and cigarettes in payment for these duties. Sometimes he would work at night in the Children's Club, using the Internet. One hairy-legged Arab decided that he wanted to write a letter to President Clinton. Hanuman took on the task, and he wrote a fairly decent missive asking Billy to assist the Arab. The Arab claimed he had been a victim of Saddam Hussein's repressive regime, and that he could help expose Saddam's crimes. Apparently he knew where they were developing the chemical and nuclear weapons; as a child he had clambered round various caves and canyons and he'd seen where stuff was kept. Then he was caught and had some sort of laboratory experiments conducted on him. His family had been executed, and he was the only survivor. Hanny scratched his chin and added a footnote promising that the Arab would give better head than Monica. The Arab didn't understand the contents of the letter, so he bought Hanuman a bottle of beer. He never got a reply, which wasn't exactly surprising.

Then Durachkov moved in with us. He had been putting up with the skinflint Jew who moved into Stepan's room for ages; the three of them had lived together for a while. The Jew eventually got to him with his constant economising, as well as banging on all the time about the environment, the disruption of nature's balance, the greenhouse effect, Greenpeace, global warming, and terrorism in Israel. The Jew had come to Denmark with one aim – to learn the unique Danish language. He had already learned Italian, German, Swedish, and "now it was time for Danish." He was an adherent of the idiotic notion that the language of the Scandinavians was the forbear of Indo-European languages. The language of the Vikings, that is. And not Swedish, not Norwegian, but Danish specifically. Although I suspected that he propounded the same theory in Sweden, that Swedish was the linguistic forbear, and then in Norway it was Norwegian, whereas in Italy he had a completely different theory, and so on. He claimed that he was a professor of linguistics and that he had written three hundred academic papers! What about exactly, he didn't say. One day he muttered something in passing about how he had always been interested in linguistic anthropology, the thesaurus, and the advent of myths. Particularly the concept of Dreamtime found in Australian Aboriginal mythology. He would say all this as if it were completely obvious, as if there were no need for any explanations, as if it were widespread, open knowledge. He came across as a very serious, learned person, and he always had a dignified air about him. He would leave long pauses as he spoke, sometimes between every syllable, as if trying to send his interlocutor into a trance. But he was so niggardly, so incredibly stingy! He even rationed his grains and flour. He would take one of the bags, open it up, measure the flour out by the spoonful into another bag, then he would divide it up – X number of spoonfuls per day, thus enabling him to work out how long his supplies would last. But he didn't hang around for long, just slightly over two months; it would have been easy enough to measure the length of his stay with us in spoonfuls of grain and flour. He would definitely have known exactly how many spoonfuls he had consumed throughout the course of his time in Denmark.

He wore silly ties which he must have washed three hundred times, and a crumpled old jacket with a large checked design, and corduroy trousers (one time I caught sight of him in jeans, but only once). He had such a huge collection of socks that it would take you less time to count the stars in the sky. But he would never need them all, because he wore every pair until they were disturbingly threadbare. He must have stocked up three hundred years ahead!

He latched on to me and Hanuman, pestering us for condoms; Hanuman's leather briefcase was stuffed full of them. One time Hanny conceded and gave him a handful. The Jew asked for more, but Hanny challenged him gruffly, "Why do you need so many? What are you going to do with them?"

"That's my business," the Jew retorted.

"Sod off then!" said Hanuman.

We spent ages speculating as to why he needed so many condoms. But then it became clear. One day we saw him wandering round the beaches at Trend and Grenaa, where the campsites were full of German tourists. He was approaching them and pestering them to buy condoms, repeating, "Safe sex, gentlemen, safe sex!"

Durachkov put up with all this until one day the German authorities summoned the Jew to return so they could complete the investigation into his case, which had been put on hold when he fled to Sweden. No doubt his case was pretty flimsy. And completely hopeless, of course. They probably sent him back to his home country, wherever that was. His nationality wasn't in any doubt, but he was just as likely to have been born in Odessa as Aktyubinsk.

So the Jew was taken away. And he left nothing behind, absolutely nothing. Even Durachkov's cupboard somehow went missing. But that wasn't important, the main thing was that the Jew himself had disappeared. Durachkov breathed a sigh of relief. But they didn't give him the chance to relax and savour his solitude, they immediately moved an Iranian guy in with him. "Looks like they want to keep us on our toes," Potapov concluded. Ivan ran away from the Iranian after just one day! He couldn't stand it there any longer, so he moved in with us.

He erected a bunk above the Nepali's bed, crawled up on to it, all elbows and knees like a little monkey, and turned his back on the rest of the world. He fell completely silent. I didn't even ask what had happened with the Iranian, he just shut himself off, he didn't say a word. It felt awkward broaching the question. He just lay there, his large, bare feet poking out from under the quilt, his long, yellow nails on display. It made me cold just looking at those feet, I couldn't bear to think what it would feel like to expose my feet for so long. He had such long, yellow nails, with some kind of fungal infection and scaly skin between his toes. And such bony heels. But if his feet were horrible, disgusting to look at, then I didn't dare to look at my own. I was afraid they had already started festering. I hadn't checked them, I hadn't so much as peeked at them in ages; maybe they'd already turned putrid? They certainly stank to high heaven. We were saved by the open window, and the fact that I kept my feet hidden under the quilt. I didn't dare look at them, and had decided that I wouldn't do so until absolutely necessary; not until hell froze over! I was afraid I would witness something truly horrific. And the idea of showing them to anyone else was really frightening, even more so than looking at them myself.

Durachkov liked to natter, and he talked mostly about himself and about Mikhail; he would say his sister was lucky to have a husband like Mikhail, that he was just the kind of guy you needed to have around, that he was a dab hand at anything, he could do whatever he put his mind to, you name it and he could do it, he was a real catch, not just any old guy! In fact, Durachkov couldn't think of a single thing that Mikhail couldn't do. Sometimes he would describe Mikhail as his sensei, his mentor, his master. I tried to listen attentively, if only to distract myself from my wretched feet.

Ivan said that he had started out as Mikhail's apprentice back when they were trading in stoves and fireplaces, they installed them for rich Russians, assembling various manufacturers' fireplaces, tile by tile.

"You need brains for that," Ivan would say, "you need to know which bit to put where. They're all different, they come in all sorts of shapes and sizes, some of them are made from marble, and God knows what else. It's not as easy as it looks. You need experience for that kind of thing!"

The work was well paid, but there wasn't always a lot to go around. There weren't many people who could afford that kind of fireplace, and pay for a proper craftsman to come and install it. Especially not a craftsman like Mikhail! Sometimes they had no work for ages, and they went hungry. Then they started doing casual decorating jobs. Sometimes they only got paid in food, it didn't seem right to take money off pensioners.

"That Mikhail is a noble soul," Ivan would say, "he'll hang wallpaper for an old grannie without taking a penny off her, although he won't say no to a bite to eat, if she puts something out."

And then there was the meat stall in Moscow, or you could even say it was a shop...

It was all lies, of course. I didn't believe a single word which that False Ivan said. He made it all up, he wasn't even called Ivan. One time I heard Mikhail shush his wife after she addressed Ivan as Gavrila, then he took her into the other room and they spent a whole half hour in there; he was most probably instilling in her the importance of maintaining the conspiracy. From then on she chose not to speak in company at all.

Maybe he did have a meat stall somewhere, but it definitely wasn't in Moscow. Maybe it was a proper stall, but in some hole like Kremenchuk. Or maybe it wasn't a stall at all, he just hacked meat to bits at some market for a pittance, that was what he called his stall.

Ivan talked about himself as well, but not much, a lot less than he talked about his older companion, his pot-bellied benefactor. We actually knew almost nothing about Ivan himself. Or at least what we knew was murky and inchoate, barely credible, more like a fabrication. We knew that his father had deserted the family when Ivan was very young, that he had a taste for boozing and carousing, and that one time he'd gone on a binge which he never came back from. They had lived in various cities – his mother was always tearing off somewhere new, constantly in search of something. Ivan was conceived in Komsomolsk (his father was doing time there), and he was born in Pionersk, but all he could remember from there was the hot dry wind blowing through the city at night, like someone working bellows... the storm beating at the shutters, and the steppe, all around was humming steppe. And then the deathly lull which followed, the moon hanging in the sky like a bloodied yellow disk, merging in Ivan's mind with a five-kopeck piece. His mother was a freelance journalist, she got by on bits and pieces of work which came her way. Sometimes she wrote articles, but more often she would have to type out someone else's work, or do the photographs, or sometimes she would just develop someone else's photographs. They didn't give her any independence, and she never managed to get close to the editorial office where the independence was dispensed. The only reason they kept her on was because she never needed to be given the cameras and photographic equipment, which were always in short supply. She got hold of everything necessary herself, and then she printed her own and other peoples' pictures. And she also had a talent for thinking up headlines. She could come up with wonderful headlines which had people cooing in delight. She would often be asked to think up a good headline for some lousy, dull article; she would read the article through, and then, barely pausing for thought, she would fire off a perfect title. They all sighed in admiration. But she was so tired of her own articles never making the cut that she started to persuade herself that the headline was more important than the article itself. And so when she thought up the headlines for other people's articles, it was almost as if the article became her very own. She anyway suspected that all the articles in the Soviet newspapers and journals had been written by one and the same person. Even if that were true, then at least she could make sure that they had different headlines. As similar as the articles

184

were, you could sometimes be surprised and come across one which was alright.. Ivan couldn't remember if she read the articles herself, but she definitely glanced through the headlines. She would also say that there was no need to write whole articles any more, that there was no longer any need to compose them from scratch. There was already an abundance of templates written to cover every eventuality in Soviet life. All you needed to do was change the names here and there, think up a new headline, and then you could dispatch the same article to the printing press again and again.

"New headlines, that's all that Soviet journalists need these days!" she used to say.

She didn't last long anywhere. She got restless. The place they lived the longest was Yermak, long enough for Ivan to get to the fifth grade in school. He even had a stepdad there, Uncle Sema, an invalid. Eternally unshaven, gruff, a whiff of booze on his breath. He didn't party much, never ventured far afield, and was always easy enough to find: by the beer barrel with a pint of draught in his hand, the place where the fields slope downwards towards the banks of the Irtysh. Where the damsons and sorrel grow, the same place where Ivan and his friends played in rusty old cars, pretending to be tank drivers. Where a drunkard could doze off on the old car seats if he got drowsy in the midday sun. Uncle Sema slept there sometimes, his single leg and two crutches poking out of a smashed car window. The kids occasionally grabbed his crutches and shoved them through car windows, playing machine guns with them.

Uncle Sema drank so much beer that they called him the Tapeworm. But they would always top up his glass for him. He had his own tankard which he kept close at hand. And he would let anyone who was so inclined top it up for him, which they normally did with the words, "Respect to our Hero of Soviet Labour", or simply, "To our hero". He would never drink himself drunk, he never got smashed, he never drank himself silly, he just quietly hobbled about on his crutches, and somehow he even managed to save some of his pension and put it to good use, buying things for little Ivan and his mother. They lived pretty well, quietly and peacefully, but eventually she got bored. At some point she met a visiting reporter at the local newspaper office, and like anyone travelling on business he wasn't averse to a bit of fun, and so she went off the rails. When he left she fell into a depression, only surfacing to wail, "Shit, this Yermak of yours is a yoke around my neck!" Then she packed her bags, grabbed little Ivan, and headed off to the bus station.

They criss-crossed the whole of the Soviet Union. And she took pictures of everything! In the evenings she would lay out the photographs in front of her like a tarot reader with her cards, she would pick them up with her long thin fingers, and examine them, rearrange them, with Ivan sitting by her side the whole time. They could sit like that for hours on end, looking at the photos and chatting, never getting hungry. They explored the forest steppes and plateaus, he travelled by every possible form of transport, on a little donkey down dried-up mountain streams, squinting at the Kazbek mountain, by camel to the fabled desert wells! Once, he saw someone eat a raw fish without even gutting it! Each Soviet republic had left a certain impression on him, which was captured in her photographs. Those impressions survived, if not the photographs. In Kogalym she got mixed up with yet another travelling man, this one worked on a building site, and he would visit for two to three months at a time and play at being her husband, although for Ivan his visits meant regular punishments in the form of press-ups and wall squats. Then he would leave to play at being the same thing for someone else God knows where. And she would go out of her mind, looking for someone to take his place, getting tangled up with yet more travelling men, drowning her sorrow with more moonshine. By then she had started suffering from delirium tremens, and she even started taking tablets for it. And she got into smoking strange substances with strange characters. She and Ivan lived with one old bloke for a while, but he slid further and further into infantilism. First, he collected empty bottles, then plastic bags, then cigarette butts, then nails and glass shards, then corks and bits of wire, anything he could lay his hands on. But he approached it all pretty seriously, thoroughly tidying his cellar and shed, painstakingly laying everything out on shelves and in boxes, so that no one ever suspected him of being crazy. They all thought he was a normal old man who had a tendency to mumble under his breath, but was fastidious and orderly. So it came as a surprise to everyone when he snapped. One day, when he'd had enough of shuffling about, he sat down by the window, and started rocking backwards and forwards, looking out over the street, singing a sad song to himself. Then he began to spit at passers-by, effing and blinding, and chucking all the stuff he had collected out of the window. After that he went out into the yard, climbed into the sandpit, and started playing with the kids. The old ladies tried to shoo him away, but he pulled down his trousers and started shamelessly flashing his wares about. That was when they came for him. After that, Ivan's mother took to the bottle. Ivan went to do his military service, and that's where he was when he got the news that his mother had poisoned herself. He served on the Caspian Sea as a diver, crawling about the ships' hulls and scraping the barnacles off. After work, everyone smoked weed or drank cannabis milk. Some of them would shoot up harder stuff. They listened to "new wave" music, the so-called political rock, they played cards, and they boozed it up. Then he went back to Kogalym, to help with the never-ending building work. There he hooked up with Mikhail, who had turned up at the same building site, lured by the money just like those itinerant workers who Ivan's mother mixed with. And so Ivan got bogged down there too, mixed up with the wrong kinds of people, which is when it had all started. What exactly that "all" was, he never explained...

In the mornings the Arabs went to wash, Potapov yelled at Liza on the other side of the wall, while the Nepali had stopped getting out of bed altogether, he just lay there lazily asking Hanuman random stuff, and Hanuman replied wordlessly, snorting something which sounded like it could be in the negative. Outside our window was the bare field. Wet snow was falling, then rain. It carried on like that until they moved in the new lot. They were Serbs, and with them came endless booze-ups.

The Serbs could smoke and drink with the best of them, and to start with there was ganja doing the rounds as well. Without noticing, I got sucked into this enchanted existence, and I lost myself in it. I made myself some new friends, lads from Krajina, who would vividly recount the horrors of the war. One of them was a rock fan who spoke in quotes from Tarantino films. The other one was a football fan who knew the entire history of the game, from the very first World Championship to the most recent one (including all the statistics, like who scored the goals and in which minute). Me and the third one had a strange relationship. He would poke his head out of the window and call my name, then I would poke my head out and ask what he wanted, and he would say, "Shit, man!" and I would reply, "Such is life," at which he would conclude, "Life is shit!"

There was a gypsy called Goran among them, he stole so much that there were legends doing the rounds about him emptying entire shops of their contents. And he drank even more! But as much as he stole he never had enough money for drink, because he just drank so much. He couldn't drink alone, he needed company, he needed a party, something raucous, with singing and entertainment laid on. That's why he kept a whole gang supplied with booze, he took a horde with him wherever he went, and he dragged anyone he could into the shenanigans, myself included. And what about me? I just wanted to dissolve into the madness, into the revelry, to lose myself. So I was happy to join in. I drank cheap Carlsberg with them, I belched with them, trying to be the loudest, and I made roll-ups with them (trying to be the fastest). I munched crisps, and chucked them into the sink, trying to get the most in, I spat at a target drawn on to the wall with coal, I bawled their Serbian songs with them, and it didn't sound too bad. When Goran drank himself silly he would yell fitfully, "I'm a gypsy from Belgrade! I'll fuck them all! All of those pigs. And their mothers too! NATO, UN, the Yanks... they bombed us, I saw it with my own eyes! I'll give it to Clinton, understand! Who are those Americans to bomb us? Who the hell are they? I know who I am. I'm a gypsy from Belgrade. I'll slash their throats if I want to. I'll rob them blind. I'll rip off anyone I want to. I'll burgle a bank if I have to. I'll slice Clinton's balls off so quick he won't notice them go. What's it to me? I don't give a fuck! I lived in that cardboard city in Belgrade. I was locked up for three weeks. I don't give a fuck! I'm no one, you got it, no one! A gypsy, nothing more. But who are they? Who are they to bomb us? It's obvious who I am – I'm a gypsy. I lived in a cardboard box. No food, no warmth, no roof over my head. Then I went on the nick and ended up in the clink. At least I had a roof and some grub there. Although it's best not to get caught twice, the second time they won't bother putting you away, they'll just beat you to death. They don't give a fuck. What's a gypsy anyway? He's no one. Beat him like a dog and chuck him in the ditch, if he crawls out throw him back to die. That's the gypsy fate. Free as the wind, that's why I've got no rights. That's why I came here, to Denmark. Let them give me my human rights, documents, a house to live in. I've got no home. But I don't need one! Fuck the house! Just give me my driving licence! *Permis de conduire!* You got it? My car's my home! Start her up and I'm off. I'll nick some petrol, and I'll find the route. And there's guaranteed to be vodka, and songs, and parties, and a laugh on the way! A good time guaranteed for all, understand...!"

It all started when Goran came round to watch a video. We still had the same old television set which was so sensitive to the room temperature. It was of unfeasibly large proportions, heavy, wooden, with the varnish peeling off in places, and the tube was playing up, so the colours were weird, not right somehow. Although the faces which materialised on the screen were always blurry and elongated, the gypsy came round. Despite the fact that our video player was old and sometimes chewed up the films, he came round. And he came because the television screen was seventy-eight centimetres across, or so he told us. I wasn't sure if that was true, maybe it really was seventy-eight centimetres. I didn't care. The funny thing was that the reason he needed such a large screen was to watch Cicciolina, the famous porn star, fornicating with a dog. He wanted to see the details. He wanted to make sure that it was for real, that there was no fakery, no funny business, no editing, that all the bits went where they were supposed to. So he sat there, a metre from the screen, eyes goggling, watching what was going on between the girl and the dog, yelling, "A motherfucking dog! Cicciolina with a dog!" and he slapped his knees and scratched his crotch. The whole time he was sweating so profusely that I forgot all about my stinking feet.

He was short, ugly, pot-bellied, dark-skinned, long-haired, with an earring in one ear, and a distended earlobe with a little star tattooed on it. He had a big nose, like a crow, and always had a rapacious, greedy, lusty look in his eyes. He drank so much beer that it was sickening to behold; it made you queasy, especially since he was always drinking the cheapest stuff. There were places you could get discounted beer, Potapov knew all about them, you could get a crate of Carlsberg at a knock-down price, it was probably past its best, but the Serbs didn't care what they poured down their throats, what grade of fuel (if a man is no Mercedes, he'll run on any old piss).

And so Potapov bought several crates of that beer. And he started selling it by night, making the most of the fact that there was always some piss-up going on in the building right under his nose. Whenever they ran out of fuel and needed a top-up to continue the burlesque, there was no way of getting hold of anything, because it was night-time and the last kiosk had shut a couple of hours ago – that was when Potapov would show up with his beer. He would always spin some yarn that he had bought it for himself and wasn't planning to sell it. But they started persuading him, and without pausing long for thought he would give in and sell the beer for three times what he'd paid, the greedy son of a bitch! Then he asked for the bottles back so he could cash them in, and he used the money to buy more beer!

But that didn't last long, because Goran and the rest of them revolted. Samson, the little Ethiopian who everyone called Tupac, was particularly incensed. They all quickly got into debt to that enterprising Potapov; they were constantly going to see him at night to wheedle just a couple more bottles, bro But then they thought up a ruse and started treating Potapov to beer as well. And of course that fool drank with them, he even asked for the bottles back. The idiot! He started asking all those pissed blokes and the drunken gypsy for money to pay for the beer they'd drunk together! Cretin, or what? He even started bumping up the bill, adding on the cost of everything he had drunk himself, oh dear me! And then those bottles went flying, right at his head. He hid at his place, and the piss-up turned into a riot. They knocked out the kitchen windows, kicked in the front door, and smashed the light bulbs. The next morning Potapov was the first to run to the staff office and complain about Goran and the Ethiopian, how they had kept his family awake, how they'd smashed up the kitchen, boozing all night, singing "Killing me softly…"

Potapov and Goran were at war for three days, giving each other wolfish looks, but nothing much changed. Goran carried on thieving and drinking just as before. But now he stocked up on crateloads of cheap beer himself. It took three or four men to carry them in, and they made plenty of noise in the process. They slapped the crates down on the table, sparked up their cigarettes, ripped open the crisp packets with an appetising rustle, prised the bottles open with other bottles so the tops went flying out of the smashed windows, then they drank, sang and drank, and drank and sang "Killing me softly…"

But then Potapov and Goran unexpectedly made up. This is how it happened: the grass we bought in Christiania ran out, so the young Serbs were left without any marijuana to smoke. They'd all had enough of the cheap beer by then. Even the porn was starting to lose its lustre…

It looked like they were ready for something big. Me and Hanny felt a change of mood, a kind of deflation, a slowing in the tempo… up until then their wild revelry had been constantly gaining pace, climbing upwards, scaling a steep slope, until suddenly it started losing ground, slipping backwards, rolling downhill. And since we wanted to carry on riding onwards and upwards on that jolly train without making any effort ourselves, but steering the party in the direction we wanted to go, we decided to tell Goran about a cheap brothel we knew. It was full of Russian and Moldovan prostitutes who you could reach an understanding with if you brought a bit of speed with you. Those whores had a weakness for that stuff. Goran listened, and his mouth started to water.

The Serbs got fired up with the idea of going to gallivant in a big city for a change.

"There's nothing to do in Farstrup, it's a hole!" they yelled.

"Those two Danish hookers will go with anyone, and they're rough as hell!"

In any case, what self-respecting Serb is going to go where Somalians and Arabs have been before him, and God knows who else, heaven forbid it could have been an Albanian, no fucking way! And it would be good to have a snort or a puff of something too, that beer was starting to give us heartburn. The gypsy said he knew a few places in Aalborg where we could get hold of some powder or grass, but how to get to Aalborg in the middle of the night...

"It's fucking miles away, and we haven't got a car!"

"The Albanians have got one!"

But what self-respecting Serb will get into a car if Albanians have been there before him? Hanuman hinted with an air of mystery that the Albanians were not the only ones who had a car. Goran didn't like riddles, so he asked Hanuman straight out, "Who else has got one?"

"Hmm, that Russian."

"Which one?"

"Mikhail"

"Aha!"

"But he's got no number plates!"

"So what! Number plates are a piece of piss! No problemo!"

"But even if you get hold of number plates, you won't be able to talk him round."

"I will! I could talk anyone round! I could talk the Devil himself round, you'll see!"

He got up and walked out. I followed him.

It was night. Potapov had constantly been complaining about the racket, about his headaches and insomnia. I wanted to see how the gypsy would go about talking to the embittered Russian in the middle of the night. Potapov opened the door, and at that moment I witnessed the gypsy's instantaneous transformation, I saw his mastery manifest itself! A sickly-sweet, obsequious smile spread across Goran's face, he came over all unctuous, and he started to act as if he could barely stand on his two feet, as if he were dead drunk.

He said, "My russky bro, sssory, lissen 'ere, basically it's like this..." and then the gypsy told him that there was some big business in the offing.

"Wooork! You got it? Okay bro, work for everyone! Everyone will get work! For you, for me, for him! For your wifey if you want! Work for our guys – but it's a secret, not a word for now – get it? You got a car?"

"Yeah, yeah, I'm selling my car," Mikhail blurted.

"Oh! What a stroke of luck! I was looking to buy a car! How much to me? I'm your bro, remember! How much will you sell it to your bro for?"

Mikhail gave the gypsy a disdainful look as if to convey doubt that he could be in any way related to that swarthy, long-haired freak. He said that he could give Goran a discount, but no more than three hundred kroner!

"Hmm, OK, but I want to try it out first!"

"Well why not, how about tomorrow morning..."

"No, right now! We've got some business to take care of in Aalborg, we can try out the car at the same time, let's go!"

There were so many of us packed into the car that not only was it hard to breathe, but thinking was difficult too, even our thoughts were cramped. The gypsy took the number plates off the Albanians' car. He did it in a leisurely but professional fashion, and with a vengeful air, as if he were performing a military sortie back during the war.

He spent the whole journey lying about business of some sort, referring intermittently to speed and hookers, and he talked about selling cars, and about some guy who printed passports.

"A Serbian guy," he said, "passoporto Horvatski! Better than a Slovenian one, or a Yugoslav one! He puts you on the plane himself – visa inclusive! If you want to go to Canada, he'll do you a visa for Canada. If it's Malibu, he'll make you a visa for Malibu! You ever heard of such good service?

He'll come with you to the airport, check your passport in that X-ray thing himself, he'll go there with you. If you get past passport control, you pay him your money. If you don't, you give him nothing. A full guarantee, no funny business, understood?"

He went on and on about the possibility of going to Canada, about getting a job in Canada, about his numerous relatives who were already working there, putting down roots. And he made sure to casually slip in plenty more references to hookers and speed. Potapov greedily lapped it all up, completely forgetting his animosity towards Goran and his ethnicity. He was completely in the gypsy's power.

We drove round all the dives of Aalborg in search of speed. Eventually we arrived at the building where Mario's brothel had been, an old lady opened up, we asked for Olga or Natasha, and they promptly sent us packing: "At night! What the hell are you doing ringing at night! You idiots!" It was unclear what had happened to the bordello. Where could it have got to? It had been right here, ringing with idiotic laughter and "Oi, I'm going to piss myself!" But it was possible that we got the wrong house. Even in the daytime everything in this town was somehow off beam, twisted, muddled. At night we didn't have a hope in hell, Hanuman couldn't make anything out. Wet snow was billowing around us, and there was a wild wind whistling. Goran had managed to properly mess with Hanuman's head, so much so that Hanny was mildly in awe of the gypsy, and he couldn't properly apprehend where we were, or where we were supposed to be going. The gypsy had somehow managed to twist things so that it seemed not only that Hanuman had told him where to get the speed, but that he had wanted whores and speed himself. So now Goran was obliged to get hold of both for his "Indian brother", and as Hanuman's "gypsy brother" he was ready to pull out all the stops, to go for broke to please his "Indian brother", who was already indebted to Goran, because he had got hold of the number plates and was now driving him from drug den to drug den.

At these drug dens sleepy-faced, pot-bellied, long-haired gypsies would surface, basically doubles of Goran. They exchanged some words in their own tongue, but of course no one else could understand what was being discussed. Goran would return with his arms spread in resignation, adding, "Facking motherfacking town! Is no amphetamine! Is no marijuana! No whorzz! No naffing! Is shit!" But there was no guarantee that these places were in fact drug dens, or that the gypsies he talked to were dealers or had access to drugs or whores, there was no guarantee that they were even talking about amphetamines. Maybe they were talking about their own stuff, who knows what gypsies talk about between themselves.

In the end we went to some bar where they sold hash, with a picture of an old man climbing out of a poppy head painted on the wall. There we met the fat old Irishman Hugh again. I told him what we were looking for, and he confided that he had grass on him, lots of grass, and that he could let us have some at a reasonable price, if we bought, say, one hundred grams straight out. I told Hanuman. Potapov pounced on me, insisting I tell no one (the others were still sitting in the car, they hadn't wanted to step out into the rain, they were already thoroughly pissed off). Potapov hissed in Hanuman's ear that he should buy the grass straight away, that he shouldn't let such a good opportunity go by.

"Or lend me some money," Potapov insisted, "lend me all your money! Then I'll buy the grass, sell it, and give you your money back, I promise!"

By now Hanuman was so fed up with everything and everyone that he gave him some money. Potapov spent it all on grass. We waited ages for him to return through the grotty alley down which he'd followed the Irishman. Eventually he appeared, soaking wet. We drove back in silence, having told the rest of them that we hadn't found any grass. We didn't hear another squeak out of Goran about buying the car, and it looked like Potapov couldn't care less any more. His eyes were ablaze, his hands shaking. When we got back those shaking hands skinned up the first joint, and it went round the group, which consisted of just Hanuman, Durachkov, Potapov, and me. The grass turned out to be potent, a bit too heavy. I got mired in thoughts, and quickly zoned out.

The next day Mikhail started dealing the grass. The Ethiopian was the first customer. Potapov was obviously a bit wary about announcing to everyone that he had grass to sell, and he was too scared to open his own drug den, in case the Georgians or Armenians came and hassled him, or torched the place. So he gave me a joint and told me to go looking for people and bring them back to him, or just to hint where I'd got the joint, where they could buy themselves some grass.

I invited Samson to have a smoke, he was known to love the stuff, even more than he loved women and booze. We smoked the joint between us, and the walls started swaying. The grass turned out to be not just potent, but a bit dodgy too; the Ethiopian felt it as well. He didn't hang about long, he left, staggering, with the words, "Oh, right then, I'm going to have a lie-down, mamma mia!" He lurched forwards, and went on his way, sticking close to the wall. Now I was alone, and I had started feeling sick. I was swamped by a turmoil of thoughts, and I regretted that I'd smoked the grass, I felt lousy, a little scared even. I poked my head out of the window and breathed in greedy lungfuls of air, I wanted to go somewhere, anywhere. I left the building, and walked past an Arab, who said, "Hi, my friend…" I left the building, shut the door, but it turned out I hadn't actually left, that I was still inside. Then I opened another door, without realising that I was about to enter the building where the Armenians and Georgians lived.

I walked nonchalantly past the kitchen, where a thieves' coven had just sat down to a game of cards. They said, "Hey, you, what do you want?! What you walking about here for?! You stoned or something, motherfucker!" I walked back down the corridor, and left the building again. But I couldn't shake the feeling that I hadn't fully left, that I was still locked in somehow. I walked into the field, through the mud, searching for that special door for ages. Somewhere in the middle of that field, soaking wet from the snow, I suddenly realised what I was looking for, and I recoiled in horror. What really scared me was that I had been hoping to find a door through which to exit this world, a way of leaving forever. I stood there in the field, snow falling on me, and I remembered Hugh's slanted eyes, and his words: "Careful with this grass, they used a special fertiliser on it."

I couldn't remember how I got back. When I came round I was taking a shower. After that I spent ages lying in bed, staring at the ceiling, repeating to myself, "We have lived for many years, we are friends of old," but I couldn't remember how the song went from there, so I just repeated the same words over and over again...

Then Samson the Ethiopian reappeared and asked where I had got hold of the stuff. I told him that he could buy some for himself, I saw doubt cross his face, and so I told him how much, and where from, and it started from there.

Business was so good that Potapov barely managed to roll the joints in time. He sold the stuff for nearly three times what he paid for it! And he cut it with tobacco too. But it didn't last long. All the camp inhabitants who had a soft spot for grass quickly ran out of money. The Georgians and Armenians got a whiff of what was going on and started calling on Potapov, and telling him, as was their way, that they would pay him later – "sometime soon" – but of course they never did. Obviously he couldn't turn them down, and they visited him in droves, more than anyone else. Eventually everyone else got in on the act. When Potapov realised what was happening he got angry and announced, "That's it, all gone!" and started smoking the grass furtively on his own. We helped him of course…

When the grass was all used up he gave Hanuman some of the money he owed him, weeping in exasperation. Not only had he failed to get rich, he'd made a loss.

"At least we had a nice smoke," said the simple-hearted Durachkov, trying to console him.

But Potapov would have none of it: "Get lost, you."

2

"We're all goners here you know, all goners," Hanuman said, pouring me some wine.
I took hold of the glass, but my hands started shaking. I was so weak that I couldn't even bring the glass to my lips, and I spilt the wine.

"Ehhh, shit, what are you doing…" Ivan said.

I croaked, "The glass was hot, what are you trying to do, kill me or something?"

They said that they were trying to look after me, so they had made me some mulled wine, to help me make a quicker recovery.

I tried to drink the wine, which they had tossed some chilli and other spices into, probably cloves and masala, but it didn't help. I started feeling worse and worse. Now and again Hanny, Potapov and Durachkov demanded that I open my mouth. They peered into the gaping cavern, shaking their heads and tutting.

"Awful," they said, "Dear me! What awful glands!"

Thank God they didn't pay any attention to my teeth, teeth which I hadn't cleaned for months, teeth which I tried to ignore myself. Sometimes I wondered what I would do if I got toothache, where would I go? It might be possible to treat my glands by loafing about in bed and gargling for a while, but you couldn't fix teeth that easily. Teeth wouldn't stop aching just like that, not without medical intervention.

I sometimes heard Potapov and Durachkov talking between themselves, and they spoke a lot about teeth, about the fact that – thank God – dental services cost them nothing. They didn't have to pay a thing for medical services, they were part of that privileged group, eternally needy refugees, the poor, *les guignols*. But they also said the Danish hated them, because they saw them as dossers, and unfairly so. I couldn't help thinking that it was pretty close to the truth. They didn't pay to see the doctor, and they didn't work. They didn't have to worry their heads about a thing, they got money for nothing: they were basically skivers! But, dear God, if the Danish could take one look into the asylum seekers' dreams. If only they could hear the roar of the asylum seeker's stream of consciousness. If only they knew how turbulent, how terrifying, that torrent was. Those waters were full of rocks and debris, they carried the asylum seekers' fears in suspension, and the silt pressed on their spleens. If only the Danish knew how badly their heads ached, then they would have forgiven them anything, anything at all, even petty theft.

Potapov confirmed my thoughts: "Heaven forbid that they should ever experience skiving like that! Even in Hawaii, even at the thermal spas of Baden, even in heaven!"

Let me explain… to start with, let them see how they like living in a hostel with Albanians and Serbs. Even if that hostel is situated in heaven, but there just happens to be some Albanian asshole there. Secondly, let them try living in a hen coop, where you have to shag your wife in the public showers. In the shower room, with the Iranian kids trying to peek in, because they got the knack of unlocking the door with a coin. In the shower room, in a rush, just a quickie! Come as fast as you can and wash yourself down…

vile! Thirdly, try getting treated by a doctor who turns those free services into a form of torture, or refuses to help at all, because he hates refugees, just like everybody else.

They said that Eddie the Iranian went to the dentist once and they pulled the sorry sod's tooth right out. Apparently the tooth was so far gone that there was no point mucking about. They decided to extract it, nothing else for it. When he got home he discovered they'd pulled out the wrong tooth! He thought about hiring a lawyer and kicking up a fuss, but they said the service had been free of charge anyway, and if he wanted they could put things right and pull out the tooth which they were originally supposed to pull out, and anyway the dentist knows best... got it, idiot? He turned down their offer of having a second go, sure they could do some more extracting, but where was the guarantee that they wouldn't mess it up again... you could end up with no teeth left!

Occasionally I would look at Hanuman and remember that time back when we'd been living at Hotello's and he'd pulled out a tooth for one of our guys, Freddy, an African from the Congo. He had such bad toothache that we didn't sleep for a week, he didn't let us, he wailed so much, he crawled up the walls and slithered back down them like a jellyfish, and his nails, which he never trimmed, left cat-claw scratches in the plaster. In the end Hanny decided to put him out of his misery, he grabbed a pair of pliers, and told him to open his mouth and sit still for a minute. Freddy took one look at the pliers and declined the offer. But Hanny gave him some weed to smoke, and yanked the tooth out while he was stoned. I still shudder to think of those pliers. They were the kind you use to pull out nails, big, jagged, jutting nails. People used pliers like that to take cars to bits, they were oily, dirty, horrific. Back then I promised myself that if I ever got toothache then Hanuman would be the last to know. Because he might just try and come to the rescue. The irony was that Hanuman wasn't very good with his hands, he tried less than anyone to assert his manliness, whether by knocking in or pulling out nails. But as soon as he heard that someone had toothache, he reached straight for the pliers!

So Hanuman, Potapov, and Ivan were standing there staring into my mouth and sighing, and I was thinking, "Yep, things look pretty bad, things have reached rock bottom, but still, but still, even if my glands are in a bad way, even if the situation is really dire, even if it doesn't bear thinking about, its still better than them finding out what's up with my feet! Who knows how they would react if I took my boots off and revealed my feet? No, best not to even think about it. No, let my glands be swollen! Best to concentrate on the glands and forget about my teeth! My feet even more so! Let my glands be swollen! Best that they be the cause of my high temperature, not gangrene! Because at least a tooth can be removed by an amateur, in a domestic environment, without the need for specialists, but once you start sawing away at feet it needs to be done above board, by a doctor, in a hospital! And once you're there, you won't wriggle out of having a chat with the police either. No, best to perish, to perish and quietly rot away, completely and in entirety. At least once you're dead you won't feel any pain. No sawing, no extracting, none of that needed! You just lie there, tranquilly rotting. And no one cares. That is if you hadn't got round to fitting yourself with gold fillings. Because if you did, then sooner or later they will come for those fillings. But if not, then no one gives a shit, they forget all about you. They're not sure if you ever existed. Ha-ha! A perfect state of oblivion! The less those filth-calling-themselves-humans take an interest in you, the better. The less they remember you, the better you rot! You won't give a toss about a thing. Especially not about someone's gold teeth!

Meanwhile, I was feeling worse and worse. The wine didn't help, it just seemed to bring on the sickness, and made me sweat continuously. And there was a draught coming from the window...

I was feverish, and I felt painfully exposed. But I could think clearly, I could analyse the situation, I could even make cutting comments in my hoarse rasp, although it sounded horribly different to my usual voice. Whenever anyone came in, I would croak in their faces: "So, scum, come to check if I'm dead yet?" My bile poisoned the atmosphere, everyone tried to leave as quickly as they could, and most of the time I was left to myself and the loneliness which sapped my will.

It felt awful, and I was exhausted from the constant nakedness, from the heightened tactility of my soul, it was as if someone had torn off my skin, leaving the nerves exposed; they were hanging from my skeleton like unclad power cables draped over a fence. I couldn't sink into delirium or even fall asleep. I looked around the room with reddened eyes, and I was fully aware of everything going on, and that was more distressing than any nightmare. Because in my condition, which had suddenly become more acute, more inflamed, the reality which surrounded me, as I perceived it, seemed more bizarre than ever.

I kept asking, in my weak voice, for the window to be shut, but Hanuman wouldn't yield and just repeated, "The window has nothing to do with it! You'll be better in no time. You've been much worse than this, hundreds of times before! And everything was just fine, and you recovered eventually."

I hissed in response, "Yes, yes, I did, but the window was never wide open like that!"

But he would have none of it. He didn't want to listen. He couldn't care less. He had his own stuff to take care of, much more important stuff. I had already been written off, like a corpse. All that remained was to take me to the field and bury me under the maize. He had already fetched a spade for that very purpose. He had already thought the whole thing through. Ivan and Potapov would make perfect gravediggers. It looked like he was counting on their help. Evidently the plan was for them to bury me.

Potapov feigned sympathy, and assisted insincerely in their attempts to cure me. He asked me to stick out my tongue, at which he would nod his head and sigh and then send Ivan to buy more cheap beer, just a couple of bottles, and – while he was at it – to steal a bottle of strong wine, "the same as before, remember" ... "yeah, yeah, alright." Ivan was a dab hand at that, a real master. A champion! He didn't arouse any suspicions. He had such a naive face, such a timid expression, how could you ever suspect someone with a face like that of stealing? But he did steal, he stole that vile wine. And plenty of it! Every single day, you could put money on it! I still remember that wine: fortified plum wine. It gave me such bad heartburn. It was the worst possible plonk! A hefty, bulbous bottle with a little brass goblet nestling in the cavity in its side. It was incredibly cheap in Denmark, it was Denmark's national wine.

Hanuman warmed up the wine, and chucked some chilli into it. Meanwhile Potapov fried the bacon which Durachkov had nicked at the same time, drank some beer, and sprinkled a pinch of herbs of some description into the wine. When they gave it to me to drink, I summoned up my last remaining energy to tell them that all this might have been caused by me overdoing it on the grass. I once had an abscess, and had to have my throat disinfected. Apparently I nearly died from it. Potapov said it was probably best I didn't smoke at all, if I had such a dodgy throat.

"Especially through a water pipe," he added. "And we were smoking through a water pipe just before you fell ill. There you go! The wine fumes must have caused it!"

"How?" I rasped. I wanted to hear this nonsense through to its conclusion.

"Smoke," he said, expanding on his theme, "the smoke which was infused with wine fumes must have caused it! In general, it's probably not advisable for you to drink wine, even hot wine, and especially not with spices in it! Those chilli peppers will destroy your throat! You'll definitely end up snuffing it like that."

And so he confiscated my wine, and I hissed at him, "Just close the window, please…"

The rest of them agreed with me that we should close the window, but Hanuman found a dozen reasons why we shouldn't. One of them made me wild with anger. "The window needs to be kept open," he said, "so as to continuously ventilate the room, otherwise we're breathing the same air as the patient!" he explained, pointing an accusatory finger in my direction. "We might get infected too. We need to freshen up the room, drive the microbes out!"

That sounded a lot like what he had said about the old man's corpse. Hanuman was keeping the window open now just as he had done back then. I didn't even have the strength to voice my indignation. All I managed to say was, "I'll perish! I'll get an abscess! And who's going to take me to the doctor then? You won't manage to call one out in time… you won't even try, you son of a bitch! Because you'd get nabbed. You'll just watch me fade away, telling me the same things you told the old man: 'Oh, you're much better now! You look fresher! You've got some colour in your cheeks! You look much better than an hour ago,' I'm right, aren't I?"

Meanwhile, Potapov said that if any incisions needed to be made, then he was on hand, he even had a suitable instrument, he'd found a pretty decent scalpel at the rubbish dump.

That didn't make me feel one bit better. I asked them again – to avoid any complications and any surgical or God knows what other kind of interventions in my throat – to please shut the window! But they wouldn't. And so I got sicker and sicker. That was when Mikhail first tried to sow a seed of discord in my mind. He came to see me and tell

205

me what an idiot the Indian was, how dumb he was, how he didn't understand how ill I was, and that the window should be kept shut. I asked Mikhail to shut the window, and he obliged. But at that very moment Hanuman came in and opened it again. Mikhail tried to stand up for me, but Hanuman sent him packing. As soon as the door slammed behind Mikhail, Hanny closed the window, came up to my bed, and asked what Mikhail and I had been talking about; Hanuman had been in the toilet and had heard Mikhail use his name three, maybe four times. I asked Hanuman to keep the window closed now. He kept it half shut for a while, but then he opened it again. We slept just as before, with the window wide open.

One time Mikhail sent Ivan to see the nurse, hoping she would give him medicines of some sort. Ivan pretended he had a sore throat, he lied that he had a temperature, and all the rest of it. But she just said he should drink some water and sent him on his way...

"The bastards!" said Potapov, "these quacks say exactly the same thing to everyone, whatever the problem, just drink water, let the body fight the illness, let it purify itself with water!"

"That's because they're proud of their water," I said. "It's the cleanest in Europe, after all!"

On the third visit the nurse gave Durachkov some sort of powder, but it didn't help me one bit. I was beginning to lose hope.

3

I was lying on the top bunk, as if I was in a sleeping carriage on a train from Farstrup to Oblivion. I lay there, heading nowhere, while Hanuman continued his journey to Lolland. He wouldn't stop raving about Lolland. I was fading fast, and he continued to burnish those same old fairy tales about Lolland.

That's right, Hanuman carried on yakking with people on street corners, collecting more and more fables about Lolland. Now it turned out that he knew some people who had once been there. He'd met them a while back, but they lived in Aalborg now, and apparently they'd once scraped together the money and taken off to Lolland. I didn't give a damn about that. I wasn't planning to go to Lolland. I just lay there under the standard lamp and the narrow bookshelf. I lay there under that lamp like a corpse in a mortuary. I lay there waiting to get some kind of infection, something fatal which would turn me into a real corpse. I was waiting until my cells started dividing, until the tumour started to grow, until the necrosis started, until the pus poisoned my blood and I departed for the other side. But no, I thought, it wouldn't be that easy. I hadn't been able to walk for ages now, so I would have to crawl there, dragging my legs, my poor old legs, behind me...

I lay there under that standard lamp, sinking deeper and deeper into depression. By now I was so indifferent to everything that I didn't even notice we had ended up completely empty-handed again. Once again it was because of Potapov. Somehow he had managed to persuade Hanuman to buy another car. Had he no shame?

This time he said that we needed to resume our food trips, and he was right that we had nothing to eat. But by then I couldn't care less about food, I was ready to perish on the spot like a Paris *clochard*, putting up no resistance. But Hanuman was different. He was always hungry. For him having a good feed was important. To be more precise, the availability of food was more important than satisfying his appetite, or stuffing his belly. Knowing that he had food on hand buoyed him up psychologically.

I had somehow recovered... or at least it felt like I was

well. Hanuman had the ability to persuade me that I felt better, he had his way with me like some kind of snake charmer, and I was hypnotised by him. I really did start feeling better. The Nepalese cat refused to feed us any more. Ivan had no money left, because Potapov kept getting him mixed up in all sorts of dodgy business. They bought a hundred-odd lotto tickets, and ten grams of hashish, and then sat there smoking, checking their tickets and talking nonsense. Then the hash was all used up, and they couldn't get hold of any more. The Jutland ticket machines seemed to have conspired against us... they stopped accepting our fake tickets. And rumours started to circulate that some guys in uniform had appeared from somewhere and were stopping the buses which the asylum seekers used, checking the tickets, scanning them with some kind of gadget to see if they were fake. A lot of people got caught. The fines were apparently astronomical. No one wanted to go legit; one hundred kroner a journey was more than we could afford. That's why we needed another car! After that last nocturnal excursion to Aalborg with Goran our old Ford had refused to start...

Potapov started pestering Hanuman again. He started going on about some guy he knew who had milk to sell.

"He's got his own farm, get it?" said Potapov, his voice oscillating between a bellow and a plaintive whine. "And what does that mean? Well, to start with it means milk, and really cheap milk. And if you buy it in canisters, twenty litres at a time, then you get a discount, a massive discount. So, we need to get hold of a big fridge from the scrapheap, for starters," he said, counting off the tasks on his fingers, "and to do that we need a car. If we're going to move milk about, we definitely need a car. Maybe we'll have to transport milk to the other camps too, maybe we can sell it for more there. That means big money. And money doesn't grow on trees. Zhenya, translate for him!"

"He understands," I said.

"He understands fuck all!" said Potapov.

"Me understand very good," said Hanuman, mocking Potapov, "but what do we need so much milk for?"

"I told you, he doesn't understand... maybe he understands the words, but not the general meaning!" Potapov started bellowing again, switching to ropey English. "To start with, is many families in our camp, and the children needs milk. And not the kind you get in the shops, but proper, fresh milk, full-fat. Plus it's going to be cheaper. And seconds, we can make different dairy products, cheese, and... Zhenya... what's *tvorog* in English?"

"Curd cheese," I replied.

"Right," Mikhail continued to pile it on. "Curd, you get it? There's no curd here, no one even knows what curd is! Zilch – in the whole of Denmark! We'll be the first! We'll give them a curd revolution!"

"A curd revolution?" Hanuman started cracking up. This really was an unexpected addition to Potapov's repertoire.

"Yes, we can patent it!" Mikhail said. Naturally he claimed to know how to make *tvorog*, and cheese too.

"We'll have a monopoly! And believe me, people will buy my cheese. It's better than the Swiss stuff! And thirdly," he continued, now hugging Hanuman close like a brother, "we need a car to go and fetch grass and hash. Who knows, maybe we'll buy some grass and sell it like before. But this time we won't let anyone rip us off. And fourthly, we'll go and collect bottles, and food, and go to the scrapheap too. Maybe something interesting will turn up. Who knows, maybe a satellite dish, or a computer, eh? It has been known. We haven't checked out the scrapheap in Skive for ages, and there's usually all sorts of stuff there. It's like King Solomon's Mines! You can sell a simple satellite receiver to someone who's got a yes for a good price. The main thing is to find the receiver, you can always find a buyer. But to find a receiver you first have to drive round a few scrapyards. And to do that, you need a car!"

Hanuman was evidently so tired and so hungry, or so in need of a smoke, or he was just so pissed off with everything, that he gave Mikhail all his money (or nearly all of it), and they bought a car. For seven thousand kroner! That is, they forked out everything they had, but of course they still ended up owing money. Mikhail promised to hand over his pocket money every month, one and a half thousand kroner, clearly counting on us to bail him out. He was convinced that the car would start paying for itself in the first few days, as soon as he started selling the milk. They bought the car from those same Georgian guys, and again it came without number plates, without an MOT, without anything! The Georgians just fobbed Potapov and Hanuman off with a note, apparently written by some Danish guy, in kid's handwriting on a piece of exercise paper, which said that the owner of the car guaranteed that the number plates and MOT were valid for the next three months. Hanuman didn't like that note one bit. It also said that the car had almost completed its MOT, that it was in the process of being registered, or that it might be registered soon; it wasn't clear. But it didn't make any difference what was written or who had written it. If you're going to buy a car off drug addicts, and for that kind of money… I didn't want to know about that car, I didn't want to see it, I refused to ride in it, I even refused to go outside to look at it, despite all their persuading. They had gone and bought a car from drug addicts and thieves, for eight thousand kroner! Some people step in the same shit twice, others do it their whole lives, every single day!

Obviously they had ripped Potapov off again; they even promised to make him some number plates.

"Right, listen here my friend," Murman said. "Did you know that our Vaska is a mechanic?"

"Vaska?" Potapov asked, failing to understand.

"Yes, yes, my friend," said Bacho, "didn't you know that our Vaska is an engineer? Hey, bro, where you been living? On the moon or something?"

"Yes, yes, my friend," said Murman, "Vaska is the business! He's such a good mechanic, he's an engineer, a real handicraftsman, don't you know? He'll take a piece of steel and make you such a nice pair of number plates that no copper will ever tell the difference! You'll never get stopped… you'll be able to drive about without a passport for the rest of your life! Without a *Syn!*[20] Without anything! And your children! And their children too!"

"Just give me the money, my friend," said Bacho. "Everything will be just fine…"

Potapov gave him the money, and the very moment the banknotes changed hands the Georgians stood up, and without another word, as if by prior agreement, they got into the car, their car, and drove off. They didn't show their faces for a while; they had gone to their heroin den for the week. When they eventually reappeared they kept asking for more money, and Potapov had to hand the brutes a bit of everyone's pocket money, all for that beaten-up BMW. Who cares if it had leather seats and wooden knobs and a CD player; who gives a shit about the interior, what's the point of all that stuff if you're just going to drive around scrap heaps and fetch hash? Every single time that Potapov gave the Georgians more money they disappeared for several days, and he kept hoping that they would shoot up and get so high that they smashed themselves to bits in a traffic accident, because they drove like maniacs. But they kept coming back, completely frazzled, a shade yellower, a sprinkling of snow on their coats, foaming at the mouth, hazy eyes. They asked for more money, and Potapov would moan, "My family, my family, I've got a family to feed." But he would always pay up, because he had no choice. And so we didn't have enough money to buy milk, even though we'd found a massive fridge, which could barely fit in our room. It had to go in our room because there was no space at the Potapovs'. Not only was there no room for a fridge,

20   MOT certificate (Danish).

there wasn't even enough space to put a chair down to sit on. His room was stuffed to ceiling-height with all sorts of junk. A while later they paid a visit to the bins outside the Brugsen store, and they found some meat, loads of chicken meat, whole chickens, enough to stuff the boot full, and then the fridge too, and those chickens turned out to be totally edible!

Our Nepali cat agreed right away to come and eat with us, and so spices, rice, and bread appeared in our kitchen, but we were still feeling washed up… and the rest of them – not me – desperately needed a smoke. And so Hanuman decided to start selling the chicken, to try and scrape together enough money for two or three grams. But the chicken wasn't that presentable, it had a bluish hue, and there was a bit of a whiff coming off it. A whiff of rubbish, of the bins. No one was going to buy chicken like that, not even at five kroner a bird. And so Hanuman came up with a particularly ingenious plan. One time some guy, he might have been a Pakistani, or maybe a Nepali, had come to the camp selling mutton. He also had bags of ready-made, frozen plov for sale. The plov was made from meat, rice, vermicelli, onions, olives, raisins and lots of spices. It was cooked up in one big batch, frozen, divided into bags, and then it was ready to sell. The Arabs loved the stuff, but the one who really adored it was the crazy Iranian. He couldn't cook, all he knew how to do was boil macaroni, although he could never fathom why it didn't end up salted.

Counting on there being plenty more idiots like that, Hanuman and Nepalino cooked up a similar concoction (using chicken in place of mutton). They flavoured it generously with chilli peppers and spices, including curry powder, garlic and ginger, so that it was barely noticeable that the meat wasn't quite fresh – the spices concealed the smell. They sold it all with no problems, then they made some more, and sold that easily again, and then they trundled off to Aalborg. They spent two days there smoking hash, then when they were back we all sat together in our room, chopping up chicken, slicing onions, cooking on our little hob, and then things really heated up, despite opening the window we were gasping for breath, the room filled up with a thick column of smoke, and a strong smell of curry. Even Potapov couldn't stand it, he told us he was allergic to spices, he faked a sneezing fit so well that his eyes started watering, and then he ran off. We carried on making and selling the bags of plov until we had used up our supplies of chicken.

We ended up without any money again, but we did have hash. Just a little bit. Our Nepali cat stopped feeding us, because we hadn't given him his share of the profits from the plov. They offered him some hash, but he turned up his nose, he told us that he didn't smoke it. It wasn't that he didn't like hash, he was happy to have a puff now and again, but only when he had food. Because as soon as you have a smoke, you want to eat. So now he wasn't going to smoke hash, because there wasn't any grub. If we had some grub, then why not, he'd have a smoke, and then he'd have a good feed as well. But he didn't want to spend his savings, and he was wary of eating that dodgy chicken, so he wouldn't smoke, he wanted money instead. But no one gave him money, they needed the money for hash! When Nepalino started whining about grub and hash Hanuman told him to shut it, he gave him a kick up the backside, and nabbed all his remaining rice, onion and spices. Nepalino got in such a huff that he not only stopped eating with us, but talking to us too. He left, he went on the scrounge, wandering from kitchen to kitchen, chatting to people about this and that, and we later heard that the Algerians gave him something to eat in return for oral favours.

So we had nothing to eat. We decided to defrost the last remaining chicken, and while it was defrosting everyone got so stoned that they forgot their names. And I fell asleep hungry. I woke from hunger, and wanted to eat so badly that

I would have happily started chewing a towel. And my feet were hurting again. I peeked under my quilt and saw they were bleeding too. There was a smell of putrefaction. When I poked my nose back over the edge of the quilt I witnessed this muted scene: Hanuman, Potapov and Durachkov standing there, staring into the saucepan which Hanuman was holding in front of him. In the saucepan there was a chicken, and on their faces there were looks of apprehension and revulsion. This was the last of the chickens.

"No, we should chuck that one," said Hanny.

Potapov objected, "What do you mean chuck it? Fuck that! Chuck out a whole chicken?"

"Well, OK, if you want it, have it, eat it yourself!" Hanny said. "Take it, I don't care! I choose life!"

Then Potapov placed one hand on the chicken, like it was a Bible, looked straight at Hanuman with his honest eyes, and said, "Some time back, me and Ivan were in Siberia, we were fitting a fireplace. The house was out in the countryside. And it was winter. The snow was piled up high all around. When we stepped outside all we could see was snow, endless snow, there was no way of getting back to town or the nearest shop, the snowdrifts were higher than our heads, all around. We finished our food supplies in three days. And the snow's still falling. We couldn't get out from there. Then the hunger started. We ate nothing for a whole week, we thought we were goners. But then one day a cat showed up, a mangy old ginger cat. Ivan coaxed it closer, here puss-puss. Then I whacked it with a spade. We made soup out of it, we lasted two whole days on that soup. The salt and pepper helped to mask the cat smell, they've got glands of some kind, some sort of secretions, that's how they mark their territory. Zhenya, explain it to him, about those glands…"

"No way, go to hell, sadists!"

"Don't you be too fast to judge, a cat's life is not equal to a human one," Potapov said indignantly.

"I couldn't care less! I don't want to hear another word! Maybe I would have eaten a cat in that situation, but I wouldn't start telling people about it afterwards, you understand?"

"OK, let's forget it... anyway, it's all about the chilli. Let's cook this chicken up with chilli pepper and curry powder, then we'll be able to eat it!"

Hanuman rubbed his chin, and said, "Yeah, technically it's possible." But he added that even if we managed to hide the taste, that wouldn't make the chicken any fresher, and if the food was already contaminated, then the spices wouldn't change that, but we could at least try...

They studded it with garlic, boiled it, fried it, steamed it, they did everything imaginable to it, but the smell only seemed to get stronger. The more effort they put into preparing it, the more it stank. At that point it suddenly dawned upon me – that chicken smelled just like my wretched feet! And that realisation made me feel even more lousy!

They started to eat it. I wanted to eat too, I wanted to eat really badly, but I couldn't control the retching which began at the thought of having the minutest morsel of that rotten rooster. But they were eating it with more and more gusto, they even started smacking their lips contentedly. As I watched them I felt I really had to eat something, even if I got food poisoning, I was ready to eat anything. And so I agreed to try a little bit...

And then I lay there sweating, tuning in to the sensations in my stomach, feeling like I had just eaten a Mexican mushroom, not chicken. I lay there, expecting to soon start feeling really bad. And about an hour later I had so tormented myself with thoughts of food poisoning that I started feeling sick. No one else got sick, just me. So badly that I got a temperature. Then I chucked up. Vomit, and blood. Oh, I felt so bad! But I had felt so good as I screwed up my eyes and sank my teeth into that chicken wing! I had felt lightness, warmth, a homely feeling washing over me...

But there was too much chilli, so much that I couldn't taste a thing. And thank God that I couldn't, that was why they put so much chilli in, so that you couldn't taste it. If they hadn't somehow masked the taste, there was no way anyone could eat that chicken.

Later, after I had thrown up, they said to me reproachfully, "What was the point in eating it if you were going to spew it all up? We can't sell it like that!"

And they looked at me with such hungry gazes, just like the shipmates must have looked at poor Richard Parker before they ate him alive.

4

Ivan and Potapov started making regular trips hunting for bottles. But since Mikhail had a family to feed (and he was still paying the Georgians for the car), none of the proceeds made their way to us. We got almost nothing, nothing except for the milk and tea which Ivan stole on a regular basis. He would usually grab something from the rubbish container when he passed by too. Sometimes there were potatoes, then Hanuman fried them up with onions, and a generous sprinkling of black pepper and chilli. He made his tea, with milk and sugar. And that's how we lived.

Every morning we listened to the Muslims' prayers, the shuffling feet, running water and the cries from the other side of the wall, just as before.

That poor child, that poor little girl, I thought. She seemed to be locked in that room day and night, she never came out. How old could she be? Maybe six? They brought her here from the sticks in Russia. There wasn't much known about their life back there. Judging by what Potapov said they had lived in lots of different places – and he couldn't lie all the time, sometimes he liked to talk, especially after he'd had a smoke, and you could just about make out the truth through a cloud of lies. His wife had a room in some kind of hostel, where she lived after running away from home; she left home because she was so fed up with her stepmother, who had taunted her remorselessly, and because her brother had raped her, or so Potapov said. First she worked as a seamstress, then she made pasties in some bakery, she had various jobs here and there, then she got together with some bloke who'd done time, he was a driver when they met, he delivered the pasties, and he was probably the father of her child. While she was pregnant, he had been killed by his mates to settle a score, or because they'd fallen out over divvying up some proceeds, or out of principle, or because he had sullied their thieves' honour, and now Liza, the dead man's child, was in the power of this despot.

"That girl's got a really poor appetite," Potapov would complain. "I don't know what to do, what I'm supposed to give her to eat. She won't eat porridge. That's understandable, the oats here are so crap, you wouldn't feed them to a dog. She can't stand the sight of meat. Sometimes she'll have a little nibble of fried potato, but only sweet potato. When we lived at the dacha – it was Ivan's place, we lived with him – it was really cold, and we had nothing to eat, and one time all we had left was a single onion. So I fried up the onion, and we ate it like the Buratino family. And she ate that onion, oh how she gobbled up that onion! That's right… and here we've got everything you could want, but she won't eat a thing! She won't eat pizza, she won't eat meatballs or sausages, she chucks the sausages down the back of the sofa! When we tidied up the room we found a whole stash of pizza. The same thing happened at the dacha near Moscow. We got infested with rats thanks to her. And a rat's no laughing matter! They can chew off your ear while you sleep! And they can suffocate a child, that's what a rat's capable of, make no mistake! And the ones there were this big…!"

It made me angry, because the bastard was saying all that stuff just to protect himself. He was shielding himself from criticism, trying to justify his tyrannical ways, his ill treatment of the child, trying to justify the whole situation, all the horrors of camp life. The situation he had gotten his whole family into. The hole he had crawled into, and dragged his family into after him. He justified all of that stuff by fretting about his family. He managed to twist it so that he was apparently concerned about the girl's well-being, he was just trying to bring her up right, to raise her properly. Some upbringing! And if he sometimes raised his hand at her, if he sometimes resorted to violence, then that was in her best interests too, of course it was. Potapov could see the look of rebuke in my eyes, but I never said a thing. I couldn't care less about Liza, I just wanted to be able to sleep in the mornings. Just sleep, without having to listen to that shouting, his bellowing, and her wailing. I just wanted to sleep; I was thinking about myself. Couldn't he do his child-rearing some other time of the day?

It didn't bother me at all that he was ill-treating her. I had already started to hate her. It was because of her that I had to lie there in torment, that I couldn't get to sleep. I just told him that he shouldn't shout at the child. I advised him to go and see the nurse, he'd get an appointment with the doctor, he could go and talk with the doctor. Maybe they would work out what was wrong, maybe they would recommend some kind of diet, or prescribe some free medicine.

"No," he said, "free medicine? Dream on. We've already been given all the freebies on offer. What more could there be? There won't be any more freebies, things can only get worse from now on. She's refusing to eat out of principle, just to ruin everyone's mood. She's got a little devil living inside her, understand? A contrarian sprite! She's doing it to rile us, she's mocking us. She does it out of spite, always the opposite of what we ask, and she lies non-stop. She mucks everything up, breaks stuff. Her favourite pastime is squeezing tubes of stuff. She'll grab the toothpaste and squeeze, squeeze, squeeze with a look of pure bliss on her face! I've seen it myself, eyes all misty, misty-eyed, all moist and foggy. Who knows how she'll turn out? She was conceived with a convict, after all! She could grow up to be some sort of slut. I had this expensive glue, I used it to fix my boots, other rubber things, it was multipurpose stuff. And she went and squeezed the whole lot out. And as soon as we started investigating who it was, she started trying to wriggle out of it. She'd say absolutely anything. She'll lie so brazenly that you'll even start doubting yourself. But I can see right through her, she can't take me for a ride, and she knows it, I give her 'what's for' for those lies…"

And he beat her. Sometimes so hard that it left bruises all over her body. He was consumed by rage. Then afterwards he would complain, "That little vixen, she provoked me again, makes me hate myself, I'm hitting her and I feel bad, I start going out of my mind, but I can't do anything about it, it just comes over me, like some kind of trance, she'll lead me to sin, one day I'll end up beating her to death…"

I listened to him beating her, and waited. I was waiting until he really did beat her to death. I dreamed about seeing his face afterwards, sodden with tears of horror. I imagined him trying to resuscitate her with an infusion of chilli peppers, or by injecting vodka into her veins, or rubbing her quivering body with gelatine, drawing symbols on her ears and heels. I so much wanted to see him in a state of panic and indecision! I listened to the commotion on the other side of the wall, and waited, waited to hear his muffled cries: "What are we going to do? What the fuck are we going to do?" I wished him the very worst, I just hated him so much. But I couldn't care less about the girl. I really couldn't.

She was actually pretty strange. Sweet, but with a certain oddness about her. Quite pretty in her own way, in a childlike way... blond hair, you could call it flaxen, pale skin with thin veins fanning out, and the clumsy frailness of a fawn. She was learning to ride a bike, wearing a cap with a large visor, and she would run her fingers up and down it so eagerly, as if to give us a sign that everything was going to be OK. Then she would fall off the bike, she would fall so forlornly, narrowly avoiding injury. Mikhail yelled at her, he would yell until his voice was hoarse and harrowing. He would yell until he was driven to distraction, until the blood rushed to his face, and his features were distorted. For the climax of the scene he would theatrically manoeuvre his massive seal-like body on to the grass and start fanning himself with the cap which he had torn off the girl's head, and she would stand there, shoulders hunched, trembling, lifting her hair from her face and wiping away the tears. Once the fit of anger had subsided he would douse himself with liquid from a bottle and tell her, now in a weary tone, that she had ruined his day off. It was true that she had ruined an ideal which he had created for himself: of a father striving to bring up his daughter well, teaching her how to ride a bike... but this wretch had to go and antagonise him! She just had to go and spoil everything. How dare she! She would sob and hiccup, and he would carry on at her until he was wild with rage: "Turn the peddles, you idiot! What about the handlebars, idiot! What are the handlebars there for, idiot!" He would hiss through clenched teeth, "Turn! What are you looking at?" But again and again she would trundle off the path and into the bush, staring ahead vacantly as if in a trance, and then, after a short delay, crying would emanate from the undergrowth. It was almost as if she was waiting for a minute or two, thinking about how best to resolve the situation, how to behave so as not to rouse her father's anger. But his anger would flare up immediately, he was just waiting for something, for the most trivial pretext, to lose his temper. For him, any insignificant trifle was reason to explode. He clearly savoured the rush of blood, he was so ready to burst into expletives that it seemed he was fulfilling a need. Hanuman once said that Mikhail was addicted... he used an exotic-sounding scientific term which I promptly forgot.

Liza's language skills came on quickly, even if it wasn't at all clear which language it was... the children at the camp spoke a strange tongue which was a mixture of Danish, English and German, a toxic, volatile mix, laced with Serbo-Croatian expletives. It was the ugliest, the weirdest, the harshest of tongues – the language of our Cro-Magnon forbears! And it was only comprehensible to the kids themselves.

At home Liza would often mix some Serbo-Croat in with her Russian: in place of *seichas*[21] she would say *ovde*, in place of *zhdi*[22] she would say *počekaj*, and, of course, she would always say *razumem*[23]. In their family, they had their own private language, and the repulsive Albanian word *prchik*, meaning "fart", somehow took root. Just as in any other family they used a lot of euphemisms, and family nicknames too. Mikhail was called Mickey Mouse or Santa Claus, Masha was called Ma-ma-ma!-Mam-mmma-Mariaa-Ma-ma-ma... They didn't worry much about speaking correctly, and parasitic loan words would inevitably invade their speech and make themselves at home, even Arab words like *khalas!*, *akharam!*, *khabibi*, *Yallah! Yallah!* Whenever Mikhail wanted Masha and Liza to hurry up, he would shout at them *Yallah! Yallah-a-a, khabibi.*[24] He would sometimes return from the scrapheap and ask his wife in Serbian *šta radiš?* to which she would reply *ništa* , with the stress on the first syllable. And this rubbed off on Liza too. When her Kurdish friend asked her, "Why ya faza don'buy ya sony play station?" it was unlikely that Liza knew which

21 "Now" (Russian).
22 "Wait" (Russian).
23 "Understand" (Serbian).
24 "Come on, come on, my little one" (Arabic).

language she used in her reply: "This is not your biznes, my frien! Razumesh? Never spor meg hvorfor! Hvorfor your fazer never fuck your mazer? This not meg biznes! I give no shit! Why you live in camp! Nobody know, hvorfor ikke pozitiv, and your fazer eat shit, derfore ikke penger, nema ništa! Go ask your fazer why he eat shit and vask hans ass!"[25] Following which they would start lobbing stones at each other. They would take up position five metres apart, squat on the ground, staring each other straight in the eye unflinchingly like two dogs, and they would grope about blindly, scooping up the gravel. Then they would push themselves upright, and, lurching forwards, fling handfuls of pebbles at each other, yelling, "I kill ya bitch! I kill ya fucking bitch! I swear ya dead before night come!" And no one said a word, everyone walked straight past, gazing blankly at their shoes, even their parents walked past... first Maria, on her way to the laundry with the washing, then Mikhail, hunting obsessively for the spanners which he had lent to that damned Goran, that accursed gypsy... and then he was gone, disappearing round the corner, paying no attention to the hail of gravel right behind his back.

Parents didn't worry much about their children at the camp. The fathers were preoccupied with their asylum cases, hatching various schemes, trying to decide whether to flee a bit further, devising nutritional plans, diets which would allow them to save a bit more money, writing letters to the Directorate, or other places too, to their relatives, hoping they would come up with something, fill in some

25 "That's none of your business, my friend! Got it? Never ask me why again. Why does your father never fuck your mother? It's none of my business! I don't give a shit! Why are you living in this camp? No one knows why, you haven't got a yes, and your father eats shit, because you've got no money, you've got nothing! Go and ask your father why he eats shit, go and clean his arse!" (a mixture of broken English, Danish and Serbo-Croat).

form, send some documents which might save their house of cards from the whirlwind of deportation. Or they just spent their days in a state of deep depression, lapsing into drunkenness, descending back into depression, and so the cycle continued, day in, day out. In other words – they had no time for children! The mothers would constantly be washing, cooking, gossiping, squabbling, warring over the washing machine, battling over the dryer, fighting for their turn at the hob, for space in the fridge, for anything and everything. They waged their women's warfare, and had no time for children either. And so the kids were left to their own devices, and rapidly forgot their native language, concluding that it no longer served them any purpose. They swiftly learned the camp slang, faster than it took them to grow up, and they grew up faster than their asylum cases were decided. They turned into louts, like that little Albanian kid, for example. They got into petty theft. They got caught, their parents gave them a cuff round the head, then they went off thieving again, sometimes their parents would put them up to it, or use them as cover, like Potapov... he always made Liza wear a little rucksack when they went to the shop, telling her, "We need to do a bit of shopping, and we need to do a little sopping." The word "chopping" had passed into their vocabulary from the Bulgarians, who spoke garbled English. They would always say "chopping" when in fact they bought nothing at all, they just stole. And for some reason Mikhail would use that word as he led Liza to a less exposed corner of the shop, where there were no mirrors, and stuffed the rucksack full of meat, cheese and coffee, which they calmly walked out with.

Hanuman liked Liza. He often spoiled her. When we had money he would buy her ice cream, Chupa Chups and cola. He took pictures of her, sat her down on his knee, took her into town, and they went on walks round the little lake together. They would pause for a while next to the old Armenian, who showed them his fish, and told them about the huge pike he once caught. Hanuman would say the strangest things to Liza. He once said that he was going away to Argentina soon. There were loads of palm trees there, everyone drank maté and danced the tango. And so he danced the tango with her, and sang her some Sinatra. "Would you like to come with me?" he would ask, and he would answer the question himself, telling her that even if she didn't he would kidnap her. He said that he would get a big suitcase, lie her down in it like a doll, and take her away to Argentina. She would fall asleep in Denmark, in her parents' room, and then wake up by the sea under palm trees on a golden-yellow beach in Argentina, where everyone there would be dancing the tango, and she would quickly learn to dance the tango too. Soon she would be the best tango dancer in the whole of Argentina... And he did another turn with her, crooning, "Don't cry for me, Argenteeeeeeeeeeeenahh..."

Liza laughed, but her laugh was kind of wrong, hysterical, not like a child's laugh...

Later I told Hanuman that the child already suffered from strange fantasies, so it wasn't a good idea to infect her with that Argentina nonsense as well.

It was true, she really did have a lot of strange fantasies...

One time the Potapovs went into town to sort some things out, and they left Liza with us. She sat on Hanuman's knee and talked to me in Russian, while Hanuman smiled idiotically, from time to time doing his Russian imitation, loudly declaiming "Kto! Pochemu?? Kuda???!!!"[26] – this was supposed to be a send-up of Liza's stepfather.

Liza sat on Hanuman's knee, talking about the time she went with Mummy and Daddy for a walk round the pond and the weather wasn't very nice and it was cold and there was a bug crawling on the path in the sand and Daddy didn't see the bug and he squashed it but the bug was big so how could he not notice it and he had a lot of feet and

26   Who! Why?? How???!!! (Russian)

if I was a bug I would have so many feet that I could hold a Chupa Chups with one foot and ice cream in the other and cola in the third one and a ball in a fourth and I wouldn't have to go to school bugs don't go to school do they and bugs don't have parents who feed them porridge bugs don't eat at all do they why would a bug eat if it can just crawl like that across the path but then someone would have to go and crush the bug just like Daddy crushed that one then there's no more me...

After that I fell into a kind of stupor. It happened after I had overhead Mikhail speaking with Ivan... or not exactly... Let's say that it was after Mais had left for Germany. He spent ages getting ready to go. For a long time he couldn't bring himself to leave. He spent a whole year planning. He was working out the route. Actually no, it was two years! Everyone got totally pissed off with him. They were longing for him to just sod off and leave. But Mais couldn't just go to Germany. He had to do something big. So that people would remember what kind of guy that Mais had been. So that everyone who had ever lived in the Farstrup camp would say, "There was once this guy called Mais, oh yes." Before leaving for Germany Mais definitely had to get his hair cut.

Back then there was this sporty black guy from the Cameroons who cut hair at Farstrup. Jean-Claude, a real brute! He was ugly: not only did he have goggling eyes, like a toad, not only did he have warts all over his face, but he also had some kind of abdominal hernia, which for some reason he liked showing off to everyone. And he had mounds of muscles hanging off him, you wouldn't even dare stand next to him – if all that came crashing down on you they would never find your body. And he was incredibly flexible too. He'd strike a jaunty pose, one leg up on the windowsill, he'd have a scratch of his balls, which were practically tumbling out of his shorts, then he'd roll his T-shirt over his stomach, up to his chest, stroke a nipple and poke about in his hernia for a bit, inspecting it, while casting oily sidelong glances at the Arab girls. He had probably ruptured himself while lifting something unfeasibly heavy, and now that hernia was, to no small degree, a source of manly pride for him. It served as evidence that he was capable of tossing something on to his shoulder which was so heavy that others wouldn't even dare try and lift it! It was his unique marker of machismo. He cut hair for money, and he had clearly decided to invest in his business and buy some clippers. Some guys buy a car, but he didn't want to throw his money about, so he bought himself some clippers, and started to cut hair for the guys who raced around in cars. He shaved his own head bald, and he would try to persuade others to do the same: he'd go up to some hairy guy and start to tease him until he was ready to go under the clippers for twenty kroner. Mais didn't take care of his appearance, either out of stinginess or laziness – it's still not clear to me which. But one day his partners in crime gave him a dressing down: Hey, you don't look the part, my friend! You don't look like one of the lads, we're not taking you on the job! You look like some sort of tramp! Mais had to go on the job again so that he had some money to his name when he eventually sodded off to Germany.

He decided to get his hair cut, so he had to go and see the black guy. Mais hardly spoke English, and the black guy only spoke French, for some reason he didn't like speaking English, whenever he switched to English his lips would curl, and he would talk with an air of disdainful condescension, as if he were talking to someone who was mentally retarded. He liked me because I never said a word to him in English! That's why he called me *mon frère* and cut my hair for free. We got to know each other after he started looking after the stolen goods. I was the one who persuaded him to do it, and he would always say that he did it out of respect for me. Back then I performed the role of interpreter for all the camp crooks, and would talk the black guys and other francophones into buying stolen stuff, or at least into looking after it and selling it on at their own price. I got nothing, or nearly nothing for that, apart from a chance to practise my French, and a free ration of food. On this occasion I accompanied Mais to the hairdresser to interpret. As ever, on our way we stopped for a while by the map of Europe which was hanging up in the hall. As ever, Mais pointed out the place where he would eventually cross the border. "Right there, see my friend," he said. "Mais will go alone, completely alone. Across Jutland, Zhenya-djan, Mais will go. Right here, brother-djan, he'll go. Oh, and here's where Mais will cross the border, my friend. Alone, understand, my friend, completely alone, no one else will come, at night, through the forest, that's how, brother-djan…"

"Yes, yes," I would say, nodding, yes, yes… and we headed off to the hairdresser's.

Jean-Claude sat Mais down in the corridor, daintily fixed a cloth round his neck, lightly touched his hair, and announced that it needed a wash. I translated, and Mais said, "Why does he need to wash it? Tell him just to cut it! Tell him I'll wash it later – what's the point of washing it twice a day, it's a waste of shampoo! Tell him to just cut it!"

I gently asked Jean-Claude to make a start on the haircut. He asked how to style it. Mais asked for a number zero.

"Aha," said Jean-Claude. "Then he'll be like a real Parisian."

I translated for Mais. It was something to see his eyes light up.

"Oh, yes, yes, yes," he said, "of course! Like a Parisian! Just like our Aznavour, like our Djorkaeff! They're real Armenians, you know! And proper French guys all have Armenian roots! They're the ones who ran from the Turks! The Turks wanted to annihilate us Armenians, leave behind nothing but a stuffed doll in the museum! Look, they'd say, there used to be this race called Armenians, and now all that's left of them is this stuffed doll! But they didn't succeed! They didn't succeed! The Armenians were the first in Europe to convert to Christianity! The first! You get it, right? That's how it was! The Turks couldn't slaughter all of us! They slaughtered the Kurds! They slaughtered the Assyrians! They slaughtered the Byzantines! But not us! That's how it was, you get it?"

"Right, right," I agreed with him. You had to agree with whatever this well-versed young man said, otherwise he could go for the jugular, this stuff was sacred to him, it got him so agitated, so worked up. But I was just trying to stop myself from bursting out laughing.

Meanwhile Jean-Claude had started grumbling, "Too much dandruff, it's no good, I'll have to wash his hair! He probably washes it once a month!"

"Tell him to stop yakking so much and do his stuff! Tell him to just cut my hair! I'm in a hurry! What's he going on about?" said Mais.

I said that the hairdresser was expressing his admiration for his hair, it was so oily, so beautiful, it just seemed wrong to cut it. I told Jean-Claude that his client said he had an itchy spot, he recently had some sort of eczema. Jean-Claude grew uneasy, "Then I probably shouldn't cut his hair at all? It might be catching!"

"What's he stressing about?" Mais asked.

I said that the hairdresser had spotted an unusual lump on Mais's skull, he was worried that he might cut the vein if he shaved that bit.

"It's nothing, tell him to go ahead – that's just where I was dropped as a kid!" Mais said. "Anyway, what do you think of Kasparov, Zhenya-djan? Eh? No one plays chess better than him, right? Karpov's just a kid, right? Listen, they say that Kasparov once beat a computer. He's a motherfucker, right? A real master, brother-djan, right? I see he's doing adverts for watches now – Rolex! Hey, I wonder how much he got for that, what do you reckon?"

Meanwhile Jean-Claude was effing and blinding. He was shaking so hard from rage and revulsion as he cleaned the dandruff out of his clippers that you could see his skin twitch, like ripples running across a horse's coat on a windy day. To me he seemed not so much naked, more like his skin had been stripped from him. It didn't end there, because when Jean-Claude finished and asked for his twenty kroner, Mais calmly said, "My friend, tell him that I'll give it to him later – tomorrow, or sometime later..."

And he didn't pay him for a whole two weeks, not until Jean-Claude turned up with his crew and kicked up a stink. They would never have had the nerve if they didn't know just how important it was for the crooks to have a place to store their stolen goods. Tiko also knew all too well that having a storehouse, a safe storehouse, the kind which the cops wouldn't come and shake down – that was vitally important. You would only be searched if you had been caught before, and the Cameroons and Congolese never took risks. The Algerians were on the nick, the Moroccans were on the nick, they were impossible to work with, they would rob you blind themselves. But the Cameroons and Congolese – never! The blacker the African the more restrained his behaviour. Tiko stole a lot and sometimes he got caught. They searched him from time to time. The last time they confiscated everything, even the stuff he bought fair and square. And so it would have cost him to fall out with the black guys. He looked morosely at Mais, sniffed the snot right up to the back of his flared nostrils, and said, "Give him the money, otherwise I'll give it to him, then you'll owe me!" For some reason he said that in Russian, so as to make sure that the Russians, the Georgians, the Kurds, and the black guys who understood Russian all knew of his decision. Feeling the pressure of the whole camp on him Mais reached into his pocket, muttering expletives in Georgian for some reason.

This encounter took place shortly after Mais had

received a videotape – a kind of video message – from an acquaintance of his who had left for America and then gone into business, or started some racket, or hell knows what it was. Some sort of stick-up operation. Mais brought the tape round one time. Hanuman put it into the machine, and we witnessed the following scene: a large room – evidently in some villa – a pack of yobs with Armenian exteriors, some glamorous girls, and this is what they were up to. One guy, who Mais said was his schoolmate, went from briefcase to briefcase, opening them up and shaking dollar notes from them, then the girls jumped about in the dollar bills, they danced half-naked in them and rolled about on the floor, which was carpeted with green banknotes, while the guys poured champagne over them. At the end of the video that same guy shouted something to Mais in Armenian, shook the gold chain round his neck, flashed his gold teeth, rolled his eyes, moved his nose so it looked like a beak, and flashed his teeth again. It wasn't clear what he was shouting but the video had a stupefying effect on Mais. His face dropped, then he turned ashen grey, then he turned black, he looked like a mummy which was about to disintegrate. He shook like a paralytic, muttered indistinctly, paced round the room repeatedly approaching the window, swore in Georgian for some reason, banged his fists on the walls and the table, kicked the chairs, closed his eyes, moaned in despair, smoked, and tried to yank his own hair out, but there wasn't any left. Then he tried to bite his own elbow, but he couldn't. He left, forgetting to take the video with him. Hanny whacked it on again. But then Mais came back, took it out of the machine, and stamped it to bits right in front of us, he smashed it to little pieces! (What a shame, I thought to myself, those scenes were priceless!) Mais stopped eating, even when he was offered food for free. He just lay in his room, shaking from fever, smoking, suffering from some illness, and a little while later he pressed "stop" on his asylum process. That's to say he asked for his case to be wound up, and went back to Armenia – that video had clearly made that strong an impression on him. That's the story of how Mais left for Germany...

Later I overheard Potapov and Ivan smoking on the sly behind our building. I was going for a number two in the bushes, and I heard Mikhail complaining about his stepdaughter, cursing, and pouring out his heart. I couldn't hear it all, some of the words were carried away on the wind or muffled by the rustling of branches. I couldn't hear Ivan's voice at all, but I could hear Mikhail pretty distinctly, and he delivered more or less the following monologue: "Damn it, just imagine, she's just such a liar! Just imagine! You wouldn't believe it, would you? But I twigged that it was her... Ah, you understand, my heart was full of kindness towards her, but she just... But it was such a good opportunity, a real opportunity, that's right... to make her my daughter officially... in my passport... Masha and I both said that she's our daughter, and that's how they wrote it, you understand... I had been longing to do it...! Ever since back there in... and now I feel nothing for her... she's a complete stranger to me, a complete stranger... I can't get through to her at all...!"

Those words of his made me sick, I couldn't bear to listen. It brought home to me that nothing ever changes. You could update ten passports, but it wouldn't change a thing. You could bury yourself in the ground, but they could still come and dig you up and take you back to Estonia! Straight back to Tallinn! That was such a dismal thought, so dismal... sometimes in a motif which bears no resemblance to our own we recognise the single truth which determines the fates of us all, a truth which is flawless and remorseless, and sends a shiver down our spines. As much as you try to escape, the end is always the same...

To try and quell the disquiet, to stop chasing those same thoughts round in circles, I took some tablets which I nabbed from Nepalino, had a smoke, and fell asleep. I slept for days on end, noticing nothing that went on around me. I didn't notice the arrival of Christmas, I didn't notice the Potapovs leaving the camp or Ivan Durachkov moving into their room. That room was where we celebrated Christmas. I had never been inside Mikhail's place before. When I first entered it I was amazed to see not only that Mikhail had turned it into some sort of pigsty, but he'd made a hole in the floor as well! According to Ivan it was a cellar, where Mikhail had kept potatoes and other stuff. Evidently Potapov couldn't resist creating a replica of the world he had inhabited back in Russia. Just like many of the other camp people. Nearly everyone did something similar, they all suffered from a similar affliction. Everyone's national origins emerged and manifested themselves in some way. But this was going too far – a hole in the ground, that was too much! I was curious about where the Potapovs had gone. Ivan told me they'd moved to the ruins not far from the camp. My heart froze when I heard that: no one could survive out there, and Masha was pregnant. She was due any day now. We had driven past that deserted house a few times, and every time I had felt a pang of horror. There was nothing in that old bunker, no electricity, no running water and a bucket for a toilet. "There is a stove," I asserted, offering an ascetic's defence. He hummed and hawed for a while before adding that they had already built a fireplace in the larger room, although for some reason it gave off a lot of smoke. Their fireplaces had never given off smoke before, but this one apparently did. "They're breathing in those fumes, they could suffocate," Ivan said, concern written across his innocent face.

Later they invited us to their house-warming. It was a short visit. The building was so old that it seemed the roof could collapse in on us at any moment. It was damp, and there was a distinct and insistent smell of death, of something which must have died some time ago. It was so awful that I spent the whole time thinking I should go outside for a smoke and then just forget to go back in. I had the feeling I should be sending someone a condolence telegram. I started to feel uneasy, as if I were trying to recall something, something which I had promised to someone, somewhere I had promised to go, something I was supposed to take somewhere, something I was supposed to do... a constant mental itch. But these thoughts were absurd, because I had nowhere I was supposed to go and no one to see, and I had long been incapable of promising to do anything for anyone, so I never did anything at all... which meant that all this must have just been me hunting desperately for a pretext to get the hell out of there, as soon as I possibly could!

The ruins belonged to the dairy farmer, Henning, who sold milk to Mikhail on the cheap. We often saw him, as the maize fields belonged to him too, and he would drive round them on his tractor. He came to the camp to pick up shit, then he would fertilise his fields, and one could imagine the satisfaction he got from knowing that the smell of shit wafted back on to the camp, in through our windows and doors.

Potapov hit it off with Henning, although it was unclear how they communicated, and unclear what yarns Mikhail had spun to the Danish guy, but somehow he had persuaded him to let them live in the ruins. The building had no windows, the walls were fecund from damp, the roof leaked. That's putting it mildly: the roof had a hole in it which looked like a missile had landed there! The first thing Mikhail did was send Ivan up on to the roof to put some plastic sheeting over the hole. They clubbed together to buy some panes of glass, and glazed the windows. They laid down some sort of artificial matting which they nabbed from the scrapheap, and put a carpet down over it. They dragged everything they could from the camp, arranged things to try and make the place as homely as possible, parked the car in the cattle shed, warmed the house through, and moved in for Christmas. They had to spend the whole of Christmas Eve dragging a power cable up from the camp, hacking away at the frozen ground, sinking the cable into the soil, bringing it right up to the house. And so now they had electricity, but no money left at all.

I shuddered when I thought about the distance from the camp to the house. They had to dig such a long trench and drag the cable all that way. How much must they have spent on the cable itself? But Ivan just smiled: it didn't cost a thing, do you think it's hard, in a country like this, where all kinds of stuff gets left lying about, to reach out and take yourself a bit of cable, even one thousand metres of it…

Hanuman started to chuckle, but then he stopped, and he seemed lost in thought for a while. And then, when that first visit to the Potapovs' was over, after we had shuddered in the bone-numbing cold, after we had inhaled lungfuls of carbon monoxide and finally fled from that dank, dismal place, he said, "That guy is totally crazy! It would be one thing to move in on his own, but he's forcing his whole family to live in that hellhole with him! They'll all go down with tuberculosis!"

When I saw the fireplace which Potapov had fashioned I realised that I had been right to doubt his craftsmanship. I probably could have created a monstrosity like that myself. It was little wonder that the fireplace gave off so much sooty smoke.

The first frosts struck, and it started to snow, so heavily that the roads quickly became unpassable. The Potapovs ended up being cut off. Mikhail was too short and too bowlegged to be able to make his way through the snowdrifts. He called Ivan at the camp using the walkie-talkie which they found at the scrapheap, and asked him to bring them potatoes from the cellar and milk from Henning.

Meanwhile, Maria went into labour, early and without warning. It took ages for the ambulance to find them because Mikhail couldn't explain how to get there, and so Maria basically gave birth at home. Mikhail delivered the child himself, as he later recounted with pride, although Maria said that he almost fainted at the sight of the umbilical cord. The ambulance came and took them all away, and brought them all back a bit later. While they were gone we waited there with Liza.

We had to spend two days at that awful place, it was horrible. There was a terrible wind, a constant crashing, juddering, creaking, singing, sobbing and whining. The power cable must have snapped, because we had to sit by candlelight. We stoked the stove; I had forbidden Ivan from making a fire in the fireplace. Hanuman cooked some food, and Liza happily ate it, without playing up at all. But then some strange things started happening, things which even I didn't expect. Liza came up to me and asked, "Do you like my new haircut?" to which I replied, "It's OK", although I couldn't really tell the difference. Then she told me she'd cut it herself. I inspected more closely, and in the murky light I could see that there were big clumps of hair missing – it was horrific. I discovered the hair by the table, it was lying about all over the place, together with some bits of paper which had been scrawled on with crayons. It felt creepy finding those things lying there together. Then I went to wash the dishes and came across the toothpaste which had been squeezed out near the sink, a whole tube of toothpaste, a mound of toothpaste smeared across the floor. I started to feel very uneasy.

Hanuman whispered to me: get your fill of thrills, Johan! You won't see stuff like this in any film, it's a proper nightmare! "Yes, yes," I replied distractedly, "yes, yes"… but that was all I said… what were you supposed to say in a situation like this? There was nothing else to say!

It looked like they had hung new wallpaper, probably to hide the dampness and unevenness of the walls. But the damp and the mould had already started devouring the paper. And as much as we stoked the stove, it didn't get any warmer. That scrawny little girl didn't seem to feel the cold, she would throw off her clothes and walk about in thin socks like a ballerina, stepping across the floor where strange shoots had pushed themselves up through the cracks. She walked on tiptoe, and danced and talked. She talked to us, although we got the impression that it was just a monologue which sounded in her head the whole time, and that she was only saying it out loud because we happened to be there, although it was possible she said the same stuff when there was no one there. This is what she said: "If I was a Danish girl I would have Danish parents they would have number plates on their car Daddy wouldn't beat me he'd buy me ice cream every day and we would go to the cinema and McDonald's I would go to school with Danish children I would have friends I would have everything I wanted even a Sony PlayStation and lots and lots of toys I would do everything I wanted Mummy would give me five kroner for tidying up my room and I would have my own room and five kroner that's five Chupa Chups or five Baldur colas and enough left over for Chupa Chups too, but now I'm going to have a brother he'll get Danish citizenship Mummy went to give birth to a Danish citizen, now we'll definitely get to stay in Denmark and I will go to a Danish school and Lia will die of jealously when she finds out that I've gone to a Danish school I don't need a friend like her any more she's so sick and crazy I don't need friends like her I'm going to have Danish friends now they've all got Sony PlayStations and lots and lots of toys we will all go to McDonald's together and the cinema and Aquapark or Waterland in our new car Daddy will definitely get a new car and number plates and money because we'll get a yes and they'll call my brother Adam because we're Christians and we believe in God not Allah and those idiots believe in Allah they don't wipe their bums with paper they wash them with water the idiots…"

Hanuman laughed for ages when he found out that

236

Mikhail had named his son Adam just to spite the Muslims. And he was almost in tears when he heard that Mikhail believed he would now get right of abode, just because they had a child! He yelled, "Oh, you fool! This isn't America or even Ireland! It's Denmark! Denmark! When are you going to realise?"

The house was full of all sorts of junk, and it seemed to proliferate in the half-light. Every time we visited there was more and more junk, and all of those objects seemed to go regularly for a wander. It never got the slightest bit lighter there either. It was hard to say what the hell was going on, what the objects were that you stumbled across; the imagination would run riot. There were the most fantastical pieces of machinery, and we managed to get a closer look at some of them… spinning wheels, threshing machines, even a mangle… a strange piece of equipment, which Potapov had hung an oil lamp above. It was a hulking great thing, it had a huge wheel with a handle on it, and two large rollers, into which, according to Potapov, one was supposed to feed the washing. Although there was no certainty that this was in fact a mangle, no one had actually tried it out. No one apart from Mikhail that is, who assured everyone that it was definitely a mangle. Nothing less! What do you mean? What else could it be? And his eyes goggled, as if he were talking about a perpetual motion machine. His honour was on the line, his right to call himself an expert in mechanics! He bent himself double trying to prove his point. It is a mangle! A medieval device for ironing the lord of the manor's sheets. That's that! There's nothing else this monstrosity could be! He would sometimes take guests up to the machine and start explaining how it worked, he would even demonstrate by inserting a pre-prepared rag between the rollers, extracting it from the other side and letting his guest feel how smooth the rag was. Lots of people had fallen into that trap, and had seen that rag pass through the rollers without it becoming in the slightest bit smoother.

As hard as he tried, Potapov's goggle-eyed demonstration didn't convince anyone that this was in fact a mangle. But he was not in the slightest bit perturbed, he continued to insist that it was definitely a mangle! He would reiterate his point at the most inopportune moments. He was obsessed with that mangle. It was his *idée fixe*! A canker on his soul. A trapped nerve in his ego which gave him no peace. He started to sense his authority was being undermined, and all because of those damned idiots sitting there in that camp, laughing at him: a mangle, what else could it be! As soon as he got out of the camp he had become hostile to the place and everyone who lived there. They were now his sworn enemies. According to him, every last one of us, our whole motley crew, should have moved out and come to rot in those ruins with him, and turned into phantoms, or if it came to that, into cattle on Potapov's farm. He would milk us, or drive us out on to his field like sheep: "Go! Go and steal something! Don't come back without potatoes!" That's how he would order us about... He was sure that a conspiracy had been hatched against him at the camp, that everyone was laughing at him... They were just waiting for him to plant his tomatoes, for his cucumbers to ripen, then they would come and steal them, steal his cucumbers, steal his tomatoes! Aaaahhh...!

There was no conspiracy. But they did laugh at him. And they would twirl their fingers at their temples. They ended up with bruised temples thanks to that fat-arsed idiot! But it made no difference to him, he carried on giving those demonstrations of his ironing theory! If only to distract his guests from the bizarre conditions which he forced his family to live in. That was why he needed that mangle, so as to distract peoples' attention from the horrors, the shadowy phantoms, the tuberculosis lurking there, from the mould, the cold, and the gloom... just take a look at this marvellous antique machine!

There was already bric-a-brac of every description there,

but Potapov would compound the chaos on a daily basis with stuff from the scrapheap and the second-hand shops. One of the things which turned up was a little cupboard, a nasty old cupboard, fit for nothing better than to be ceremoniously dispatched to the scrapheap or chucked on the bonfire. The cupboard wasn't just nasty to look at, in fact I never really got a proper look at it (other than hazy outlines in the gloom, because there was virtually no light there). The nastiest thing about it was that I kept bumping into it, if not with my knee, then my shin. Me and that cupboard grew to have a fraught relationship. It seemed to change position on a regular basis. Somehow I couldn't seem to avoid it, one way or another it would get me. An open lower drawer to the ankle! Or an upper door opening unexpectedly into my forehead! That cupboard drove me to distraction! Potapov said he needed it to hang up what he called his "work clothes". In other words, stuff that was just as useless as the cupboard itself. It would have been easier just to get rid of some of the useless junk, but he couldn't bring himself to, so he came up with a solution: he brought home yet another useless object, one of larger dimensions, in which to place all the rest of the junk! A pair of torn old baseball boots appeared from that cupboard on several occasions. One time a jacket emerged which Mikhail donned to crawl under the car (that jacket was fit only to be worn under a car). It was from that cupboard that he produced the tatty sheepskin coat which he wore when he cleared the snow from in front of his so-called garage gates, which could charitably be described as the pigsty doors.

The cupboard stood in the corner of the room, and there was a smell of benzene wafting from behind it; it hit you as you entered the room, as if there was an open barrel of the stuff standing there. That was where the generator was, which produced the electricity. Mikhail would start it up whenever someone appeared near the house, so that the cable which he had illegally connected up wouldn't arouse any suspicions. A member of camp staff called Ole often passed by; he spied on everyone, but he took a particularly maniacal interest in Potapov, who he saw as his enemy, his personal enemy, who he was obliged to bring to justice. Potapov reckoned that he had been given an order from on high, from the Department, to expose him. And so whenever anyone turned up near the house he would switch on the generator, which would roar, rasp, groan and howl like a hungry pack of wolves. The din would wake Adam, and he would start crying. I felt sorry for that baby. I reckoned that anyone who had to hear that racket every single day of their childhood was likely to grow up mentally scarred.

Once again we had ended up with virtually no money, and vacillating… until Hanuman had a stroke of genius, which led to another even bigger stroke of genius, which eventually resulted in me shaving off my beard, starting to brush my teeth, tidying up my act, and all the rest of it…

Hanuman had a telephone, a really old Siemens. It was big, battered, scuffed, but reliable, with wood-effect casing. The buttons were all worn, so that it was impossible to make out the numbers and letters, but that didn't matter. Hanuman knew the phone so well that he didn't need any symbols, he would always dial the right number without fail, by touch in the dark or in whatever condition he happened to be in. And he knew all his numbers off by heart, because it was risky to keep any numbers written down, in case we got caught. The phone numbers could be used to work stuff out. So it was dangerous to have any bits of paper on you. And clothes too, clothes which were only manufactured in the country you came from. When I arrived in Copenhagen, for example, the first thing which my uncle did was tell me to take off my Sangar cord trousers and my Sangar T-shirt, because they could be used to determine that I'd arrived from Estonia.

But regardless of how well Hanuman knew his telephone, he never, or hardly ever called anyone, because the phone never had any credit. You could receive calls, but you couldn't make them. Or you could, but for some reason it was best not to (although it was never made clear exactly why). Hanuman told me that the phone was a present from his Swedish girlfriend, and she had bought the kind of SIM card for it which worked all over Europe. He always kept it switched on, always recharged it in good time and always kept it close at hand. He was always expecting a call! And it was clearly very important that he was ready to take that call! He kept us in a constant state of suspense! He made it very clear to us that he might get a call at any moment! And it could be absolutely anyone! It could be one of his wives, of which there were an untold number, all living in different countries! We were constantly reminded of that fact, we were all made very aware that he had numerous wives waiting for him, that he was in great demand, that they were all begging him to come home, that none of them could live without him, and that this was worth far more than getting refugee status. Or even a British passport.

"Because," began Hanuman, honing in on us, "so many people have got British passports! And they're all so, so lonely! No one gives a damn about them! They spend their whole lives phoning the sex channels, ejaculating on the screen! They call the sex lines, wank off, and waste their sperm! Look into Prince Charles' eyes! You reckon he's never had phone sex? Of course he has! Just take a look at him!" Hanuman slapped his hand on to his porno mag, where the prince was depicted as a character in some smutty comic strip. "Who gives a shit about him? He's lonely! He's hopelessly lonely, and no one wants him, no one at all, the poor guy! He reckons that England needs him! How mistaken he is! England is the last place of all which needs him. They need him even less than anyone needs that Chinese heir of Prince Joachim's sitting on the Danish throne! But me, I'm different!"

That's right, no one could do without Hanuman! He was irreplaceable! It might be his mother calling, or a girlfriend from Prague, or one from Bucharest, or a wife from Australia, or India (the least preferable option), or in the worst case it might be Daddy's favourite, that's to say his brother, or even *Daddy himself*... or some illegal immigrant, or Laszlo, who still owed us money; after all, we had assembled those computers, and they were supposedly on sale, and someone was supposedly going to buy them, and Laszlo was going to call us, and then Svenaage would turn up with our money. Hanuman was waiting for a call from Greece, where one of his ideas might bear fruit at any moment, where he might be required in the capacity of manager of some newly formed corporation, or in some other role. He was waiting for a call from his mentor, they had a joint project which could lead to the construction of an amazing building, which would house the cinema of the future, which would put all other cinemas out of business, which would make Hanuman's name immortal! That's right! That very same Hanuman who was sitting in front of us on his grubby bed, rocking his leg backwards and forwards! This was our immortal Hanuman! So when Hanuman was sitting there with his mobile phone in his pocket, he wasn't just sitting there, he was waiting for a call! Hanuman wasn't just sitting there, he was busy! He had business to take care of! He had a deal in the offing! He had plans! Projects! People who depended on him! Anyone could call him, because he gave everyone his number. It might be Liberty Bushevangu, Madam Sonya, someone with AIDS, a Pakistani guy, the owner of some restaurant where he was hoping to get work; he gave absolutely everyone his phone number. He tried to convince everyone that he was important, that his help might be required, that he had several university degrees, that his services might come in handy, that you couldn't do without him, that he was irreplaceable! Need an expert in Indian cuisine? Hanuman's your man! Need to pick up secret signals from the Pentagon using a TV aerial? Hanuman's your man! Need to tune in your satellite receiver? Hanuman's your man! Need a computer specialist? Hanuman's your man! Need to set up a web page and mailbox? Hanuman's the man for the job! No one else will do. Well, maybe someone else could do it, but not as cheaply and not as well as Hanuman! He can perform any task, solve any problem, cure you daughter's angina, your computer's virus, your cat's cough, your dog's distemper, and he'll relieve your Christmas tree of fir cones and presents too! He'll teach you how to live your life, he'll initiate you into the sacred rites of yoga, he'll show you tricks, he'll teach you how to walk in your sleep or along a tightrope, and how to speak Chinese. He'll sort you out with a pardon from the Pope, a place in heaven, a room in a pyramid, or a seat on a satellite orbiting Earth, and if you want he'll get your waxwork in Madame Tussaud's, while you're still alive. Just go and see Hanuman, and problem solved! And all his services come virtually cost-free! He's the only man for the job! Him alone, no one else will do!

But his phone rang infrequently, maybe only once a month. And then he would leap up, grab the phone, and he could talk for ages, sometimes hours on end. He would inform us that it was his father calling from India, or his wife from Rome, or his girlfriend from Sweden. I was always amazed by how long these calls lasted, it seemed as if the callers weren't paying. One time he told me that they weren't, that the owner of the phone had to pay, and that the phone belonged to someone who no longer existed, or who had never existed, because it was a fictitious subscriber, a phantom who paid for everything. And all the calls went via the Internet, and his girlfriend sorted it out. Although it seemed she couldn't go quite as far as other hackers and make the outgoing calls free too. That is, he could call out if he wanted, but then he wouldn't be able to use the phone much longer, the telephone company would catch on to him and shut down the number.

I didn't understand any of that stuff, and to be honest I didn't even try to. I wasn't that worried about his telephones, I was more worried about my own poor feet! In any case, he had got me confused, or it seemed like he had got me confused, or it seemed that he wanted to confuse me in some way... or maybe it was just my paranoia playing up again. I always suspected people of trying to trick me, of pulling the wool over my eyes...

And then it occurred to me once again that Hanuman may have been assigned to me to work out who I really was, that he was working for some unidentified agency, maybe Interpol. And when that suspicion stirred within me, then every word he said seemed to have been said for a certain reason, every gesture seemed somehow contrived, premeditated, and fundamentally fake, as he was himself, to the very core. And you didn't need to be paranoid to think that. Anyone in their right mind could see it, which was why Hanuman could only exist and have his wily way amongst the outcasts, underdogs, and untouchables, the losers and outsiders of this world. I had one word to describe it all, and that word was "Hanumania".

One time he turned up soaking wet. He was carrying an umbrella, but he was still wet through. There was snow melting on his shoulders, but he didn't seem to notice. He was shaking, but he didn't notice that either. His eyes were gleaming. He said that the hard times were over, that from now on we would have money.

"Not as much as we'd like, but all the same... And who knows, it's enough for starters, to make the first push, to get the ball rolling, it'll be enough for wine and hash at least. And we'll definitely be able to eat better, that's for sure! And then if we're lucky we'll get to Lolland too, heh!"

I was sceptical. Hanuman and his delusions of grandeur,

I thought to myself, lying under my quilt, scratching. I lay there listening to him, just turning my head slightly in his direction.

He stood there tall, lean, brown, exquisite, smiling radiantly, illuminated in the light of the desktop lamp which sat on top of that useless television, the television which no longer worked, because no one heated it with the hairdryer any more (no one had the patience).

"We need a receiver," he said enigmatically.

"What kind of receiver?"

"A telephone receiver of course," he said, "just a receiver and a cable, I'll do the rest myself…"

And then he explained what he was on about. He'd gone for a stroll in the part of Farstrup where the refugees and other such scum never normally went, where the local Lolitas roller-skated, where there were proper public squares and pavements. There were often kids playing on their skateboards up there, and ravers partying. The upstanding citizens of Farstrup walked their dogs there, carrying plastic bags to clean up the shit. There was a red-brick building there; small, pretty. It was called the Raadhus, and it had a similar function to the local council in the Soviet Union. That's where they deliberated local affairs where they carried out various registration processes, where they signed documents, concluded contracts, where meetings and other such nonsense took place. Behind this building there was a box, a transmitter which housed the telephone cables. All you had to do was open up the box, which you could do using a common screwdriver, then hook up to the cables. You just had to poke about a bit, which you could do with a common pair of pliers, then you had to use the receiver to select the right line, and that was it – you could call wherever you liked, Argentina even. The main thing was that it had to be one of those phones with buttons built into the receiver. I told him that I found it hard to get excited about the idea, I couldn't see the point of it; there wasn't anyone I wanted to call, especially not in Argentina. And I couldn't understand how this was supposed to make our lives better, where the wine and hashish would come from, just by hooking up to some telephone cable, even if we managed to patch our way into the Pentagon.

He puffed up his cheeks and chuckled, "What an idiot you are! You've smoked yourself silly! Do you really not understand? Can't you see how many people there are in this camp who would jump at the chance of phoning their relatives cheaper, and risk-free? People are scared that their calls are being monitored! That the authorities will rumble who they're calling, and kick them out of the country! Surely you're not such an idiot! You've been loafing about in bed for too long! You've gone soft in the head and don't understand how the world works any more! We're going to charge money for phone calls! They'll be three times cheaper than their phone cards or mobiles, you understand? Even cheaper than the Albanians' pirated SIM cards!"

I remained sceptical about Hanuman's latest brainwave. But he succeeded in infecting Potapov and Durachkov with the idea. Although that wasn't difficult. It didn't require much effort, they were ready to swallow anything. They were clearly just waiting to be fed the latest scheme, however absurd. They didn't care what they did, just as long as they didn't have to sit about indoors, or mooch around the camp, looking at the vile mugs of the other camp dwellers. They were dying of boredom! And so when Hanny told them that there was some business which needed taking care of, they brought back a telephone receiver and some cable from the scrapheap the same evening, and found something in the car glove compartment which Potapov called crocodiles. They rolled up at the Raadhus that very night, forced open the transmitter, and hooked themselves up. They phoned Russia and India right away, chuckling to themselves. Then they took the cable and dragged it as far as the roadside, submerging it in the snow-dusted lawn and the gaps between the paving stones, they insulated it, and they concealed it under a tuft of grass. The next day they invited two Tamils who were itching to phone Sri Lanka to take a seat in their car, drove them back to that spot, hooked up the receiver without arousing any suspicions, and let the Tamils phone. They fleeced each of them for around one hundred and fifty kroner for those lengthy phone calls, and then headed to Aalborg to buy some hash.

The next day they brought a Somalian who liked calling the other end of the earth for nights on end. He coughed up three hundred kroner. Next up were the Albanians. But they only talked for a bit. As Potapov said they were too stingy to call for any longer, even if it was on the cheap.

"An Albanian is an Albanian, even in Africa," Durachkov said.

Every night they would drive people up to the phone, and then come back at daybreak, stoned.

But even if Hanuman now had money in his pocket, it didn't improve the quality of my life one bit. I ate just as badly as before, mostly what I was given, which meant rice and beans with chilli sauce, or a sausage of some sort if I was lucky. I couldn't drink anything, or smoke. The carnival of life which had whisked away Hanuman and the two Russians passed me by, and I remained studiously indifferent to it all. I knew that this latest money-spinner would wind up pretty soon. In a week or two the people at the Raadhus would look at their phone bill and see that someone had been calling Sri Lanka and Kathmandu, Kinshasa and Bangkok, and they would check their transmitter. And one of the more alert neighbours or passers-by would inform the police (there were plenty of patriots around) that some car had been parked by the Raadhus at night with foreigners sitting in it, and the next thing you know they'd stage an ambush! And then why not comb the camp too…

I shared these concerns with Hanuman and the two Russians, which made them stop and think, and they decided to wait, they laid low for a while. But then, as if by coincidence (although nothing really happens by coincidence) Bacho turned up with his phone. Although it wasn't Bacho himself, but the young guy Zenon, together with some loony compatriot who had just bought a phone off Bacho. It was a stolen phone and it didn't want to work. The Georgian had sold it to the Albanian, demonstrating that it was in working order. But when the Albanian tried to use the phone it locked. They tried everything with that phone (Hanuman winced as Zenon told him), and it was an expensive one, he had paid three hundred and seventy kroner for it (he'd knocked the price down from four hundred). The Albanian tried to get his money back, but the Georgians just said, "Why, my friend? Eh, telephone arbaiten du, you saw it yourself, sod off you twat!" And so the young guy went to see Zenon, who was an expert in all sorts of electronic equipment, and could speak all the languages commonly spoken in the camp. Zenon brought him to us.

Hanuman took the telephone, inserted his SIM card into it, and it started working.

"There you go, it works," said Hanuman. "It works with my card, chuck away your old card, buy a new one, and then phone all you like…"

When the Georgians found out that Hanuman had unblocked the stolen phone which they had managed to palm off on the Albanian before the former owner had cancelled the card, they went to see him, and asked, "Hey, how did you do that? That phone was blocked, and you got it working just like that? Show me your phone!"

Hanuman showed them, then showed them again, and then said, "Give me any card, I'll show you something…"

They gave him a SIM card which no longer worked, he fitted it into his phone and with a few presses of the buttons he activated the card, then right before their very eyes he called the neighbouring room, from where Potapov appeared, then he called his ex-wife in Bombay, then Bucharest, while the Georgians stood there gawping...

"Hey, how'd you do that, eh?" they asked, looking at me for some reason, but my mouth was wide open too, I had no idea what was happening. I hid my amazement by feigning boredom, as if to say, Show me the Seven Wonders of the World, it all just bores me! He gave them the card, they inserted it into their phone and tried to call, but nothing happened; they were flabbergasted.

"Hey, let's have a look at your phone! How'd you do that, eh?"

Hanuman gave them the phone. He was enjoying being the centre of attention. He spread his arms wide and told them that the phone was a present from his favourite wife, it had been purchased in Sweden, and it was a special phone, it could unlock any code, PIN and PUK codes, and any card would work in it...

"Hey, how'd you do that, eh? Hey, sell it to us! How much do you want for it?"

"No, the phone's not for sale, it was a gift from my favourite wife, there's no point haggling, all I can do is let you use it, but only for money..."

"Eh, what gift..."

"What do you mean it's not for sale, everything's for sale..." they said, but it was in vain, Hanny wasn't going to sell the phone, he stuck to the offer of letting them use it to make a call, but for money, only for money...

But of course they declined, for them it was a matter of principle not to spend their own money on anything. Other than maybe as a diversion while they robbed something else. Or on hash. But they preferred to steal that and other drugs whenever they could. Every dealer in town would fall prey to them sooner or later. Either they burgled his joint, or they beat him up and rifled through his pockets. But they respected me and Hanuman. Of course they would talk about us behind our backs, call us fucking faggots, stupid twats, butt-faced skivvies, pond life, bitches and fucking bastards, but they always greeted us with a smile, and they would often be pretty frank with us. At the end of the day they reckoned that we were pretty handy thieves, and that we had our heads screwed on right.

Although I think they were wrong, not just as far as I was concerned, but about Hanuman too. His head hadn't been screwed on right for a long time. But he somehow created the impression of being savvy about everything, or at least he tried to.

He could talk about absolutely anything. He could talk about telephones non-stop. He reckoned that the most important thing was not the phone itself, but having the right SIM card. One that wasn't stolen, a proper one. A clean, legit one, with a connection. The kind of card which could only be acquired by someone with right of abode, a bank account, and the rest of it, including a personal ID code, which was something we didn't have. Hanuman said that the telephony business was a real gold mine. If you could get your hands on phones like that then you could sell them to the refugees for big money. The refugees had the money to part with if you could convince them that they were acquiring a pirate phone or a phone with an unlimited call plan, which is basically what one of those phones was. At least for the first few days, that is.

The only kind of person who was prepared to go in on Hanuman's scam was someone who had nothing to lose, someone who had massive debts, or was waiting to be sent down at any moment. That kind of person wouldn't take much, just name your price, for one hundred or two hundred kroner he would sign up to a phone contract. Then you could sell the phone and the card for seven hundred or even a thousand kroner. But you had to buy the phone itself, and we had no money for that. We were washed up, on the rocks.

Maybe we had a bit of money, but not enough. I never

knew how much money Hanuman had in his pocket, that was the biggest secret of all. He would always say that you should never let anyone know how much money you had – especially women. And the less money you had, the more confident you should act, because that created an air of mystery which would deceive people and draw them in! He insisted that you should always behave as if you were standing right next to an inexhaustible well of money, and that sooner or later the well would blow, and the money would come gushing into your pocket! You could even say that behaving like that was in itself enough to make the money come your way.

And so it did. One day the Georgians turned up with a black – or pirate – telephone which had stopped working for some reason. Hanuman later explained to me that the number had been shut down, and the Georgians knew nothing about phone numbers, they didn't understand the principles of pirate phones at all… they reckoned that some wires had been soldered up inside it, so that you could phone just like that, like it was some sort of walkie-talkie, and they knew even less about cards and codes than I did, which was laughably little.

And so they brought the phone to us. Hanuman immediately twigged that we were dealing with clueless idiots, so he pretended to do some work on the phone, he fiddled about with it a bit, but eventually he summoned forth an expression of deepest regret and informed them that the telephone was broken, that it would never work again, and that they might as well chuck it away… then he threw it into the rubbish bin himself. But Bacho fished it out and said he would give it to his son to play with.

Over the next few days Hanuman observed Bacho's five-year-old son playing with that phone, he watched him shovelling sand with the phone's flip-top lid, and pushing the buttons to produce a melody, he saw the kid playing a game on it (he even helped him to play it). He looked on as Bacho's son slowly lost interest in his new toy and got more interested in other games, he saw Bacho's son beckon the Albanian kid over and say, "Goy teik tat baik iz for me, my fren, du kan teik, teik an give me my baik!", and Hanny saw the little Albanian go and take Liza's bike, and Potapov leap out and start whacking the Albanian, while the little Georgian boy stood there giggling and the phone became an even more distant memory... Hanuman pretty much watched the boy's every move, with a cunning smile on his face. Until one day the boy dropped the phone, walked away from it, grabbed the Serbian girl's ball, and ran off behind the building. Then Hanuman got up, walked up to the phone, picked it up, and came back to our room...

That very night Hanuman entered the code, found the account holder whose number he had hijacked, and made the first test call, first to India, then to Sweden, and the third to Bucharest.

"He-ha-ho!" Hanuman threw back his head and chuckled, tossing the phone up and down in the palm of his hand. "Oh the idiots, the idiots! It's good to be surrounded by such idiots! He-ha-ho!" Hanuman guffawed, and he put the phone on charge (we had more chargers than telephones, even more chargers than you would find telephones in a telephone shop).

He turned to me and asked me to get down from the bunk. Then he opened up the squeaky metal cabinet which he normally opened just once a week, took out a Gillette razor, shaving foam and shampoo, handed me a towel, and told me to go to the shower room and only come back when I was washed and shaved.

"We're leaving at the crack of dawn," he said with a stern tone. "I'm going to make the arrangements with Zenon and the driver. We've got work to do, and you have to look convincing, serious, and respectable."

When I got back from the shower, where I was temporarily detained by cuts to my neck and chin, I found a fresh, clean shirt waiting for me on my bed, together with trousers, a jacket, a coat, new shoes, all of which Hanny had just bought off the Georgians (they were suffering withdrawal symptoms and selling stuff for peanuts, just to scrape together enough cash for the next fix)…

"From now on you're going to be Russian mafia!" he informed me ominously. "We'll leave that one here," he said, nodding his head in the direction of Durachkov, who was observing Hanuman's activities inquisitively. "Mmm… that guy's face is somehow not right… it's painfully pitiful… anyway there's not going to be much room in the car, and who knows what else, or who else we'll need to find space for…"

"So then," he said, looking at Potapov. "That chain of yours, is it gold? Excellent, give it to Johan then! Only on loan, of course. Calm down! Give it to him! There you go! Try it on!"

They fitted the chain on to me, and I thrust my chest forwards.

"Wow, that's just right! Proper Russian mafia!" Hanuman exclaimed, taking a step backwards. "Wow! Do something about your face though!"

I pulled a drowsy expression, raising my eyebrows to make my forehead as lined as possible, and pursed my lips…

"That's pretty bad," said Hanny.

"Not like that…" said Durachkov.

"You never seen a proper gangster?" Potapov said mockingly, and he pulled a face which was dodgy enough to make you sick.

"No, I can't do it… No I can't… my feet are getting cold," I complained.

"Put these Ecco on! They're not just shoes, they're medicine for your feet!"

I slipped on those Ecco shoes and I immediately knew that I would never take them off again, even if they had only been given to me on a temporary basis. Not even if I got beaten up for them! Not even if I got given a kicking! I would never take them off, not ever! I would defend them with my life! I would wear only Ecco for the rest of my days! Even if I had to go without a jacket in winter, without underwear, without a hat, without the key to my flat, a flat where I'd have no money whatsoever, not even a nail to hang my coat, a coat which I anyway wouldn't possess! I wouldn't care! I would wear only Ecco! What bliss it was to ease my wounded feet into shoes like this! Oh! It felt like my feet had been reincarnated!

"There you go," Hanuman said, handing me a hairband. "Tie your hair back into a ponytail!"

I did what he told me. Hanny looked at me and said, "Wow, a real baron! Mafioso! Bravo, bravissimo! We're setting off in the morning, at six! On the dot!"

We started trundling round Jutland, going from camp to camp. Potapov was at the wheel, and Hanny and I looked for customers and charged them for phone calls. We made good money out of that. When the customer paid, Hanuman handed the money over to me in a professional manner, with an unctuous smile on his face. And in a similarly professional manner I counted the money and placed it inside Hanuman's leather wallet, which I kept in my pocket as if it were my own, if only for the time being. When the call session was over and there was no one left in the room to see, Hanuman took the wallet and counted the money again. Then he spent a while lost in thought, brow knitted and lips pursed, staring into the distance, as if he were trying to discern if the promised land to which we were striving had materialised, or trying to work out how much further this money would take us towards our dream. Then he would sigh and place the wallet back into his bottomless pocket, and he did so in such a way that I immediately lost any hope of ever seeing that money again.

Often we didn't need to spend any money on food. At every camp we would find an Indian or a Nepali who was willing not only to wash Hanuman's dishes after him, but his long-toed feet too, and that was on top of the food which they were obliged to provide, together with lodgings! They would sleep on the floor themselves, while Hanny and I slept in their beds. If Potapov stayed the night, then he would sleep on the floor as well!

My feet stank so badly that Hanuman would open the window for the night. Then he had the idea of tying cellophane bags on to them. A bit later, he bought some Indian ointments and instructed me to rub them on to my feet, and then gave me some strong-smelling red soap. He told me I should wash my feet three times a day. After that he got hold of some sort of powders for me, which I had to sprinkle into a bowl of water and soak my feet in before bed. I tried everything. I submerged my feet in boiling water, I plunged them into a snowdrifts, I rubbed those ointments on to them. Pretty soon not only had the scabs and the fungus disappeared, but the stench had dissipated too. Eventually my feet smelled as fragrant as lotus flowers. At least that's what Hanuman said.

I didn't have to do much. I just made myself look important, displaying disdain in my expressions and my gestures, and I spoke French with the black guys and English to the rest of them; tersely, gruffly, dryly informing them of the tariff. Me and Hanuman spoke Danish to each other, so that no one else would understand. As far as our clients were concerned I was a representative of the Russian mafia who had put down roots in Denmark, entirely legally. I pulled it off pretty well; people treated us with respect, awe even. Thank God that none of the Armenians or Georgians got wind of the fact that we were doing business on what was basically their turf. It all went very smoothly, we only just managed to recharge the phone in time for the next client. They made so many calls that the money poured into our pockets. But we had to enter new codes and hunt for new lines to hijack. Hanuman spent hours and hours on that...

Ten days flew past. We made enough money to stock up on hashish and wine for the whole winter. I was buoyed by a newfound optimism, and my feeling soon turned out to be warranted. One fine day Hanuman announced, "That's it! Basta! We heading back to base, via Aalborg!"

In Aalborg we bought hashish, had a smoke, and sat in that hash bar for eight hours straight, waiting for something to happen. Hanuman sat there checking out various people; he would start to show an interest in someone, only to rapidly lose it... sometimes he would approach someone and talk to them, only to return with a disappointed look on his face. I had no idea what they were talking about... But then we noticed one grizzled old drunk. He had a joint between his teeth which arrived there via a series of hands and then promptly continued its journey straight into someone else's hands. Unexpectedly, he nodded at Hanuman a certain way, and we immediately got up and took off with him. Following the tramp's directions, we drove to a phone shop, and he and Hanuman went in. Half an hour later they came out, and Hanny was carrying a box containing a new phone. The tramp got into the car with us and we let him make a few calls on our pirate phone. Then we set off again, driving down narrow streets until we reached a small square: three trees, five benches, and a kiosk...

"This is where the druggies hang out," the tramp announced with an important air, before shaking his head and adding, with a rueful note in his voice, "Oi, fackin' byad pleis tu vizit!"

I scanned the scene from left to right. There were people wherever I looked, all of them stoned, contorted, hairy, one in a raincoat standing to one side, speaking with someone on the phone, laughing incessantly... he looked cleaner and more respectable than the rest. Maybe a snoop. I didn't take my eyes off him until I was convinced he was laughing naturally, that he wasn't faking it... you couldn't be too careful... there were informants everywhere... But no, it seemed the coast was clear, the rest of them were just standing there minding their own business, there didn't seem to be any snitches about.

The spot was familiar. It wasn't our first time there… there was a cheap toilet nearby. Mikhail and I had gone to buy hash one time, and we'd stopped for a beer under the bridge. He was trying to find out more about the St. Petersburg sluts; he couldn't get them off his mind. My stories had got him really hot under the collar. He constantly came back to the subject of whores and speed, asking me again and again how we had met them. That story seemed to really prey on him. But this time we found nothing, because I suffered from topographic cretinism. I would get totally lost, with no clue what part of town we were in, where Mario's brothel was, whether it was before or after the bridge, or even what side of the bridge it was on. And so we got ourselves a couple of six-packs, and Mikhail slung his fishing line under the bridge a couple of times, hoping to catch something. Or maybe just for the hell of it. But pretty soon we needed the toilet, and somehow we ended up at one. Mikhail unleashed his mighty plume of piss and poured out his emotions, and so the urine came mixed with the bile which had accumulated in him, all the reasons he was sick of this country.

"These Danes," he spat the words out in drunken derision, "these Danes are like fattened pigs! I start shaking when I look into their shop windows! I want to smash those windows up, smash them into little pieces, smash up the whole country. Because they don't deserve this life. Those pigs licked the fascists' arses, while the long-suffering Russian people sacrificed countless lives, and shed so much blood. And now our veterans chew their millet with toothless mouths, if they're lucky! They definitely can't afford milk any more. Meanwhile, these Danish pigs are living in clover. And they shoo off the Russian immigrants with a broom while they give those stinking Arabs – the same ones who go around blowing stuff up, the terrorist scum – they hand them social support on a plate wrapped up in a humanitarian ribbon."

At this point he started swearing, and so profusely that I started feeling giddy. But then we were interrupted by a female voice, announcing in perfect Russian, "Mind your language when you're at my place!"

It felt like I was back at the Baltic Station in Tallinn, a kid who had just drunk a skinful of beer and was trying to communicate his enthusiasm for Russian expletives to random people on the street. I shuddered so hard that my flow was interrupted, and I couldn't resume. The voice turned out to belong to a middle-aged Russian woman, and we soon learned that she had been in Denmark for a while now. Notwithstanding her education (two degrees) and knowledge of foreign languages (five), she had to work in a public convenience as a so-called "lavatory concierge". Oh, my learned lady! It was completely understandable that our swearing should bother her so much. It was an assault on her ears, not least because she was blessed with a musical ear too! She had been brought up in a professor's family, she attended the conservatory, where she had to mix with bearded, highbrow, arrogant representatives of the male sex, who thought that swearing was for the plebs. Yes, plebs like me, Hanny, Potapov and Durachkov... fucking pond life. It was only natural that we made her sick. And we stank as well. We were like worms which had crawled into her public convenience just after she had polished it to a sheen. Did she have the appropriate chemical substance to hand to wipe us off the face of her polished tiles? Could she spray us with something to make us dissolve? A copper would only need to take one glance at me and that would be enough – I'd disappear! Oh, what's that she's got there? Mmm, all sorts of odds and ends! What doesn't she have there! She didn't let her time go to waste, she wiped those lavatories clean and cooked for herself on a little hob at the same time. The school of immigrant life had turned her into a new breed of human! Russian savviness plus European cunning. She saved her money, she studied the local language, she knew all the ins and outs of the Danish bureaucratic labyrinth. Maybe she even knew what the Directorate was. Maybe she had even been there – to the Directorate. What a shame that Hanuman didn't meet her, he would have fallen to his knees before her and kissed her lotus feet! Goddess Padma! Feet like Buddhist stupas. The old lady wasn't just treading water there. She was so full of energy. Every minute of her life was lived to the full! She certainly put me to shame, I could barely drag my sorry hide along, and I chewed my food three times as slowly as her. There was definitely something up with my liver, but I wasn't going to go and get it checked, even when all our adventures came to an end, even if I ended up in prison, I wouldn't go for a check-up… fuck it! The elderly woman was wearing a shawl and had a broach on her collar, and she fed us sauerkraut and potato salad, homemade meatballs and pickled cucumbers. As she brought us the food she said, "Young men, you must eat, not arouse God's ire, you must keep you language and your thoughts pure!" We chomped away and praised her to high heaven… I ate myself fit to burst.

She had French and German magazines on her table, marked with a pencil here and there. She didn't waste her time – that was for sure! A hi-fi to listen to music on? Naturally. And more texts, language courses, it was all there, from A to Z. She would praise the Danish: "You have to admire them. They value their linguistic traditions! Every diacritic positioned in accordance with the canons…" and so on. We chatted for several hours. She was in a fake marriage with some heavy-drinking Dane who kept trying to treat his liver condition but never did manage to cure it, damn it! He took her money, and she paid him. But not long to go now. A couple more years and she would get her citizenship. Her son had married a Danish girl out of love, and they were living together happily. A warm aura of worldly wisdom emanated from the old lady. I forced a crooked smile and made a crooked roll-up, and then I went outside to smoke it. I didn't want to hang around there too long, I didn't really want to see her. But Mikhail felt differently. He visited her every time he went to Aalborg. He claimed to take her presents (later I found out that the rogue was flogging her all sorts of stolen crap). He ate her sauerkraut and salads, he cursed his fate, his latest no, the threat of deportation, the lack of money, the unbearableness of camp life... you can't sleep, or cook, or sit in your room or even in the toilet, they spy on you, rummage through your things, everyone's filthy, there's roaches running about, disease is rife, you can't wash your clothes, they're always cutting off the water, the rash on my arse just won't go away... and so on and so forth...

Pretty soon she disappeared. She must have got tired of his visits. An elderly Danish chap turned up in the toilet, dressed in a black frock coat and a cap with a rosette, the polished buttons and the gilded braiding on his cap glittering. Judging by his uniform he must have been a railwayman in a former life. He even seemed to mutter station names to himself. On two occasions I went to the toilet and I was sure I could hear him naming stations under his breath: not quite Randers, not Horsens, fuck knows...

There were women shivering on the benches in that park, they all looked half-dead. I had never known that this place played such an important role in the life of the city.

"They often come to collect corpses from this square, from these benches," said the tramp.

A pair approached us. The tramp yakked with them for a while. Then they nodded and headed off to that same shop. Five hours later we had six telephones. Every one of them had SIM cards which allowed unlimited calls, that is until the druggy got sent his bill and they shut down his account...

"But no one is going to know that when they buy the phones off us!" Hanuman said, and burst out laughing.

We phoned round the camps, contacting various acquaintances of Hanny's. He started roping them into his business venture, promising a hundred kroner for every telephone sold, telling them that the price of each phone would be 1500 kroner, which they could knock down to 1250, but no less! "I'll call back in an hour..." I was always amazed that everyone in the camp seemed to have their own phone. When I asked Hanuman where they came from he told me that those phones were no better than the public phone boxes. You had to pay one hundred kroner for a phone card, then you entered the code in the phone, and your credit would quickly evaporate... it was enough for a ten-minute call to Russia, five to India, one to Australia. The most expensive country to call was America, so you couldn't call America at all with those types of phone, the cards just didn't exist.

"But at least people can call you... you could buy yourself one of those phones, then your precious uncle could call you direct instead of calling my mobile all the time, I'm really pissed off with it now. I'm expecting an important call any moment, every time the phone rings it makes me jump, then I answer it to find it's your noble kinsman once again, for fuck's sake. Time you got yourself a phone, Johan! I'll give you the money. Anyway, you're supposed to be Russian mafia now. And mafia with no phone is an anomaly. It's one thing not to have a gun, but you can't do without a phone!"

We couldn't sell those phones in Farstrup; we didn't want to shit on our own doorstep! There could be trouble when our customers discovered not only that they could no longer make calls, but they couldn't receive them either. We decided to sell the phones in the most far-flung camps. In Frederikshavn, for example. We managed to sell three phones at full price to some rich Pakistanis, our old acquaintances, who were still decked out in gold chains and still in possession of their video cameras; they hadn't been stolen yet. They bought the phones just for the hell of it, and because they thought they were buying them from one of their own, a fellow Pakistani.

In one of the other camps an Indian bought a phone just to try and please his Indian compatriot. Hanuman constantly tricked everyone. For the Indians he was an Indian, for the Pakistanis he was a Pakistani. He was happy to con all of those cretins. He detested Indians and Pakistanis in equal measure. And the more he succeeded in deceiving them, the more he detested them. You could have devised a formula which expressed Hanuman's essence: his contempt for someone was equal to the ease with which he could trick them. And the easier it was to trick them, the more contemptuous he was of them.

We laid up at the Farstrup camp for a few days, where we spent the whole time toking like troopers... and then we found another customer, this time somewhere in the back of beyond. The town had a strange name – Hunderskov. It turned out there were three or four towns with similar names, just with a few extra letters in front, like Ny Hunderskov, Nørre Hunderskov, and some others too. It took us ages to work out how to get there. Hanuman bickered with the person who put us on to the customer, he bickered so hard and so heatedly that he almost bickered up his tongue, he almost coughed it up like a piece of chewing gum! That filthy alcoholic Beer Machine didn't know which Hunderskov he lived in himself, because he was always drunk, and when he was drunk he didn't have a clue where he was! He drank away his grip on reality! He drank two whole crates of beer a day! And he still managed to stay as skinny as a tapeworm! Where on earth could he be? Maybe he was in all the Hunderskovs at once, eh? Work that one out!

"Go outside and ask where you are, for fuck's sake!" Hanuman yelled into the phone, bloodshot eyeballs bulging, bent double at the waist like he was chucking up. But it seemed that everyone made fun of that fool, everyone treated him like an idiot, they all played tricks on the old Indian alcoholic, they teased him at every opportunity. "He came to Denmark to earn enough money for a tractor!" Hanuman fumed as he waited tensely for the phone call. "He came here to earn the money for a tractor! Have you ever heard of such an idiot!"

Hanny paced up and down the room with the measured strides of an agronomist, tapping himself on the forehead with his phone. "Will he ever work out where he is? Our client is getting away! He came here to save up for a tractor, he drinks a crate of beer a day, and still stays as skinny as a tapeworm! Beer Factory! Fuck me! He's an alcoholic! He's in a constant state of delirium! The idiot!"

Eventually Hanuman found out which Hunderskov the client was in, it was Hunderskov K (K stood for Kirkegaard, or graveyard). But when we got there it turned out that no one had ever heard of Beer Machine. The telephone conversation was repeated, but by now all that barking into the phone had made Hanuman as hoarse as a dog on a chain. And in the end the person on the other end of the line explained that he was actually in Vamdrup; he'd been driven up there yesterday and completely forgotten about it, all the camps looked exactly the same... Hanuman yelled at him to get to the point. Basically, the client was in Lunderskov, not Hunderskov, and we were nearly twenty kilometres away!

We were suddenly in the money. I was sure that nothing good could come of it, but things worked out fine; life continued pretty much as before, nothing nasty happened. No one started looking for us. No one tried to get revenge over the telephones, which I reckoned must have been disconnected by now. We just started smoking a lot more

263

hash. We smoked, and watched TV. After a long period of inactivity, our television had unexpectedly started working again. Of its own accord. No one even touched it. One day we came back to our room, Hanuman yelled "fancy a suck?" at Nepalino, chucked his briefcase down and pulled off his jacket and boots. I carefully placed a bag stuffed full of stolen CDs and cosmetics down on to the floor... and the television switched itself on! The TV was showing scenes of a raging battle between protestors and police in Copenhagen. There was war in Nørrebro, guys with scarves wrapped round their faces, wearing masks and hats, running about smashing up Arab and Pakistani stalls and shops, razing to the ground anything which the owners hadn't shielded with boarding, overturning cars... and then the beautiful sight of a Molotov cocktail sailing through the air, becoming yet more beautiful as it smashed and ignited everything in its vicinity. For some reason it seemed to be the only Molotov cocktail thrown that day, and it looked like it had been thrown in such a way as to give the camera guy a good shot of it. It even occurred to me that the reporters might have mixed up the concoction and chucked the bottle themselves, so that they could film it and stoke unrest in Nørrebro. Our jaws dropped as we watched those scenes, we wished we could be in Copenhagen to make the most of the situation. But the next shot was from inside the TV studio, where lazy, fish-eyed journalists were sitting chewing over events which were already three or even five years old. We felt like we'd been tricked yet again. That was when Hanuman first came up with the idea of a strike, a hash-smoking strike. He said he was going to protest. He didn't want to hear any more about all the hypocrisy out there, it just fucked with his head. He didn't want to know what was happening in the world. He couldn't care less about Burma! Or about the nuclear tests in India and Pakistan! He didn't give a fuck about Iraq and Yugoslavia! Or about the rainforests and the greenhouse effect! Or about any of the rest of it!

"We're in a refugee camp, after all," he said. "That's more than enough! We see the people who fled from bombs every single day of our lives! We can smell their shit with our very own noses! The stuff that goes on right here in this camp is far more important than anything happening in any conflict zone! The stuff that's going on in that crazy Iranian's guts is way more important than anything happening in Iran!"

Hanuman filled his pipe and carried on, "All those bomb craters, lights blinking in the darkness, grand speeches, hostages' heads, none of it convinces me... it all seems unreal somehow, I have serious doubts about it. I'm a solipsist. I reckon it's all staged, from the Molotov cocktails to the debates in parliament. I don't believe them! Not just them, I don't believe anyone! Turn that shit off!"

I switched off the television, opened up a magazine and put my legs up, leaving my boots on. The magazine had an interview with some Danish punks who were already getting on in years, a couple of dinosaurs who refused to shed their studded-leather second skin. I'd bought it because I wanted to read about what the punks got up to and get up to in this country. It turned out that they had all smoked hash, tripped on LSD, played their psychedelic punk music, painted graffiti on the walls, and were the first to get piercings done – but that was all twenty years ago! And now one of the oldest members of the gang had gone so soft in the head that he'd started to publish comics and write poems which were like poetry written for children or, worse still, poetry written by children. There were some examples in the magazine. Even with my very basic Danish I could tell that this guy's poetry was totally devoid of any talent. This "poetry" was slightly reminiscent of Sapgir, but even with my hatred of Sapgir I felt that his idiocy – that is the stubborn persistence of his stupidity – went so far that you could almost respect him for it. But this senile punk just seemed to be an illiterate

265

idiot! He was still wearing studded leather jackets, he didn't wash or cut his hair, but he didn't dye his hair any more either, because there wasn't enough of it left. He had his own studio, his own editorial office, he printed pamphlets of some sort and he wrote songs, which little children sang. The other one recounted his past at length, stressing that he was one of the last survivors, and had his own gallery where he displayed works by modernists, graffiti artists and God knows what else. There was a whole series of pictures called *Dreams of a Schizophrenic* and judging by the little reproductions in the magazine they were worse than anything Potapov had painted.

I started to get bored, I just sat there smoking, drifting in an ocean of thoughts, unable to decide where to drop anchor. I took the pipe, inhaled deeply, passed it on... that made more sense, much more sense than any punk movement. At that point I stopped moving altogether, I just lay there. Hanny was stretched out there too, not stirring. When the hash was finished we sent Potapov to Aalborg for fresh supplies.

"Money makes money," Potapov said for some reason as he took the money for the hash. I nodded, but laughed to myself. What was the cretin so happy about? The idiot! He didn't make any profit, unless you counted the bit of hash he chipped off with his crocodile clips on the way, plus enough small change to buy himself a drink. And I was happy about that, because I found him repugnant.

5

Hanuman told me that he had found some people who arranged transport to Holland. I laughed. I told him that you could get to Holland by foot.

"Why go by foot?" Hanny objected. "They can get you there completely legally!"

He told me about some Dutch guys who ran strip joints and shipped in girls from Poland, the Baltic states, and Russia completely above board. They would take anyone else as well, but for money. And they could sort out Polish or Russian documents. Obviously the documents came from the same people who supplied the whores.

That made me prick up my ears. It sounded like it could be close to the truth. Now I wanted to know who had told him. It turned out to be a young Indian guy called Aman who had arrived from Germany. He had an uncle living there who was some sort of rich businessman. Aman had married a German woman and now he had to wait half a year before he was allowed to enter Germany legally. His uncle had contacts in Holland. All of that was confirmed by one young Afghan who had spent a long time in Holland and liked to show off his knowledge of various Dutch words, even whole phrases. The young Afghan spoke perfect Russian and he looked just like a Russian. But he was an Afghan. That was confirmed by the Afghanis themselves, who initially had some doubts about his Pashtun provenance, so they had shoved him up against the toilet wall and interrogated him. Later they said he had answered their questions very competently in the languages most commonly spoken in Afghanistan. The young guy said that his dad was an Afghan, and his mother was Russian, that's where he got his Russian language and looks from. Now they lived in Holland. What exactly they were doing in Denmark wasn't clear, but he said that it was his own business, and they didn't ask any more questions. Especially since he was friends with a ginger-nut Georgian called David, who smoked a lot of hash and was the kick-boxing champion of Georgia. He was very tall and had a really short fuse; his face was dotted all over with vicious stubble, he was hideously pockmarked, his eyes were bloodshot and watery and his gaze was like a lightning bolt which incinerated anything he looked at. David happened to enter the toilet just as that interrogation was under way, and so the interrogation promptly turned into a discussion. There were six of the Afghans, but they backed off and let Aman go. David confirmed everything Aman said. It turned out that David was also planning to go to Holland, and there was a family of Russian Assyrians together with someone somewhere who was ready to fork out the necessary money. So they would have company; there might not be room in the trucks with the whores. I asked, "Why do they have to go in trucks, if it's legal?"

Hanny ignored my question, it was as if he hadn't even heard me, his eyes had glazed over in anticipation of coming adventures. He said we should grab the opportunity while we could, even if we were only going to live in Holland temporarily, with false passports. From Holland you could get a boat to the States. His eyes goggled. There was no way you could let a chance like that get away. It was worth working for something like that. David had apparently started work already. He went to Aalborg every day to steal electronic equipment and CDs. He had already saved enough to cover half the fare. Hanuman said he couldn't make all the money himself, I would have to shift my arse off my bed and get to work as well.

"No one is going to hand us ten grand," he said. "We'll have to earn the money ourselves. Ten thousand Danish kroner is not that much if you put your mind to it. I'm sure that someone like Nepalino has got that kind of money. He's been at the camp for more than a year now, and he spends nothing, he saves every krone. The best thing would be to squeeze him for some cash. We don't have to worry about giving him a bit of a squeeze. We can use brute force on him, we're going to take off from here pretty soon. Anyway, who's going to stand up for him? The cops don't give a damn about asylum seekers. They're happy to let them sort out their own problems. Anyway, Nepalino was harbouring us illegally. So he's not going to grass us up. Even if we don't want to hassle Nepalino, we could rope the two Russians in to our moneymaking plans, eh? We could sell the car, or all their bric-a-brac, eh? Or force them to work somehow, what do you reckon? In any case, we've got something for starters. That's right, we don't have to start completely from scratch. We haven't smoked all our savings yet. In any case, we can make the odd phone call from time to time. We can make a few thousand a month from that alone. We just need to select the line, hunt for the codes, dial up, and that's it. Yes, yes... and the bottles too, and then we can start up the food sales again!"

But then this black guy came our way. A black guy who we ended up making a pile of money off. We met him via Svenaage, or rather via Laszlo. We'd gone with them to buy vodka and cigarettes from the sailors at the port again, from the Russians, and Svenaage was scared that it could turn nasty, so he asked us to come with him on to the boat.

He left us his fax number, told us to write, and promised he would write back, insisting that it cost nothing. "Fax is completely free, *absolument gratis!*" he yelled. We promised that we would get hold of a fax machine and write. He said he'd send us an order list, because he was coming back the following year to buy more stuff, and to get some stuff gratis, the more gratis the better, because he was a special customer! Eh-he, a loyal customer! Everyone said "yes, yes", smiled, shook his hand, expressing the hope that we would see him next year, *mon ami*. But after that he must have come back, crept up to Potapov's place, and swiped the torches! Evidently he didn't believe he was going to see us next year.

None of us believed it either. None of us believed that we could stand living in Farstrup that long. And no one wanted to believe it could be true! No one wanted to sit it out in that hole for another whole year! No one wanted to see Ambrose again, not at any cost! Even if he agreed to buy every last ounce of shit that we crapped in the course of that year! Even if he offered us the most astronomical price for it! We still didn't want to see him! We all wanted to run from there, we all secretly envied Ambrose for being able to leave, everyone else wanted to leave as well… each had his own destination… Potapov fantasised about Canada, Durachkov about Australia, Hanuman was yearning for Holland, but we were too late for that. The lorry left before we had finished fleecing Ambrose. They promised Hanuman they would do the passports in five months and they asked for the money up front. He gave them half and said that he would wait until the Dutch guys were ready to set off again. Hanuman promised to pay the other half five months later. I told him not to bother about me, he didn't have to pay for me. I'd manage on my own somehow, I was prepared to go on foot. By the time his passport was ready I would have made it to Germany. And from there it was only a stone's throw to Holland. I said it made no odds to me, I was happy to go anywhere, the main thing was to go somewhere, preferably as far away from here as possible. Hanuman just laughed. He said he felt bad for not paying my share. I told him not to worry. With his nose deep inside his cup, he said that we could definitely earn enough money for my passport too. We could start shifting contraband goods to Germany, if I was planning to go there anyway. I paused to think. Hanuman said he knew an Afghan guy who was headed to Germany, Sheikh-Mahmood. I had to think a bit more.

After consulting for a while (a full twenty minutes) we got up, packed our stuff, and headed to Germany.

6

Sheikh-Mahmood had spent a long time in Russia. It had taken a heavy toll on him, it had corrupted him. He had three university degrees, all of them Russian, and all of them fake, as far as I could tell. One of them was in medicine, and that was definitely fake, because he didn't know the most basic things about medicine. He didn't know the difference between physiology and anatomy, he reckoned they were the same thing! He also thought that anabolic and antiseptic were one and the same. He thought aspirins would cure his child of any illness. But he even got that muddled up quite a lot. He would say that aspirin was the same thing as Analgin. In any case, the child wasn't his. Maybe the wife he lived with in the camp wasn't his either; it seemed like she was happy to be anyone's wife for a while. She was Ukrainian, she drank like a bloke, her voice was always hoarse, and she had huge strong arms which were constantly kneading dough or mince She always wore the same clothes, she pronounced her "g"s like "h"s, Ukrainian style, and was responsible for spreading an infectious disease. The disease took the form of a set of twelve detective novels by Alexandra Marinina, which spread round the entire Russian-speaking population of the camp in a flash (the Georgian and Armenian women read them too, I saw it with my own eyes). Together with various video and audio cassettes, and Christmas TV classics, films like *Brother*, *The Irony of Fate*, or *Say a Word for the Poor Hussar*. Thanks to her you could hear Bulanova bawling in almost every building, and Russian pop bands like Ivanushki, Strelki, and Confetti belting out wherever you went. It made you want to run from there, run without a backwards glance.

The first thing Sheikh-Mahmood did when he arrived was

to cover his walls with carpets. He said that he couldn't live without carpets. A room without carpets was no better than a prison cell! But even prisons have carpets! And he should know! He'd been in every prison there was. It was all pure lies of course. Because it was clear from looking at him that he'd spent his whole life rolling in clover, and he couldn't give it up; he kept rolling from country to country, from one woman to the next, but he was never happy. He was always cursing Denmark, particularly the Danish people and the climate; he even found a causal link between the two. He talked a lot about rugs, how at the main market in Kabul they laid the carpets straight out on to the road, so that people would walk across them, and the cars would drive over them, so that dust would get into the fibres. It turned out he was an expert in textile production technologies too! The rugs were supposed to lie about in the dust, it apparently improved their quality. Just as in the well-known saying – wherever you lay your rug, that's your home...

And as a fan of rugs he liked spinning yarns, he talked a lot about Russian women, he said they were always up for it, that they'd do whatever you wanted, not like the Danish ones. Danish girls put rings in their noses, and cigarettes in their mouths, what was the use in that? He spoke about women the same way he spoke about rugs – they both needed to be laid just right...

He was headed to Germany, and then onwards to Holland. I told Hanuman right away that we should go with him all the way, but Hanuman suddenly decided that there was no sense in going to Holland without a passport. I goggled at him in disbelief, and he hissed at me, "I've already paid for the passport, I've already put down a deposit." His eyes were wild with offence. I couldn't understand what drove him, was it a longing to move through space, or his desire to possess a document which would enable him to cross the border legally, or at least semi-legally. But we couldn't have it out properly in front of Sheikh-Mahmood, even if I was burning to. I wanted to grab Hanuman and shake him, to ask what was more important: the document which he put down a deposit on so as to travel to Holland in a lorry, or Holland itself, with or without any deposits. I was ready to get moving to Amsterdam as soon as possible. I didn't need to think twice, there was nothing keeping me in Denmark, and I was ready to go. Hanuman and his sour mug had suddenly started driving me crazy. He pulled such a fishy face that it looked like he must have something rotting inside him. He didn't agree that we should go straight to Holland. By now I was boiling with rage. What was he on about? He had been planning to go to Holland, but now he had to go to Germany, as if he wanted to keep me company, to come and drink schnapps with me or something. Instead of taking off for Holland with the Afghan guy right away! What was he up to? I reached for a cigarette, but we were sitting in non-smoking. And there were law-abiding passengers sitting all around. It wasn't a good idea to argue too loudly, but I was seething. Sheikh-Mahmood broke the silence. He was still spinning some yarn. He said that he had a flat in Germany. And, I thought to myself, he was sure to have another wife living in that flat, if not several of them. It turned out he had been granted refugee status in Germany seven years ago, he'd got his hands on the holy grail of asylum, and he had social support dripping into his bank account. But that wasn't enough for him! That's why he'd gone to Denmark, so as to claim his pocket money there too. Very cosy! He had the social support piling up in his account in Germany, and he got his asylum seeker's allowances in Denmark as well! Peanuts for him of course, but watch the øre and the kroner take care of themselves! And while they were finding out that he already had refugee status in Germany, while they were checking his fingerprints and establishing who he really was, he was pocketing two thousand Danish kroner a month! Nice little earner! Especially since he spent next to nothing! He was living at the expense of his mythological Ukrainian wife, who did his washing, cooked for him, the full service, all in one, just like the Goddess Shiva! He'd already managed to travel to Norway and Sweden, where he'd put aside a tidy sum. Now he was heading in the other direction, to Holland. He could live there for half a year and save some money. And he'd get to see a bit of the world into the bargain.

He talked the whole way, with his voice lowered, trying not to attract too much attention, but doggedly and unrelentingly, without shutting up once: Norway was so boring, they'd sent him all the way up north! As far north as possible! To the end of the world! Where the ice never melted, even in summer! Where the sun shines all night! Where there are penguins hopping down the street! And seals shuffling along after them! What a place! And the people! They'll all so dozy! Stupid! Lazy! And they've granted the penguins citizenship! They register every single one! They fit them with chips! They probably have passports as well! In any case, every single one of them is accounted for, that's for sure! They look after the penguins better than they look after humans! They put them on the Red List of endangered species, don't you know! That's better than the Red Cross!

Hanuman and I yawned in indecently close unison, but the Arab just carried on, "Of course, they're all in the population register, and everywhere else too! Just like in Germany, where every dog is accounted for! Not only does every dog have a chip embedded, the police can determine who the dog belongs to from its shit! Then they send the fine straight to the owner! A fine for dog shit! Just like a parking fine, understand! You don't believe me? Well, it's simple! They give the dog a special type of food, which passes through its guts and bowels, acquiring an electrical charge which is unique to that dog! And so when the shit comes out it sends a signal! And every dog has its own

274

signal! It's impossible to get them mixed up! That's why it's easy for the cleaner to sweep up the shit, he's got a special piece of equipment for it! All he needs to do is switch it on and drive about in his car, yawning to himself. Meanwhile, the gadget picks up the signal and starts blinking, then the cleaner stops and picks up the shit, but at the same time he identifies whose dog it is, its name, address and breed, it all shows up on his equipment! And then they send a fine to the owner over the Internet! It's as easy as that! They haven't got that far yet in Norway! Although they do have penguins walking down the streets. I saw them myself! They're just like people! Nothing like dogs! Oh no! The penguin is just as clever as a dolphin, even cleverer! He's almost human! He can walk upright! But a dolphin can't walk! He just swims! Like a fish! But penguins walk, just like humans. They can even run! You walk down the street, and there's a penguin waddling towards you, huffing and puffing, you go, "Guten Morgen mister", and he nonchalantly goes "tak-tak-tak" with his beak, as if to say, "The same to you!" But it's cold there, and boring... I did see the Northern Lights, but they weren't anything special, just some colours floating across the sky, big deal!"

Sheikh-Mahmood was a famous celebrity. An important personage. He'd been persecuted for his books. He had written a number of them, in Urdu and Farsi, maybe even in Hindi, because he knew that pretty well too... he was a real polyglot! You would need more than the fingers on both hands to count how many languages he knew! He had almost finished writing his traveller's notes – "Europe through the eyes of an Afghan refugee!" It was no laughing matter! It was an epic panorama! A tome which recounted the histories of entire peoples, and an encyclopaedia of political intrigue! From big cheeses like Brezhnev and Reagan to the little boy in the street! Fate had been cruel to him, and his book was mostly autobiographical, about all the things he had experienced, all the things which had befallen his scarred hide. The hero of the book – and the narrator – was an Afghan, he had suffered shell shock, he had contracted every disease there was, from typhus to the plague, and he didn't have a soul left in this world, because the Russians had slashed his family's throats in front of his eyes, when he was just thirteen! The horrors of war, and the polished sheen of the European's boot! The stench of the camp versus the paschal, crystal cleanliness of the shops! Hunger in his homeland but abundance on the rubbish dumps of Germany! The Taliban there and democracy here! Contrasts! Contradictions! Disorientation! Spiritual turmoil! Indignity! Ennui! Our hero can't adapt to his girlfriend's European mentality. He tries to learn how to live here, but he feels the pull of his homeland, that same old nostalgia again; love and hate! Sweet poison, banishment from paradise through the hell of war into the garden of earthly delights, where the women are all morally corrupt! Where drugs make you crazy! To the world of discos, bars, prostitutes and striptease! A strange, foreign tongue, foreign people, and you're foreign too, a stranger in a strange land... and so on, and so forth...

He nattered away like that the whole journey, and at one point he suggested that a book like that might be of interest to Western readers as well as Eastern ones, then he asked, "So what do you think?"

"Yes, yes," said Hanuman. I nodded: of course, my friend, of course...

Me and Hanuman were travelling with tickets bought for a third of the normal price from some characters who had fled to Sweden. They'd been summoned to Copenhagen for some sort of interview, and they already knew that their time was up, that it was a trap, so they had decided to scarper. They sold their tickets to us and disappeared. We left with Sheikh-Mahmood, who had promised to show us where to cross the border, because he could cross any border in Europe with his eyes shut! I cursed that coincidence: we'd have been better off travelling without him! He wouldn't let me sleep. My head hurt, and it hurt more and more as he pummelled it with his version of Afghan history, his view of how the catastrophe had unfolded after Brezhnev's mistake, his prognosis of his homeland's future. Instead of white gaps on the map there was just a black hole left, otherwise known as Talibanistan! He was writing about that in his book as well, and he was writing it in English, oh yes! The Booker was already in the bag! Nothing like it had ever been written before! It wasn't some sort of Arab family chronicle! It wasn't some book about émigrés like the one written by that guy who won the Pulitzer, the one who can't string a sentence together!

I couldn't bear to listen! It annoyed me that absolutely everyone seemed to be writing something. Virtually every third person I met! Anyone who had learned how to hold a pen, anyone who knew their way round a keyboard, they were all writing something! And not just any old thing, but a book! And not any old book, but a real opus! That's right! Every other guy! And they already had their sights set on the Booker! Every other person I met! Either they were in the course of writing a book, or they had already written it, or they were about to start writing one!

He led us down a footpath, whispering the whole way that if the Germans spotted anything they might set the dogs on us.

"But don't worry," he reassured us. "Those dogs are so well trained that they won't bite, they just grip you with their teeth. They grab you by the ankle and hold on. They hold you still, but they won't bite. That's if you don't start struggling. If you start struggling, then they might bite. So best not to struggle, just to be on the safe side. And you should raise your arms as well, just in case. There have been cases where the police started shooting. And they were right to do so, because they've been shot at themselves, and more than once. So they might start shooting if they don't see your hands in the air. After all, they've got no idea what you might be carrying. I can fully understand their position. I'd start shooting myself!"

"Understood," said Hanuman. I just bit my lip...

By morning we arrived at a town which didn't seem to have a single cheap supermarket. We made our way to the railway station. The Afghan wanted to catch a train and continue his journey (dropping by at his place first, and then onwards to Holland). I tried pinching Hanny again, to suggest that we continue on to Holland too. Hanuman just shrugged his shoulders, half-irritably, half-indifferently, and said, "If you want to, go on then, go with Sheikh-Mahmood, good luck to you, but I've got money in Denmark." I was so pissed off with him. "What money? What money, Hanuman?" But he didn't hear me, he wasn't listening. He thrust out his lower lip, hunched his shoulders, wrapped himself in his jacket, rolled his eyes, and lit up a cigarette, making it even clearer he wasn't listening. The only way I could explain his stupidity and indecisiveness was that he was so cold that even the thought of going to Holland was too much to bear. The German border had taken its toll on him. And when we got to Holland we would still have to find somewhere to rest our weary bones. He couldn't bear to think about it. I said that we could rest at Sheikh-Mahmood's and then think about what to do. But he just repeated, "Not with me." I treated him to some choice four-letter words, and walked off. Hanuman and the Arab jabbered away in their own language, discussing something between themselves, gesticulating wildly like a pair of monkeys, nodding at each other like numbskulls. Then the Afghan approached me, wished me good luck and farewell in Russian, waved at us, and with the words "Ha de so bra!"[27] he departed for Stuttgart in a train with toxic-yellow curtains and sporadic bored faces in the windows. We got on the next train to arrive, which seemed at risk of collapsing underneath us; it

27   Goodbye (Swedish)

juddered and jolted, wheezed and sighed, but somehow it delivered us to a little town, although hell knew where we were exactly. It looked as if we had travelled deeper into the heart of Germany. The idea intrigued me. I reckoned that the deeper we penetrated Germany, the more chance we had of getting stuck there. Maybe we'd meet someone new, maybe we'd get waylaid and we'd never go back to Denmark. Maybe Hanuman would develop the same kind of enthusiasm for Germany as he had for Denmark. Maybe fortune would smile on us in Germany. That's how it normally went. If things didn't go your way in one country then you had to move to another, things would be just fine, at least to start with. Someone once told me that gamblers always win when the go to try their luck in a new casino.

We changed some money, then we found a supermarket and bought a load of cheap schnapps and cigarettes. We tried not to buy too much in one go, so as not to arouse suspicions. Who knew what people might think; a couple of weirdos sloping round a border town, one of them black... the Germans were a suspicious lot, someone might grass us up. Everyone had a mobile phone on them, and it didn't take much to make a call. It didn't take much to drive up and check our *ausweis*. So we didn't sit on the same bench for too long, we moved about a lot, we went to different shops, and we bought moderate amounts of stuff at each one. We went in alone, one of us waited outside with a full bag, and the other one went in to do the shopping with an empty one. Best not to trudge round the shop with a full bag, you might get stopped, they might check your bag, and then try to prove that you didn't nick the stuff, even if you've got the receipts. They might ask you why you kept the receipts. Maybe you knew you were going to get stopped? Maybe you've had a run-in with the law before? Got your papers on you? What can you prove if you've got no papers? At that point they wouldn't bother investigating whether you stole the schnapps or acquired it honestly – no papers, end of story! I was worried, I was really worried. I was really suffering, I felt sick, so ill. I was shaking, shivering, I was so hungry that I demanded, I outright demanded that we buy some bread and salad, and that I immediately got my share! Preferably Italian salad! When we walked past the German sausages my hands involuntarily reached in their direction and my stomach started playing organ music which could have put Bach to shame! I insisted, I demanded that Hanny buy me some cheap bacon to go with the salad! The cheapest possible, I wasn't picky! But bacon, for fuck's sake! Any kind would do. Hanuman coolly declined. Instead, he stole some bread and bought us each a beer. But I nicked a packet of cheese without him noticing.

It looked like we had taken the wrong train, or we had overshot by one station, and hell knows what direction we'd gone! It had taken a whole day to find the border town. We meandered along asphalt roads which had been polished to a sheen, although God knows why or who for – we didn't see a single car in three hours! There were fields either side, and there was such a bone-chilling crosswind that we had to, we just had to open one of the bottles of schnapps! We drank it straight out of the bottle to save ourselves from perishing in the cold! But the wretched stuff didn't warm us at all! Not one fucking bit! It made things worse! As soon as the liquid entered our bodies it spread such a chill that it seemed it wasn't spirit, but acid of some kind. I froze up, just completely froze up! The schnapps was already so cold that I could hardly hold the bottle. It was so frozen that barely a dribble came out, it was virtually impossible to pour down our throats. And thank God for that! I had lost any desire to drink. The schnapps was so icy-cold, so toxic, it wasn't funny! It wasn't just useless for warming ourselves up, it was unfit for external use! So when Hanny started pouring it down his throat I couldn't bear to watch. It was scary, horrific, like witnessing a suicide attempt. When I tried drinking it myself, I started to choke. That vile schnapps suffocated me. It oozed into me like hair gel, it slowly edged into my body, it slid gradually down my throat, and then it came to a standstill. I tried to swallow it, but the liquid came bubbling back up, making a bid for freedom. Any kind of moonshine would have been preferable to that cheap schnapps, even the stuff which Stepan made from those vile Danish jellies which he scavenged from the rubbish dumps. And I wanted to eat so badly, it felt as if I hadn't eaten for three whole days! I had such a sharp stabbing pain in my stomach, such a sharp pain, as if I had appendicitis and someone had already operated on it, but it just made me want to eat even more. And my feet were hurting too, I'd got them soaking wet in the deep snow when we crossed the border with Sheikh-Mahmood.

We had been walking along a railway track towards a forest for a while now… it was obvious that we'd gone off course. But Hanuman insisted on following the rails, he didn't want to turn off into the forest. It was easier to get lost in the forest, he said. I told him, through gritted teeth, that we'd got lost ages ago, and that just because we were walking along the rails it didn't mean that we were going in the right direction, that we hadn't got lost. But he continued to insist that we should continue in the direction we were going, so as not to go completely off course, and if we started wandering about in the forest we would definitely get lost, at least we were walking along a railway track which sooner or later, any moment now, would lead us somewhere!

"In any case," he said optimistically, "we're going to come to a river pretty soon! And beyond the river there are fields! And where there are fields, there's Denmark! Because as we know very well, Denmark is a small agricultural country!"

Naturally he remembered one time when we had been walking across fields – the fields where, as the Georgians told us, bulls grazed in the autumn – and we'd seen a rail track in the distance, the same one which Sheikh-Mahmood didn't dare walk down, because there were border guards patrolling nearby! He'd been warned many times about a railway track which it was best not to walk down, because you might get caught.

"So now we're walking down that railway track," Hanuman said with certainty. "But no one is going to catch us. Because the border guards are not such fools as to venture out in this weather. He-ha-ho! Why would they do a thing like that? They're sitting in their cabins drinking schnapps. They're drinking schnapps and playing cards!"

I said that was what the Germans did in American WWII films, but that things were different now! "So let's head into the forest as quickly as possible!"

"No, no," Hanuman said, digging his heels in. "Absolutely no way! We'll get lost straight away! Why can't you understand?"

But at that moment we heard dogs barking. Hanuman dashed headlong for the forest, and I followed him. Our rucksacks were really heavy, and the worst thing was that the bottles were chinking against each other, making a repugnant sound. It was such an excruciating sound! I never did know how to pack a bag, but Hanuman's rucksack was so musical that it set my teeth on edge! I could vividly picture the bottles smashing into pieces! And I could imagine the schnapps trickling down his back! Brrr! We walked across a forest clearing, waist-deep in snow. The snow continued falling, erasing our surroundings, as if a curtain had fallen, obscuring the way forwards. We could hear barking somewhere behind, but it seemed to be moving at an angle to us, it wasn't directly at our heels. We hurried onwards, and the snow fell, tracing vertical lines, tumbling downwards, sliding into our eyes, forcing its way into our mouths, we nearly choked on snow. A terrible weakness was overpowering me, and I felt sick, as if this was all happening in a dream. We hurried on, trying to make it before the veil of snow fell, and our freedom swooned before us. There was no sky, the sky and the fields had merged into one, the snow had unified the firmament and fundament, and we ran on, as if we were no longer running across earth, but across the sky. The snow was so voluminous that we couldn't feel the ground beneath us, and it continued to tumble down, chasing us; now I couldn't see Hanuman's back at all. But you could be sure that we were fully visible to those who needed to see us. It occurred to me that they might simply shoot us down, if the Afghan hadn't been lying about them sometimes opening fire. They would shoot Hanny first, I thought, because he was dark. They would spot his skin colour in their sights. They're called dioptric sights, aren't they? Of course they'd shoot the Indian first. Those lot, the darkies, the Tamils-Bengals-Indians-Pakistanis-Turks-Georgians-Armenians and all the rest of them, they were often seen roaming about these parts. But I was white, maybe they wouldn't shoot a white guy?

But no one shot at us. We arrived at a river, already soaking wet from the waist down, and we came to a standstill, because I had started puking. I fell to my knees, and I didn't have the strength to carry on, my legs were convulsed with cramp, I couldn't take another step forwards, I just carried on vomiting. I crouched down on my knees until the retching subsided. Then I looked at the slow-moving river and told Hanuman that I didn't care any more, that we could wade across, we were already wet-through, it made no fucking difference. Hanuman just chuckled, and started walking along the riverbank. He was moving like a drunkard, his feet sinking into the mud, reeling from side to side. He was walking with that heavy rucksack on his back, like an astronaut or a wind-up astronaut doll striding across the lunar surface.

We walked for ages, edging along the riverbank with no sense of purpose and no hope, because we had no idea where the path was leading us. It took so much effort to lift our feet out of the oozing mud that we didn't even bother talking. By now we had been walking so long that we could have crossed ten borders. The snow had stopped biting and scratching our faces, and a terrible lull had set in. Eventually we came to a field where the grass had been trampled down, piles of dung dotted here and there, a field full of shit. We concluded that we must be back in Denmark. We headed across the field, tripping over frozen clods of dung. The wind picked up, shoving us from behind, running ahead for a while before turning back on us, like a frisky dog. I suggested that in autumn we might be able to come and pick mushrooms in this field.

"Yes," Hanuman agreed, "if the bulls let us get close enough..."

"Where are they now, Hanuman, what do you reckon?"

"God knows. In this cold they must be in their stables, munching hay..."

But it turned out that in Denmark, in this "small agricultural country", they put the bulls out into the field even in such cold weather, because it made the fat turn into meat quicker (or so we were told). By now the thud of hooves was at our backs, and the bulls were breathing down our necks, just as in Hemingway; now our hearts were beating faster, even more deafeningly than before! I didn't know which would happen first, either my heart would burst from the strain, or my body would be torn to pieces by the bulls! I was no fan of bullfighting, that's true. I didn't like to see innocent animals being slaughtered. But these dumb beasts could trample me to death without sparing a thought, they could tear me limb from limb on their horns, and not because they wanted to eat me! So why not let them perish in a bullfight, if they were so vile and stupid. Let them die for our amusement! Stab them with swords and daggers, the brainless brutes! The bulls were running after me without knowing who they were chasing, where they were going, why they were running... they were just running by reflex – one of them started, another followed, then a third, and then they were all running. Or maybe they just wanted to keep warm. But as I jumped over the barbed wire I told myself that I would never ever go to that festival in Madrid... what was it called?... where they let the bulls loose and they run down the streets, run and run... Then I threw up again, just bile by now... and the bulls were standing there three metres from the fence... their stench reached me, and they stood there, dumb beasts, behind a fence which they could easily have torn down, but they just stood there, stinking animals, thumping the earth with their hooves. I vomited, I choked, I coughed on bile, I started seeing stars. I felt my consciousness slip away from me, my guts were being wrenched inside out...

By morning we arrived at a village. There was a flag flying outside the very first house we came to, a Danish flag.

"I told you so!" said Hanuman, issuing a victorious "He-ha-ho!"

I popped the last lump of cheese into my mouth. Hanuman looked at me and asked what I had just eaten. I said it was nothing special, just a piece of cheese...

"Ah, you son of a bitch!" Hanuman said, "oh you cunning son of a bitch, fuck me! I was wondering whether you were quietly chewing away on something, turns out you were munching cheese the whole time!"

I told him that it was my cheese.

"Oh, so the bread which we ate together, that must have been our joint bread?"

I told him, "Yes! We had an unspoken agreement that it was our joint bread!"

"And so you took an unspoken decision that it was your cheese, and no one else's! Son of a bitch! You son of a bitch, for fuck's sake!" and he added something in his own language...

"There you go again!" I said angrily, "I request a translation, translate what you just said! I won't stand for that! We agreed that we were only going to speak the languages which we both understand!"

"Yes, but I can't understand how you could do that! You had some cheese! Cheese, for fuck's sake! And you ate it! Alone!"

"Well you don't like cheese like I do…"

"What do you mean, 'like you do'? Are you suggesting that I somehow like cheese the wrong way? In some sort of perverted way?"

"Not as much as me…"

"Ah, not as much as you? You son of a bitch, you ate the cheese and then you justify it by claiming your own ardent love for cheese as opposed to my insufficiently strong feelings for the same! You crafty son of a bitch!" he said, and he added the Danish word "fedterøv",[28] and some more stuff in his own language…

"I demand a translation!"

"Fuck you! We're back in Denmark now! Go whichever way you want! Our paths diverge from here! I can't go the same way as someone who I share everything with, absolutely everything, who then goes and munches cheese on the sly, knowing just how hungry I am…"

"You're better at tolerating hunger, Hanuman…"

"I'm better at tolerating hunger… some argument that is! I'm better at tolerating hunger… I'm lacking in love for cheese and I'm better at tolerating hunger… I don't want to hear another word! Especially not about your obsessive love for cheese! I cured the wretch of every disease under the sun! I washed his underwear for him! I applied creams to him and massaged him! I treated his diseased, necrotic feet with Indian herbs! And he behaves like an ungrateful swine! He conceals his cheese from me! At an hour like this! When we had dogs and bulls and hunger and terror on our tails, the son of a bitch was secretly eating cheese, son of a bitch!" And he added a few more words in his own tongue…

"Alright, stop whingeing! Buy yourself some cheese! Or do you want me to steal you some crisps?"

---

28   Cunning (Danish).

"No, not crisps! Sausages! Steal me some sausages! A whole pack! Ten of them!"

"OK, sausages… bangerwangers it is…"

"What are you mumbling to yourself, translate!"

"I said yes-yes, sausages, for fuck's sake…"

"From the first shop we come to!"

"OK, the very first…"

"And I hope they catch you red-handed…"

"Fuck you…"

We went into the supermarket, and Hanuman bought a Chupa Chups – he couldn't have chosen a sillier thing to distract the cashier's attention, it was the cheapest, paltriest, least probable thing he could buy. And the quickest – I only had a few seconds, but I still managed to nab some sausages! We retreated to a spot where no one could see us, then the sun poked out from behind the clouds like an unseeing eye, like a cataract on the celestial cornea. I felt a pang in my stomach as I watched Hanuman rip off the packaging with his teeth like a wild beast and take out the first sausage…

"You going to scoff the whole lot on your own?"

"Yes, alone! You ate the cheese on your own!"

"Come on, that was just a little lump of cheese, but you've got ten sausages there! And we weren't as hungry as we are now! It was a long time ago! Can't you leave me just one?"

"No! I won't! Not a single one! Let it be a lesson to you!"

"Very well, scoff your sausages, you fucking bastard…"

"And you can suck your Chupa Chups! He-ha-ho!"

We started looking for a bus stop, but we quickly got lost. Then we spent ages traipsing about and at around midday we arrived at another village – a few farm buildings scattered across the hillocks, a petrol pump, and a square for playing pétanque, with a German flag flying above it…

"Fuck them!" Hanuman got agitated. He even hopped about on the spot. He stamped his feet and threw his arms in the air like malformed wings.

"Take a look at that! What the fuck is that! Are we back in Germany or something? Fuck them, the sons of bitches! So where do we go now?"

"We need to get out of here fast, look some guy's just come out into his garden, he's watching us, let's go, Hanny, let's go… everyone's got a mobile phone…"

We walked for another couple of hours and arrived at another village – this time with a Danish flag.

"Well, that's alright then," said Hanuman, cooling down. "I told you that you won't go wrong with me!"

But an hour later it was the same story – we came to another village with a German flag. It was some kind of cartographic conundrum – a real maze!

"Maybe they fly flags according to their nationality? Maybe there's a German guy living in that house, but he's living on Danish soil, eh?"

"Fuck knows, they've made a right fucking pig's ear out of it, it would be enough to trip up the Devil himself!"

"They must have won and lost this land to each other at cards a hundred times over!" Hanuman suggested.

"Aha, exactly… that's why they've dotted different flags here, there and everywhere… let's keep going, the same way the Georgians went, let's just go straight ahead, the Earth is round…"

Two more villages with Danish flags. By now the sky had darkened again. We stumbled onwards, barely able to make out our surroundings. Like two ghouls, we arrived at a road where a sign informed us we were thirty kilometres away from some town; we identified it as Danish by the diacritic "å" in the name. That was a relief…

"We're home," said Hanny, and we started walking calmly down the road.

I followed him, fuming again. His words enraged me. "We're home" – what the hell was that supposed to mean! What sort of home was it? "Home" was what the Georgians said when the heroin started spreading through their veins, that's when they hissed "home" through gritted, rotten teeth: "hooome…"

His words made absolutely no sense, just like our trip to Germany. Hanny drove me crazy with that statement. He might just as well have said "Alamo"… Total nonsense! The numbskull! None of it made any sense. I got more and more wound up, and then eventually I let loose, "What are you talking about? Why are we home? Why is Denmark our home? Why didn't we just stay in Germany? We could have lived at the Afghan's place! He promised us work, and a roof over our heads! He doesn't even live there himself, we could have lived in his flat, we could have worked in that Indian restaurant, and we would have eaten there for free, scoffing bits from the orders before they went out, and there would have been plenty of cheap beer to drink! What fucking use is Denmark to us? What's Denmark to you?"

"I don't know… I left some money in the forest in Farstrup, in a bottle…"

"To start with, it's some piffling sum, I'm sure of that. And secondly, we know the way now. We can go and get that money, find Mahmood before he's buggered off to Holland, we can move in to his place, and live in Germany for a while!"

"Let's see," Hanuman said nonchalantly. "If there's nothing for us in Denmark, we'll head back to Germany, but now I just want to eat and sleep, eat and sleep…"

It was morning by the time we dragged ourselves to the town with the diacritic in its name. Walking around, we saw a police station which looked like a museum, a library which looked like a post office, a post office which looked like a library, a museum dedicated to the old police office, and from the bronze plaque nailed to the wall Hanuman could make out that the first Danish victims of the Second World War had been executed there. There was a railway station too, but no trains.

We wandered aimlessly down the empty streets, as if in

a dream. I was half-dead by now. It was early morning, a dank morning, probably Sunday. There was lots of rubbish on the streets, the remnants of some kind of debauchery. Deserted tables outside the café, paper plates left behind, and a wine glass, empty and cracked. A hat with a bell on it on one of the chairs. Cardboard Coca-Cola cups rolling around the ground. Beer bottles which no one had yet claimed. They stood there like an abandoned game of skittles. Some of the bottles had beer left in them. For some reason they were mostly positioned under the lamp posts. Probably because people had been leaning against the lamp posts and put their bottle down on the ground next to them, to remember that they'd left it over there, by the lamp post, but then they forgot... A Dutch-orange scarf was hanging limply from one of the lamp posts, a detail which made the lamp post seem almost human, and I felt a pang again (Holland, damn!). Thanks to that scarf the lamp post looked like some sort of cartoon character. The beer bottles glinted in the light, the darkened green glass beckoning me. I approached one of them and picked it up: there was more than half left. I said quietly, "I don't care – I need a drink," and I drank it down.

Hanuman grimaced in disgust, he even turned away so as not to have to watch me drinking the beer.

We walked down the road. I picked up the empty bottles and placed them in a plastic bag. Then I spotted a frostbitten, half-eaten piece of pizza on a cardboard square by one of the rubbish bins. I could see a mushroom, and a pretty splodge of tomato on top, which seemed to be beckoning me with a woozy, wanton smile. I was so hungry that I picked up the piece of pizza and sank my teeth into it. I was worried that if I didn't eat it I might not be able to make another step forwards!

"Heh!" Hanuman made a sound which didn't quite become laughter. "You won't die from fussiness," he said in conclusion. The pizza was wooden, frozen stiff, even the mushroom was like a piece of rubber, and the tomato tasted bitter. It left my mouth in welts, and my gums bleeding...

Once we had got on to the train and travelled a couple of stops something weird started happening to my guts. I had to rush to the toilet a couple of times. When we got back to Farstrup I slept for a whole day...

I was woken by a spasm in my leg. I felt really ill. My glands were swollen again, I had a temperature, I was aching all over, and I badly needed the toilet. Hanuman was airing the room, telling me that I'd been breaking so much wind in my sleep that it was impossible to breathe. I told him that I wanted tea with milk, because my glands were swollen and I had a temperature, and some honey would be nice too. But this time Potapov had decided that he was going to cure me with schnapps, which no one wanted to buy from us. He offered to treat me so he would have unrestricted access to it. He kept helping himself to little sips, so he wasn't drunk exactly, but jolly, tipsy, and he was singing some horrible song to himself the whole time. When I asked what the song was, he informed me importantly, "Mummy Troll!" I asked him again, "What was that?" and he replied, "Oh forget it," shrugged his shoulders and walked off down the corridor, continuing to sing to himself.

We started selling the cigarettes we'd bought in Germany, but at some point we realised that we weren't going to make a profit. Hanny pointed out that since we were smokers ourselves it didn't make much sense to sell our German cigarettes cheap and buy ourselves Danish cigarettes, which were more expensive. We'd end up making a loss! Best to smoke the German cigarettes and not buy Danish ones! It was cast-iron logic, his brain worked like clockwork, like a computer! We ceased trading and started smoking the cigarettes ourselves, and we got so stuck into them that we started lighting one off the other. But those cigarettes were really dry. They blazed up like bits of straw. Ivan even started to doctor them with a wetted finger so that they wouldn't burn so fast. We smoked those cigarettes and drank our schnapps, which we mixed with *saft* (Scandinavian cordial), and we drank as if we were vying to see who could drink the most...

But I couldn't get much pleasure from it, because I could remember the road we had travelled. According to my inebriated deliberations cheap schnapps and cheap cigarettes just weren't worth the suffering which we had endured on our travels! And even if we had made a profit, it still wouldn't have been worth it!

Those thoughts made me so upset that I gave up trying to do anything. I stopped answering questions and asking them too. I ceased all forms of communication, I didn't react to anything. I gave up shaving and washing, I stopped getting out of bed, and I remained in that condition until our train entered spring, which brought with it two Serbian girls who were called Jasmina and Violeta.

Part Three

1

February 1999 was a month of heavy snowfall. The Danish newspapers and TV clamoured about it nationwide. They wrote and they blared away that even 107-year-old Mrs Vibeke Struse couldn't recall such snow, and despite her advanced years she was still of sound mind and had a crystal-clear memory. Her memory reached back to the deepest depths of her childhood, to when she was three years old. She could remember when the last Jutland wolf was killed and hammered up on the doors of the tavern, the last tavern to succumb to Tuborg. She could remember her great-great-grandfather opening a bottle of beer with his teeth and spitting out the very first metal cap. She could remember the sailors coming back from the three-week storm of 1908 (they didn't look happy, more humiliated, as if the elements had abused them). She had to live by candlelight and brands during the two world wars, she knew the true taste of bread and cheese. She could remember how they shaved the women who had slept with the Germans; "like sheep," she would say. She remembered the time when people walked across the ice from Copenhagen to Malme. She remembered people eating horsemeat during the famine. "They ate it with guilt written on their faces, as if they were eating human flesh," she would say. She remembered all of those things, but she couldn't remember snow like the snow which fell in February 1999.

The roof collapsed over Potapov's ruins, but no one was hurt, thank God. There was so much snow piled up in the middle of the kitchen and living room – where the notorious stove was busy pumping out smoke – that it caused a flood when it melted. Unfortunately for Liza, she was the only one at home when it happened. She got such a fright that she climbed into the wardrobe and started shrieking harrowingly. When they got her out of there she said that the Abominable Snowman had come to steal her away. Potapov suffered a fit of rage, and gave that stupid little stepdaughter of his a good beating. Then he grabbed a bucket, but he couldn't manage on his own. He chucked it in, and for a while they lived there like that, ankle-deep in water, fully dressed the whole time.

I saw it with my own eyes, I saw them eating in the kitchen, when Ivan and I came to fetch the meat. Potapov kept it in the hallway, which functioned as a freezer room. And it did so in an exemplary fashion, it should be said, since it was so cold there. The little stove in the kitchen only heated the room half-heartedly – they lived in such freezing conditions!

They would sit round the table having dinner, surrounded by water… with snow falling through the hole in the roof. The beams sagged inwards, the plastic sheeting flapped about and rustled in the wind. It resembled a scene of people eating out on their veranda, or having a picnic somewhere, you would never think they were sitting at home! There was open sky above them, and the moon and the stars were literally peeking into their plates, but the three of them just sat there in silence, calmly eating their soup. Only that they were dressed in winter clothes, of course. Maria was holding Adam in her arms, and she had a hat on her head. Liza was even holding her spoon in a mitten-clad hand. Mikhail was also wearing his hat. He didn't even look up at us.

"Wait a minute," he grunted tetchily.

He unhurriedly finished his soup, and then, wheezing and belching, he came with us, shining the torch beam into the darkest recesses of his ruins, which were rammed full of shabby, ancient, furniture. We took a piece of meat wrapped in plastic, or rather he gave it to us. He picked it up off the floor, brushed the dirt off it, had a sniff and said, "Should be alright", as if he were handing us something for the dog. I started to express my doubts as to the freshness of that piece of meat, which Potapov wanted five kroner for.

"It's half price to friends. The Arabs give me ten kroner for it," he said defiantly.

"It's not about the money, or about Arabs," I said. "They don't care what they eat, as long as it's not pork. We'd be willing to pay twenty kroner, if it were a bit fresher. Anyway, how can you charge us for it, the meat's from the container at the rubbish dump, as we know very well! We're not like those Arabs, who think that you bought it or stole it. They don't know where the meat's from. But we know! We're the ones who put you up to hunting for meat at the dump! It doesn't make any difference if you drove there yourself!"

Potapov didn't want to hear it, shrugged his shoulders and said, "But I have to pay for the petrol!"

"What's that got to do with it!" I yelled at him, "You can get to the container on foot!"

"Not me," he said, wheezing and whining, "I can't go on foot! I fetched the meat by car!"

"I don't care if you went by helicopter!" I said, refusing to let him off the hook.

He turned away, with the words, "If you don't want it, don't take it. Eat beans instead. I haven't got time to waste with you. I've got loads of stuff to do. No rest for the wicked…"

Ivan offered to pay for the meat later. I half-heartedly said it was too bad about the roof, could we help in any way? Mikhail said it was OK, worse things had happened, he would manage somehow, and he hurriedly shut the door…

The Serbs started disappearing from the camp, one by one. To start with they stopped drinking and taking drugs. All apart from one of them, Aleksandr, who they took away in an ambulance following his latest overdose. They didn't bring him back. People said that he was sent to some sort of penal drug addiction clinic. He had exhausted the patience of the police, who didn't bother sending him down for every misdemeanour, but just issued him one more fine, and reminded him he was in the waiting line to do 150,000 kroner-worth of time, and that if he carried on stealing then he would just extend the time he had to do. And he kept on extending it. He kept on stealing and getting caught. He didn't care how much more time he clocked up. He knew that the longer the term, the longer he would stay in Denmark. Maybe in prison, but still in Denmark! And that was important, very important, it was vitally important! Because, as he told us, "Better to do time in Denmark than in Sarajevo, the prison there is no fucking joke!"

"Yes," I said, "that's right. The longer he spends in prison in Denmark, the longer he will live. Because he won't be shooting up so much, maybe he'll even come off the stuff…"

"With his past form – not likely," said Mikhail, scratching his beard.

"He won't come off it, no way, he won't," said Ivan. "That one will be injecting until the end of his days – until he's dead and buried, that's for certain!"

They gave Goran a room in some hostel which was no better than the camp. It was like being back in his homeland! The place was packed with gypsies just like him, from Bosnia and Romania. They drank together, sang together, and jabbed each other with their knives for want of anything better to do! He was also in the queue for prison, so he could do his time! And oh, was he looking forward to that! He was looking forwards to it like a sailor looks forwards to getting back to dry land, or like an ordinary person looks forwards to their holidays.

"Ah, I'll catch up on my sleep!" he said, "at last I'll get some time off work!"

The rest of the Serbs started to plan where they should go, where to take off to, and they began to put some money aside. But they couldn't agree about going to Holland, which is where the three of them who were heavy rock fans wanted to go. Two of the other ones who were older and wiser, wanted to go to Switzerland. The Serbs spent a long time deliberating, yelping at each other in the kitchen, staining the ceiling yellow, in the end they fell out, and decided that the ones who wanted to go to Holland could go there and the rest would go to Switzerland! But they were later spotted boarding the ferry for Sweden! I wasn't sure how to explain it. Maybe their geography was really that bad, or maybe they just wanted to sneak off from the others.

Mikhail spent January and February painting a big picture, a huge, really intricate painting, which was commissioned by Svenaage. He was a fan of hard rock and fast motorbikes, which was something he and Mikhail had in common. Just as he didn't hide his tattoos, Svenaage didn't try to hide his past, which may have been shady, but was at least untarnished by any prison terms. Svenaage looked after the teenagers at the camp, and took refugees round Denmark to see the sights. Sometimes he took people to the lake, where they tried to catch the fish, but they were so overfed that they didn't go for the unnaturally large worms which were on sale by the lakeside. Those places were called "Put 'n' Take". But despite the promised good catch, the fish didn't go for the bait. The large, plump trout, which were abnormally large and plump, just swam about near the hooks, flicking their tails from side to side.

In the picture, which Svenaage had commissioned out of some kind of charitable considerations, he was supposed to be depicted seated on his motorbike, which was a chopper. He would be sitting there wearing his studded leather jacket, wrapped in a scarf of some indeterminate colour, with a pipe between his teeth. Mikhail asked Hanuman to take a photo, then Hanuman went to the computer room to scan it, and he placed Svenaage on his motorbike by a canyon in a desert in America. Svenaage was in raptures. Mikhail asked him to choose the size of the canvas. That was a cunning ploy, because it meant that Svenaage was pretty much obliged to buy the canvas. And canvases were expensive. But he wasn't stingy, he paid for one of the larger canvases. When Mikhail realised the scale of the commission he scratched his turnip-head and said "Mmm..." And so he painted the picture. He drew a grid, sketched the outlines of the photograph, and then started painting square by square, like some kind of colour-by-numbers. Progress on the work was painfully slow.. But Potapov was in no hurry to show his woeful work of art to his client. He painted slowly so as to put off the moment of being found out until some time in the unforeseeable future. So that when that moment finally arrived Svenaage would be so tired of waiting that he'd be content with any old daubing. But the picture turned out pretty well. The desert was best of all, the sand dune and canyon made quite an impact, and the motorbike wasn't too bad either. You couldn't tell if Svenaage was a good likeness – he was wearing a helmet, which was a clever fix. I'd seen worse things hanging up in Danish flats when I was cleaning toilets with my uncle. Svenaage was so undiscerning in matters of art that he didn't care what he put up on his wall. And he forgot that he hadn't been wearing a helmet in the photo. But that wasn't important! Now he could invite his drinking buddies round and show them the picture, telling them that it was painted by a Russian guy with whom he had traversed the deserts of America, and that this was in Nebraska.

As Mikhail painted, he smoked hashish and told all sorts of stories. Not only did he smoke the hash, he did a bit of dealing too. He had acquired some loyal customers in particular the Kurds who smoked on the sly from the other Muslims, and the Iranian guy Matthew, who we nicknamed Holmes.

Matthew never took his pipe out of his mouth, not even when he ate. And he ate all sorts of crap, so called "lazy food", because he couldn't cook to save his life. He would boil spaghetti and ask why it was always stuck together in a lump. He told us that whatever he cooked always ended up tasting like shit, total shit! That's why he always ate sandwiches. He would come into the kitchen carrying plastic bags full of food, then lay out a long row of sliced bread along the two worktops, asking anyone else who was in the kitchen to move to one side. Then he would put a piece of pre-sliced cheese on to each bit of bread, and continue moving up and down the row, placing pieces of sausage on top of the cheese, after which he would sprinkle on spices and place a second slice of bread on top to complete the sandwiches. Then he would take ages to eat them, a really long time, moving up and down the row, sometimes reseating himself to do so. But then he found a solution to the problem – he started eating packet soups, and cheap Chinese noodles. Although even then he couldn't wait until the food was ready, and the noodles crunched as he ate them. The crazy Iranian drove everyone up the wall with his strange, stranger than strange behaviour; everyone ran a mile from him, including Ivan. But no one revealed why it was impossible to live with Matthew, no one mentioned anything specific, apart from the smell he exuded. He never washed and bought piles of second-hand clothes, which he never washed. He would put them on in the shop and then walk straight out, dressed in them. He emanated a specific smell of clothes which had been festering in a heap for too long. On top of that everyone said that he was crazy! A total psycho. And they said he wanked a lot too. As well as that, he pestered them with idiotic questions and shouted in his sleep!

He had a taste for gambling, particularly at cards. One time he got completely trounced. He lost everything to Arshak. The Armenian deftly made the Iranian part company with all of his pocket money. He knew that the Iranian liked playing cards and had played with him now and again for small change, while also messing around with him and pretending to be a young simpleton. And then on payday he fleeced him completely. Matthew was left with nothing to eat. No one was prepared to feed him or bail him out, because everyone hated him. He started stealing food from the communal fridges, but was caught the very first night and got a whack. Then he stopped eating completely. After five days he went to the staff office and fell to the floor, pretending he was fainting from hunger. He crawled around asking for some money to buy food, or at least to be given a food package. Svenaage was the only one to show him pity. He took him to the lake and made him go fishing. But Matthew couldn't even fix a worm on to his hook, so he didn't catch a thing. Svenaage gave him his whole catch and bought him a load of noodles. Matthew sold all the fish and sloped off to play cards with Arshak. He lost everything just as before and swore never to play again.

Arshak looked around thirty, he was a hairy, muscle-bound ape, and alongside him Mais was like a skivvy who was kept on a short lead. Arshak twisted him round his little finger just like rosary beads. Mais was nimble, but Arshak was some kind of viper. Despite his massive proportions he could flit through an open window like a bird, and he'd nick anything out of the cupboards which was of any value or of no value at all, and then flutter back out, leaving no trace apart from the smell of his sweaty body. He was so solidly built and looked so threatening that Hanuman didn't dare get on the wrong side of him. Arshak would have been more than happy to start something, he was a total cut-throat! He was always looking for an excuse to kick off. Sometimes he would just nab money or mobile phones off the Tamils. If he spotted one of the camp runts talking on the phone by reception then he might grab their phone card, or he'd ask to make a call and talk until the credit was finished. If they asked him "vay may frend?" he would reply menacingly, "That's vay may frend. No si kart iz kaput? Go bay nu kart, twat!" He was always wearing that vile loutish leer, like some kind of mask. He was a proper thug who dreamed about growing up to be a gangster, just that no one gave him the opportunity. He complained there were no real warriors in the Danish criminal community; he meant the Russian or Armenian gangs. But there were, they just didn't want to take him in. He wanted to pull off some big jobs, do some real work, he was fed up with filching tracksuits and irons. He went to the gym, pumped iron until he was giddy, until a huge vein appeared on his forehead, then he walked out with that vein bulging. When they asked him to pay for the gym he refused, so they stopped letting him in. The last time he was there, when he already knew it was going to be last time, he secretly opened a window in the corner, and that night he stole everything he needed to continue making that vein bulge at home.

One time Arshak stole a wallet from a fat old Serb, which had all his takings in it. The Serb used to bring food to the camp and get very agitated and sweaty as he sold it. It was clear that he didn't feel comfortable selling food to his own lot, because he had been an asylum seeker until recently too. Arshak bided his time, waiting until the Serb had sold all his stuff, until the poor sod was about to leave, and then he chucked some kind of tin on to the ground, to lure the Serb out. While the clumsy Serb climbed out of his car, huffing and puffing, to go and have a look at the tin, Arshak crept into the car and nicked the Serb's wallet from the glove compartment. The Serb sat there in tears for a while, begging the camp dwellers to give him back his money, because he wouldn't be able to carry on trading now, and his boss would kill him for being so sloppy. But of course Arshak didn't give the money back. He walked around for a whole month with a self-satisfied grin on his face, boasting, "Silly Serb, he's just as stupid as an Albanian, he fell for that tin of condensed milk, the twat, and he kept his money in his glove compartment, what an idiot!"

Arshak would go round the camp asking to borrow videocassettes off people, and if someone gave him one, he would go up to one of the wimpier camp inhabitants and he wouldn't back down until they bought that video off him.

He would send his dad to go and see the Tamils and ask them to call the ambulance for his wife, because she was so ill, and the camp's only public telephone was broken. If the Tamils produced mobile phones, the old man would walk off and a little later Arshak would turn up and help himself to the phones.

The old man was called Grey Hare – Liza had given him that nickname. Grey Hare was of diminutive stature and short-sighted, he limped, he spoke in a nasal voice, and he had a funny moustache which was as thick as a brush (people even joked that it was the moustache which made his voice sound strange). And he always wore the same old moth-eaten grey suit. When he took a liking to someone or wanted to impress them he would take them to see his collection of clothes. Sometimes he would invite people to tea or even the *dalma* or *tamale* his wife made – they were really mouth-watering! And then he would casually reach into his wardrobe, and start up: "By the way, I've got this one jacket, here, how's that? Not bad? I'm not sure if it suits me though? What do you reckon? What about this one? And then there's this blue one, how's that? It's got nice buttons; I only got it for the buttons..."

He had loads of expensive suits in his wardrobe which he and Arshak had nicked from the Kaufmann and Illum clothes stores in Copenhagen, back in the days when the shop assistants were naive enough to trust their detector alarms, and didn't suspect that with a pair of pliers you could easily prise off the plastic discs which triggered the alarm.

Grey Hare was grey, in patches. He was balding, but only in patches too. He was dirty, smelled of sweaty feet and armpits, scratched himself, and often cleared his throat to give himself an important air. He frequented the local second-hand shops, and never bought a thing but always left with loads of stuff, because it was so easy to steal from those places – he couldn't resist the temptation. You could see him every evening at the supermarket rubbish bins or by Farstrup lake. He went fishing even if there were blizzards blowing, just because it was free. They said that back in Soviet times he'd been some sort of technologist, maybe an engineer. His wife was a Russian teacher. She was the biggest thief in the family. Every single day, sometimes even twice a day, she would go to the shop and load up her trolley. Then she would hide behind the crates of Coca-Cola, and place the contents of the trolley into her bottomless bag. And then she would leave, paying only for a loaf of bread. She had a simple justification: she had to earn back the cost of their journey, they had invested so much money, there was no work to be had, and now they had hardly any money left.

They started to have some bother from the cops, who wanted to deport them together with the other Russian speakers – the Armenians were placed in the same category as the Russians, and assigned the number "120"; that's what they called the Russians, the "one-hundred-and-twenties". At that point they took a radical decision – to sacrifice Arshak's mother's well-being in order to stay put. Rumour had it that it was Arshak who broke her leg. It meant that she was no longer deportable, so the police stopped hassling them. But she still managed to get to the shop every day, just as if she were going to work, hobbling along with her bag slung over her crutches.

Mikhail painted his picture, Ivan and Hanuman hung out with him, and I dropped by every evening for a few puffs, so I could fall asleep in the corner, on a dilapidated and very soft armchair. I didn't smoke much, and only so that I could crash out and sleep – if not for twenty-four hours a day, then at least twenty. So that I wouldn't have to witness everyday life at the camp. So as not to have to think about anything.

We would discuss camp life, and how the place was fast becoming more and more Muslim. I say "we" but I was only a peripheral member of that "we", in the same way that your elbow sometimes makes it into the corner of a photograph. The camp was already three-quarters Muslim before we got there, but now the non-Muslims were being ejected in droves, and the others were fleeing, fanning out across Europe, leaving like fleas hopping off a body sprayed with insect repellent, so that the camp became basically pure Muslim! And three times dirtier than before!

They prayed for days on end, and they ate nothing while the sun shone, but by night they would come crawling out and start stuffing themselves in the kitchen, and they would never clean up their mess behind them. The kitchen was so filthy that I hardly dared go in. There was a terrible stench, scraps of food lying about all over the place, flour everywhere, like a baker's or a mill! The camp staff had even resorted to threats – no pocket money unless they tidied up! A sign to that effect appeared in every camp building, but it didn't scare anyone. The staff weren't allowed to force people to tidy up, and everyone knew that very well, so no one bothered, and they got paid their money all the same. When the Muslims weren't praying, they listened to tapes of prayer songs, and sometimes they even played them backwards. They messed about with those tapes like little children, but some of them thought it was blasphemous, so they swore at each other and had heated debates on the subject! They consulted the Koran and yelled at each other. They kicked up a scandal over the slightest thing. Of course they did, they had to direct their energies somewhere! After all, they didn't have wives with them! And the tension was palpable; that was them waiting for their cases to be decided. Waiting for the Directorate to bestow its benevolence upon them! They prayed and they prayed... They flitted up and down the corridors with their water bottles ever more frequently, more and more puddles formed in the toilets, and the bruises on their foreheads grew more vivid and hideous!

At some point Hanuman became very pensive. It started with him tapping his foot. That measured tapping would even wake me sometimes. I would think to myself, still half-asleep: surely one of those gimps hasn't crept under Hanuman's wing again. But when I looked down I saw Nepalino, rolled up into a ball under his pile of quilts. I looked over at Hanuman. He was lying there, stretched out, tense, with a strange, absent expression on his face. He lay there knocking his left foot against the metal pole of our bunk, his empty gaze fixed on the open window. He didn't even notice that I was looking at him. That was a bad omen. Then he started singing to himself, and some words surfaced, barely audible. The melody sounded familiar, I'd heard it somewhere before. Not from him, but earlier, during my childhood. For some reason I pictured fences, poles, branches covered in hoar frost, and garage walls, stretching along the road where we lived in Pääsküla, outside Tallinn. Towering birch trees harbouring crows' nests. Marshes, covered in piles of rubbish, with gulls circling above. That melody stirred memories which had long been buried by the sands of time, and it felt pretty spooky! It went on for several days, and I started to feel more and more uncomfortable. That melancholic refrain sucked me in like a quagmire. But then suddenly it stopped.

Hanny jumped up, yelling that he'd been stained by the damned sheets. He leaped into the middle of the room and started twitching, twisting, contorting himself, as if he was possessed by demons. He wrung his hands. Then he showed me his elbows, his knees, and arse...

"Look," he shouted, "There's dye all over me. It's these blue sheets! And the green quilt cover! The red pillowcase! What sort of bedding is this! Curse these Danes! I've faded!

I'm coloured! Blue like Jesus! Like Krishna! That's what their fucking bed linen does to you! Soon we'll all turn into vegetables!" Then he went to mooch around the camp, slamming the door as he left.

He would pick holes in everything, making mocking jokes or caustic comments. He started hassling Nepalino, threatening to shag him up the arse, but Nepalino locked himself in the shower room and wouldn't come out for ages. Then Hanuman bought himself a crate of beer, which was always a bad sign. It looked like he was searching for the next big idea. But he couldn't come up with anything at all. He sloped round the camp, looking for a way to realise his dream. And his dream was that all those people who had spat in his face or at his back would one day see his dazzling smile wherever they went, that it would adorn every bus, tram and skyscraper, and loom over them from overhead screens: "Hallo, it's me, Hanumancho!" But he couldn't find anything in that vipers' nest which might have brought his dream closer to reality.

"This lousy place is killing me!" he said.

On top of that we'd smoked the last of our damned cigarettes, so we had to get our arses into gear again! At the very least we had to pay a visit to the rubbish bins to fetch bottles and food!

"This camp is stifling me!" he snarled. "It's brought my migraine on again! A bloody migraine! My head's like a Halloween pumpkin, for fuck's sake!"

And then he took to wandering round the corridors again, singing to himself, and putting videos on, although he didn't watch them, he just switched them on and walked off. He slagged everyone off constantly, including me, and one time we nearly fell out…

It happened because of a jigsaw puzzle which Ivan brought home from the scrap heap one time. He started trying to put it together, but eventually he gave up, and so for want of anything better to do I decided to try and complete it myself.

Then, early one morning Hanuman woke up, saw me with the puzzle, laughed, and started picking an argument with me: "Doing that puzzle makes our predicament positively penal, because prison is the only place where people waste their time on that kind of nonsense! It's the most pointless pursuit imaginable, invented for kids, cretins, and invalids who have nothing better to do!"

In the end we decided to have a wager. He said that with my feeble mind and fumbling fingers I wouldn't be able to assemble the thousand-piece puzzle in five days. No way! No chance! He ribbed me so hard that I even got offended. And – it should be noted – it was the Nepali's muted giggling which really made my indignation boil up and erupt (looking back, I'm sure that they must have conspired against me – I'm sure of it! – because they'd started speaking their own language a lot when we were together). For some reason I insisted I would be able to assemble that puzzle. Hanuman promised to pay me one thousand kroner if I could. But if I couldn't I would have to eat five fresh chillies, big ones, which he would select for me himself.

"I'll go to Copenhagen for them if I have to!" he exclaimed. "I'll get hold of some chillies which will give you worse hallucinations than those cosmic magic mushrooms!"

I parried with bravado that there would be no need for him to go to Copenhagen. And I started assembling the puzzle. It went pretty well; in just a few hours I had already made good progress. The picture was materialising before my eyes. After a day you could make out its basic outlines. Hanuman realised that I was on top of the task, and he started doing everything possible to disrupt me. He sent idiots to come and see me with the absurdest questions, like "Where can we get hold of some broccoli round here?" He brought Svenaage round with a bottle of vodka. He dispatched Nepalino, who informed me with a feigned look of horror that the police had come, then pointed at the open window and said feebly "Run! Run!" Meanwhile,

Hanuman was waiting behind the door, ready for me to jump out of the window so that he could come in and defile my masterpiece.

It truly was a masterpiece. It was the picture of my dreams, the azure dreams of an idiot. It depicted a cove, with dizzyingly blue waters, a yacht, a beach of golden sand, palms on the beach, and cliffs, atop of which some large, gaudy Ara parrots had convened like the jury in a kangaroo court. Suspended in a murderously monotone sky above them was the dazzling sun. I assembled that picture, telling myself that if I completed it and won the bet then my dreams would come true: the yacht would be mine, I would bathe my feet in the waters of that cove, and wash my dirty socks there too.

But I didn't finish it. There was one piece missing. It just wasn't anywhere to be found. I turned the room upside down looking for it. I got Ivan on the job as well. I sent the Nepali hunting under every bunk. I called the Chinaman to come and have a poke around as well. But it was useless, completely hopeless. Nepalino sorted through his papers, lazily shrugged his shoulders and went off to inform Hanuman that I was starting to panic. Ivan was too drunk to look for anything. I got nothing from him, not a word of sense, all that happened was that his key ring fell from his trouser pocket. He just distanced himself – how was he supposed to know! He'd found the puzzle at the scrap heap, after all. Maybe it was incomplete to start with! How could he have checked? You can't check it until you've assembled it!

Hanuman brought me those chilli peppers. Attractively presented on a saucer. End to end, in a cosmic smile. A ticket to clinical perfection. But I refused to admit defeat. I wasn't going to eat those chillies. I maintained that I would have succeeded, if it weren't for... But Hanuman wouldn't have a word of it. He kicked up a fuss. He huffed and he puffed, inflating himself like a balloon, smoke and sparks came flying from him. He insisted that according to our wager I was supposed to assemble the puzzle in five days!

"Assemble!" he shouted, "I repeat, assemble! In its entirety! But I don't see it! I don't see that you've finished it! The picture isn't complete! You lost!"

I told him to go to hell, and we didn't speak to each other for several days.

The snow melted, the fields blackened, the first real spring rain fell, and I went out for a walk in the wet, waking forest. I heard the forest weeping and birds rustling amongst fragrant rotted leaves. I saw cracks appear as the frozen field arched its mighty spine. I saw the fog crawling across the fields, and I found myself thinking, "So, we survived winter, what next?" I looked around me and felt revulsion. I was afraid to raise my eyes and see what lay ahead. I had gone into the forest feeling a strange, suppressed desire – to lose myself, to lose myself in that forest like a character in a fairy tale, to meet some sprite or other mystical creature; my despair had awoken the child in me. But of course nothing happened. I went back to the camp all the same, I peeked out from behind the bushes to check the coast was clear, then I went up to our window, climbed in, and got into bed. Hanuman asked me if I'd had a good wank, out there in the forest. That was him trying to make it up with me, his overture. I hissed "go to hell" at him through gritted teeth. He continued musing out loud on the subject, as if he were talking to himself. "I don't understand how anyone could go for a wank in the open air? In the forest? How's that possible? What would you feel like as you did it? Anyone could be watching from behind the trees." I wanted to shove my fingers into my ears and run. But I just lay there, I lay there with my eyes shut, listening to the sounds of camp life. The voices, the doors slamming… and whenever I heard tires crunching across the gravel I tensed, I listened in, waiting to hear whose voices would follow, which door would slam, which direction the footsteps would go in, and what kind of footsteps they were: confident ones measuring out the floor proprietorially, or soft, stealthy ones... I could only relax when I heard the wheels departing, then I would collapse into a fitful sleep...

We waited for the spring move – the mass influx of new refugees. We were hoping for something new, different faces, new ideas, fresh blood and new stories. We were waiting for more idiots to make money out of, to con. Or people who could give us some useful pointers, people who had useful connections. We hoped that there would be more decent folk, and fewer representatives of different faiths. But it was the opposite. A load of Iraqis turned up who had endured the Baghdad bombardment. They had glazed-over gazes, faces frozen in horror, hatred in the wrinkles round their lips. Then there were two Russian families. One decent, quiet-natured musician and his family, who were swiftly sent to Sweden. And an awful pair from the sticks: young, scruffy, uncouth, hot-tempered. They quickly got into a really nasty scrape, and fled to Germany. And two more Serbian families, with two girls who were real beauties, a couple of pearls: Jasmina and Violeta...

2

It was the middle of April when I saw them – Hanuman and Jasmina – walking down the concrete path, past the cherry trees which hadn't yet thought about blooming. He was gesticulating, and she was smiling. He was wearing his blue jeans, and a dark brown, iridescent shirt with cufflinks. He wasn't wearing a tie, but he somehow created the vague impression that one might be present. His leather jacket had zips like a handbag, and the leather was clearly soft and expensive – no one normally wore jackets like that in a refugee camp. It was a poser's jacket, it looked like it could have cost as much as fifteen thousand kroner, from the leather goods department of the kind of shop which mere mortals never entered, not even out of idle curiosity. That jacket made him look like a film star. Nepalino had cut his hair masterfully, and Hanny had then styled it with two bold movements of his virtuosic hands, completing his resemblance to the world-famous Indian actor, Bachchan. In that jacket, Hanuman could go up to any cabriolet in town, and without really trying he could convince anyone at all that it was his. No one would suspect you of lying, if you were wearing a stunning jacket like that. As soon as I saw Hanuman and Jasmina together I realised that she was doomed, it was clear to see. Hanuman had conquered her. Already. Right there. On the asphalt path by the unblooming lilac bushes, next to the puddle where the crows were paddling. As he spoke his hands flitted about like birds, his chin jutted forwards, his lips moved like waves, and his eyebrows arched upwards, like the wings of his high-flown phrases. He had already captured her attention, her imagination and her heart, and now he was juggling it in his hands. The capitulation of the flesh was just a question of time and the right circumstances. It was a question of time just like the expected blossoming of the lilacs. It was clear that the girl was all his.

I behaved gallantly and avoided superfluous questions as I shook Jasmina's hand. Hanuman introduced me as "the Russian writer who writes in English", and her as the perfect superwoman. He said that we were going to go into town right away, that a certain Violeta would join us at any moment and then we would all head into town together to let our hair down, because today was Friday and all normal people let loose on Fridays.

"And why are we any different from them? We have to cling on to our humanity whatever happens, don't you think? The fact that we're illegal immigrants, and that you're refugees doesn't make any difference. We're human beings first and foremost! Maybe we're even more human than those people with passports and six-figure bank accounts! Anyway, we're going to Aalborg! We're off to Aalborg! To Aalborg!"

We went to every nightclub and disco on Disco street. We danced, Hanuman flared his nostrils and pursed his lips, he rolled his eyes and jerked his knees. I just put on the appearance of dancing, I rotated my torso as best I could, but my movements weren't far removed from kindergarten gymnastics. Jasmina and Violeta enchanted us with their litheness, and I fell completely in love with Violeta's waist, with her wave-like form, with the smooth transition from girlish midriff to her buttocks. There it was – the transition from poetry to prose! The transition which I made that very evening, as my hands gripped her waist and slid down her butt... mmm, her eyes blazed up, and she said something, although it seemed as if she said it to herself, and it seemed it was something like, "Ooh, that feels just right!"

I later found out that they were only sixteen, although they had claimed to be nineteen to get the full social support, instead of half of it, as children. Violeta had long black hair, but Jasmina had even longer hair, and it was just as beautiful as Violeta's. They both had beautiful eyes, but Violeta's eyes were black as night, whereas Jasmina's eyes shone like the glow of distant summer storms. Violeta's eyebrows had been applied in thick brushstrokes, but Jasmina's were delicate slivers, resting on her brow. Violeta's lips were blossoming buds, but Jasmina's lips were thin. Violeta was shorter than Jasmina, but Jasmina's breasts were perter than Violeta's ample, low-hanging bosoms. Jasmina rose early, while Violeta went to bed after midnight.

When we got back to the camp Hanuman told me that he didn't want to sleep alone any more. That we had to do something about the situation, we had to get shot of our feline Nepali friend. We had to organise a party! A celebration! We needed to find the key to their fathers' hearts! Those girls will make us millionaires! I didn't ask any questions. I had no idea how those two girls could make us millionaires. But I decided to trust his feelings, his instincts. If that was what he said, then that was how things should be. We dispatched the Nepali to Astrup, telling him that it was just the place for him, that there was a black guy with a big fat dick waiting for him there! And that if he didn't get a move on and sod off then we'd sweep his chimney pipe for him! Not personally, of course, we'd invite Arshak to come round and do the job! Upon mention of that monster Nepalino immediately said, "No, that won't be necessary thank you, do want you want, I'm off to see my uncle," and he left once he'd got his next pocket money, paying for the ticket himself. That very same evening we forked out a few hundred kroner and put on a party in our room, or you could have called it a foursome, because no one other than Jasmina and Violeta were invited.

We listened to music, we had a whole heap of CDs which we showed to the girls and chatted about with them. We showed them our collection of videocassettes, of which we had more than one hundred, including some of the most recent releases; we had a fantastic collection of films copied from the pay-per-view channels. The girls looked at us as if we were the most sophisticated guys in the village. Which we were, because there was no one else in that village with jackets like mine and Hanuman's. Or who said the kind of stuff which me and Hanuman said! No one else could smile at them like us, or look into their eyes as devotedly as we could! And they fell for it! They fell like Berlin and Troy! They couldn't withstand the assault! Hanuman took Jasmina in Potapov's car, he took her for a ride in that car, he took her away somewhere, and that's where it happened. And I fell for her right there in our room.

Of course I didn't do anything in particular to make it happen, I never did anything which might later cause my corroded conscience to torment me. I let her do everything. Such is my seedy nature, and I have always been proud of it, because I am yet to meet a more devious sod than me on the face of the earth. A sod who could do so much vile stuff and yet preserve his conscience in a state of anabiosis and his heart pure and unsullied. Who could be so comfortable with himself! Who could be vile like a gentleman! Who could maintain the appearance of decency. Who could be so rotten to the core and not suffer in the slightest. Who could dismember someone's soul without messing up his nice white shirt-cuffs.

The next day we watched *Shakespeare in Love*, drank Coca-Cola, and ate popcorn. The cinema in Aalborg was small and almost empty. Then we sat outside a café, and despite the chilly weather the girls ate ice cream while Hanny and I drank beer. Hanny spent the whole time explaining what kind of country Denmark was, and what kind of country Sweden was. The sleepy woman at the kiosk yawned, stepped outside for a smoke, and observed us with drowsy curiosity. Hanny told us that he would show us the difference between Sweden and Denmark right away. He went up to the woman at the kiosk and asked for a cigarette. She pulled a grimace as if he had tried to sell her a crocodile, she didn't even bother answering, muttered something to herself and turned away, choking on smoke and indignation. Hanuman came back to us and announced, "Welcome to Denmark!"

We spent ages walking down a road with an incredibly noisy wedding party whizzing past us, and Hanuman's story about Prague was also somehow celebratory and never-ending. We walked down the old streets, which were narrow and packed full of funny little Japanese people in caps and raincoats, with miniature cameras on their chests. Hanny yelled, "What do these people hope to photograph here?"

The wind tousled Jasmina and Violeta's hair, the sunlight played off the studs and zips on Hanuman's jacket...

And then we stood on a bridge with an endless stream of cars and bikes flowing over it. A cat crept by, hiding and spying out for imagined pigeons. Some guys stepped out of a musical instrument shop carrying a guitar, flashing cymbals, and an amplifier. The two at the back were lugging a massive keyboard like it was a coffin, edging forwards with penguin steps...

For some reason we stood motionless on the bridge, unable to choose which direction to go in. We could hear some drunk underneath us speaking to someone, gesticulating with one hand, a bag in the other; someone seemed to answer him, then he carried on talking. We couldn't see who he was talking to, they were standing under the bridge, directly beneath us. We couldn't hear what we were seeing. Then I realised that it was because the world had been submerged in the sound of an approaching train, that was where the deafening silence was coming from. And suddenly I started to feel anxious, my heart sunk, I felt trapped within my inner world, I wrapped my soul up tight as if sensing the onset of a strong wind, a chill, and I thought to myself that I was about to sink to the bottom.

I looked at the gesticulating tramp with his string bag, at the looming locomotive, and I thought to myself that this may be how the world speaks to us, even if we don't notice, and we don't attach any importance to it, we just think that it's a drunkard talking with God knows who, while in fact... But fuck it! What difference does it make? What difference does it make what's really going on! Sod it all... everything inside me slammed shut from alarm, my nerves quivered at the sight of the advancing locomotive, I was afraid to think about it any more...

We carried on flowing, we just flowed down the road with our ice cream, and then we watched films again, listened to our music, talked about books. At the Internet café Hanuman showed them emails that he had apparently received from three distant parts of the world, including

317

New Zealand, from a tribe of cannibals who invited him to become their chieftain, because it was only under his guidance that they could become vegetarians and shake off their dark primordial past. He showed them emails he'd sent himself, signed off as Salman Rushdie, or as Maharishi Yogi, and as Bachchan, as well as emails from Madame Sonya. We described some of these as obituaries, because they informed us which of our friends had died, and they did so in a reproachful tone, as if we were to blame for their deaths. We also deployed letters written from the refugees' cultural centre in Copenhagen, and from a newspaper which printed our articles or which used Hanuman's photographs alongside other peoples' articles, like the ones written by that fat four-eyed Serb who sometimes availed himself of Nepalino's services.

One day Violeta and I were walking by the lake, with the wind ripping past overhead, shaking the raindrops from the whispering branches, when Violeta asked, "So you're waiting for Hanuman's uncle in America to send you your green cards?"

Unruffled, I looked at the ducks, and replied, "Yes, we're waiting for them to arrive. And for one or two other things as well…"

Although Hanny hadn't warned me about anything like that…

In fact mention of Hanuman's American uncle caught me off guard. Evidently the two girls discussed what went on when Hanuman was with Jasmina and I was with Violeta. But in general I didn't need to be forewarned of those surprises. I knew how to react. And thank God my reactions were still intact. Otherwise Hanny wouldn't have wasted his time knocking about with me. Violeta said that she'd dreamed of going to America all her life, she even knew how many states there were! That was the kind of enlightened young girl that she was!

I didn't think that I'd fallen in love. Sometimes

spontaneous urges blaze brighter than desires which have been smouldering for years. Sometimes a lost lamb comes your way, you intertwine in a dark, narrow backstreet, and you do everything, everything that you want to, because in those moments you are entitled to, and you are not alone in thinking that, the girl who surrenders herself to you completely in the darkness concurs. Even those moments seemed more vivid than what Violeta and I had. But we did have something. A certain touching tenderness. It made me feel like a real man again, after a whole winter of half-waking, sexless existence. If, heaven forbid, some black guy were to rear up in our path, making lewd gestures which deserved a punch in the face, I was ready to do it.

We listened to music for hours on end, drinking cola, mixed with the final drops of schnapps, smoking the last remaining German cigarettes, which Ni found when he was dusting under Hanuman's bed with his rag. We smoked our last cigarettes and transitioned smoothly to tobacco. Hanuman used the rolling machine, making joints and pontificating as to why Bowie's "China Girl" was more popular and cropped up on TV more often than Iggy Pop's version. He rolled the joint and talked pretty coarsely, arguing that Iggy wasn't as pleasing on the eye as that slick dude Bowie, because Iggy looked like a little monkey, whereas Bowie had an intellectual air... although Bowie liked monkeys himself, he wrote abstract books about them, and painted even more abstract pictures. I stayed quiet most of the time, I just listened to Violeta, stroked her belly, touched her fingers and hair, and smiled tenderly at her, catching her gaze and earning her kisses in reward for my silence. Meanwhile, she told me that genuine feelings shouldn't be suppressed by social norms or rules of decency, or by ethics either, because feelings were like fire, and they couldn't be controlled, and so on... She gesticulated comically as she spoke... But Jasmina said that you could control feelings, and then they went into Serbo-Croat, and

I was the only one who vaguely understood – not the overall meaning, but the shadow of a meaning, not the actual words, but a pantomime of words. What I understood was not what they were really saying, but what I imagined that two sixteen-year-old girls would say on that subject if they were Russian. And some of the words were familiar, or at least they sounded kind of familiar.

I stopped listening and started feeling sad. Unexpectedly, completely unexpectedly, I was shocked at the realisation that I was the only Russian in the room. And that there was no one in the camp who I could talk to about Tallinn. Or with whom I could at least refer to the town, or not even the town itself, but the environs. If I were to idly recall some detail, or to identify some trivial feature which was typical of Danes and common to both Scandinavians and Estonians, then I wouldn't have anyone with whom to share that thought. And then that unsaid thing would itch away inside me, it wouldn't burn up, it would carry on smouldering, stinging me. It would choke me. No one knew that I was from Estonia, not even Hanuman. That didn't mean that I really wanted to talk about Tallinn! Quite the opposite! But the fact that I couldn't talk about Tallinn, that it was impossible to talk about it (or about Narva or Kohtla-Järve), that fact alone wore away at me, tormented me, compelled me to say something. Sometimes I would half-open my mouth on the verge of asking, "What about Tallinn, have you ever been to Tallinn?" Or sometimes the word Tallinn would almost trip off my tongue in place of Copenhagen. It was like when people say "Let's go to into town!", or "They went into town", meaning that they'd gone to the nearest large town, and everyone would always know which town they were referring to, if they had been living near a certain town all their lives. Everyone had their own big town. For some it was Bombay, for others it was Los Angeles, for others it was Sydney, or Irkutsk. Before I came to Denmark that town had always been

Tallinn. So when I wanted to tell Hanuman that we should go to Copenhagen, or to Aalborg, or to Odense, I would sometimes inadvertently say Tallinn instead of Copenhagen. I would automatically compare Scandic Copenhagen with the Viru or Olympia hotels, for example – simply because I had nothing else to compare it with. That was the kind of clod I was. A total cripple! Hanuman was right when he said that life had subjected me to worse abuse than a medieval torture chamber. That was indeed how it was. Two years had passed and I still hadn't got used to the idea that I was no longer in Estonia, at the campsite in Nelijärve or Otepää for example, but hell knows where, some place called Jutland in Denmark. When I had a proper smoke I would sometimes be so far gone that I was sure that if I got on a train or bus I would arrive in Tallinn in a matter of hours. As if Tallinn were just round the corner, a couple of stops away. I had to keep myself in check the whole time. I became my own warden, even when I talked with Hanny. Even with him I had to watch every word. Otherwise I might blurt out one thing or another, and then away we go… On no account could I rupture the hermetic seal of my new identity, my new persona, or relax the discipline on which the legend depended. It was like believing in God. If you were going to be a believer, then it wasn't just at certain times, on Sundays, but every single second of your life! If you let your discipline go, then the legend could lose its credibility. The legend would start to disintegrate. That legend was what gave me strength, what helped me to carry on. According to the legend I was from Yalta, and no one apart from Mikhail Potapov knew where that town was. No one in the whole camp had ever been to Yalta! I had something in my past, even if it was an invented past, which no one in the camp shared with me! It was a unique form of isolation, it felt so sad. There weren't words for it, it was impossible to describe how lonely I would sometimes feel. Especially when we were alone with those girls – my

321

sorrow was so acute. The loneliness held me like a drug, it suffocated me and I didn't know how to deal with it. But I wasn't lonely for lack of someone to chat with about shared friends, to remember the good old days with. To hell with that! I didn't want to remember anything. Neither the good old days nor shared friends. I was happy to forget them all. If only it were possible to surrender one's memory at no cost, with no risk of losing the layers of essential information! If only one could forget selectively. If only it were possible to fall into a lethargic slumber for one hundred years! Or to die and wake up in another world! And ideally as another entity, like a droplet of dew on the stem of a coral plant! Even there, even as a droplet on a coral stem, I would still be me! More so than here in Farstrup, in the garb of one Yevgeny Sidorov. In Farstrup I no longer had any roots, I couldn't even feel the ground beneath my feet. It was more than being free, I had almost ceased to exist! My life had become a kind of dream! It was like a hallucination. And within this dream, within this hallucination, I was almost an invisible man.

I wasn't scared of death. I didn't feel I was descending to the depths, because I was already there; I had already left the realm of the living. To everyone else I was Yevgeny Sidorov, sometimes Eugene, sometimes Johan, sometimes Zhenya. But not one of those was my real name. And no one, none of these fellow travellers, none of these personas in my anecdotal life, knew what my real name was. Nor did my old friends and my relatives know my new names and nicknames, they didn't even know where I was (other than my mother, who was in on the conspiracy and didn't say a word to anyone). No one knew the details of my stray-dog life (not even my uncle, who was the only one who would have rejoiced at the knowledge). No one knew what I was doing, who I was with, or where. For many people, as it later transpired, I was long since dead, feeding the worms. I was so stone-cold dead that people had even started to memorialise me. They remembered me like they remember their favourite singers. Maybe no one recalled my poetry, but some aphorisms, verses and metaphors were still doing the rounds. Or sometimes people would recall parts of their own repertoire, but ascribe them to me, and then they would acquire an added cachet, or become redolent of a lost epoch, which is what I represented for them. My failed jokes and one-liners had seemed silly at the time (which they were), but people later remembered them and repeated them like lines from a song, and then they discovered something in them which had previously passed unnoticed, some sort of hidden meaning, something portentous. I was that far gone for them all. But as far as I was concerned I was still alive, even if only partially – to a lesser degree than before. I was less myself than at any time previously. When I lost my name, most of my personality went with it It was as if it had evaporated, like the scent from an old bottle of perfume. The vessel was the same, but the smell had changed, now it was bitter and repulsive.

I hadn't heard my real name spoken out loud for more than a year now – and for several years it had been just an empty sound, bearing no relationship to me. True, there was a guy in the camp who was my namesake. He had exactly the same name as me, the same as my real name. And he was a dolt from Rostov region. His wife was misshapen, young, and she spent the whole time baking cakes. He was a young guy too, and was constantly showing us photographs from their wedding: there they are stepping out of the registry office, she's wearing some weird tatty dress, and he's got some shoddy jacket on. Then they're on the threshold of their house, and the door is hanging off its hinges, and there's a crooked drainpipe with a dent in it, and a lopsided porch: vile! And she's standing there in her white dress, but you can see from her crooked grin that she's already pretty merry! A nightmare bride! And in her features, in her physical form you can see sickness, you can see alcoholism.

She and her husband smoked a lot of hash and drank cheap fortified wines. They listened to all sorts of stupid music, like the crap Russian pop band Agatha Christie. He used to shoot up sometimes too. He hassled the Georgians to sell him drugs. One time he handed them some cash, and they ripped him off, they brought him a syringe full of some cloudy liquid. They'd probably been brewing up the dregs of their heroin, so they just gave him some of that. He injected himself with that crap, and then complained that it wasn't kicking in. The Georgians responded, "It's not working for us either, must be a duff batch!" But they would stumble about the camp, dozing off in mid-sentence. Then he got beaten up. By the Armenians. He was the one who started it. They were drinking together, smoking, and he kicked off. The Afghans came running to tell us that they'd heard shouting and scuffling coming from the Russians' room. So they told me to hurry up and find out what was going on, because I was the only Russian in the camp that day. I ran there on my own. When I came round the back of the building I heard, "You cunt, I'm gonna fuck you up the arse right in front of your wife! Cunt! Got it? Then your wife's gonna suck the lot of us off, right in front of you! Got it, you cunt?"

The situation was dire, to put it mildly... but I was too afraid to knock on the window. I stood there in the darkness listening to them battering the Russian guy. Then I ran off to look for Tiko. He was that guy's best friend in the camp. But Tiko was playing billiards with some horrific, gorilla-faced Armenian, the one who had brought that mob to the camp. I ran to see Hanny and asked him to call the police. But he refused to use his phone.

"The police will trace the number! You're out of your mind! I'm not a complete idiot! Phone from the call box! I haven't got a phone card! Best not to get involved!"

I approached the door on my own. I could hear what was happening on the other side, I could hear the sounds of someone being raped and beaten. I grabbed hold of the door handle and twisted it, then I knocked on the door.

"Hey! Open up! Stop that!"

But of course no one paid any attention. I just stood there listening. You can imagine what torture it was. This was the only person in the camp who I had any kind of connection with, albeit distant, imaginary even, but a connection... A person with whom I had some sort of mystical, anthroponomical bond, even if known only to me. A person who had the same name as me, and they were raping him. And his wife too. And I was standing behind the door, listening to it happen! It was a nightmare! I ran off to see Tiko again: "Hey! Your crew are getting up to some bad shit there..."

He went and sorted the situation out. He turfed his guys out of the room, and told them to get the fuck out of the camp! As far away as possible! But it was a bit late now: the Russian guy and his wife were so badly bruised that they made a horrific sight. As it turned out, no one actually got raped, but still... they soon left for Germany, and nothing more was heard of them. Nothing at all, and that was for the best, because it enabled me to forget them more quickly, to forget them once and for all, and not to experience any pangs of my fading conscience, a conscience which was dying with my former self, along with all the principles which had been forcibly instilled in me.

It was as if I was living under a shadow, the shadow of my fiction, under the umbrella of a lie, which reinforced with every passing day and made all the more credible. It had grown, fanning out like the branches of a tree. But no one, no one at all ever got to the truth, no one could catch me out, no one could pin me down. I was as slippery as an eel; I was emotional, and therefore credible. I portrayed nostalgia with just the right shade of gloominess. I painted such a colourful, vivid picture of Yalta, I described it in such flowery terms, that no one had the slightest suspicion that

I wasn't telling the absolute truth. Moreover, I had actually been to Yalta once, in my childhood, with my mum; we'd spent a whole week there. And when you're a child a week can seem like several years! I absorbed that town into my pores. And then later Yalta was featured so memorably in the film *Assa* that I couldn't go wrong. And in any case, I wasn't a refugee, so no one expected me to lie. I had no grounds to dissimulate.

Over those few days I told Hanuman three times – God help me! – that I was incapable of feeling any tenderness towards others, let alone love. I told him that I didn't love Violeta. That I couldn't care less about what happened between us, I didn't care one little bit! "What's the point of it all? Where is it all heading? Who would want to be with me? Why am I here? What am I waiting for? Why don't I just chuck it all in and leave? What's the point of the camp? Why are we languishing here, tormenting these poor girls?" At that moment Hanuman started inflating his cheeks and guffawing! Later I realised that his reaction was contrived, fake. He was working the bellows of his mirth with ungrounded self-assuredness. With implausible assuredness, even. He told me that we were slowly and surely progressing towards our goal, the goal which required no mention, because it had been mentioned so many times before, and therefore he wasn't going to trouble himself with excessive mentioning of what our goal was, and so on… that was all just high-flown bombastic drivel, nothing more. In reality he needed a companion, a partner in misfortune. So as not to feel so lonely. Or so that his own lost life didn't feel like such a drama, because there was this Russian guy called Eugene, there was Nepalino, Ivan on the top bunk, the family next door, the Serbs – what more could you ask for. He treated the situation he was in like some sort of sociological phenomenon, an instance of some form of psychological deviation, he saw himself as an observer, a scientist who had immersed himself in a world of perversion to study a sickness against which he had a secret immunity. He had a simple stratagem for getting hold of a passport which would allow him to flee to America, the homeland of illegal immigrants. That was the standard immigrant syndrome – so many others suffered from that same sickness, which made Hanuman feel less alone. So the drama of his life was no longer just a personal drama, but a drama which involved the whole of society! And society was supposed to show concern for his well-being, and pray for him and everyone else like him. It was truly awful. That was exactly how the whole situation suddenly appeared to me, and I'd come to that understanding after having a really good smoke. I got really stoned and suddenly saw everything clearly, as if Hanuman were suddenly made of glass. I realised that he was incapable of climbing out of that pit of illegality, of escaping that *clochard* existence. But I didn't know why that should be. Maybe he had been sucked into a vortex, a psychological vortex, and been taken in by an obsession with being outside society, not just an outsider, but someone who was completely outside the hierarchy. Because a person who has no status can have no relationship to any social hierarchy. This wasn't like being an outcast or a tramp, at least a tramp once belonged to some social strata, from which he had then lost his place, the glue of social utility which bound him had come unstuck. But we were different, we were still capable of doing something about our situation, but we were directing all our energies against having any place in society, a society which we had never belonged to anyway, because we were outsiders wherever we went. And so Hanuman needed a companion on that drifting iceberg.

But once the last wisps of smoke had wafted from my lungs I forgot all these revelations. I reverted to my former mode of thinking, devoid of any clarity and characterised by short-sightedness, an inability to look deeper, and a tendency to reach conclusions based on fleeting fragments of phrases, of which there far were too many to make any sense of. All I could do was react. And I tried to vindicate Hanuman and myself too. I explained away the drama of his life. I gave in to apathy. I was a paralytic, an invalid, and the camp was my wheelchair, my leper colony, my loony bin. Hanuman was one of the patients who was mobile enough and crazy enough to fly the coop for a few days, to go off and get plastered and shag cheap hookers... but he would still come back when he felt the hunger pangs. Back then I was so dim-witted and indifferent to everything that I didn't notice that he was afraid to admit that he was lying to himself, more so than he was lying to me! After all, deceiving someone else might be a misdemeanour, but if you deceive yourself – that's a sin! Because to deceive someone else you need to first deceive yourself. Sin spreads from a corrupted soul, it begins when you stand face-to-face with your conscience. If you warp the truth, if you crush your conscience like a handkerchief in your hands, then sooner or later you will end up blowing your nose on it.

That was what was happening to us, in those crazy Hanumambo days in Farstrup, throughout spring 1999, in the theatre to which we had lured those wonderful Serbian girls... Those two pure souls, whom we had poisoned with high hopes, in whom we had kindled a flame, a dream, a belief in the possibility of America, in British passports, in success, in money, who we had subjugated with our silver tongues, our fancy clothes, our practised gestures, our smiles and the twinkle in our eyes... Oh, ours were the eyes of swindlers! Of fraudsters and imposters. Without promising anything certain, we seemed to promise much more than someone who promised less and kept their promise! Because our non-promises were bigger, much bigger than promises which could be kept!

Jasmina and Violeta were dreamers anyway, and they truly believed that their dreams might come true. But we only needed those beautiful dreams to addle their brains, to contaminate their souls! To paralyse their wills! To intoxicate them! Those poor little girls! Maybe we were guiltier than paedophiles? If the heavens were a little bit lower then we wouldn't have escaped the bolts of lightning either…

But if there's no Devil, I thought to myself, there can be no God! Without sin there can be no virtue! The sky is there to cast rain and snow upon the earth, and the earth is there to swallow up that rain and snow, as well as rogues like us, and innocent girls like Violeta and Jasmina.

3

May 1999 got off to a terrible start. That year spring was somehow warped and buckled like a bad Polish road; the months trailed on like a tailback of heavy-goods lorries. Our days were burdened by the wearisome state of anticipation; they became noticeably longer and more futile. The limpid rays of light which entered and fragmented through our blinds seemed to reveal the full hopelessness and misery of camp life to us with ever greater lucidity. That was when they evicted the Potapovs from the ruins. They had only just got the dog which Liza and Maria had always dreamed of, and the dog had only just started getting used to the Russian language and to Russian ways, as well as to the strange name "Dolly" which they'd given it. It had just about resigned itself to the awful conditions, and stopped trembling with its whole puny frame, and wetting itself on the rag which Potapov put down for it in the entranceway (the cold storage!). And then they were asked to leave. The owner, Henning the dairy farmer, came round and rudely asked them to get packing. Potapov later recounted to us that the Dane had called them gypsies several times, and also said something about Mikhail selling stuff illegally. Bikes of some description. Meat, and a sack of potatoes which someone had nicked from the neighbour in a car without number plates. Then there was something about driving without a licence, and fines. And now they had gone and got themselves a dog! They had a dog living with them! There had been nothing agreed about keeping animals! Dogs were not allowed! In other words – sod off! The Potapovs got more and more rattled, while Henning stood there, hands smoothing the pockets of his overalls, ordering them to leave: "Russo, skynd dig! Jo, Russo, Jo!"29 That was only to be expected. Trouble had clearly been brewing for a while. And it was brewing in the camp office, from where the order had been issued: the Potapovs are to live in the camp, and nowhere else!

They started traipsing backwards and forwards between the ruins and the camp with their things. They had to lug some of them on their backs, because they wouldn't all fit into the car. They must have made around thirty trips. There wasn't space in their room for all the stuff they had accumulated over the winter, so they dumped some of it in our room, and it ended up looking like a second-hand shop, or some sort of lapidarium. Mikhail gnashed his teeth and cast wolfish glances from side to side as he dragged his stuff into the camp; he could feel the mocking gazes of the Albanians and Arabs on him, he knew that they were just waiting for the chance to have a tongue-wag, to laugh at someone's expense, and now they had the perfect material, the perfect raw ingredients for some new anecdotes. Sink your teeth into those juicy morsels! The Russians are moving back into the camp! They spent winter at the ruins, but now they're back!

They got so knackered dragging their stuff back that they asked us to help. But Hanuman announced that he wasn't <u>going to lift</u> anything heavier than his briefcase. And he

29   Russians out! Come on, get a move on (Danish).

wasn't capable of walking more than one hundred metres due to chronic exhaustion. I said that my feet were hurting, that my toes were hurting unbearably: once again it was blisters, fungal infection, all the rest of it. I could have thought up a hundred reasons. Not least that Hanny and I couldn't risk being spotted, not by anyone! That was the biggest reason of all! No one could argue with that!

The two of them, Potapov and his wife, trudged backwards and forwards, shifting their things, all their stuff, all that junk, and eventually they had moved back in. And a strange smell moved in with them, which I assumed they must have picked up from the ruins. I assumed it was the smell of the damp, of moss, mould, and dog. And it started to spread. I was the first to be overpowered; I woke up one morning, unable to breathe. At first I thought it was the fertiliser wafting off the fields again. But once I had sniffed the smell a bit more, started to comprehend its essence, I realised it was different; it was the smell of something mouldering, something decomposing, something long since dead. The smell grew in potency and started expanding its domain. By now I was not the only one to notice it and wonder what it might be. The smell became more and more sickening, it was much like the smell of chunder, and it wasn't just hanging in the air, it was clearly coming straight from the Potapovs' room. I decided to ask Ivan what was going on, what the stench could be. He said nothing, he just shrugged his shoulder slyly, guiltily, and said nothing. It was clear he was hiding something, that he knew something but was hiding it. Eventually the smell acquired eye-stinging acridity and gave Hanuman an asthma attack, at which point he whacked his foot against the wall, and with chest heaving and in tears, he yelled, "Even that dead old man didn't stink as badly as you people on the other side of the wall!"

Potapov appeared, sneezing and rubbing his eyes with his handkerchief. He came into our room, red in the face, shaking, and said, "That's it, I can't fucking stand it any longer! Fuck that!"

I felt a chill run down my spine, and I froze in horror. Suddenly I realised that I hadn't heard Potapov swearing for several days, and nor had I seen Liza, or heard the dog whining. And his wife Maria hadn't come out to do the cooking either. Surely not!

"I can't fucking handle it any longer! I'm allergic!" Potapov yelled.

"What's going on, explain yourself!"

"Masha's dyeing silk, she's doing batik, scarves for old grannies, to order, with a Russian design. But that dye stinks! It's a fucking nightmare! It's unbearable! I can't stand it any longer! That's enough! Put a mattress down for me here!"

We swiftly told him where to go: "Get lost! Go to hell! Fuck off, motherfucker!"

It turned out that his wife wasn't bad at batik, she knew the right techniques, she had studied it somewhere, done some courses. So she could sew, knit, all the rest of it, she was a real Jill of all trades, a handicraftswoman, a proper little clever clogs was our Masha! Potapov had the idea of going into production, making scarves and shawls. He bought a load of silk and paints with his and Ivan's money, then he fashioned a frame to stretch the silk across, and set up a little home workshop. He had Masha sew the silk, then dye it, then who knows what else, everything just as it was supposed to be. She worked twenty-four hours a day. Potapov kept his business a secret until he started to find the smell of the dye physically unbearable. He said that it had been just about tolerable to start with, but then towards the end of the tin the paint got thick and clotted, and that was the bit that fucking stank, that was what made you want to puke. What's more, they had a three-month-old baby in the room with them, Liza, and the dog, and they sat there without any ventilation, breathing in that crap day in, day out. I reckon that if the old grannies knew the price of making those shawls and scarves, they would have wanted Potapov behind bars for treating his family so inhumanely.

When Hanuman found out he stopped even saying hello to Potapov, he just called him all kinds of bad names, like "motherfucker", "son of a bitch", "sistersleeper", "bloodsucker", "bloody bastard", "blasted bastard", "fucking miser". He used a lot of different words, but the general sense was the same.

As well as that smell, the camp started getting dirtier and dirtier. I rarely left our room, and when I did go to the kitchen one time, I decided I would never go back. I refused to countenance that the food which Hanuman and Nepalino brought me was made in a kitchen where the hob was covered in a thick layer of black grease, with a slice of tomato stuck to it. Where fat was spattered everywhere, with little sesame seeds suspended in it. On the walls! On the windows! On the ceiling! Everywhere! Leftovers! Sausage skins! Fishtails in oil! Footprints left by massive military boots, all over the floor and the ceiling, long since dried fast! Pubic hair in the rubbish bin! Rice! Pubic hair on the windowsill! Salt! Pubic hair and bits of bread roll on a sheet of baking paper! Flour! Fuck knows what else! It was a tip! And it stank to high heaven… I'd never seen such filth! Even the tramps at the Pääsküla rubbish bins were cleanlier than the Arabs and Albanians who lived in our building!

Eventually the cockroaches came. The first one appeared out of the blue, on a blue table where one of the Albanian women had just been kneading her dough. The handsome, fat, black roach came scuttling across the white-floured surface, swiftly followed by a Somalian who came beetling along behind it, raining down blows with his slipper. The Arabs observed the proceedings, chuckling to themselves; they had no idea what was to follow. A second and then a third cockroach appeared by the sink, but they didn't generate the same reaction as the first. And then roaches started crawling out of every nook and cranny, although for some reason everyone reacted calmly, as if it were inevitable, necessary even, the same way they would react to excessive bodily hair or a skin rash. In the end the roaches overran the whole camp. And Hanuman came up with a good word to describe the place: "cockroachium". But that didn't make us feel any better!

Ivan told us about one time when he'd gone to the kitchen to make himself some tea... No, he must have been sent there by Hanuman... yes, Hanuman sent him; he wouldn't have gone of his own accord. Hanuman sent Ivan to make him Indian tea with honey and cream, because Hanuman was starting to get one of his migraines, an "evil migraine", as a sleepless Hanuman told him that night, "the kind of migraine which all Indians get when they move to Europe... you wouldn't understand," he told Ivan, who hung on every word that Hanuman said, and worshipped him like some kind of guru. "It's a particularly vicious kind of migraine which people get when they move to northern climes... for Indians that migraine is as commonplace as homesickness... but it torments us worse than any homesickness!" Ivan was prepared to wash his feet and massage his back, he'd have happily fetched him water in a sieve if he was asked to! He was so mesmerised by Hanny that he would do anything for him. I'd heard about that migraine a thousand times, starting from the day we first met. According to Hanny, that particular form of migraine normally started in his left temple, then it would spread like a cobweb across his whole left hemisphere, and as a consequence he went deaf in his left ear, or he went blind in his left eye, or almost blind, or he could still see, but it was like looking through a fog. He couldn't eat anything, he had difficulty controlling his left arm and left leg, the headache not only ruined his appetite, but made him nauseous, and sometimes he said that it made him vomit, but he was probably lying about that bit. He asked Ivan to go and fetch him tea, because tea was all he could stomach; he couldn't eat, but he could drink tea, yes... So then, Ivan entered the kitchen at three o'clock in the morning, and at first he couldn't understand what was going on. The whole kitchen was quivering, it was completely black, it was moving, it was alive. He thought he must be dreaming. At first he couldn't comprehend that the whole place was coated in cockroaches, scurrying about all over the place. It looked like the cloud of locusts he had seen flying from Kyrgyzstan to Turkmenistan when he was doing his military service there; it was as if a swarm of locusts had flown into the kitchen and decided to stay for dinner.

News reached the camp office, and the pest control squad turned up and spent several hours sprinkling everything, chucking us out of the building. Me and Hanuman and three illegals from Sri Lanka hid in the field behind some tall bushes, and we stood there smoking. Hanuman was talking to the Tamils, the wind picked up, it started raining, and then the whole camp got rained on. The pest control team left, and the asylum seekers went back into the camp buildings, which now stank worse than Potapov's dyes. They spent several hours sweeping away piles of cockroach corpses. The Albanian and Somalian women started cooking straight away, although they had been warned to wait at least twenty-four hours. There was a queue trailing from the nurse's room for several days – people had given themselves food poisoning. From then on we only cooked in our own room, even if we were only boiling water for our midnight tea.

Something else happened that May... one day Liza and her Kurdish friend came running up to our window, each trying to out-jabber the other... there's something! Over there! In the rubbish container! But it took us a while to realise what was happening, our minds refused to assimilate, to process, to comprehend, or to fully believe what the two girls were yelling, "A horse's head, and hooves!" Being lovers of the macabre, fans of naturalism, Hanuman and I went to check if it was true. And indeed, in the container, amongst the paper and cardboard, together with the rest of the rubbish and in the same kind of black bin bag, lay a huge horse's head (in fact I reckon it must have been a pony's)! And the hooves. There was a lot of blood, a lot of blood had collected in the base of the container. And there were rats heedless of the people who'd gathered around, huge grey rats that were scurrying and scampering about, squeaking and licking the blood.

That month the Potapovs were forced to give up their dog: it was forbidden to keep animals in the camp. They managed to keep their rat concealed in a jar, but the dog got spotted. Anyway, some strange things had started happening to that dog. Potapov punched it, kicked it, choked it, and chucked it around like a ball, yelling at Liza the whole time, "Look, you stupid little girl, I'll grab you and strangle you just like this dog, if you insist on not eating!"

Then they started keeping the dog outside in a cardboard box under the window, but it kept getting out and trying to slip back in when the door was ajar. And if it didn't succeed it would try and jump in through the window. But if the window was shut fast then it would simply stand on its hind legs and shuffle round in circles, whining. Then it started to howl, bark, snort and whimper. I couldn't sleep. It drove me wild. I longed for Potapov to put it out of its misery. Sometimes the window would open and Potapov's massive paw would appear, beckoning the dog in, and with a yelp it would jump inside and calm down for a while. But events soon took a really nasty turn. One day Mikhail turned up at the camp office with a big bag. Opening the bag, he produced the dog and placed it on the camp director's table with its rear pointed towards the stunned director's face. And then Potapov proceeded to demonstrate that the dog had been – as he put it – raped. He pointed at evidence of forced entry into a certain part of the dog's anatomy, arguing that the proportions of whatever had entered must clearly have been greater than those of a dog, and that in his opinion it could only have belonged to a human, and not any human, but a human of Arab or Albanian origin. The camp staff didn't even ask him to explain his strange theory, they simply told him to remove the animal and himself from the office forthwith. They had a good laugh after that. But they fumed at him too. They sputtered in disgust. Mikhail's appearance with his dog aroused the full panoply of emotions! Svenaage was the one who told us. He couldn't believe it either, that someone could go and…

"No, Michel, no!" he cried, "no, it's not possible! It's too much, my dear, no! A donkey, a mule, a big dog even – that I could understand. But a little dog like Dolly, no way, Michel, no my dear, no! That's going too far, even for the Arabs! You've got a sick imagination!"

Mikhail did indeed have a sick imagination. He was eager for his theory to be proved, and for a major scandal to erupt. He insisted that either Hanuman or I, or both of us, write a lengthy article on the incident, and he was ready to find witnesses! He said that we urgently needed to take photographs of the dog, in particular of its affronted bits! "We have to arrange a medical examination!" he yelled, his eyes goggling, flailing his crabby claws. It looked like he would have been prepared to rape the dog himself, so long as he got his scandal. Scandal! In all the newspapers! Featuring him as the dog's owner, of course!

Pretty soon some Danish folk who lived near the camp took Dolly in. She had clearly pressed herself upon them. She could often be seen playing with the Danish kids outside, and Liza sometimes went there to play with Dolly, until Mikhail forbade her from going. One time he went to pay them a visit. He informed them from the doorstep that he had paid five hundred Danish kroner for the dog, and if they were going to take her then as owner he was in his rights to expect "compensation", as he put it. And then he left, brusquely shoving his wallet into his breast pocket. Flexing his double chin. Mutedly clearing his throat.

Later, when Potapov passed the yard of Dolly's new owners on his way to the shop, he would often call her, and I saw the dog start at the sound of his voice, then it would begin to shake, as if it were possessed. It glanced around distractedly, crouched down with its tail between its legs, and it pissed itself. My God, I thought, what had that poor animal had to suffer!

4

Jasmina's father would often come round to see us. He wanted to discuss some important stuff, since we were considered to be pretty knowledgeable in questions regarding legal and illegal immigration, and in everything else related to crossing boundaries, including the boundaries of decency (Hanuman had earned us that reputation, of course, he tirelessly sought to enthral anyone we met). Hanny called Jasmine's father Zdravko, because he couldn't pronounce his name properly, he couldn't get his tongue round it, which meant that I couldn't get my head round it either. Zdravko was exercised by one question alone: where was the best place to go if he wanted to do nothing at all but still get good welfare payments. Hanuman kept telling him fairy stories about Sweden. These stories inflamed the old Serb's imagination, especially since he had already heard similar stuff from other sources. The Serb also said that he needed to study English, he mumbled something about how English would be useful wherever he went. That made me shudder. He really was prepared to end up anywhere at all, and he imagined that English would be his best insurance policy; he had convinced himself of the fact. I could have told him that there were thousands of places in the world, millions of boarded-up cells in every country, where English would definitely be of no use to him whatsoever – but I obviously kept quiet. He was so pitiful, you could have crushed him with a single sentence. He always looked awkward, huddled up, chewing his lips. He would come round with a cheap bottle of Danish vodka, fill his pipe, and ask Hanuman to tell him about Sweden, India, Greece, the countries where he, as a Serb, had not been, but definitely wanted to visit, if only in his imagination, or so that he could at least sense the nearness and attainability of those countries with someone who had lived there. He thought that our conversations would help him learn English too. He would ask loads of ungrammatical questions. And he never got a straight answer to them. If there was some word he didn't understand then he would turn his perplexed, ashen-grey face to me and ask, in Polish for some reason, "Co to jest?" For him I was both teacher and interpreter, even though I had never once taught anything to anyone, and had never interpreted a word, since I knew neither Serbian nor Polish nor Romanian. I quickly got tired of his company. The last straw was the Australia saga. Rumour had reached the Serb that several families at the Gudme camp, where they held mostly Serbs and Albanians, had written some sort of appeal and sent it to Australia. And very recently, after waiting two months or so, they got invitation letters and had successfully set off for Australia – for further investigation into their cases. The Serb was so entranced by that fantastical story that he couldn't wait to emulate the success of the trailblazers from Gudme. He asked Hanny to find out everything he could about the chances of emigrating to Australia. So Hanny printed out several kilos of paper from the Internet, handed them to the Serb, and told him that they were the documents which he needed to complete and send off to Australia for consideration. The Serb took one look at all the tables, at the laws, at the paragraphs of text, at the graphs, the diagrams, the questions and the blank forms, and he said, "Fuck me, bureaucracy! Catastrophe!"

And then he was on Hanuman's case, tearfully imploring him to help him make sense of it all. Hanuman and the Serb filled out those forms together. They spent whole days at it. It was complete idiocy, as Hanuman himself would yell as soon as the door shut behind the old Serb, "The idiot! He thinks that he and his family are going to get into Australia! The cretin! Look!" and he shoved the other papers which he had printed from the Internet in my face.

"Look! Take a look at these articles! They're the findings of a special commission investigating the camps! The closed camps! The closed camps in Australia! Closed! They keep people in those camps for up to seven years! They have to live there like Indians in the reservations! They don't let them anywhere near the main towns! Not without authorisation! Nowhere! That's right! They live in reservations! In the desert! They can't see a lawyer! They don't have the slightest idea how their cases are progressing! Less than three weeks ago there was an interview on CNN with the director of the Australian equivalent of the Directorate, and he was wriggling out of answering the questions, claiming that they don't have any closed camps! The lying scum! And they had his back against the wall! Photos! Video clips! Witnesses! All the rest of it! And this lot want to go to Australia! It takes ten years to process a case there! And then, and then… then they'll get bugger all! They'll get to eat rabbits and sow maize! And worst thing of all… at least here in Europe if you get deported, if you get sent packing, then you can go somewhere, you can go home if it comes to it, but there, there you get herded into a reservation, and then you've got no chance! You won't be going home! Or any other place! They don't even deport people *Nach hause* from there! They don't give you right of abode or any work! But they don't send you home either! Because it's too damned expensive! Because there are so many of them, so many that if they deported all those refugees from the deserts, the Australian state would bankrupt itself and they would have to slaughter all their kangaroos and sloths, because they wouldn't have anything else left to eat!"

So all that red tape and paperwork related to Australia was pure madness as far as Hanuman was concerned, nothing more. He was quite sure of that.

Jasmina's mother Bogumila was a tall, slender woman, with a pointed nose; canny but quiet-natured, and she cooked very well. Just like Violeta's mother Borislava. The two families decided to complete the forms together and send them for consideration to Australia, and all that hassle benefitted Hanuman and me only insofar as the Serbs brought us food, tobacco and booze, in return for our help filling in the forms. But God, it was so tedious! It was totally pointless! Completely hopeless! I could hardly bear to look them in the eye and see the fear there. Warped, feverish, sickly faces. Faces ravaged by fear of deportation, as if by endless insomnia. And so the hope of losing themselves in Australia, of gaining some sort of status, that foolish hope washed over them and gave them an unnatural high, like cocaine. Violeta's mother said that they had some relative there, and Zdravko would chip in: "We're going to stick together, we'll stick together, you're always best off together... that's right, isn't it?" he would say, looking at me. I nodded, of course. And I made myself sick. I found myself repulsive because I happily took food from them, helped them to translate those documents and fill out the forms, but I did nothing to dispel their silly illusions, although I didn't encourage them either. Towards the end Hanuman and I were speaking Serbian better than they spoke English. It was funny watching the Serbs talking hurriedly to Hanuman, shouting over the top of one another, and Hanuman holding up his hand with fingers splayed, as if he were pushing back an invisible wall, maintaining his gravitas and urging them: "Polako, polako!"[30]

Meanwhile Zenon and his family got a yes – at long last! Zenon immediately found himself work in a hotel, ostensibly as a waiter in the restaurant. Everyone chuckled at that: Who would he be serving, if no one ever went there? Whenever he turned up at the camp (he kept on coming, out of boredom), they would ask, "Hey, how much did you get in tips yesterday?"

They got a huge relocation allowance and went round the shops buying furniture.

Masha got caught red-handed with a pair of pants. She had apparently gone to buy a present for Mikhail but once she was in the shop she discovered that she'd lost the one hundred kroner which Mikhail had given her for his present, so she decided to nick something. But instead she got nicked herself. I heard the cursing on the other side of the wall; I didn't so much hear it as feel the walls of our hen coop shaking. I thought he was going to kill her. He had reached the end of his tether in that camp. When I heard that Maria had lost the money which Mikhail gave her, it occurred to me that maybe he had nabbed it out of her pocket himself. When I floated the idea with Hanuman, he immediately agreed, yelling, "He could well have done it! Not only could he have done it, he did do it! He actually did it! The fucking bastard did it!"

Potapov could easily have done it, I had no doubt about that; moreover, I was sure that he had done it too! Potapov was so greedy, and he despised the entire world so completely, that doing something like that was just fulfilling a basic need for him!

Soon they deported Jasmina and her parents, before they had got their reply from Australia. They deported them just like that, they turned up early in the morning, at

30 Quiet, quiet! (Serbian).

seven o'clock, gave them twenty minutes to get their things together, sent them straight to Kastrup, to the airport, and then put them on a flight to Sarajevo, most probably, with a change in Berlin or France, I'm not sure, those routes could be pretty odd. Sometimes they deported people to Serbia via Spain. Or they would send an Albanian via the Arab Emirates. One Serbian family was sent home via the Faroe Islands, and then they ended up getting asylum there! There was even a film made about them.

Hanuman got a bit depressed, but he handled it like you would a cold after a bullet wound. It had to be said that those people had started getting on his nerves; it was a relief to get rid of them. Friends like that can be worse than bad neighbours. But Hanuman still couldn't resist going on a drinking binge, and a smoking binge too. And he smoked all sorts of crap, because there was nothing else to hand. He had to make do with roll-ups soaked in milk extracted from wild poppy stalks, which he gathered from the local back gardens. The Georgians had already lopped off all the heads. It was madness! I didn't ever touch the stuff, I was sure you couldn't get high from it. But he insisted that it got you oh so high: "Ooh yeah, so high my man!" I shook my head, agreed with whatever Hanuman said, sympathised with the Serbs… Violeta cried, she said that mummy was going to be deported too, they'd applied for asylum on humanitarian grounds, because of her mother's ill health, but the investigation would be over in a month and then they'd be deported too. That was that! The fairy tale was over! We would never see each other again. I sighed, and thought to myself, "Oh, how tedious… how miserable, how miserable and tedious…"

By now Hanuman was stoned out of his head and pretty witless, so he told her not to give up hope, to go and seek her fortune in Sweden, and that she should go there alone, after all she had submitted her application in Denmark as a child…

"No, she said, we applied as grown-ups…"

"As grown-ups," I thought to myself with a smirk: those two little kittens…

"Well, submit your application as a child in Sweden then!" Hanuman yelled. "They're not going to take your fingerprints… You can just say that you're an orphan or a gypsy, that you can't read or write, you don't even know which country they brought you from! It's all the same to gypsies! The whole world is their camp! Borders and states mean nothing to them! Think up something awful! Tell them that Muslims executed your parents! In Bosnia or Bucharest or somewhere! Is there anywhere they don't persecute gypsies these days? Tell them that you almost got sold into prostitution, to some paedophiles or something! Spin them some yarn like that, and cry, cry as much as you can! The canals are full of water in Sweden, they like that kind of stuff there, so cry! Drown them in tears! Let them shed a tear or two as well! That stuff still works, give it a go!" and, following Hanuman's advice to the word, she burst into tears, and started lamenting, "I don't want us to break up! I don't want to go alone! What am I going to do there alone? Without you! Without mummy!"

By now I wanted to leave, but Hanny stopped me with his gaze, and said to her, "Find yourself a nice rich local guy, some Swede. Or some local ex-Yugoslav! There are loads of guys like Ibrahimovic there. Some pedigree stallion… or actually a Swede might be best! There are still more of them than there are foreigners! For now, at least! So it's not too late, you can find yourself a proper Swede in Sweden! Get married to him! And if he pisses you off, just wait until you get your passport, and then dump him! Once you've got your passport you'll get given a flat, you can take out all sorts of study loans from the bank, you'll get yourself an education, you're no fool after all, then you'll get a job! Then you'll find yourself a better man! You'll be able to start living like a proper person!"

"I don't want it to be like that!"

"What don't you like about it? Any which way… what's the difference? All means are justified when your time's running out and deportation is round the corner! Eh?"

"But it's like selling yourself!"

"Well you know my dear, everyone sells themselves, everyone! Especially the artistically inclined! Artists, actors, they all sell themselves! Just take a look around, all these squeaky-clean millionaires are rotten to the core, there's corruption everywhere, corruption! The world is a market – a huge market! The Indians sell their cooking and religion, they sell their statues and their sandalwood Buddhas, he-ha-ho! The Chinese sell their kung fu, their zen, God knows what else, their tea, for example! The Japanese sell their electronics and their astrology! The Americans sell hamburgers and weapons! The French sell postcards of the Eiffel Tower! The Italians sell postcards of the Tower of Pisa! The Egyptians sell their pyramids! We're all selling something! The clever guys sell for the highest price possible! Everyone in this camp is trying to sell their homeland in return for a yes! And you're a real beauty! You're a work of art in your own right! So sell yourself for such a good price that it leaves no nasty mercantile aftertaste! Sell yourself like a piece of jewellery! Sell yourself like a diamond or a pearl! But sweeten the deal with some emotions, with some illusions! Convince yourself that you love the person you're sleeping with, that you don't need his passport, or his wealth, or his country with its redistributive social security system, but that you really love him. Choose the route of the lesser lie in the name of the greater good of your child, who you can conceive here, with the person you love. I mean Eugene, if you still love him…"

"That's why I don't want to go anywhere without him! Come with me, Yevgeny, let's go together!"

"No," I said, shaking my head, "no, I can't…"

"But why? Why don't you want to come? What's keeping you here? What is there here for you? What's stopping you coming with me?"

"I don't know, I just don't feel the urge. Maybe I'll go somewhere, maybe I'll go soon, just not to Sweden… or maybe I will go to Sweden, just not now… give me a week or so to think it over, OK?"

"But do you want us to have a baby?"

"No, definitely not, I'm quite sure of that!"

"But why?"

"Because I know this world well enough, and the better I know it, the more I despise it. I don't want my child to have to sell itself. I don't want to bring a soul into this world, to give it flesh and blood and thereby the conditions for its putrefaction and its suffering. I don't want to go hunting for souls which dwell in other spheres. I don't want to get involved with what could be considered…"

"OK, I understand, it's all perfectly clear!" and she left, slamming the door behind her.

"You idiot," said Hanuman. "You're an idiot! You're such an idiot! You could have gone to Sweden with her! You'd have got a baby, and a yes. But you… you're such an idiot…"

"I don't want to, I just don't want to! You have to understand! Better to be an idiot in your eyes than to behave like a pig, to use her, to make a fool out of her! You've got to understand, she does have a future…"

"…in which there will never be anyone better than you," he said, raising an eyebrow and an index finger. "That's it, conversation over! End of story! You're an egomaniac, but you're a stupid one! Because your egomania doesn't even bring you any returns! It's more to your detriment! You don't even know how to be egotistical properly! Because you're playing at humanism, at honest, conscientious humanism! He-ha-ho! Euge! So you reckon you're no hypocrite. You reckon you're pure! He-ha-ho! That's right, your conscience is clean, but you're happily sleeping in shit! You're an idiot!

346

Better not to sleep at all, and have your conscience torment you, but over in Sweden! Lying in a feather bed. With a beautiful wife, and a child, and a bottomless bank account! Better that than to have nothing at all and to sleep calmly, free from any pangs of conscience… but in shit! You really are an idiot, Eugene, a total idiot… you're not bad at chess, you write, you have good ideas, sometimes you manage to pull the wool over peoples' eyes, but what good is it all if you let an opportunity go when it presents itself, if you don't make that winning move when you're playing the deciding game against the Almighty! You'll surrender your most valuable piece – that girl, that queen – to Him. And you'll condemn yourself to endless further games, which you may not win, at least not as easily as you could win this one. There she is! Take her! Take her right now and go to Sweden. By the time they twig who you are and all the rest of it, while the papers are being processed, while the computer chugs away and your case goes to court, by then she'll have a belly the size of a watermelon, she'll have the baby, and then that's it, how are they going to deport you then? You think they'll send her to Serbia? Or you to Russia? They'll never separate you! You're a family! You've got a kid! You can stage a suicide attempt! Or check yourself in to the loony bin with a case of depression, reason impaired by grief! And that's it! The passport is in the bag! Job done! Didn't I tell you? I told you that those girls would make us millionaires! If not me, then you! What an opportunity! Take her, and you're sorted! And wherever you're sorted, I'm sorted too! I'll move in with my Swedish bitch, live with her for a while, then we'll see what comes up! You can't let a chance like that go! Go on, go and catch her up, go and make babies with her immediately, and then you'll get everything you ever wanted, over in Sweden! They're humane there, and she's just a kid – all the more reason! You're a unique couple by any standards! If she had a kid at that age in Serbia or in Russia, then you know, you or she could be… but in Sweden they'll take you in and shower you with blessings. But you're too much of an idiot… Oh, he wants to be so pure and upright, so true to himself, don't you know! But what good is that to anyone? Who benefits from that, apart from you and your conscience? Does she? No! Do I? Definitely not! So who does? Only you! You! You're an egomaniac! And a pansy! What are you after? What do you want out of life? Why don't you take that girl? You're already slept with her! So have a baby with her, and marry her! You'll help her, and drag yourself out of the gutter into the bargain, you idiot!"

"You don't understand… I don't want to taint our relationship with deception!"

"But you've already tainted it quite nicely, you've already pulled the wool over her eyes pretty well!"

"Yes, but I haven't yet destroyed her life!"

"So don't destroy it! Do everything you can to make her happy! Deceive her, and make her happy! She wants to be deceived! They all do! The whole world, all human relations, are built on deception! Any kind of communication is pure deception! What's the point of philosophising? Go to Sweden, they'll take you in, and you can start your new life!"

"No – how will I be able to look her in the eye? How will I be able to sit across the table from her, share a bed with her, for the rest of my life? I might still be thinking about it on my deathbed, about how I deceived her, how I used her as a ticket to a better life… And what about the child? How will I live with that child? I'll spend my whole life looking at it and thinking that we only conceived it to get asylum in Sweden! I won't be able to live with myself!"

"Nonsense! It's all just sentimental nonsense! I don't want to hear another word of it! You're far too Russian! And all you Russians are idiots! Total idiots! And you know what the most annoying thing is? As much as we try to help you, it doesn't make a sod of difference! You won't change! It's totally pointless!"

5

Potapov and Ivan started snorting some sort of cheap cocaine which Bacho had got hold of. Bacho had links with the real Danish mafia, which was as comically minor league as he was himself. After spending three months in a real Danish prison he came out hard-boiled, crooked, and well connected. He also had a ring on his finger and a dragon on his left shoulder. He started walking round his building in a body-warmer, patting his tattoo and saying, "You know what this means inside? Status, you got it! Fucking respect!"

He kept coming to see me with letters from his new Danish friends, which I translated for him. It was as if they'd been written in a secret code! They referred to various boxes, which would be delivered in containers from Germany, and stored in some bunker somewhere. Sometimes they referred to onions instead of boxes. One time they featured fish which had to be delivered to the Arabs at the market. When I translated them (and he demanded that I translate everything word for word, he practically counted the words) we would normally end up with awful nonsense, total gibberish. But he would listen to me, nodding and commenting, "Right, OK, got you, well that's pretty much all clear my friend! Many thanks!" Then he would grab the letter and disappear for a few days. He would return ashen-faced and weary, he would come to see me with the latest letter and offer me some cocaine. I turned it down, explaining that my head wasn't quite right anyway, that I didn't feel like cocaine, I turned it down. He would reply, "Well, as you wish my friend, it's your choice…" But as soon as Ivan saw the cocaine he asked where he could get hold of some. Bacho offered to get it for him, because the person he bought it off didn't want any new customers, he already had his regulars, "…so just give me your cash, my friend, and I'll fetch it myself, I'll go and get it right away, just add a bit on for petrol…" Ivan paid him with a single banknote, and as usual Bacho promised that he would bring back the change "right away or in a little while", which he never did. Then he came back with the cocaine, told Ivan that there was no change and that he shouldn't expect any, "… here take the change in kind…" and he offered to fetch some more cocaine right away "…if you want some more, if you've got the money, no point hanging about, give me the money while you've got it…!" Ivan or Mikhail gave him more money, he took it and came back with more cocaine, and so it continued…

One look at those grey pellets was enough to piss Hanuman off: "What are you snorting, you idiots! It's poison! It's crap!" They ground, pounded, sweated and pulverised for a while, then they snorted the powder with their heads craned backwards, as if they were using nose drops. And for some reason they snorted it through a five hundred kroner note, as if that made any difference! Then they patted their fingers on the dust left behind on the mirror and dabbed it on to their gums, they rubbed it right in.

Pretty soon they started getting toothache. Mikhail was constantly touching his teeth, wiggling them with one finger, checking to see if they were loose. He stood in the corridor, touching his teeth, he would touch them and say, "They are wobbling, shit, I wonder why?" Or he would sit on the porch, smoking and touching his teeth, he would sit there and say, "Damn, they really are wobbling!" and he would utter it in such amazement that it made you want to punch him in the face. Ivan said his gums were swollen and had started bleeding too. Mikhail reckoned they had scurvy, all the symptoms suggested that it was a serious case of scurvy. And it was probably due to a lack of vitamins. How long could anyone be expected to live off that muck from the rubbish bins? No fucking wonder they had scurvy! So Potapov started peeling potatoes and boiling up the skins, then he would eat them and force everyone else to eat them too, even his wife and Liza, whose teeth were fine. He said it was down to the poor-quality food, people ate all sorts of crap in Denmark! All of it was low in calorific value! Because of course all those organic foodstuffs were low-calorie!

"Us Russians can't survive on that kind of food! We need proper meat, understand!" he said as he cut down spruce branches to brew into juice. He drank that juice and forced everyone else to drink it too, pointing out that it was a recipe from Jack London.

Towards the beginning of August, Hanuman started spreading rumours that the end of the world was approaching; he wanted to taunt people, for want of anything better to do. He went to one of the camp buildings and gave a speech warning about an imminent eclipse, and pointing out that eclipses are omens of coming troubles. Then he went to the next building, and people followed him there. When he was inside, he struck a soothsayer's pose and said, "Behold, you fools! The time has come to test your spirits! The ultimate ordeal is about to begin, and innumerable unpredictable things will descend upon your ignorant heads, you bastards!"

Then he deployed a few quotations, ostensibly from the Bible, and said that all the signs indicated that the end of the world as predicted by Nostradamus, Sai Baba and Vanga was nigh. Then he went to the next building, this time with even more people tagging along. Eventually he brought everyone to our building, and Ivan, Potapov and the Arabs all cropped up in the crowd. Now Hanuman embarked on a speech about Y2K, about the coming computer apocalypse, about the war of the machines, and nuclear warheads. He also said that humans were the worst parasites on the body of Mother Earth, and that by enabling the existence and condoning the activities of such a highly developed parasite, Earth was basically committing suicide.

"Steel yourselves, you fools!" Hanuman bellowed. "The time has come to test the strength of your hearts! The living will devour the dead! And the dead will be more alive than the living! I see black snow! I see bloody skies! I see flocks of carrion crows and packs of hyenas! There will be cockroaches on the throne! Maggots in the innocent maiden's loins! The Antichrist is coming! The Antichrist is coming! On crutches, with bandaged head!"

And then he calmly went back to our room.

But it had its effect on the Arabs. According to them Allah had made man, and everything which Allah did was for the best, that was how it should be, Allah couldn't do anything bad, because Allah was kind, Allah was good, so if the end of the world was meant to be, then let it be, no eclipses needed, eclipses had no part to play, if the end of the world was coming, then it would be Allah's doing, because all things which happened were Allah's will, he was unable to do anything bad, because Allah was good, Allah was kind, and if everyone died, if bombs started to fall, it was because Allah had decided it would be thus, and it was good. "We'll definitely go to heaven, and if the rest of them down below fry, let them fry, the infidel must burn, for that is Allah's will, and it is good, because Allah is good."

Mikhail was standing there with a piece of glass, gawping at the sky; he was trying to observe the sun through smoked glass, roughly as he had seen it done in the film about Lomonosov. Naturally, Potapov had to see the eclipse. He had to witness it himself, with those narrow Tatar eyes of his. He had to see the light receding, and the darkness advance. But he was not the only one who had to see it; he took everyone out on to the field with him. His whole family. They even carried little Adam out there. Mikhail held Adam in one arm and looked at the sky through his dirty piece of glass, from time to time bringing it right up to his five-month-old son's eyes! He handed out bits of smoked glass to the others too, forcing them to look up at the sun through them just like him. Including Ivan, who they made sure to include because he was virtually a member of the family, as they kept reminding him. They stood there, looking up at the sky, necks craned backwards, holding their pieces of smoked glass in one hand, squinting, and shielding half of their face with the other hand, and for some reason their mouths were contorted into ugly shapes. Mikhail looked upwards and commented, "Maybe it's the last eclipse we'll see… maybe it's the end of the world, who knows… the Indian wouldn't have said all that stuff for no reason… India is the home of ancient wisdom… that's where it all began…"

Of course Potapov just had to observe the sky, and in the same way he had to believe in Hanuman's soothsaying. Once again he used it for his own gain: he started spending all the money which Ivan had put aside for his escape to Holland. Having seen enough mass deportations from the camp, Ivan had come to his senses and begun to save. And he wasn't going just any old place, but to Holland. He came down with a bad case of Holland just as Hanuman and I recovered and stopped thinking about Holland altogether. But then fate intervened. Ivan remembered the Dutch guys, and the family of Assyrians who had gone to Holland in the back of a van. When they got there they sent an email to everyone to inform them of the successful completion of their journey. The Assyrians were from Moscow, the father was one of those old New Russians who had become destitute. They fled Moscow to save their skins, and mainly for the sake of the kids. The mother and father still spoke Assyrian; the children couldn't. But they still managed to get through the immigration interview by pretending to be halfwits who couldn't speak any language properly. According to their email, crossing the border was "easy!", tricking the cops was like "taking candy off a baby!", and the camps in Holland were fine, they had everything you needed. And what they needed was a decent-sized bedroom, and a sports club, and they wanted football boots right away, because their lads couldn't live without football, that was the reason they had chosen Holland. They wrote to Ivan and told him to drop everything and come to join them immediately, because camp life just wasn't the same without him: they had already lost a match to someone there, because their goalkeeper was a butterfingers. The refugee championships were just round the corner, and without a defender like Ivan they had no chance of winning the cup, so Ivan was told he had to come. And so Ivan had started to save. Hanuman promised to hook Ivan up with the right people and managed to convince him that he was no longer going to Holland himself, and that the down payment he had made for the passport and transport could somehow be transferred to Ivan. Hanuman said that he'd have a word with the people and that he'd dispatch Ivan in his place, if he gave him the same amount of money which Hanuman had already laid down. Ivan immediately gave him three thousand kroner (Hanny later admitted to me that this was much less than he had paid himself, because he'd been ripped off yet again). Ivan corresponded with the guys in Holland himself. They wrote back that "the bastards don't pay much in Holland, less than in Denmark," and that "the beer here is fucking piss." But the babes you saw walking about were apparently enough to make you cream your pants! At that point Ivan started saving obsessively. Mikhail didn't like that one bit. He didn't plan on going anywhere himself. And he couldn't handle the fact that his errand boy might just get away, taking his money with him – money which Mikhail could otherwise help himself to, using the pretext of "family". He tried to talk Ivan round, to dissuade him. But then he decided it would be best to somehow commandeer his savings. He didn't yet know how to do it exactly, but he was sure there was already more than a thousand there! If not two! The less he really knew about how much Ivan had saved, the more it seemed to his fevered imagination. Maybe it was already two and a half thousand? Or even a full three? He'd been saving for a full two months now... three and a half! Just think how much cocaine and hashish that could buy! And now there's this eclipse! Global collapse! The deluge! The end of the world! What's the point of saving money if we're all doomed anyway! Might as well spend it! And so somehow Mikhail managed to twist Ivan's arm – they headed off to Aalborg, bought a load of hash, and started smoking it. I helped them a bit, although only a little bit; I was so wasted from the heat that I didn't need to smoke, I just sat in the same room as them and listened to their halfwit banter, and felt totally spaced out. They quickly smoked up all their hash. The heat was terrible, and it was accumulating, it was threatening to unleash something truly awful, it was promising to be horrific! Hanuman told us that in Los Angeles people were dropping down dead in the streets! In the City of Angels the ambulances weren't managing to clear up all the bodies in time! Animals were snuffing it in such quantities that they had given up trying! There were corpses lying about rotting. Fires breaking out all over the place! Siberia was engulfed in flames! The Amazon rainforest was burning! Some kind of foul-smelling plague was on the loose!

"But in Mexico," he yelled, "meanwhile in Mexico they're throwing snowballs at each other! That's right! They're chucking snowballs about! A snowstorm passed right through the centre of Mexico City! Nothing of the sort has ever happened there before! How do you like that! Get ready, you idiots! He! Ha! Ho! The best is yet to come!"

I couldn't bear to listen. Potapov did nothing but drive back and forth to Aalborg buying hash. But he couldn't smoke it any more because he had such a bad cough. I shuddered from head to toe when I heard it; he had gone hoarse, and his coughing sounded like the barking of a chained dog. By now it was unbearably hot indoors. The roof of our building was incandescent, and if one of the kids' balls ended up on it, it burst immediately. Everyone hid in the shade. The only people who were out in the open and playing badminton were the Tamil queers who had just moved in to the camp. Nepalino, who was not too sporty, was always the third in line to play. If the shuttlecock ended up on the roof, Nepalino had to climb up a ladder and knock it down with a pole, trying not to touch the roof; Radenko had been careless when he climbed up to get a ball and had ended up with burns!

Tormented by boredom and the stuffiness inside, I went out into the field wearing my flip-flops. That way my feet could breath, they weren't festering, and it felt good. I was soaking in sweat, but my feet were fine. The sun had slid behind the moon a little, as if it were swooning, and it looked pretty cool! I said to Mikhail and Ivan, "What about having a smoke of your grass, some of that ditch weed?"

"No," said Mikhail, "it's too soon."

And he looked up at the sky.

"Why's it too soon? What's the difference, if we're all doomed anyway. Let's at least boil up some cannabis milk!"

"Now you're talking!" said Potapov.

And so we headed into the field to look for the grass, which Mikhail had planted himself, as he liked to boast. Mikhail and Ivan started meandering through the field, and we ended up hell knows where, but eventually we found a couple of plants and yanked them out of the ground. Unfortunately they were wimpy specimens, we would need seven or eight of those minimum, otherwise it might not be enough. But at that moment I trod on a snake, and it sank its teeth into my foot. I distinctly felt the poison flowing into my flesh. I kicked my leg out. The snake came unstuck, dropping off like a big leech. For a few seconds I hoped that it might just be a bundle of wires. But it became clear that it was a snake when it started slithering; it slithered off. And then I said quietly, "A snake just bit me…"

"A snake bit him!" Ivan yelled in a panic.

Mikhail grabbed a stick and started whacking the ground around my feet.

"Eh! Uh! Ah!"

I started hopping about and yelling, "Idiot! What are you doing! You fucking twat!"

But he carried on pounding my feet with his stick. Then he started hitting the ground around himself and dancing a Cossack dance with a face which was so pale and frightened, it was a sight to see! I howled at them, "What are you doing, you idiots! Someone has to suck the poison out of the wound!"

They stood there rooted to the spot, staring at me and shaking their heads, "No way, we can't! We've got open wounds in our mouths!" and they opened their mouths to show me their bleeding gums.

I started wailing, "Take me back, for fuck's sake, take me to Hanuman! Where is the nearest road out of this forest? Ditch those plants! Take me back! Look where you bastards brought me!"

One of them started tugging me to the right, the other to the left – what a pair of idiots! I ran off in a random direction, and arrived back at the camp before them. I bellowed, "Hanny, snake, suck!"

Hanny looked at me as if I was raving mad, and asked me, "Suck what?"

"Look, my foot! Snake! You've got to suck!"

Hanuman shrugged his shoulders and told me I was making it up.

"Hanny! Those idiots saw it happen, they'll turn up any moment!"

At that point Nepalino popped up beside us, and, suddenly plucking up his courage, he said scornfully, "If he'd been bitten by a real poisonous snake he'd be dead by now! But no such snakes exists in Denmark! You'd have to be bitten by all the snakes put together to end up dead!"

And he chuckled out of the corner of his mouth. For some reason Nepalino seemed to think that I was some sort of outdoor survivalist. He blurted out his thoughts, turned round and started plodding back to the kitchen to see if he could get a free feed off anyone. I yelled at him, "Fucker! Hey! I said hey! You! Fucking bastard! Come here! You like to suck – have a suck of my toe!"

Nepalino half turned and said lazily, "Danish snakes are about as poisonous as mosquitos. Don't be silly. Don't panic. Wash the cut. Stick a plaster on it. It'll hurt for a while, and then it will get better. This isn't Nepal or somewhere..."

And he padded off, jingling the keys in his trouser pocket.

"Fuck the lot of you, bastards!" I yelled at them, looking down at my foot. I could see it visibly swelling. Hanuman crouched down, and asked, "What pattern did the snake have on its back?"

Breathing heavily, Mikhail said, in Russian, "It was a smooth snake!"

Hanuman couldn't understand of course.

"If it was a smooth snake" Ivan said, also in Russian, "he would have already been..."

"It was a young smooth snake, a young one," Mikhail insisted.

"It wasn't a smooth snake, or a viper, it was a grass snake..."

"What do you mean, grass snake!" I yelled, "you reckon I couldn't feel the poison going in?! What sort of grass snake is going to bite?"

Hanuman rose from his squatting position. I hadn't ever seen him look so serious.

"Yes," he said, "it's serious, we need to go to the doctor's..."

"No," I said, cutting him off, "I'm not going to any doctor's!"

"Ivan," said Mikhail, "run to the doctor's, tell him that you got bitten by a snake, ask him to give you something for it!"

"How am I going to prove it... I haven't even got a wound on my foot..."

"I'll give you a couple of jabs with my knife!"

"You know where you can put that knife!"

"Stop fucking about! We've got to get moving!" I said, panicking.

"Where to?"

"I don't know! But my foot's swelling! It's getting bigger the whole time! Come on, let's get in the car, we're going into town!"

Hanuman produced his mobile phone and dialled a number, which is something he never did, and said something fast in Hindi. Then he called another number, and spoke a bit more. Then he called a third time, spoke for a while, and swore in his native tongue. Then he called again and spoke for a long time. Then he swore again, called another number, and started speaking English, "You're our last hope," he said, "I don't know who else to try, everyone else has sent us packing. We've got a snakebite to deal with! Antibiotics? Penicillin, you say? Where can I get hold of some? Well, his foot's swelling up, it's ballooning with every second... come and see you? We'll come right away! Quick, let's get in the car!"

"Which one?"

"Yours you idiot, start her up, take us to Aalborg, look lively!"

"There's no petrol in it..."

"Have you got any brains in your head? Quickly!"

We got into the car and quickly filled up at the Georgian's place; when we presented him with my swollen leg, which was already a right sight, he sympathised with my predicament, and didn't charge us anything. By now I was feverish; my nerves were shattered, and my temperature was rising... poison, poison, poison!

The car barely chugged along, and I was sure that it would end up being my hearse; it was only an hour and a half to Aalborg, and we'd already been travelling a whole three! A whole eternity! It felt like death was already inside me, and everything around us was happy to abet her.

Eventually we arrived in town. Mikhail suffered from worse topographical cretinism than Hanuman and me put together, and he couldn't find the street called Godthaabsgade. Oh, what a name, Good Hope Street! When we stopped and asked passers-by the way, no one could understand which street we were looking for, because none of us could pronounce that never-ending word properly, and so the hope which had nestled in that name turned its back on me and slipped away. By now I was almost raving. I felt as if I was already three-quarters poison, that I already contained two or three litres of poison! That I would soon begin to rot from the inside, or start visibly decomposing!

By the time we turned up at the right place I could no longer use that foot, which was now three times bigger than it had been! The pain was excruciating! They lifted me up, and my leg flopped downwards, it was so heavy that it felt like it was going to drop off. In fact the other leg, and my arms, and my head felt just the same, my head could easily have rolled off down the street, to be scooped up by some tramp like a cabbage! They carried me past some cars, two lamp posts, and a person who was standing between the lamp posts, a telephone to his ear and his mouth open; he followed me with an unblinking gaze. It occurred to me that he was about to inform the necessary people about my death, and then the people with telephones would be stood down, or they would get a new tasking to follow someone else.

They carried me into Hugh's flat. He was sitting at the table with some guy called Paul – no one bothered to introduce us... both of them started inspecting my foot. Then Paul said, "Well, well, it's just like what happened to me, it's like that Ebola, remember? I almost died back then, my capillaries were bursting, the bleeding started moving along the foot, under the skin, the foot swelled up, the tumour moved up my leg almost as far as my vital organs, my thigh swelled up in a flash, if it wasn't for the serum, I wouldn't be sitting here now..."

Hugh gave me some penicillin, three tablets, and he put my foot in a bowl of water with some kind of powder sprinkled in to it. Ignoring us, he started consulting with Paul: "What should we do?"

"What do you mean? We've got to save the guy..."

"I can see that myself... we have to save him, but how?"

"We need to have a think..."

They were properly pissed, a sea of beer bottles had spread out around them, leaving no room to stand, not even on one foot. Paul stretched his lips and all the slack skin on his face into an expression of complete indecisiveness. Hugh goggled, wiped his greasy mouth, and inhaled sharply, inflating his whole body. Paul twitched the only line on his forehead and said they had to go to the doctor's, if they wanted the guy to live. I rolled my eyes and said that I would rather die than hand myself in to the cops.

"Why bring the cops into it?" said Paul. "There are doctors around who won't say a word to the cops."

"We don't know any doctors like that..."

Paul said that he would call someone, but he didn't have a telephone. Hanuman produced his phone. Paul called, spoke for a couple of minutes, explained the situation to someone called Zuzu, and said that the foot looked awful, that the guy had a temperature, he wasn't making any sense, he was practically raving...

"Bring him to you right away? Got it, he'll be brought," Paul said, and then he got up.

He instructed that I be taken to the car. My foot bumped along the floor like a dropped anchor. It even seemed they were carrying it separately for a while, like a baby. But still, but still – damn it! – I couldn't avoid knocking it against the car door! Seven hours later I was in Huskegaard.

But how I suffered during that journey!

I was tossed this way and that, I had hot flushes, I felt nauseous, I threw up, and I couldn't shake off this vision: an unknown street, with a huddled pack of lapdogs, and whenever they ran to the right I felt sick, whenever they ran to the left, I had a cold flush, and wherever I looked, there they were, running along, relentlessly. It was so horrible, there was such a sense of inevitability about it, a feeling of foreboding, of a terrible, horrific end which would befall me as soon as that pack of lapdogs dispersed. That would have been the worst thing which could happen! The most inconceivable and the most terrifying! It seemed as if I was flying somewhere on pellucid, barely visible wings. I came to when Hanuman started shaking me; he was trying to wake me, to force me to speak, to hold on, while Paul was saying, "Oh, now he's all blue, he's getting bluer, that doesn't look too good, it doesn't look good at all, actually, fuck me, it looks fucking terrible!" At that point I fell into delirium. I was aware of someone tugging my foot and whispering something, there was singing coming from somewhere, something was moving about, something was flowing, flowing into one ear green and coming out of the other blue, and it was all seething, and I was seething with it...

I came round as the doctor removed a strong-smelling wad of cotton wool from under my inflamed nostrils; I was suffocating, sweat was pouring down my face, and I could see an old man, a really old, really decrepit old man, he was standing there saying something in Danish to a worried-looking woman in a shawl. If I understood him correctly, he was saying that there was only one thing which would help me, if they used it right away, and that he had some, but he didn't know if I was allergic, and if my heart would take it. The woman in the shawl said that if they didn't try, I would die, but that if they did, then at least I had a chance.

"Well," said the old man, "if I inject him and he dies, I could be prosecuted!"

"Aha, so someone else should do the injection?"

"That would be best..."

There was no one in the room, no one apart from the three of us and Hanuman, but he wasn't in a fit state to do the injection, especially not into the vein, because, as it later transpired, they had got him properly stoned in the commotion. I instantly came round and asked them to give me the syringe! The doctor silently broke the tip off the ampule, filled the syringe, and handed it to me. The room was swimming; I summoned my strength, found the vein, then I saw blood spurt into the syringe and shoot up it, but I didn't bother taking a sample, I just squeezed the contents of the syringe straight into my arm, with assuredness, with finality, without worrying that I might miss the vein, or that anything else bad might happen... and it was already working, it was working, full speed ahead! What freshness! What freshness! What lightness! I had no idea what kind of antidote it was, but it took me higher, I was so high, higher than I had ever been in my life!

"Hey, doc," I said, "you didn't mix anything up, did you? That wasn't fentanyl by any chance?"

The doctor looked at me – now he had parchment skin and eyes the colour of rubies – and said, "Best you don't know what it was exactly, and best you never use it again, not ever..."

The room was dancing in front of my eyes, and I had trouble comprehending where I was, and who the people around me were; I didn't want to eat or sleep, I didn't want anything, I just asked for cigarettes, which sometimes got mixed up with joints, but I smoked whatever I was given. I drank tea, green tea which an incredibly tall, skinny black guy brought me, while masks stared down on me from the walls, showing me their long serpent tongues, laughing in my face and whispering. Night spun round me, people flitted past, there was African music playing somewhere, people dressed in strange clothes danced round me, people were smoking, smoke was floating round the room, and I was floating with it, then dawn broke, and suddenly I felt weak, and I collapsed into a deep sleep...

The doctor squeezed the puss from my foot, and I bawled.

I bawled like a child. Visions bubbled up in my mind. The pain painted pictures. I imagined that explosions were going off in my mind, and that walls, towers and bridges had sprung up. It was delirium, the real thing! For some reason it seemed that the doctor took some sadistic pleasure from the procedure. He turned up punctually every day, gave me the penicillin, put my foot in the bowl of water, took off the bandage and started pressing.

When the doctor left and I was on my own, enclosed by those damp, bare walls, I started feeling so bad, so lonely, so scared, that I wanted to hang myself. Firstly, I couldn't comprehend where I was, and why I felt so cold the whole time. I had a heap of quilts on top of me, and a radiator beside me; it didn't give off much warmth, hardly anything, but there was something coming from it! That was the whole point, that was the problem. The radiator was working, but I couldn't get warm, I didn't feel any warmth from it. I was shaking. The fear that something wasn't quite right with me started gnawing away at me... panic welled inside me. I couldn't shake off that fear, not a fear of death, but an inchoate fear of losing my foot. Secondly, my foot really had gone numb, which multiplied my fears and fed my speculation. And thirdly, outside it was raining torrentially, there was a wall of rain, and an unpleasant musical dripping noise was coming from inside the room itself. The rain was creeping into the room through the roof, which was also rattling and rumbling noisily; the rain was dripping on to the floor, merging with the discoloured damp patches on the broad carpet, which was worn bare in places; the rain dripped on to the table, on to the newspaper which someone had abandoned unfinished and left to turn yellow back on 16 June 1985; the rain dripped on to the chairs, which were positioned as if someone had just been sitting on them. Or the chairs may have been there for a hundred years already, those people had stood up and walked out, leaving the chairs as they were, and no one had touched them since, preserving their historical positions like museum exhibits, as a mark of respect, while only the rain dared to drip on them, on to their bulging sprung seats, on to their curving armrests and the roses on their backrests. I looked at those silent chairs and I couldn't shake the strange sensation that even if one hundred years had already passed since those imagined persons had left, they still had to come back, they would definitely return, and they could do so any time, any time whatsoever, they could return at any moment. And the monotonous dripping sound reinforced that sensation, it increased the sense of expectation. Papers of some description had been left lying about, huge stacks of paper and files, folders, printouts, presentations, speeches, reports, abstracts and write-ups from seminars. All of it was in English, but it was impossible to work out what it was about! There was all sorts of nonsense. It was hard to believe it had been written by real people. It read like some sort of science fiction novel! There was stuff about a conspiracy, a global conspiracy against the whole of humankind, about some elite which oversaw everything, absolutely everything, from economic crises to social development, education, intellectual history, revolutions, religion, wars; everything, they had absolutely everything in their power. That small handful of people controlled all of humanity, and all our dreams as well: including mine and Hanuman's. This elite apparently intervened in the DNA of every single person, they had created McDonalds and McBurger, set up the Spar kiosks and Spar banks, they dreamt up the Internet, computers, cockroach races and the Cannes festival, they planted ideas for films in the minds of Hollywood and Bollywood directors, they controlled our behaviour, telling us who to sleep with, and even who to befriend. This elite controlled everything, even death itself. Which meant that common people, idiots like Hanuman and me, had to sacrifice our lives for them, so that they could live forever, all these Rockefellers, Rothschilds, Fords and Bilderbergers, these princes and princesses, lords and ladies, the fucking elite. I wouldn't have even wiped my arse with those papers! In any case, the weather was getting worse and worse, there was something ominous in the air, it was constantly gloomy, the roof was shaking, somewhere something was rumbling, grating, moaning; it seemed like a storm was brewing, and obviously that had also been pre-planned by that masonic lodge, by that coalition, by those idols. Water was streaming down the walls, but it wasn't simply trickling in any direction, it was being directed straight into my bed, the bed felt damp. It was horrible. And I was hungry too. Once a day some old guy turned up; he was tall, gangly, bearded, tousled, toothless, and he was dressed in a huge raincoat with traces of dust, lime and soot on it. He brought me tea, bread, and plain white rice, carrying the plate in his gnarled hand. He put the plate down and pushed it towards me, then he sat down on one of the chairs, paying no heed to the dampness and the rainwater dripping on to him, he sat there, looking at me and around the room, breathing through his open mouth, like a fish. He would sit there for a while, a bead of sweat dripping from his nose, not saying a word, and then he would leave, only to return the next day and repeat the whole process: the tea, the bread, the rice, the silent contemplation, the nasal breathing. Every single day he would come and sit with me in the damp, produce a droplet of sweat from the tip of his nose, and leave, only to come back the following day. And so on, without end... I was going out of my mind.

I spent a whole week like that, with no idea where I was, or where Hanuman could be. I didn't even have any idea where the cursed Irishman Hugh was. It later transpired that having decided that my life was no longer in danger Hanuman had relaxed and opted to unwind by joining Joachim, Frederic and Joshua for a smoke of their superstrong grass. While they were chatting he had an interesting idea. Someone mentioned that Luke made chapattis, but no one was sure that they were the genuine thing. They started to discuss how to make chapattis, and at some point they recalled how the Kurds made their shawarma kebabs, and then they concluded that if you were to wrap meat, salad and tomatoes in a chapatti, you would end up with some kind of shawarma or tortilla. At that point Hanuman yelled, "What an idea! What a brilliant idea! You could call it a CHAPATILLA!" and he left to put his brainwave into practice in the local restaurants. He completely disappeared from view. As soon as he left, a torrential downpour began, and all the hippies covered their logs with plastic sheeting, or dragged them under roofing and covered that with sheeting. They forgot all about me, about Hanuman, about everything. According to Hanuman the downpour had prevented him from realising his concept, and from coming back to see me. He settled in Avnstrup at the fat Serb's place. While he was there he wrote a newspaper article about what happened to the money the refugees were given (what they spent it on, or if they didn't spend it, where they sent it, and by what means). In that article he also wrote about how refugees whiled away their time while waiting for a decision on their cases. He wrote about violence at the camps, and about what the kids got up to. He wrote about the parcels home full of stolen goods. In that article he wrote about the unhygienic conditions at the camps and how the asylum seekers were entirely to blame for them. And he wrote about lots of other stuff: the horse's head in the container, the grass, the fertiliser. About the stench, the puddles in the toilets. And he did all of that in forty-three lines with a single photograph of the Farstrup camp taken from afar – that was it. At the same time he combed Copenhagen for people who might back his new idea, or help him to devise another one. He wanted to find his old acquaintances, the ones who sold boring old rice and chicken curry, something like a Chinese takeaway, but Indian style. He wanted to meet them and explain his new idea. The Chapatilla! Just wrap some meat and a bit of lettuce in a chapatti, pour some sauce and dressing on it, and it's ready! Twenty-five kroner! Twenty-five kroner of pure profit! Pure genius! He raved about copyrighting his idea, about opening a chain of fast-food joints called "Hanuman and Sons", and some idea was buzzing round his brain about an international project, something like the "Chez Guevara" café concept. Only that this time he had thought it up for himself. He had intoxicated himself, duped himself, driven himself mad. He believed that his star was in the ascendant. A smile was slowly forming on his face, ready to be displayed on TV screens and posters, to be unfurled from skyscrapers and at every bus stop, on every form of public transport, in every country of the world. He was already imagining how all those people who had spat at his back or straight into his face would tear their hair out! That smile was intended for me as well. He wanted to laugh at me: "He-ha-ho, Johan, you fucking bastard!" He was ready to guffaw in my face, because I had mocked his dream! Me, the one who was perishing from paranoia and a putrid foot in that draughty castle. He who had doubted Hanuman's genius! Obviously, huddled there under a mountain of stinking quilts, I was in dire need of his Chapatilla and his iceberg-sized smirk! He had to show me that he had been right all along. He had to jeer at me. I had to pay for my lack of faith. I was like the wise fish in the fairy tale, keeping to himself at the bottom of the lake, I was a misanthrope and a pessimist. I had to be punished, I had to be taught a lesson, my nose had to be rubbed in the resplendent facts, because I had said too many times, "Hanny, by the time your dream comes true the people who you want to tear out their hair at the sight of your on-screen smile won't be around any more, or they won't have any hair left to tear out, or you won't have any teeth with which to dazzle them, or even if you get false teeth fitted so you can flash people a smile and inspire awe in them, they will already be too old to care, they won't give a damn, none of them are going to look at the radiant Hanumancho and see that same guy who they fucked over one time, or they simply won't want to admit that the guy in the posters with the dazzling smile is the same Hanuman who they humiliated in some dungeon in India all those years ago!" Oh dear me! So now he was in a hurry to prove that I had been wrong! To prove that he was an almighty god! To prove that he could survive anything, and become a millionaire from nothing! Without doing the lottery, or playing bingo, or going to a casino or appearing on *Who Wants to Be a Millionaire?* He could do it! And now we all had to acknowledge that fact! Pretty soon Hanuman's visage would light up the sky in place of the sun and the moon. And so as to realise his dream as quickly as possible, he gave up on me. He forgot all about me. He left. He deserted me, lying alone in that castle, in a hot fever. Completely alone! He didn't even check if I was alive! He didn't care, he couldn't care less, that Hanumaniac!

They suggested that I stay at the castle for a while. While my leg healed, while things sorted themselves out. They sympathised with my predicament, took pity on me and made an exception for me. Mister Vinterskov (my ancient carer) said that when I got better I could do some work to pay the rent. He needed some people to help round the castle: there were repairs to be done, and some sort of seminar coming up. He didn't have time to dilly-dally, to weigh up the pros and cons and check if I was a "good person". He told me how things were going to be. Even if I wasn't a good person, I would have to become one immediately, if I wanted to live at the castle! That was the condition. I had no choice. And so I agreed.

Me and Mister Vinterskov hit it off. We found that we had several languages in common. He even spoke pretty good Russian! This is what he would say about his Russian skills: "I speak it badly, I can read a lot, but I understand even more!" I had never met anyone quite like him! He would come out with all sorts of random stuff, on any subject at all. His thought processes were probably pretty similar! He was already over eighty, so it was only to be expected. Although he was still in pretty good shape. Once he had plucked up the courage to talk to me we found out a lot about each other. He told me about India, about Africa and Paris, about Pavel Florensky, Father Sergius Bulgakov, and the Second World War, as he remembered it. This was no ordinary human, he was a walking museum, a library, a real Babylonian. Nothing I said could surprise him. Although perhaps there was one thing... I told him that I couldn't reveal my real name or the country I came from, and had my reasons. He agreed with my conditions: he would call me by my invented name and wouldn't ask too many questions... I told him that I'd had some bother back home, and described it in general terms – gangsters and corrupt police – obviously I dressed it up and embroidered it a bit. I told him that I had to sit things out for three years or so, until the limitations period had passed. He nodded sympathetically, muttered into his beard, bit his lips, rubbed his hands together, and then he informed me that his monastery was prepared to take me under its wing, to make me its first refugee member... "You'll be under our protection, in a church refuge, even the police won't be able to touch you here!" he added emphatically. Evidently that was why I was needed in that castle: to help give the ruins the appearance, albeit phantasmagorical, of some kind of monastery! I agreed to take on the role of refugee, which immediately elevated my status amongst the others in the village. I thanked him with all my heart and rejoiced... at long last!

He brought me books. I asked him to bring me some Kierkegaard, explaining that I had already read a little. I even remembered once reading something about Abraham, then I recalled something about the sickness of the spirit before death, that the self, the ego was the sickness of the depersonalised spirit, and that freedom consisted of freeing oneself from everything personal, freeing oneself of the ego, undergoing a Buddhist form of regeneration to achieve freedom and so on… The old man agreed, bit his lips, and added some thoughts of his own… It turned out that the papers I'd found in the cupboard were reports from the seminars which he organised at the castle. People came from far and wide every year, even from as far as India… All those ravings which I had unearthed, about inserting chips into people, about achieving total control – incredibly, they were the work of real, live people, people who were perfectly sane, not lunatics. The old man documented it all in detail. He told me that his seminars were dedicated to anti-globalism, and something else as well, to spiritual emancipation, to harmony, to self-improvement, and other such dross, I couldn't get my head round it all. What stunned me was that he really believed that everything had been planned in advance, absolutely everything – the recent history of humanity, the entire course of events, all of it! In order to exercise total global control a group of individuals (billionaires and political elites) had devised a painstaking plan to divide the whole world into subordinate sectors, so as to control everything from behind the scenes, pulling the strings of their chosen puppets. The old man's grand prediction was that soon everything would change, and the world would end up under the umbrella of a single global government.

"Yes," he said, "the European Union is just the first stage in a far-reaching programme, the first step towards the unification of the whole of planet Earth – the aim is to enslave the whole of humanity. After that will come the African Union. Then, most likely the United States will be unified with Canada and Mexico, which will of course require the introduction of a single currency… After that Eurasia will be unified… That's right, Russia as such will cease to exist, instead there will be a United States of Eurasia… It will include Ukraine, Belarus, Kazakhstan, Kirgizia and the rest... China, India and the nearby countries will also form a union of Asia and Oceania, together with Korea, Japan, and Oceania of course... then there will be the Pacific Union, that's right... That will make it easier to maintain control... As Ford said, if humankind needs a crisis in order to organise a new world order, then we will organise one, by whatever means necessary..."

...And on top of all that, it turned out that the eugenicists were behind everything! I could hardly believe my ears! Why not just say it was aliens? But I didn't have the strength to joke. I was in a state of shock. And anyway, the old man seemed deadly serious. This was no place for joking! He counted off the names on his taloned fingers: "Rockefeller, Rothschild, Ford." I gulped after every one: "Bush, Blair, Stoltenberg, Clinton..." That was already more than enough, I had no desire to hear about sterilisation or cross-breeding, I didn't want to know what would become of the East, of Australia, and the rest of the world... I didn't want to hear anything about the coming technological revolution, about the depopulation programme, about the impending attacks, the wars, holocausts, crises, about the maelstrom which was being prepared for us by evil monsters, by the midgets in crystal limousines. I shoved my fingers into my ears so as not to have to hear the revelations of that Nostradamus. My eyeballs were bulging out of their sockets from the strain, and my guts had almost turned inside out (so I shoved them back up my arse, blocking the passage with my fist!). I was sure that either he was raving or I was hallucinating! The old man gurgled on for a while, before gradually falling silent, he finally shut down the fountain, there was still some murmuring coming from somewhere in the pit of his stomach, a sucking sound like plumbing, but eventually that stopped as well. He stuttered to a standstill, his shoulders slumped forwards... and I breathed a sigh of relief. I must have looked awful by now. Our conversation had left me drained. He let me rest and didn't appear for a few days. When he eventually came back, he didn't make too many demands of me. He must have realised that in my weakened state the kind of information he had imparted was too much of a burden. In order to properly absorb that kind of stuff you needed plenty of spare calories, and the constitution of a leopard. I didn't have either. I could barely move. Him and his talk of global dominion were the last straw! It took me a week to recover. I turned over escape plans in my mind. I tried to work out how I could get to Odense, and where I should head after that... But eventually I decided to wait. He didn't say anything further on the subject, which suited me fine. He gradually dropped the topic altogether, he just came and tossed logs into the stove, and sat there in silence, rubbing his ugly fingers together, and tugging at his beard. He poured me tea, dripping beads of sweat from his nose, and then carried the plate away in his gnarled hands. I preferred talking about poetry, about various other vague and pointless things which were as far removed from eugenics as possible; I spoke to him about my quest for freedom, about the strange journey which Hanuman had got me mixed up in, about the bizarre lifestyle we had adopted over the last two years. The old man listened and seemed to be moved. I told him about how Hanuman and I had been going against the flow, trying in our own way to stop the world on its axis.

"That's exactly why we need a new world order," Mister Vinterskov said with a grin, "so that no one gets left at a loose end... so as not to have the likes of you knocking about...!"

"Yes, yes of course," I said and continued elaborating on my theme. I gesticulated, pursed my lips, cast my gaze up at the ceiling, from where the ideas were raining down, like pigeon droppings mixed with rainwater. And I embroidered all of this drivel with bits of existentialism, the "Parable of the Raindrop", and some other stuff which I had heard from

Hanuman. I even used Hanuman's gestures, his phrases, sometimes I even kicked off from his springboard "cos you know man", which brought a barely concealed smile to the old man's stern lips, a smile which appeared fleetingly, like a seagull hovering above a wave before disappearing behind the severe, craggy seascape. The old man had clearly taken a liking to me; I couldn't fail to notice that. There was a certain type of person who seemed to like me for no particular reason, there were people who fell in love with me immediately, without even knowing why – Hanuman had spoken to me on that theme. "Just that as a rule those kinds of people have got nothing to offer you," he added, "or me, or anyone else... It's like in prison. It's just that sometimes amongst all the hopeless fools you will come across a more or less decent lamb, from whom there is nothing to be gained nor to be lost... They're just ordinary people like you, and that's that..." Be that as it may, I thought to myself, I don't care, the main thing is that they don't gob into my heart. I had also taken a liking to the old man, as far as I could tell he was the holy fool type, a Don Quixote, and he wasn't planning to shaft me. As well as that, it seemed he liked the way my mind worked, my lively, bold train of thought, which moved at a gallop while I was physically unable to get up and walk round the room. He liked my boldness and my cockiness, because he was a kind of botanist-experimenter who liked to cross-fertilise ideas, religions and languages, of which he knew more than a dozen. Once I started to get by without medicine I was able to walk around a bit, with the help of a stick. As soon as the rain stopped we started going outside and we even did some work together. We would go to the willow garden, get down on all fours like dogs, and pull up the weeds around the trees. There were hundreds of them there. Every day from morning to lunch we would weed the garden, on all fours! Our hands ended up grazed and bloody! We would break our fingernails! We would sit on his porch and, just like kids, we would show each other the wounds on our hands, talk about the mortality of the flesh, and the immortality of our souls, which were made stronger, were tempered by such ordeals. I got to meet lots of new people. There were slightly more than a dozen houses in the village, knocked together from bits of junk. Some of them had been built lovingly, the others willy-nilly, in a hurry. They were hovels, there's no other word for it! Most of the houses had once been train carriages. But it was hard to tell; they'd been so well done up inside, and covered with layers of insulation on the outside. The best house belonged to a Japanese guy. A genuine Japanese house with little lanterns hanging from a cornice all around the edge – in any case, it seemed genuine. A guy called Henrik had a pretty decent place too: a prefabricated Swedish house, delivered direct from Sweden. He made a point of telling me as soon as we met, "My house is the only proper one in the village, made in Sweden!" If he had been a Swede himself he would have been sure to declare his house Swedish territory, and there'd be a Swedish flag hanging from it! But there weren't any Swedes in Huskegaard! Even in Huskegaard they couldn't stand the Swedes! The inhabitants of Huskegaard pretended to be different to everyone else, but those hippies were just as Danish as the people living in blocks of flats or residential properties in the big cities, towns or villages, whether in Copenhagen or the farms of Jutland – they were exactly the same! Maybe they were a bit weird… but so what, it made no difference, just like it made no difference if they smoked grass, they were exactly the same as everyone else in Denmark, end of story. Joshua rented three square metres from Henrik, and Henrik charged him for it on a punctual basis (the sum of money was calculated according to a special formula which Gunter the German had come up with, and it took everything into account, even the amount of air which Joshua inhaled!). Either that or Joshua would pay by doing cleaning work and gardening. One time Joshua and I had a good smoke on the porch of that little Swedish house. We got pretty stoned. But Joshua just carried on rolling joints. And it didn't look like he planned to stop. "Now we're going to get even higher," he said, "now we're going to get really high." He really loved his grass, and he would probably be able to score wherever he was, even in the Antarctic. We smoked everything he had, but that wasn't enough, he wanted one last high. So we scraped together some change, and went to see the German, then we went to Ivonka, and in the end we managed to roll a nice fat joint, smoke it, and sit there admiring how well-tended and pretty Henrik's garden was. I was so zonked that I was able to observe that garden from two viewpoints simultaneously! From the porch, and from one of the castle towers. And I couldn't work out where I really was: in one of the towers of the castle or on the porch of Henrik's house! Joshua told me that he had done so much work in that garden and worked so hard. He was constantly repeating, "I planted so much, I planted and planted, and I weeded even more! I cleared all sorts of weeds, some of them you could probably only find in Polynesia! And all because I had no money to pay Henrik…" He had worked the land so hard that the garden had started to look really good, incredibly good…

"A proper enchanted garden, isn't it?" said Josh. "You can just imagine Africans or Indians turning up with their kids, it's as if the garden was created especially for them, they're going to turn up any minute and start frolicking with tigers, lions and panthers, just like in the Jehovah's Witnesses' magazines…"

I almost split my sides with laughter!

One quiet night Hanuman came creeping into the Huskegaard village. He had barely managed to drag himself there, swaying from side to side like a drunkard. He sat down on a bench outside the commune building and stretched out his legs. He stretched them and flung his head back so that his huge Adam's apple jutted out like Kilimanjaro. He was completely feeble. He was drained, like a randy tomcat after a lengthy rampage, his eyes brimming with unvoiced implorations, his stomach empty and his loins lightened. He had frittered away all his savings. He had snorted them up his nose with some druggies on Istedgade Street. And he'd shagged some Nigerian woman again, for forty-five kroner an hour. She was a refugee, married to a German guy, or that's what she said. But that wasn't important; she had wide cheekbones, huge nipples like gooses' feet, and broad splayed toes. How could he resist! She wore jeans, her backside was flat but wide, she had broad swimmer's shoulders, and really curly hair. What was he supposed to do! She was coarse and haughty, short-tempered and loud. In other words, she was pure dynamite! Half of the male population of Avnstrup had slept with her, and if you took into account that it was a transfer camp, with new refugees regularly being delivered and dispatched, then she must have worked like a mill on that river of human lives which was fed by tributaries from all across Europe, the East, Asia and Africa. Everyone knew her, because she had been living there for nearly a year, and almost as illegally as Hanuman. She had an arrangement with a black guy who took payment from her for the room and something on top, as her pimp. For some reason he wasn't sent on anywhere. He was registered in Avnstrup. He'd been there half a year already. Everyone said that he was a spy, a police agent, a grass, not a real refugee. Maybe that was true, but it was certain he was a pimp! And he dressed appropriately in gaudy, glittering clothes with his collar turned up, in a hoody, covered in chains, rings, bracelets, and his teeth were metal too. It really was hard to believe he was a refugee. He only came to Avnstrup twice a month, to collect his money. Nothing else interested him. Nothing whatsoever! No one knew where he went the rest of the time. He didn't talk to anyone, apart from giving them the occasional piece of advice: "I advise you to think before you speak," or "I advise you to keep your mouth shut and your ears open," or "I advise you to count you money carefully before you give it to me." That was how he spoke, he didn't know any other way. "He's just pretending to be from the Cameroons, he's really from America," the woman told Hanuman. "Only black men from America treat their women like that! Only American black guys call each other 'nigger'. An African would never say that to another African, not even as a joke! But that guy says nothing else!" She had big eyes and long fingers with nails which curved inwards. She was taller than Hanuman. She had bulging eyes like a toad, said Hanuman sentimentally. It wasn't comfortable to shag her upright. She had a strange smell about her, she didn't wash very often. But that was "all right". There were lots of discomforts at Avnstrup. There were plenty of grounds to complain. For one thing, it was cramped. And this girl had jutting ribs and a protruding tailbone, so they couldn't fit into the showers together. But she didn't like going there on her own, it was boring, she said. "What am I going to do there alone?" she asked, and burst out laughing. She had a grating laugh, like the call of some nocturnal bird. Spittle collected in the corners of her mouth as she spoke and she would suck it in noisily, especially if she was talking heatedly on the phone, and especially when she switched to her native tongue. When she spoke her own language she could only shout, she wasn't capable of talking calmly at all. "Only dead people speak like the people here in Europe speak!" she would say. "Where I come from even dead people don't talk like that! Where I come from even the dead sound more lively than people here in Europe…" She fired off the words with a percussive sound, and those words made a deep impression on Hanuman. To him it seemed they were accompanied by the sound of giant parrots flapping their invisible wings. He was entranced. She suffered from claustrophobia. It really was cramped in the shower cubicles in Avnstrup. That much was certain. Like a coffin. She and Hanuman tried several times, but sod all came of it... they didn't manage any washing or fucking. It was as cramped as a cupboard! She squeezed herself into the shower as if she were trying on a coat, the whole thing was silly. They tried several times in the middle of the night. But it was Ramadan, and there were sleepy, grubby, bearded, singing, snivelling, slow-moving Arabs, Kurds and Albanians about, and hell knows who else! They paid too much attention to everything, but to him in particular. Or at least it seemed that way. They kept asking him how his case was going. They stood in front of him, half-asleep, mouths open and eyes half-closed, swaying like zombies, asking the same questions again and again. Who, what, how much, what stage, had he got a no, a second no, had he made an appeal, what about deportation, a food pack, how, what, why? This, that, and all the rest of it! They wanted to know everything. They were suspicious, and they had to know every single detail of his affairs. He was plagued by misgivings: what if they grassed him up? He wanted to run, but his animal passion for the curly-haired Nigerian woman held him back. Together, they used up all his money. He stayed with her until there was nothing left! They traipsed around the nightclubs. She flirted brazenly with Danish guys right in front of his eyes. And she had no qualms talking about it. She didn't spend a krone of her own money. She snorted a lot of speed. They necked some tablets which gave him diarrhoea and made her horny. She never smoked a single cigarette of her own. And he never smoked a single cigarette of hers. Whichever way you look at it, he never fucked her for free. He had to pay for everything. The last of his money went on her taxi from the nightclub back to Avnstrup. The moment he handed the money over to the taxi driver she slammed the door in his face. And then he went roaming about like a jackal, looking for somewhere to kip. He found nothing, so he got on a train and came to Huskegaard. He was lucky – he hid from the ticket inspectors in the toilet. He admitted that he had cried in that toilet from humiliation and lust. He was getting withdrawal symptoms from her, he couldn't resign himself to never seeing her again, never feeling her body next to his. And there was something languishing in the depths, some unuttered swear words... She was called Deba, which meant "God abides with us"! He meandered from Odense to Huskegaard on foot (nearly twenty kilometres). When I saw him he looked like a phantom. I even thought that I was still asleep and that I was dreaming, that I was looking at a carpet which they'd taken out and put on the bench by the commune building, that it wasn't actually Hanuman, that Josh's grass had hit me that hard and any moment I would adjust the focus and what looked like Hanuman would turn back into a carpet which had been put out to be cleaned. But no, it was him. He had tears in his eyes, and his Nigerian woman was dancing in those tears, mocking him. I winced and invited him into the castle. I fed him with what I had. He ate little, and warily, sluggishly. I looked him up and down, and he looked at me. Eventually he flaked out. He slept almost a whole day. Then he spent a long time smoking a joint with some Lithuanians, saying nearly nothing, just tapping his foot the whole time; his heel was constantly tapping, as if it was working an invisible spinning wheel.

Someone called him, and he was on the phone for ages, answering monosyllabically, then he abruptly wound up the conversation, switched off the phone, and crashed out again.

Ivan appeared in Hanuman's tracks with an even more awful story of what had been happening to him. And so the three of us settled at the castle. Ivan started working ten hours a day, either patching up someone's roof, or laying flooring, or chopping wood, or painting walls, and he did some plastering at the castle as well. He would laugh at himself, saying that he was doing work therapy, so that he could feel like a proper person again. Hanuman did nothing, he just lay there, singing his song to himself and reading the reports from Mr Skov's seminars and the other papers which I dug up in the cupboards and drawers. He liked that stuff, and kept asking me to bring him more. I brought it, he read it, and he laughed at what he had read. And then, most probably under the influence of what he had read – and what he had smoked – he started dreaming up films, writing the scripts in his mind, growing more and more distant from us, losing touch with reality...

One of those scripts occupied him for a particularly long time. I even got the impression that he was hallucinating, given the clarity with which he saw every detail as he filmed it in his head. He could spend ages talking about his characters, their life stories, and the events in the film. Towards the end he realised that it wasn't just one film, but a whole series of them. There were several protagonists in the script, and they started having dreams which were somehow connected, even though the characters themselves weren't linked in any way, and knew nothing about each other. At the same time strange events started taking place around the world: UFOs appeared in various places, catastrophes of unprecedented scale began to occur, soothsayers and miracle workers appeared, and other such overblown nonsense... It was all leading to the moment when the world would tumble into an abyss, Armageddon was fast approaching. Meanwhile there were miracles and other such silliness happening at every turn, you could bump into an alien in the lingerie shop, or ride a tram with a miracle worker, or visit another world as if you were going to the cinema or a museum, or buy a ticket to Sirius, or go for a trip in a time machine... and it was all quite affordable. Quite independently of one another the characters who were only connected by their dreams track down the magnates who were behind all the miracles and who staged the whole spectacle, the show, in order to distract people from the approaching catastrophe, so as to keep the human masses firmly in their grips. They said don't worry, whatever happened they had time machines, and space flight, and salvatoriums, and other worlds, and miracle workers who would save humankind from the plague, and aliens who would rescue them from global cataclysms... But the heroes of the film knew that it was all rubbish! They engage in a struggle with a web of official agents who are simultaneously trying to hunt down the heroes; they enter into open conflict. The protagonists establish contact with one another, and join forces. They coordinate their campaign. One of them is a doctor. The other is a politician. The third one is a solicitor. The fourth one is child with truly phenomenal powers. And so on... Obviously they save the world, which had been heading for the abyss because the magnates were staging all those miracles using technologies which dangerously depleted the planet's energy resources, and the miracles were nothing more than mass hallucinations, which happened simultaneously in different locations. That was Hanuman's script. He was possessed by it, and it dragged him away from normal life for weeks on end. He had started raving. He was wide awake and raving! He had fallen into a trance. He was watching his very own serial. It was worse than what happens to ordinary people when they get hooked on some idiotic soap opera. It was worse because he had his own soap opera running in his head: he wrote it, he filmed it, and he watched it round the clock! Numismatics, or astrology, or reading the tea leaves had nothing on it.

6

We somehow got by on the money which Ivan was paid. Me and Hanuman just vegetated, we did nothing for Mr Skov or for the benefit of the commune, or even for ourselves. Ivan would pound away at some wall for a while, then he'd go off and fiddle with something else for a bit. I was kind of writing a book – that is, I was sustaining the myth in the old man's mind that I was writing a book, which was supposed to be related to the topic of world dominion and other such nonsense. Hanuman had fallen into a lethargic slumber.

Having parted company with his film, and feeling empty, exhausted and horribly lonely, Hanuman fell into a deep depression, a depression which was probably worse than anything I had ever suffered. When I looked at Hanuman I could tell that he was in a bad way, that I had it easy in comparison, and sometimes I even summoned up the enthusiasm to smoke some grass with Claus.

But it didn't last long, because Hanuman's depression continued to worsen, his headaches drove him crazy, they left him stupefied, sometimes he moaned for hours on end, and when we brought him tea, his favourite tea with honey and coriander leaves and some other herb, he pulled such a hideous expression, as if we'd given him fermented horse's milk. Although maybe he would have had a sip of horse's milk...

It was raining endlessly, and it was dark and spooky in that damp, chilly castle. Ivan stoked the stove, but it only gave off heat for three hours, and over a radius of no more than three metres, before the coals went out and stopped giving off warmth altogether – the stove was completely useless. Ivan went from room to room, gathering parts from the remains of various stoves, hoping to assemble one decent stove from them. He went missing for whole days.

We hardly saw him at all, and we saw even less in the way of results. Nothing changed, the stove still didn't work. I got the impression that Ivan was pulling our leg, he was pretending to be busy, to be looking for stuff, but in fact he was sitting in some storeroom somewhere, masturbating for days on end. Hanuman hadn't left his room for a whole month, and I had forgotten when he last spoke to us. He seemed to say only two or three words a day. He just lay under his quilt with his teeth chattering, tapping out his song with his foot, groaning whenever his migraine started again. Outside the rain was pouring down unremittingly...

Soon Ivan stopped working or going anywhere at all. He smoked so much grass with Joachim and Freddy that he wasn't fit for work. He took to his bed. He buried himself under his quilt and didn't show his face. I couldn't stand being in that room any longer, it was too much like a ward in a mental hospital, so I ran away from there, deciding to fill in for Ivan by knocking away with the hammer and pounding at the wall. I was promised fifty kroner an hour. I was supposed to knock a hole in the wall so that someone (I didn't know who it was supposed to be, maybe no one at all) could run a pipe through it. The arguments about how to acquire the pipe were yet to flare up at the commune meeting – no one explained to me what the pipe was for, or where it was coming from or where it was going, and anyway I didn't give a shit! I just got up earlier than usual and started pounding away. I quickly got into the flow, I just got up, pounded away, drank some tea, had a smoke, and carried on pounding. And my life somehow had a new-found simplicity.

Hanuman was even more down in the dumps, at some point he just completely switched off, something inside him came to a standstill, he stopped talking and singing, and then he stopped eating. He stopped reacting to anything. He didn't notice anyone. Not me, not Ivan... Even the bats which flew into our room didn't seem to bother him.

Sometimes it seemed he was smirking, but looking closer I could see that it was just the shadows flitting across his face, just shadows... The guys came to see us, sat down by Hanuman's bed, smoked and talked, but he didn't notice them either. Mister Claus burned some magic incense next to Hanuman, which made us all feel high, but Hanny just lay there, polishing the ceiling with his glassy gaze.

Claus reckoned that Hanny was just unwell, and that it would soon pass. Claus said that he had also loafed about like that for months when his wife went off with some bastard. To start with Claus smashed the guy's house to bits, then he torched it, then he kicked the bloke about in the dirt, then he gave the bitch a divorce, then he got stoned, and then he started smoking non-stop, just lying in bed. Joshua or Freddy and Joachim brought him food, bought stuff from the shop for him, cooked it, and smoked with him, they even moved in with him, they didn't want to leave him alone, they stopped all the mucking about and held a vigil by his bed, but he was zonked out, smoking and eating on autopilot, and talking to himself and staring at the ceiling, but he couldn't later recall how time had passed or what he'd been doing while he was in that depression. All he could remember was that he had smoked a lot. But he had no idea what he had eaten, or what he had said. Patricia and Jeannine also looked in on Claus during those tough times and massaged him – no funny business, just a massage – and they tidied up around the house and fed the dog as well. But he didn't talk to anyone, everyone said that he hadn't uttered a single word to anyone over the course of several months. He might have mumbled something to himself, earnestly and scornfully, but no one could remember what it was. Otherwise he just smoked, stared at the world with his empty, glazed expression, and that was it. "They thought they had lost me, they thought I would hang myself, but I didn't, I recovered... and Hanuman will recover too," Claus said tenderly, placing his hand on the quilt, patting Hanuman on the shoulder, adjusting the quilt and saying, "Of course he'll recover, he'll get better, I'm sure of that."

Mister Lee said the same thing when he came floating into our room chasing a rare butterfly which he had been stalking with his net for three days, clad in his dressing gown. He stood by the bed, listened to my account of what was happening, which involved a short overview of Hanuman's life up to now, his erotic dreams, his passion for photography, his first experience with a lady who was much older than him in the shadows of his small photo studio, illuminated by the occasional flashes of a red lamp, as well as his expedition through the mountain villages of Himalaya, where he was brought flatbreads sprinkled with cannabis seeds by fairies dancing in gay dresses with lilies woven into their hair from which hummingbirds and butterflies fluttered, not to mention his journey to New Zealand, where he danced with aborigines, and transformed himself into a multicoloured fountain. From there he went to the island of Crete via the island of Bali, where he had wandered through the gloom on to a showground full of fireworks and other pyrotechnics while a carnival was in full swing – and when it all went up in smoke, he came out in one piece and was taken for a New Avatar. I spoke about his life on Cyprus and Capri, about his wives in Bucharest, Prague, Riga, Gå on the outskirts of Stockholm, about everything which had befallen us in Denmark, our travels from Frederikshavn to Copenhagen, from Copenhagen to Farstrup, up to Aalborg, down to Langeland, to Svendborg, Silkeborg, and eventually to Huskegaard. Mister Lee listened, attentive and unruffled throughout, frozen in a fixed pose: his right hand was raised, holding the net, and the long sleeve of his dressing gown, which looked like a ceremonial robe, had slipped down, exposing an elbow with a wart on it. He had shifted the weight of his body on to his half-bent right leg, while he was holding his left leg in the air – he was the spitting image of Mercury! He let me finish, and then he said, "His mesolimbic system has collapsed, that's all. The patient used narcotic substances in excessive quantities. He also suffered overexposure to gambling, both in the casino and with his own fate. Recklessness, thrill-seeking, risk-taking, an unhealthy obsession with making money from nothing accompanied by an ever greater gift for spending it – all these things led to mental exhaustion. He needs peace and quiet, tea, and weed. It's not psychosis or a coma. It's just his nucleus accumbens. Nothing more."

Hanuman slept for days on end, occasionally eating something, occasionally smoking, but mostly just lying there staring at the wall or the ceiling, his leg twitching under the quilt... Ivan and I were losing hope that he would ever come round...

But eventually he did. And this is how it happened.

By now I had pounded the wall for long enough to be able to go and unwind properly somewhere – I'd earned it. Whether it was honest labour or not, I had done what was expected of me, and nothing had ever been agreed when it came to how long I should pound for or how much time I could take for fag breaks. And so Mr Skov paid me part of my wages, although he kept back most of them to pay for rent and food (for all of us, including Hanny-Manny). I came back with the cash, waved it at the others, and told them that I planned to go and let loose somewhere.

"Hey, big guy, how about you?" I said in Hanuman's direction without expecting a reply. I just talked as I got dressed, and by now we were used to talking to him without him answering. We'd got into the habit, and so on this occasion I was just talking in his direction in the same way as I would talk to anyone else.

"No," I said, "we won't be taking Ivan with us, just you and me, just like before, like the good old days, eh? We can go and shoot up, if the thought of heroin doesn't make you sick. We can go and sit in a coffee shop, have a smoke and a drink, do some people watching... we could have a game of chess or nard or backgammon, what do you reckon? Or maybe you'd like to go to a restaurant? An Indian one? Or how about some hookers! What would you like to do? I've been pounding the wall for thirty days, ten hours a day, we're flush with cash, let's go and let loose! Come on, don't just lie there saying nothing! Answer me, you son of a bitch!"

He looked at me and his gaze slowly became more focussed. Then he came round, he got out of bed, took a shower, shaved off his beard, plucked some hairs from his nostrils, combed his hair, brushed his teeth, took a fresh shirt – a brown, sparkling one – out of his suitcase, put on a light spring jacket, adjusted his gold bracelet, applied some moisturiser to his face and some gel to his hair, twisted his ring so that the aquamarine stone faced outwards, clicked the heels of his Camel shoes, and followed me...

Patricia and Jeannine dropped us in town. They looked at Hanuman in amazement, they couldn't understand where he might have appeared from. They asked if he was a guest, but he told them he'd been living at the castle for three months, that he was officially registered there, that the rent had been paid on his behalf, that he was a completely legal inhabitant of Huskegaard! Then they asked which room he was living in. He told them that he didn't know, that he had been in a deep meditation which he had surfaced from only a couple of hours previously, and now he needed to visit the nearest energy nodes in order to replenish his reserves; he had expended so much energy during his travels through other worlds that he could barely speak, he needed time to recuperate.

The streets of Odense were glazed with rainwater, the sunbeams were beating downwards, trying to break through, but they were refracted by the puddles, reflected back in fragments. We had a smoke in the coffee shop. Hanny stared at everyone, his gaze brimming with irony, his smirk becoming ever more enigmatic. He somehow resembled a large fish which had poked its head out of the water and was contemplating whether to become a biped. By then we had worked up a good appetite. On the way to the restaurant Hanuman told me about various visions he had seen while he was in suspended animation. He told me that he had now gathered enough wisdom and strength to get back to work... "He-ha-ho!" he exclaimed. Now he would show everyone what's for and whip their asses too! He had come up with a great idea! Such a good one! He was about to tell me about his idea, he had already opened his mouth in order to utter forth the magic word, but fate intervened, and in place of the magic word came a swear word, in place of a revelation a profanity came flying from his lips. And so I didn't find out, and I would never find out, about the visions which had visited Hanuman... And all because of a damned Indian restaurant! Because when we got near enough for Hanuman to make out through his glasses what was written on the windows and the door of the restaurant, instead of the revelation came, "Fuck me in the mouth!" and his eyes glazed over, full of rage. Written across the front window was the name of the place, "Chapatilla Restaurant"! And right by the entrance stood an Indian man resembling a pompous turkey, with long whiskers and a burgundy turban, with a broach nestling in the thick folds of cloth. With palms pressed together ceremoniously, and bowing low, he invited all to enter and sample the Indian cuisine. He was glistening, his silks shone, his face was radiant, his cheeks had the hue of tea, and his ivory teeth flashed. And he was the one Hanuman flung himself at, fists flying, yelling, "You bloody bastard! You motherfucker, tell me who's running this goddamned place! Tell me which son of a bitch is sucking my blood, taking my profit! Who's the thief that stole my idea! Show him to me! Show me the bloody bastard!" Some Indian guys came running out of the restaurant, chattering like magpies, flapping their robes, slapping their sandals. Then the owner appeared, bearing the tight gaud of his belly before him. He tooted something through greasy trumpet lips. Everyone fell silent. Then they began to ask Hanuman what was going on. Hanuman started jabbering away even more frenziedly. He threw himself full on at the restaurant windows, like Alexander Matrosov blocking the German machine guns with his chest. I had no idea what was happening. I was afraid that they would reach for their mobile phones, either the restaurant staff or some pedestrian would make a call, just to be on the safe side... One of the Indians, the smallest and puniest, started to interrogate me, obviously assuming I was Danish. I reckon that if there hadn't been a white man present (me), and if they hadn't assumed I was Danish (the first and last time that ever happened), they would have done Hanuman over straight away, and there was no telling how things would have turned out, although things were pretty bad as they were. They couldn't have been much worse! And so I spluttered something in Danish, which they kind of swallowed, but they asked me to repeat it in English, to avoid any misunderstanding. I explained to them that it was the Chapatilla which had driven Hanuman wild with anger, because he was sure that it was his invention, and eventually they grasped that Hanny thought they had stolen his idea (although it was so hard for them to believe that they even doubted they had understood his Hindi properly). And then they told him (and me) that he was a lunatic! A maniac! A schizo! Because there had been a restaurant of that name, with that menu, functioning for ten years already! And not only did the menu feature the Chapatilla, which was first made in Berlin in 1987 by an Afghan of Indian origin who was now rolling in clover, in silks and in carpets, and was living happily ever after. It also contained similar culinary creations such as the Chapatiletta, the Chapatimama, the Chapatipulka, as well as many other variations on the chapatti theme...

Hanny was gutted. At that moment I recalled how his bros

had tossed him that idea, and Joachim's face materialised before my eyes, with his cheeky, mischievous expression... I realised that he had tricked Hanuman...

I had never felt for a friend like that before, not for anyone! I had never felt pity as I felt it for Hanuman at that moment... Eventually they managed to calm him down, and then they politely asked him to come in and try the Chapatilla for free. Clearly they wanted us to put the argument behind us, to demonstrate how civilised they were, and how understanding about the mental condition which they all assumed the Hanumaniac to be suffering from. They produced their certificates, they wished Hanuman *bon appétit*, they showed him photos from ten years back and the first Chapatilla which the restaurant had made, displayed under glass like an oyster in a laboratory retort. Hanuman apologised anxiously to everyone, he apologised profusely and looked distracted, distraught, like a scolded child... he ate that Chapatilla with tears pouring down his face, and as he ate he said he hadn't tasted proper fresh Indian chillies in ages... he broke down completely... "Your chillies are the finest in Denmark!" he bawled. "Yes, yes! The very best in Denmark! They bring tears to my eyes!"

We paid them of course. Hanuman ordered me to give them one hundred kroner for emotional damages, but I gave them only twenty, I handed twenty kroner in loose change to the guy outside the restaurant.

Hanny walked ahead of me, his chest thrust forwards, tugging at his braces, his left elbow jutting outwards, wrist resting in his trouser pocket. He walked with a bold, broad stride, paying no heed to anyone. But he was walking to his doom, because from now on Hanuman was on the way down!

But he still hadn't reached the depths, this still wasn't the very bottom... he carried on falling, getting submerged in silt and limestone, enveloped in clouds of sediment. From that moment on he continued to fall, sinking ever deeper, losing his dignity, his spirit, his hope, until he was a lost soul, a one-time thrill seeker who had become just a refugee, soon to be nothing more than a *clochard*...

After our spree in Odense he took a firm decision to hand himself in to the Red Cross, with the ruse that he was Hanuman Pardesi, a native of the Pakistani part of the Punjab who had grown up in different places, studied here and there, and then taken the faith, becoming a Jehovah's Witness. Having made the application he left Huskegaard, and left me behind. I was stunned! I looked on in amazement as he got into the car with the Jehovah's Witnesses, who had been calling in on us regularly, bringing us their brochures, which weren't even any good for chucking in the stove, because they wouldn't catch light. Hanuman had cosied up to them, pretending that he had believed all their mumbo jumbo for ages, then he went to one of their gatherings, following which he jumped into their car and drove off with a smile on his face, waving goodbye to me with his birdlike hand. I was in shock. It took me several days to pull myself together. Hanuman was no longer a part of my life! I was completely alone...

7

A while later I went to Farstrup to see Hanuman, having received a horrifying letter from him, a letter which could only have been written by a madman. Apparently, he had sprouted a tail! Straight out of his anus! It was causing him terrible inconvenience. It had become far more problematic to perform his bodily functions. It was a nightmare! According to the letter, Hanuman's tail was already the length of a little finger, thin, gristly, pink, and highly sensitive. "Just imagine, Euge! What am I going to do? How am I going to look people in the eye? I've locked myself indoors and I don't venture out at all! Soon I'll turn into a real monkey, my bodily hair is already much thicker! My hands are deformed! My forehead is sloping! Just look at how terrible my handwriting is!" (His handwriting really was awful, unspeakably awful, at some point it broke off completely, and the letter continued down the straight rail tracks laid by Nepalino's typewriter). "It's some kind of malign mutation. I've got no idea what it could be. I can't explain it at all. How did it come about? How could something like this have happened to me? What might have caused it? Maybe it was the drugs? What about you? Have you had anything similar? I've never heard of anyone in our family suffering from anything like this! It's horrific. The metamorphosis is progressing with every day. My speech and my brain functions are deteriorating. You can see for yourself how poorly I'm expressing my thoughts. If only you could see what I have become. I'll soon lose the gift of speech altogether! Oh, Euge, it's some kind of punishment! The gods are laughing at me... you have to save me, Euge!" That letter filled me with horror. I decided to go and see Hanuman straight away. I found him at Nepalino's place, just as before. He was lying in bed. On the floor by the bed was a full ashtray, and a cup of tea. No signs of any mutations. But he was definitely dejected and disorientated; he looked awful. His face had turned a greyish hue. His eyes were sunken and inflamed. His mouth was agape, and he had a vacant expression. At first I felt very uneasy, but Hanuman quickly put my mind at rest. He told me with a wink that he'd written that stupid letter in the hope that the camp staff would intercept it and conclude that he'd gone mad, which would help him get a yes decision on his case. But it didn't turn out that way. No one cared what he had written or who to. No one was intercepting the letters he sent, nor did they bother opening the ones he received. It made him indignant: his rights weren't being violated one little bit! He couldn't appeal to the European Court of Human Rights in Strasbourg. He had no grounds on which to rebuke those damned Danes. Their treatment of him was beyond reproach. Such was their indifference towards him, such was their assuredness that he would soon be deported that it wasn't even necessary to pressurise him. Everyone was convinced that he was healthy and that he would soon be sent home. Their belief in his imminent deportation was so strong that they didn't apply any pressure on Hanuman at all. There was no pressure whatsoever, because there was no point in exerting any. What was the point of pressurising someone who had already been morally crushed? What was the point of using pressure against an Indian whose self-abasement had gone so far, who had so completely lost his dignity, that he was happy to call himself a Pakistani? What was the point of pressurising someone like that? He was already as flat as a board! He was as smooth as the asphalt on the German autobahn! You could drive right over him! You could seal him up in an envelope and send him back to India as a letter! He was already completely flattened. Everyone was just waiting for him to hand himself into the authorities and confess to being who he really was. And then they would lead him ceremoniously to the airplane, and, just like an old man, they would sit him down, pat him on the cheek, and say, "God tur, Hanuman!"[31]

He was horribly depressed, he had mummified himself, barricaded himself in with cushions, with five mugs and a teapot on the floor, and he lay there smoking the cigarettes which Nepalino brought him, feverishly tapping out the melodies of various tunes with both feet, endlessly mumbling to himself... He didn't even go to the toilet, he just pissed in a bucket, which Nepalino then carried out. As soon as he saw me, he yelled, "You're just in time! My Nepali wife is leaving me! Now there'll be no one to proffer

31   Bon Voyage (Danish).

the poor madman a match!" Then he whispered into my ear, "Nepalino's got beer in the fridge, but he's stopped giving it to me... Do something!"

His eye wandered round the room like a fish. I recognised the familiar glint. I sat down next to the Nepali, shifting his pile of paperwork to one side. I hugged the catlike creature round the shoulders and asked him where he was off to.

"Surely our little scoundrel hasn't got a yes?" I asked, tapping Nepalino on the back and coaxing a shy smile out of him.

"No, no, what are you talking about! When have you ever heard of a Nepali getting a yes. He's being deported! Plain old deported! That's right, isn't it? He can tell you himself..."

But Nepalino was silent, his back turned to us, maintaining his fucked-off dignity. He took a mouthful of water, lifted one of his legs and hugged his knee close. He was wilting, he was melting in our combined projector beams of muscular attention.

"Why don't you tell him? It's your third deportation order, you've been through all the appeals procedures, and you've already packed your case to go to your uncle in Copenhagen. That's right isn't it, my little scamp? You're planning to dump me? Hey, roll me one too..." Hanuman broke off, noticing the pouch of tobacco and grass in my hands. He reached a paw towards me. I sat down next to him, and let him have a sniff. He inhaled long and deep, savouring the pungent, resinous aroma.

"Magnificent!" he finally pronounced.

Suddenly our Tamil friend came in. It was immediately clear that he was out of his mind, terrified; he was even shaking. He was dressed as before, in a heavy sweater tucked into his trousers, his trousers were pulled right up to his waist, and he kept pulling them further and further upwards – he looked like a toddler in a romper suit who had wet itself. He looked pretty bothered, and I could tell that something wasn't right. He sat down on the bed next to Nepalino, opposite Hanuman and me, and Nepalino budged up slightly for him. The Tamil immediately started jabbering something in awful English. I took a closer look at him: he was thinner than before, and hairier, his eyes were inflamed and had a deranged look in them, he was talking twaddle about Germany, Flensburg, Frankfurt, Padborg, and he constantly repeated something about the border, the border, the border. He said "principally" after every word, and it sounded awful, because the word got snagged on his lips and bristled there like a burdock, he couldn't get the better of it, he just spat it out and started over again; it even seemed that the only reason he was speaking was to be able to repeat that idiotic word again and again. It was hard to understand what he was saying, because there were more Danish and German words in his English than English ones, but it was still English. It was a German hotchpotch cooked up in an English gravy.

Overwork, I thought to myself. Their scam must have taken its toll. And I started to examine the large spiral wood shaving on his sock.

I asked him about the work at the factory, but he just shrugged his shoulders and left, saying nothing more than, "Bootlegging, that's the business to be in!" Nepalchonok also seized the moment to get away, darting off after the Tamil. I looked at Hanuman, who said, "Yep, these days its hard to get a yes on humanitarian grounds, even if you're mentally disturbed. There are so many crazy people around that no one's going to take you seriously. There are so many psychos that they no longer see it as serious grounds to grant leave to remain. There's so much competition that it's enough to drive you to despair! Anyone who gets a deportation order immediately turns out to be crazy, and before you know it they've whipped out a doctor's certificate, a genuine certificate from the doctor. Plenty of them arrive at the camp with certificates, and they start faking at the very first interrogation! Some of them even turn up at the cop shop fresh out of the loony bin! They start faking it in the middle of town, in the pedestrian precinct! They go into a trance or they burst out in hysterics! They get taken in... and then it turns out that they're refugees too... Well I never! Take that Bengali, for example! He's not a Tamil, he's Bengali, as the police established. He's hiding out here illegally, he's got a pile of cash which he just sits on because he's scared of leaving the camp! He's got genuine paranoia! He thinks he's being followed! Look, over there in those bushes, outside the window, he can see the police sitting there! He's lost all self-control! But I've got one more idea, maybe it's my very last idea, before this place drives me completely round the bend..."

"What kind of idea is that?"

"What kind of idea would you expect from me? I want to squeeze that Bengali for all his money, I'll ask him to give it to me for safekeeping... yeah bro, just give it to me to look after for a while... I'll tell him that it's safer with me than in any bank, so why not just give it all to me. And then I'll take off..."

"Where to?"

"To Lolland!"

"To Lolland?"

"That's right, to Lolland! To step out of the frame for a few days, fix my health in the swimming pools with the girls and cocktails... I'll take his money and run! And he won't find out, because he doesn't have a clue what's going on any more; he'll forget everything, all of it, all about his money, all about me, because he's a total idiot, a total fool... Only thing I'm worried about is that he's already given the money to someone else, or he's buried it somewhere and can't remember where... Anyway, we'll have to find out..."

"To Lolland, you say? But why Lolland?"

"I told you, I want to feel like a proper person again... I want to gather my strength... I want to fill my lungs with fresh air... I want to see the whole picture... maybe some things will become clearer... After all, there are all sorts of opportunities right under our noses, all we have to do is reach out and grab them! We've done it so many times before! The main thing is to make a start!"

"OK... But it's a pretty long way from here... all the way to Lolland... First you have to get to Zealand... and that's no mean feat..."

"That's what I'm saying, we need money... have you got any?"

"I've got a bit..."

"Right, enough said."

"Can't you get there from Blomstrup? Have you thought about that? Are there ferries from there to Lolland? Maybe Svenaage knows someone who could take us by boat?"

"What boat?"

"You remember, he once told us that he knows some fishermen there with motorboats, they go out almost as far as Langeland, Aero, all the way to Germany... the catch is better there... What was he prattling about fishermen?"

"I can't remember..."

"Maybe they'll give us a lift to Lolland?"

"Come off it... to Lolland by boat? Svenaage? Are you having a laugh? Best you go scrounge some more beer off Nepalino instead..."

"Right, but where is our little friend Nepalino off to then?"

"I told you, he's going to Copenhagen, to lie low for half a year or so... And then he'll take some fresh editions of Nepali newspapers, he'll put on his nice outfit which was purchased in some Nepali shop complete with Nepali receipt, and he'll show up at the cop station again. And once again he'll say, 'I'd like to make a new application, I went back to Nepal for a while, but they started persecuting me again...' All by the book, half a year back home, and you've got a new case. I'd do it myself, but I've got nowhere to lie low... Apart from maybe Huskegaard... Listen, put me out of my misery, go and fetch that beer!"

"All right, all right…"

I left the room, and the Nepali was standing there in the corridor like a school kid, picking his nose, and standing kind of crookedly, sideways on to one of the doors as if he was eavesdropping. There would have been plenty to listen to in that campful of queers. As soon as I looked at him he yanked his finger out of his nose.

"Hey, Nepalino! Come here! Feel like treating me to a beer? Eh? A little reunion drink! Chin-chin baby! *Skynd dig, bøsseven!*"[32] I said, and the Nepali went to the fridge…

As we drank the beer Hanuman slowly explained what had been happening. It turned out that the situation was much more fraught than I had imagined. He had gone as far as to declare a hunger strike. And he'd declared it to the Danish Red Cross, to the whole world, so everyone knew about it, even the Dalai Lama. You better believe it! Hanuman's affairs had got really out of hand, and he had been driven to extreme measures. He had sacrificed his physical well-being. Now he was worried that things might have gone too far. When he handed himself in to the authorities he had said that he was from Pakistan, just as he had planned. Once they had checked his details, the police invited him to a routine interview. They told him that he was a liar, because the street where he claimed to have lived didn't exist, and neither did the city of Chahmadur, where that street was supposed to be situated. It was all totally made-up! Not a single word of it was true! All complete lies! Apart from the word Pakistan… But they had major doubts as to whether he had ever been there! The police told him that if he didn't start telling the truth, they would put him in pre-deportation detention while they established his true identity. And so he lay there waiting to be locked up; the cells were packed full of fantasists just like Hanuman, there wasn't room for him yet. As usual, he would have to wait. And so he was waiting…

32   Gay friend (Danish, Copenhagen slang)

I sent the Nepali to fetch another bottle of beer.

"What's wrong?" I said when Nepalino pulled a face. "How about one for the road before you set off to Copenhagen?"

The little green-skinned frog went to the fridge. Hanuman carried on griping and telling his story. He cheered up a bit as he swigged on his beer, musing that he should have gone about handing himself in a bit differently. He should have played at being a psycho from the very start, he should have pulled off something spectacular in Copenhagen, like faking a fit in the Illum department store! He could have rolled about spewing blood in the midst of all that luxury! Or tried to slash his veins in a supermarket! Or staged self-immolation! Or something else, it could have been anything, anything at all...!

No, he hadn't been thinking straight at all, and he should have been, he really should have been... He immediately started trying to rush through a marriage to someone, as he had previously planned he joined a sect of missionaries, he started chasing some young Danish girl, who people called the Tank behind her back because she was unfeasibly fat and unwieldy, like a tortoise! But at least a tortoise isn't pushy and sharp-tongued like this girl was, she was a real scourge, *mamma mia!* Tank sent Hanuman packing, she didn't believe a single word he said. In general it seemed like Hanuman had lost his charm and powers of persuasion; nothing went right for him any more. He stopped trying to curry favour with the preachers; they weren't any help anyway, they just sucked his blood and his time. He gave up on them, he started drinking and going on binges, and then he decided to go on a hunger strike... But he didn't even manage to convince the nurse that he had a mild form of schizophrenia.

By the time I arrived he had made himself completely miserable contemplating the sad lot of the asylum seeker, so he was really happy to see me, imagining me to be the harbinger of better times to come. I sent Nepalino to fetch another bottle of beer, so that we could drink to the good old days, but he refused, claiming there were none left. At that I advised him to pull out a couple of notes from the bundle he kept stashed somewhere on his person, and to go and fetch a couple of bottles of beer from the Albanians at the cafeteria, and make it snappy! Before we asked Arshak to come and help us out...

"Not Arshak, my friend, no need to call Arshak," Nepalino mumbled, turning even greener, before adding meekly, "Right away, there'll be beer right away!"

And so we had beer to drink once again, and Hanuman told us that he was living out the last days of his journey, or that's how it seemed. He had an unpleasant sensation just below his left shoulder blade, a very unpleasant sensation... he had felt something similar one time in Bucharest, when he'd ripped off a gang of gypsies. He had sold them a thousand fake dollars in exchange for two hundred grams of gold, after which they nearly killed him. He had to give everything back, phone up his father in India, and ask him to pay the ransom! That was the first time he heard daddy hemming and hawing: "You could have thought up something more original," daddy had answered... In the end his Romanian wife had to pay them all of the money she'd earned toiling as a stripper in Germany for two and a half years! So now he had a similar feeling, as if he was on the verge of a physical collapse, as if he'd come to the end, or very close to the end! Now there was nothing left but to be led away to prison, and to perish there, quietly, like a cat...

Nepalino brought Svenaage to see us, with a six-pack of beer. Svenaage sat down on the bed next to Hanuman, and he was clearly already very drunk, he was barely making sense, he rolled his empty eyes, his mouth was open, and he didn't shut it, he just gulped agitatedly. He opened a beer for each of us and told us that there was a Russian ship in port again... For fuck's sake! He never got time to dry out!

He'd just managed to sober up a bit, and there it was, the Russian ship was back! Before he'd even managed to finish the last lot of vodka, there they were again – the Russians! When would it ever end? It was unbearable! But all of that washed over Hanny, he just carried on bemoaning his fate, talking about his sense of foreboding, about some fateful mistake he once made, after which life's road had become a lot bumpier, and started veering all over the place. The Dane slurped his beer, and sighed. Once Hanny had stopped grumbling I sighed as well, and announced that I too was about to take an important decision. I told them I was pissed off with the whole situation, with absolutely everything, that I'd had enough of crawling on Europe's underbelly like a flee, with no home and no family – no, enough was enough! "Come on, you guys! We've got to come up with something!"

Svenaage nodded his head sympathetically and tried to look understanding, but he didn't really pull it off. I patted him on the knee, he patted me on the neck and sighed, and then tears welled up in his eyes...

The next day, before he'd had time to sober up, when he was still steaming drunk, Svenaage invited us to the port, to the Russian ship. He literally dragged us there, asking me to translate what the sailors were saying, because as usual they didn't have two words of English to rub together, and as usual he was scared they would rip him off. I went there with him and we bought a few cartons of cigarettes and a crate of vodka as usual, then we sat down to drink it at Svenaage's place. Hanuman smoked more than he drank, but he got drunker than he smoked, and eventually conked out. At that point he mumbled, "Man's soul is immortal, but it is not given to him for all time, man is but a vessel for the soul's safekeeping, because the soul is a precious thing, and most important of all is to care for it properly!"

That was obviously part of the gibberish which the Jehovah's Witnesses had used to brainwash Hanuman, but

Svenaage said, "Yes! True words, because the thing about life is…"

"Life is a staircase," Hanuman interrupted. "Either it leads upwards, or it leads downwards, but it's easier to go down, which is why we are heading down, and only a rare few go up, the ones who focus on the question of the soul's salvation…"

"Yes, yes," said Svenaage, sighing.

"And that's why I am going to St. Petersburg!" I suddenly blurted out.

"Where? What for?"

I started explaining to Svenaage that I had spoken with the guys on the boat, and they were heading to St. Petersburg in two days. I was hooked on the idea, I told him, because I had a girlfriend there, an ex, the love of my life, and I wanted to see her again. I didn't know her address, but there was always the phone book, and all sorts of agencies. I'd phone everyone with the surname Lepa. I'd go to every single theatre and cinema, and if she'd changed her surname I'd look for her by her first name, and I'd go through every single Anna in St. Petersburg, and if necessary the whole of Russia!

"But I will find her!" I said, striking my fist on the table. "I'll definitely find her! I'll fucking find her…"

Svenaage clenched his fists too, and said, "I believe in you! You'll find her! A guy like you, *for helve*,[33] you'll find her…! But what for?"

"Because, because… if only to find out how she's doing… is that just a silly whim?"

"Hey, hey… Johan, you're a sentimental one! And I mean that in a good way!"

"Yes… I know… I agree… Is it a stupid idea? Yes! But so what…"

I spent a while telling Svenaage the story of my imagined romance with a non-existent girl called Anna.

33   Hell yes (Danish)

By the end of the story Svenaage was pissed out of his head. He looked at me with genuine awe and eventually asked when I was planning to leave.

"In a few days... I've come to an agreement with the captain, I just need a certain amount of money, not much at all... although I won't be able to get hold of it in two days, so I'll have to wait for the next ship... but I'm definitely going to go!"

I rapped my fist against the table.

"I fucking will! Whatever it costs me! I'll get the money..."

"How much do you need?" Svenaage asked sympathetically.

"I'm eight hundred dollars short," I said dejectedly.

"It's not so much... I... I'll lend it to you," he said.

"Listen, Svenaage, we're old friends, I don't want to put you in a difficult..."

"You're not putting me in anything... Eight hundred dollars? That's peanuts to me! Johan, you don't need to thank me... I'm sure you'll send it to me when you can... now some other guys are a different story, but you'll definitely send it back... what's the problem? Johan, me and you are old friends! Friends, you understand? You might be my only friend! Maybe Hanny-Banny as well, and that's it! Who else is there? Laszlo? That Hungarian Serb, the motherfucker! Ugh! Fuck that! I'm not even sure how much of a Serb he is! Maybe he's not any sort of Serb after all! We should check! What kind of friend is he to me? He's the kind of guy you have a drink and a natter with... But you – you're top blokes! To me you're really decent guys... Friends... I know you'll send me the money, Johan, and that's that..."

"Yes, Svenaage. Of course I'll send it to you. Without fail!"

A few hours later Hanuman and me were on our way out of the camp. Hearing our footsteps, the Albanians peeked out of their windows. I pulled my head down low, hoping that this would be the last time. Hanuman was holding his coat collar tight against his neck, and squinting. I had eight hundred dollars in my pocket, and a shadow of sadness playing across my face, while the bleak dusk of Denmark's sorrow hung above us. I was burdened by a sense of anticipation, which had bubbled up and spread across my skin in goosebumps. It was the expectation of some major exploit, a sense of anticipation which had long been lurking in the deepest recesses of my soul.

Jean-Claude came with us, lugging a duffle bag on his shoulder which looked more like a massive boulder. He had got some sort of free gym membership in payment for something, so he had packed his bag and set off. As soon as he saw us he started telling us about a particularly cocky young Nigerian guy who had just arrived in their building. He spoke about him with marked distaste (maybe it was because he had to speak English). Jean-Claude told us that the guy had already tried to flog the same communal vacuum cleaner three times, and two bikes as well; there was hardly anyone who he hadn't tried to rip off since arriving! He was a real reprobate! I glanced at Jean-Claude's huge bag and for a moment it occurred to me that he might have taken all his belongings with him, just in case! He carried on telling us about the Nigerian guy: the scumbag had already managed to sell something in every building of the camp – something he had simply swiped from one of the other buildings. He couldn't be stopped! There was no point giving him a beating, because he immediately came up with justifications and excuses! He was a slippery sort, like a snake in Vaseline! But the camp wasn't enough for him! He wanted to branch out further afield! So he found some amenable Danish guy, managed to win his trust via the Bible, and moved in with him.

"The Danish guy recently went away on holiday for two weeks, I think to Spain, although I'm not sure, and just imagine, that crook rented his flat out! To some gullible

Afghan and his family! And he didn't bother with any paperwork, he just took half a year's rent up front and disappeared!"

"He-ha-ho! That guy will go far," Hanny said, shaking his head. "If he doesn't go the way of Icarus!"

"With giant steps like that he could end up ripping his trousers," I added.

Once we arrived at the bus stop, and Jean-Claude had gone on his way, Hanuman gripped my hand, and it felt like he was trying to hold on to me.

"So," he said bitterly. "I guess you'll be on your way then…"

"Wait," I said. "What's that nonsense? Where am I supposed to be going? What are you talking about?"

"Hmm… you're leaving aren't you? For St. Petersburg, isn't it?"

"Hmm, what are you talking about Hanny, have you smoked yourself silly or something? What's that about St. Petersburg? Hey, pull yourself together! We're going to Lolland! Eight hundred dollars! Paradise, booze, girls! Man, you wanted to step out of the frame! To see the whole picture! You wanted to recharge your batteries, didn't you Hanny? Look, our bus is coming. Cheer up! We've got two or three days of fun waiting for us! You could do with unwinding and forgetting all about this nightmare for a while… this place has really got to you. We're off to Lolland, Hanny! To the Danish Ibiza!"

Hanuman forced his bloodshot eyes wide open, the clouds of insomnia immediately dispersed, and a spark of life blazed up in them. He flung his head back and opened his fishy mouth: "He-ha-ho!" Hanuman guffawed for all to hear, then he took a deep breath, slapped me on the shoulder, and said, "So we're off to Lolland, Euge! At long last, we're going to Lolland? To the Danish Ibiza? To step out of the frame, to see the whole picture? Euge, you son of a bitch you! Hah, you really are a son of a bitch!"

Hanuman slapped me on the shoulder again, and tears of happiness and gratitude came to his eyes. He boarded the bus with an important air.

"To til Lolland!"[34] Hanuman exclaimed to the driver jubilantly.

---

34   Two to Lolland! (Danish).

Translator's Acknowledgements

When I last met Andrei to discuss the translation of *Hanuman's Travels* I handed him a copy of *Vladimir Nabokov, America's Russian Novelist*, written by my father George Hyde back in 1977. This gift had a special personal symbolism. My father was, amongst other things, a scholar of Russian literature, and it was he who first suggested I study Russian at university. This choice then led me to a career in the British Foreign Office, which eventually brought me to Estonia, where I discovered Andrei Ivanov's work. Nabokov was the subject of Andrei's university dissertation, and an important influence on him as a writer. I would therefore like to thank my father, and the two people who are at the centre of my life in Estonia, Airi and Theo. And of course my mother, Barbara.

Translator's Biography

Matthew Hyde is a literary translator from Russian and Estonian to English. His translations have been published by Pushkin Press, Dalkey Archive Press (including the *Best European Fiction* anthology for the last four years running), *Words Without Borders* and *Asymptote*. In 2018 he was shortlisted for the John Dryden translation competition and the Estonian Cultural Endowment translation prize. His writings have appeared in *Europe-Asia Studies*, *In Other Words*, and *Asymptote*. Prior to becoming a translator,

Matthew worked for ten years for the British Foreign Office as an analyst, policy officer and diplomat, serving at the British Embassies in Moscow, and Tallinn, where he was Deputy Head of Mission. After that last posting Matthew chose to remain in Tallinn with his partner and son, where he translates and plays the double bass. He has recently recorded an album of his own compositions with leading Estonian jazz musicians, Nordic Blues, available on Bandcamp.

Remember the Translator!

Vagabond Voices continues to celebrate translations and its translators. It is proper that translators are occasionally invisible (particularly when the reader is busy suspending disbelief), as their task is to present the authors and not themselves to the reader. But the actual words are not the authors', but the translators', and it is also proper that the reader recalls the presence of this intricate and generous craft.
www.vagabondvoices.co.uk/think-in-translation